STD

ALLEN COUNTY PUBLIC LIBRARY

3

D1555206

Fiction
Kidder, Jane
Passion's ki

"D   Vic
you p

"No   eck.
"I like the feeling of you against me."

The next thing she knew, her mouth was being covered by soft, warm lips. She felt her hard riding hat being tugged off her head; then, as if by magic, her hair tumbled down her back.

Victoria wanted to pull away, knew she should pull away, but somehow she couldn't find the strength. It was as if she was using all the energy in her body just to stay conscious as Miles continued his sensual assault.

"Miles," she moaned, "you—have—to—stop. . . ."

To her surprise, he did. Mortified by her wanton behavior, she set her features in what she hoped was a no-nonsense posture and said firmly, "Mr. Wellesley, I cannot continue to allow you to—"

He buried his lips in her hair. "Don't," he groaned. "Don't say anything to spoil it. We didn't do anything wrong. We kissed, that's all, and there's nothing wrong with that."

"Maybe not in America, but here in England, it just isn't done."

"Well, it must be done once in a while," he snorted, "or none of you Brits would be here!"

* * *

Praise for *Passion's Gift*:
"Outstanding . . . A sensuous, delightful read full of splendid characters and raw, human emotions."

—*Rendezvous*

"Passionate and absorbing."

—*Romantic Times*

"Five stars!"

—*Heartland Critiques*

JANE KIDDER'S EXCITING
WELLESLEY BROTHERS SERIES

MAIL ORDER TEMPTRESS   (3863, $4.25)
Kirsten Lundgren traveled all the way to Minnesota to be a
mail order bride, but when Eric Wellesley wrapped her in his
virile embrace, her hopes for security soon turned to dreams
of passion!

PASSION'S SONG   (4174, $4.25)
When beautiful opera singer Elizabeth Ashford agreed to care
for widower Adam Wellesley's four children, she never
dreamed she'd fall in love with the little devils—and with their
handsome father as well!

PASSION'S CAPTIVE   (4341, $4.50)
To prevent her from hanging, Union captain Stuart Wellesley
offered to marry feisty Confederate spy Claire Boudreau. Little
did he realize he was in for a different kind of war after the
wedding!

PASSION'S BARGAIN   (4539, $4.50)
When she was sold into an unwanted marriage by her father,
Megan Taylor took matters into her own hands and black-
mailed Geoffrey Wellesley into becoming her husband instead.
But Meg soon found that marriage to the handsome, wealthy
timber baron was far more than she had bargained for!

*Available wherever paperbacks are sold, or order direct from the
Publisher. Send cover price plus 50¢ per copy for mailing and
handling to Penguin USA, P.O. Box 999, c/o Dept. 17109,
Bergenfield, NJ 07621. Residents of New York and Tennessee
must include sales tax. DO NOT SEND CASH.*

PASSION'S KISS

JANE KIDDER

ZEBRA BOOKS
KENSINGTON PUBLISHING CORP.

ZEBRA BOOKS are published by

Kensington Publishing Corp.
850 Third Avenue
New York, NY 10022

Copyright © 1996 by Jane Kidder

All rights reserved. No part of this book may be reproduced in any form or by any means without the prior written consent of the Publisher, excepting brief quotes used in reviews.

If you purchased this book without a cover you should be aware that this book is stolen property. It was reported as "unsold and destroyed" to the Publisher and neither the Author nor the Publisher has received any payment for this "stripped book."

Zebra and the Z logo Reg. U.S. Pat. & TM Off. The Lovegram logo is a trademark of Kensington Publishing Corp.

First Printing: May, 1996
10 9 8 7 6 5 4 3 2 1

Printed in the United States of America

To Rebecca Rosas who, as acclaimed author Rebecca Paisley, delights her readers with her wit and imagination and who, as my dear friend, Beckie, delights me with her warm and gentle spirit.

Thank you for all the laughter, joy, and astronomical long-distance phone bills you bring to my life.

This one, Beck, is for you.

Chapter 1

"I never thought I'd say it, but if one more simpering maiden flutters her eyelashes at me tonight, I just may bolt and run."

Alexander Shaw, the fourteenth Earl of Chilsworth, looked around the crowded ballroom in amusement. "Oh, come now, Miles," he chortled, returning his gaze to the man standing next to him, "you've only been in England three weeks. You can't be bored with the Season yet. Besides, think how devastated all these hopeful ladies would be if you suddenly bolted and ran. Why, you're the most fascinating tidbit this group has had to natter about in years."

Miles Wellesley's blue eyes narrowed with distaste. "I didn't come all the way to England to be a 'fascinating tidbit,' Shaw. I came to buy horses to take back to Colorado and so far, I haven't done nearly as much of that as I've done of this." Frowning, he glanced around the crowded, flower-bedecked ballroom.

"I know, I know," Alex soothed, not in the least perturbed by his friend's contrary mood, "but your grandmother has gone to great lengths to properly introduce you into society while you're here and you're just going to have to put aside your snobbish American prejudices and go along with it—if for no other reason than to please her."

Miles nodded resignedly, his eyes drifting over to an elegant old lady seated regally on one of several high-backed chairs set strategically around the perimeter of the massive, gilt-columned room. Catching her grandson's affectionate look, Regina Wellesley, the Dowager Viscountess of Ashmont, inclined her head in his direction, a small smile tipping the corner of her mouth.

"So, have you seen anything you like yet?" Alex questioned.

"You mean horses?"

"Yes, Wellesley, I mean horses," he laughed, "although I'd actually be more interested in knowing if you've seen anything tonight that you like."

Miles looked around the ballroom absently, then shook his head. "Sorry to disappoint you, old friend, but there's nothing here that interests me. And as for horses, there's only one I'm really interested in, and I haven't had a chance to personally see him yet."

"Oh? You're interested in a horse you haven't even seen? Who would that be?"

"His name is King's Ransom."

"King's Ransom!" Alexander burst out. Then, seeing Miles's scowl, he lowered his voice. "You mean Pembroke's King's Ransom?"

"Is there another King's Ransom besides Pembroke's?"

"Well, no, but I just couldn't imagine you setting your sights on that horse. Why, he's one of the finest Thoroughbred studs in England. I'm afraid you're barking up the wrong tree, Wellesley. You'll never get your hands on him."

Miles shrugged. "Maybe, but you never know. Every man has his price. At this point, I'd be satisfied just to be introduced to Pembroke so I might set up an appointment to look at the horse. At least that would be a start."

"Well, old boy, I just might be able to help you in that regard."

"Really?"

Alex inclined his head toward a portly man with a florid face and thinning blond hair who was striding energetically toward them, hauling two breathless but determinedly smiling young women along in his wake. "The Honorable Sir John Pembroke," he muttered.

Miles looked in the direction in which his friend gestured and smiled with surprised pleasure. "You don't say," he murmured, straightening his shoulders. "Well, things are finally looking up. And just who might those two lovelies with him be?"

"Quit pawing and stamping," Alex chuckled under his breath. "You'll find out soon enough."

Turning a smiling countenance on the man bearing down on them, Alex held out his hand. "Sir John," he greeted as the threesome swooped in amid a swirl of taffeta and a wild fluttering of fans. "How nice to see you." Nodding to the breathless girls, he added, "Lady Georgia, Lady Carolina, how lovely you're both looking tonight."

Miles bit the inside of his lower lip to squelch the surge of laughter that threatened to erupt upon hearing the girls' outrageous names. Taking a closer look at the tittering, pink-cheeked blondes, he decided they must be twins since it was virtually impossible to find any marked differences in their pretty, blushing faces.

"May I introduce Miles Wellesley," Alex said graciously. "Miles, I would like to present Sir John Pembroke and his daughters, Lady Georgia and Lady Carolina."

Again, Miles fought back his amusement, quickly bending over the girls' limply extended hands. "A pleasure," he murmured as he brushed the back of their gloves with his lips.

"Been looking forward to meeting you, young man," Sir John boomed.

"And I you, sir."

Sir John nodded at this acknowledgment, then continued, "Went to school with your father, you know, and I never knew a finer man than James Wellesley. It's just a damn shame that he and that lovely mother of yours abandoned us to set up in the Colonies. How are they, anyway? Still struggling along in the wilderness?"

A brief vision of his parents' spectacular Colorado ranch with its twenty-six-room house, six barns, eight outbuildings and thousands of acres of rolling meadows and fields flashed through Miles's mind. "You could say that," he answered wryly.

"And are they *really* happy over there in the middle of nowhere?" Pembroke prodded.

"Very happy," Miles confirmed. "Colorado is a beautiful place, and they've carved out quite a comfortable life for themselves."

"I've heard that," Pembroke sighed. "Indeed I have. Still, I do miss James's company. There's not a man in all of Britain who's a better companion on a hunt or a night in town than your father. And I always thought your mother was the prettiest girl in the shire. Had designs on her myself, until your father set his sights on her." He shook his head wistfully. "I never knew a man with such luck with the ladies. Once James Wellesley decided to set his cap, the rest of us just had to give up the game and look elsewhere."

"Oh, Papa, really," Carolina gasped, snapping her fan shut and giving her father a sharp rap on the arm. "You're going to embarrass poor Lord Wellesley to death, talking that way about his father!"

"Not at all." Miles laughed, turning his clear blue gaze on the mortified girl. "My father's charm is as legendary in America as it was here. It's a difficult legacy to live up to."

"Oh, I don't think you have to worry too much about that, Lord Wellesley," Georgia interjected boldly.

"Mind your manners, miss." John frowned, then turned his attention back to Miles. "So, I hear you've come home to purchase some horseflesh to take back to America."

Miles smiled tolerantly. It never occurred to the aristocratic members of his grandmother's social set that anyone would actually prefer living in America over England. When he'd

3 1833 02838 2908

attended college at Eton his classmate's belittling of his American roots had, at first, offended him greatly, but over the years he had become so accustomed to their biased views of "the Colonies" that their subtle little jabs no longer bothered him.

"I'm afraid you have that backward, sir. I didn't come *home* to buy horses to take back to *America,* I came to *England* to buy horses to take *home.*"

"Well, yes, then; have it your way," Sir John blustered, giving his elegant silver brocade vest a jerk. "I suppose you do consider America your home, although it's difficult for me to think of your father and mother as anything but the blue-blooded Brits that they are."

Miles smiled amicably. "I'm afraid that if you met them today, you'd find that they've both turned into red-blooded Yankees."

Sir John cast him a pained look and opened his mouth, as if to further protest this possibility.

"For heaven's sake, Papa," Georgia interjected with a little giggle. "There's nothing wrong with being American. After all, Carolina and I are half-American ourselves."

Miles's eyebrows rose with surprise. "Really?"

Carolina took advantage of Miles's momentary attention and stepped in front of her father. "Oh yes," she gushed. "Many years ago Papa took a trip to America and brought our mama back with him. Sometimes he tends to forget the fact that Mama was born and raised in Virginia."

John threw his daughter a jaundiced look. "All right, my dear, you've made your point." Turning back to Miles, he said, "Tell me about your plans while visiting, Mr. Wellesley."

"It's *Lord* Wellesley," Georgia corrected.

"No, your father is right," Miles said. "It's *Mr.* Wellesley."

The sisters looked so crestfallen that Miles had to struggle to keep a straight face. "But it *could* be Lord Wellesley if you wished it to be, couldn't it?" Carolina asked hopefully. "After all, your grandmother is the Dowager Viscountess of Ashmont."

"Yes, I suppose if I stayed in England permanently, somebody could come up with some sort of title for me," Miles admitted, shrugging with disinterest. "But since I'm only here for a short time and have no claim on any of my grandparents' lands or titles, it's just plain Mr. Wellesley." Turning back to Sir John, he said, "As for my plans, I'm looking into purchasing some good English breeding stock to cross with native American horses in order to get a better quality riding horse, but one that still has the strength and stamina to endure the rigors of ranch work." Bowing to the ladies, he added, "Please excuse me, ladies. I hope the topic of animal husbandry doesn't offend you."

Georgia and Carolina smiled up at Miles coquettishly and shook their curls, trying their best to look interested now that the conversation had drifted away from themselves.

"That's an intriguing possibility," John agreed, noting with some embarrassment his daughters' ill-concealed infatuation with the handsome American. "I have an idea that might be beneficial to both of us. Why don't you come spend a few days with us at Pembroke House? You and I could discuss your plans further and I could show you my farm. As I'm sure your grandmother has told you, I have some of the finest blood stock in the whole country, and I might have an animal or two you'd be interested in."

Hearing their father issue this unexpected invitation, Carolina and Georgia immediately turned dazzling smiles on Miles. "Oh, please say yes, Mr. Wellesley," Carolina cooed. "We'd so love to have you."

Miles grinned at the obviously smitten girl. "Thank you, Lady Carolina." His gaze flicked back to John. "And thank you, sir. I'd be most honored."

"Carolina and I will plan some entertainments while you're visiting," Georgia assured him excitedly. "That way you won't die of boredom, spending all your time in that smelly old barn."

Miles forced a reluctant nod, hoping the two debutantes

wouldn't overdo it on the entertainments. Finally he was going to have an opportunity to get a look at the horse he had heard so much about, and hopefully transact the business he'd come for. The last thing he wanted was to have his time taken up with more soirées and house parties than his grandmother had already forced him to attend.

Sir John noticed Miles's lack of enthusiasm at Georgia's suggestion and quickly stepped in. "Let's wait and see how much time Mr. Wellesley has before we begin planning any parties," he suggested.

"But Papa!"

"Just wait and see," John repeated, his tone placating. Clearing his throat, he turned back to Miles. "Until tomorrow then, Mr. Wellesley. Say, about dinner time?"

Miles nodded. "That will be fine. Ladies," he added, executing a perfect courtier's bow, "it has been a pleasure."

Georgia and Carolina curtsied prettily, then reluctantly allowed themselves to be herded away.

"Quite a pair, aren't they?" Alex chuckled as the girls disappeared into the throng of dancers.

Miles turned on him with a wide grin. "Carolina and Georgia? Why in the world would a proper British couple name their daughters after two American states?"

Alex shrugged. "As they said, their mother is from America, and she's very proud of it. She may have lived here for nearly twenty years, but she's never really thought of it as home. I think giving the girls those unorthodox names was her way of reminding everyone of her heritage. Though rumor has it that it's always been something of an embarrassment for Sir John, and probably for Lady Victoria as well."

Miles looked at Alex quizzically. "Lady Victoria?"

"Oh! You haven't heard about her?"

"No. Should I have?"

Alex took a sip of champagne and smiled broadly. "Let me put it this way. Lady Victoria Pembroke is probably the most

unique . . . and most difficult woman in the shire. She's Sir
John's eldest daughter—by his first marriage. She's consider-
ably older than Georgia and Carolina, but still, she has a way
about her that makes her deucedly interesting."

"More interesting than her sisters, I hope."

"Infinitely," Alex assured him. "In fact, Lady Victoria has
the reputation of being something of a bluestocking, as well
as being a damned fine horsewoman."

Miles's eyebrows rose with interest. "A good horsewoman,
eh?"

"Probably the best in the shire."

"Is she married?"

"Heavens, no."

Miles looked at him curiously. "But you say she's older?
How much older?"

"Old enough to be on the shelf."

"Oh." Miles sighed, his interest quickly waning. *"That* old."

"Wellesley! How unchivalrous of you to put it that way.
But, yes, I'm afraid Victoria has reached the age where she is
definitely considered a spinster."

"Is she here tonight?"

"Not a chance. She hasn't attended one of these functions
in ages. After three Seasons in London with nary an offer for
her, I think she finally just gave up and retreated to Pembroke
House for good."

"Three Seasons with no offers?" Miles gasped. "My God,
does the girl have warts?"

Alex burst out laughing, giving every eligible girl in the
room an excuse to turn around and covertly ogle the two of
them. "No warts, but she's always been willful and outspoken
to a fault, and what man wants a wife who's bound to fight
him on every issue that might arise?"

"What man, indeed?" Miles agreed. "Thanks for the warning.
I'll be careful not to raise her ire while I'm visiting."

Alex waved a dismissive hand. "You'll probably hardly see

her. I guarantee that the States will have your time so monopo-
lized that you'll be lucky to find a minute to see that horse you
want to buy, much less Lady Victoria."

"The States?" Miles guffawed. "Do you mean Georgia and
Carolina?"

Alex nodded. "That's what everyone calls them, although
they don't know it, of course. But isn't it the perfect moniker?
It's long been a matter of great speculation among the men at
the Club whether they actually do share the same brain or just
appear to do so."

Alex's outrageous comment sent Miles into another peal of
laughter. "Oh, Lord, Shaw, that's rich! Tell me, are they twins
or just look-alikes?"

"Oh, they're very definitely twins. In fact, if you ask them
about it, Georgia will be very quick to tell you that she is
exactly two minutes older than Carolina. For some reason that
I've never been able to understand, that's quite a source of
pride to her."

"Sounds like a rather insignificant accomplishment to me."

"Absolutely," Alex agreed, "but the very fact that they seem
to find such delight in the most insignificant of matters is part
of their charm."

"Really?"

"Really. I'm sure you'll find them to be a most amusing pair.
Most people can't tell them apart but if you look very closely,
you'll notice that one has blue eyes and one has green. Also,
Carolina's hair is a bit darker than Georgia's. Once you see
Lady Pembroke, you'll understand where they get their beauty.
They look just like her."

"And is she as much of a coquette as her daughters?"

Alex wiggled his eyebrows meaningfully. "Absolutely, so
you'd better watch yourself. Once Lady Fiona gets a good look
at that blond hair and those blue eyes of yours, you could find
yourself with far more female attention than you're bargaining
for."

"Lord, Alex, you make it sound like I'm casting myself into the midst of Sodom and Gomorrah!"

Alex chuckled. "I'm sure it's nothing you can't handle, Miles, old man, but I think you'll find your visit to Pembroke House interesting." He chuckled, adding, "Very, very interesting."

Chapter 2

"So, my dear, I understand you're going to spend a few days with the Pembrokes."

"Yes, I am." Miles took the cup of tea his grandmother offered and sat back on the plush settee, looking around appreciatively. All his life he'd heard his father talk about Wellesley Manor, with its huge, high-ceilinged rooms, graceful Regency style furniture, and hand-rubbed mahogany woodwork and silk wallpaper.

Even now, sitting on the mauve velvet settee in the grand salon, Miles found it hard to believe that he was actually here, and that the elegant old house was still every bit as beautiful as his father had described.

His reverie was broken by his grandmother's next question. "When are you leaving?"

"This afternoon," he responded, focusing his attention back on her. "Sir John has some horses he thinks I might be interested in, so he invited me to come take a look. Since I had nothing planned for the next few days, I decided I might as well go immediately. They're expecting me for dinner."

Regina Wellesley smiled. "Are you sure it's horses Sir John wants you to look at, and not his daughters?"

Miles set down his teacup and looked at his grandmother. "I beg your pardon?"

"Those girls of his—Atlanta and Savannah—or whatever their names are."

Miles chuckled and gazed fondly at the imperious old woman. "I believe you mean Georgia and Carolina."

"Whatever," Regina shrugged, waving a dismissive hand. "Sir John is anxious to marry them off, especially after he was unsuccessful in his attempts to betroth Victoria, so you would be wise to prepare yourself for an onslaught of feminine wiles."

Miles's eyebrows rose with interest. "I take it the ladies Pembroke aren't favorites of yours?"

Regina sighed. "Actually, I think Victoria is a perfectly charming and discreet young woman. But those other two . . ." Her voice trailed off meaningfully.

"I know what you mean." Miles chuckled. "But, I don't think it will be so bad. After all, I'm there to find horses, not a wife. I probably won't even see the girls, and if I do . . . well, I guess I can survive a couple of days spent with two beautiful women fawning over me."

Regina threw him a jaundiced look and shook her head, trying hard not to laugh. "You're just like your father, Miles; too handsome for your own good and shameless in your knowledge of it. But you're right, you'll probably have a perfectly wonderful time, and I hope you do. Just be careful not to let Florida and Virginia's compliments go to your head, or you might find yourself entangled in a web from which even you won't know how to extricate yourself."

"Georgia and Carolina," he corrected again, "and don't worry. I'll be on my guard every minute."

Regina's expression turned thoughtful. "Don't misunderstand, Miles. Nothing would make me happier than to see you find a suitable girl and settle down here in England, rather than returning to America. And if you decided to pursue that course,

I doubt you'd have much trouble in attaining your ends. After all, you are everything a well-bred young lady looks for in a husband. You're charming, wealthy and have an impeccable lineage. But as much as I'd love to see you make a match, those two are definitely not what I had in mind."

"You needn't worry," Miles assured her again. "The only thing I'm interested in acquiring from Sir John is horses, and at this point I'm not even sure about that."

Regina nodded, relieved to know that the two empty-headed Pembroke sisters had obviously not turned her beloved grandson's head at the ball. "Do you have any particular horse in mind?" she queried.

Miles leaned forward, warming to this new subject. "As a matter of fact, yes. Pembroke has a stud named King's Ransom whom I have a definite interest in."

To his surprise, Regina broke into an amused peal of laughter. "You and every other horseman in England, I'm afraid." Noting Miles's immediate dismay, she quickly added, "But that's no reason why you shouldn't make an offer, if you like him. I haven't heard that Pembroke is interested in selling that particular horse, but one never knows. If there's any truth to neighborhood gossip, Sir John could probably use the money that selling a horse of that caliber would bring."

"Oh?" Miles asked, his crestfallen expression lightening. "Are the Pembrokes having financial trouble?"

"So I've heard," Regina confirmed. "I've known Sir John for years and years, and although he's a delightful man, I don't think he has much of a head for business. Back when your grandfather was alive, Pembroke was always approaching him with some wild investment scheme that, according to him, would triple our fortune in a matter of months. Thank God Charles was wise enough never to get involved; the results were nearly always disastrous. On top of that, rumor has it that he's nearly beggared himself trying to keep Fiona and those girls attired in their fluff and finery. I'm afraid the man is quite desperate for funds."

"That's good to know," Miles acknowledged, "although I wouldn't take advantage."

Regina threw him an appalled glance. "Of course you wouldn't. Offer Sir John a fair price. Just don't let him horn-swoggle you into paying more than an animal is worth by making you think he is doing you a favor by selling."

Miles studied his grandmother closely for a moment, his mouth curving in a wry smile. "Tell me, Grandmother, did you advise Grandfather like this when he was purchasing horses?"

"I?" Regina gasped. "Advise Charles Wellesley? Hardly!" Closing her eyes, she sighed, the faraway, wistful sound of a woman remembering a much-loved man. "Sometimes, though, he would seek my counsel, and then I always did my best to help him."

"I wish I could have known him," Miles said quietly.

Regina opened her eyes and nodded. "I wish you could have, too, Miles. He was a magnificent man. Your father reminds me a great deal of him. In fact, most of my seven sons do, and now that Charles is gone, it's a great comfort to me to see how he lives on in his children and grandchildren."

"You loved him very much, didn't you?"

"Yes," she answered unhesitatingly. "But somehow 'love' has never seemed a big enough word to describe the way I felt about Charles. Like most young people of our time, ours was an arranged marriage. Despite that, we eventually came to love each other a great deal. Not at first, mind you, but eventually. Your father and mother share that kind of love, too, and I hope that one day you will find it yourself." Lifting an elegantly bejeweled but arthritic finger, Regina brushed away a tear that had formed during her fond reminiscence.

"I hope so, too, Grandmama."

A teasing glint came back into her eyes, and she pointed her finger at him warningly. "But not with one of those Pembroke twits, please!"

Miles drained his teacup and set it on the table. Walking over to his grandmother, he leaned forward, giving her an affectionate kiss on her wrinkled cheek. "Don't worry, darling. Baltimore and Boston aren't my type at all."

"Baltimore and Boston? I thought you said they were named Georgia and Carolina."

"They are," Miles chuckled, "and you knew it all the time, didn't you?"

Regina shrugged elaborately, but the little bubble of laughter that escaped her belied her disinterested gesture. "Poor dears. How could they have grown up to be anything but vacant and insipid with such ridiculous names!"

Miles's grandmother insisted that he make the short journey to the Pembroke estate in her luxurious coach. Although he would have preferred to ride, Regina wouldn't hear of it, reminding him that in England no gentleman of quality would travel thus, carrying a clothes satchel on his saddle and arriving at his host's manor on horseback, like a servant back from a day's leave. Miles finally agreed to take the coach, amused, as always, by the British penchant for correctness, even when dealing with the most insignificant of situations.

As the well-sprung vehicle, emblazoned with the Wellesley family crest on its side, neared the perimeter of the Pembroke land, Miles rapped sharply on the ceiling, signaling the driver to stop. Leaning his head out the window, he called softly, "Don't go up to the house immediately, Clement. I want to stop at the stables first."

The coachman threw him a surprised look. "The stables, sir? *Before* you make your presence known to the Pembrokes?"

Miles grinned. "Yes. *Before* I make my presence known. I want to take a quick, private look at the horses."

Clement's lips twitched. Obviously the young master from America was as savvy as his grandfather had been when it came to making important investments. More times than he could remember, Clement had driven Lord Charles around the countryside while the viscount made "private" inspections of horses in which he had an interest.

"As you say, sir." Clement nodded, carefully concealing his satisfied smile. "We'll go directly to the stables."

Several minutes later the coach rolled to a stop in front of an ancient but well-maintained stone barn. "Here we are, sir," Clement announced quietly. "You do wish for me to wait, don't you?"

"Please," Miles nodded, stepping down from the coach and looking around. He was impressed by what he saw. The imposing barn was immaculate, the hitching rails and mounting blocks in perfect condition, the window frames painted and the great old stone building freshly whitewashed. The area directly outside of the massive doors was set with flagstones that showed signs of having been recently hosed down. The smell of fresh hay, well-oiled leather and healthy horses filled the air. Miles sniffed appreciatively, thinking that there was no smell in the world sweeter than a clean barn.

Turning to Clement, he said, "I shouldn't be more than ten minutes."

Clement nodded, then drove around to the side of the barn, where the large coach would be less noticeable to passersby.

Miles entered the cavernous building and paused, allowing his eyes to accustom themselves to the dim interior. Directly in front of him was a wide aisle flanked on either side by large, airy box stalls. As he moved down the lane, several horses poked their heads out of their stalls, greeting him with soft nickers.

At the fourth stall Miles paused, drawing in an awed breath as he stared at the sleek-coated bay stallion within. This had to be King's Ransom. Glancing at a shiny brass plaque nailed to the stall door, his assumption was confirmed.

Miles smiled and reached out a hand toward the horse's outstretched head, allowing the stallion to sniff him. "You really are everything they say you are," he murmured, rubbing his palm lightly over the horse's velvety nose. He moved a step closer, looking over the stall's front wall to get a better view of the stallion's legs and hindquarters. His interest only increased as he studied the horse's conformation.

Quietly sliding open the stall door, he stepped inside, running his hand over the stallion's coat and glancing occasionally at his head to see if he pinned his ears back or bared his teeth at the unknown intruder. King's Ransom eyed him a bit warily, his nostrils flaring slightly, but his ears remained pricked forward. Miles smiled with satisfaction, as pleased with the horse's temperament as he was with his looks.

Miles was squatting down, running his hands over the stallion's front legs, when he was startled by the shrill sound of a woman's angry voice from outside the stall.

"What are you doing in here?"

Nearly jumping out of his skin, Miles shot to his feet and whirled around to face his accuser. Trying desperately to hide the guilty look he knew he must be wearing, he smiled and answered, "How do you do? I'm Miles Wellesley."

The woman stared at him coldly, her mouth tightening at his evasive answer. "I didn't ask you who you are; I asked you what you're doing here. Get out of that stall immediately before I call the stablemaster."

Miles's eyebrows rose indignantly. Who did this girl think she was? Obviously, based on the fact that she was clad in worn riding breeches, a dingy long-sleeved blouse and dusty boots, she was some sort of hired help, although it was a bit unusual to find a woman working in the stables. Perhaps she was the daughter of the stablemaster or one of the senior grooms.

Miles's eyes swept over her slender form assessingly. Her face was smudged with dirt and her thick, dark hair was pulled back in an untidy bun, pinned loosely at the base of her neck. Still, despite her bedraggled state, he could see that she was pretty. Her eyes were large and luminous, and he guessed that her mouth, when it wasn't pursed as tightly as it was at this moment, was soft and full.

Still, her haughty expression and tightly folded arms

bespoke a woman reaching far above her station, and Miles was not about to obey her imperious command. Standing solidly in the doorway of the stall, he announced, "I am a guest of Lord Pembroke, miss, and I can assure you that there is no problem with my being here in the barn. As I said, my name is Miles . . ."

"I know who you are," she interrupted rudely. "I've heard all about you."

Miles stopped in midsentence, astonished by this unexpected announcement. "You have? From whom?"

The woman ignored his last question and continued on as if he hadn't spoken. "Furthermore, I don't care who you are or how wealthy you might be or how many horses you think you're going to purchase from this stable, King's Ransom is not for sale. Now, get out of his stall."

Miles had had enough. Although he was American to the core and secretly disapproved of the strict British class system, he was not about to take this kind of rudeness from anyone, be they servant or peer of the realm. "That will be quite enough," he snapped, unthinkingly repeating his grandmother's favorite expression when upbraiding a servant. "You already seem to be aware of who I am and the purpose of my visit here, so I see no further need for discussion. I don't seriously think you want me to call Sir John down here to validate my legitimacy in being in the barn, so I suggest you return to your duties— right now."

The girl's mouth dropped open in stunned disbelief. "Why, you . . . you arrogant American boor! You're all the same, aren't you? You think that because your family is rich and influential and because you are the rage of the social season that you can do anything . . . say anything . . . take anything . . ."

Miles's eyes narrowed. "And just what would you know about my success or lack of it with society?"

"Oh, I've heard," she spat. "You're all anybody talks about anymore. Miles Wellesley this and Miles Wellesley that. I've heard all about how handsome you are, how popular you've become, how all the hostesses are vying for your attendance at their functions and how every silly girl on the marriage market is trying to gain your attention." She paused, her eyes roaming insolently up and down the length of Miles's muscular physique. "Frankly, I don't see what all the fuss is about."

If Miles hadn't been so shocked by the girl's audacity, he probably would have been furious. Instead, he found himself trying to think of a way to counter her misguided impression of him.

Suddenly a little needle of mischief pricked him and he smiled, a blinding flash of sparkling teeth and blue eyes that had melted female hearts on two continents. "Frankly," he shrugged, "I don't see what all the fuss is about either."

The girl blinked in surprise at this unexpected admission. "Well," she blustered, "I guess it's somewhat comforting to know that at least *you* don't believe all the nonsense that's being said about you." She cocked her head to one side, throwing him a considering look. "And I suppose *some* of what they say about you must be true, or they wouldn't all be saying it."

Miles stepped out of the stall and pulled the door shut. Taking a step closer to the girl, he murmured, "Suppose you tell me just what they're saying, and I'll tell you whether it's true or not."

She studied him for a moment, as if trying to decide whether she wanted to play his game. Then, with a challenging lift of an eyebrow, she said, "I've heard . . ."

"Wait a minute," Miles interrupted. "Before I put myself in the position of having to defend myself, which I strongly suspect I am going to have to do, I'd like to know from where this wealth of information you seem to have about me has come. You say you've heard things about me. From whom?"

"From everyone!"

"But who is everyone?" he asked, throwing his arms wide. "Do you mean the other workers in the stables?"

She looked at him in bewilderment for a moment; then a

small smile spread across her face. "Yes, of course, from the stable men . . . and from people at the house, too."

"Oh, I see. I am the object of servants' gossip, am I?"

Her smile widened. "As far as I can tell, Mr. Wellesley, you're the object of everyone's gossip—servant and master alike."

"And what are they saying?"

"Lots of things," she hedged, turning to run an affectionate hand down King's Ransom's nose.

"Such as . . ."

She turned, her expression again challenging. "Such as how you've come here with your big American ego and your big American wallet to try to buy every decent piece of horseflesh in the shire and then quietly move it out of the country."

"I see," Miles said, frowning. "What else?"

"Oh, there's lots more."

"Such as . . ." he said again.

"Such as the fact that you're an incorrigible rogue and that all the debs are making perfect fools of themselves over you, hoping to catch your eye."

"Oh? And have any caught it?"

"I'm sure you'd know the answer to that better than I," she returned.

"But what have you heard?"

She hesitated a moment, then plunged on. "Actually, I've heard that a few have, and I've also heard that you've taken shocking liberties with several of them."

"Shocking liberties!" Miles blurted, genuinely confused. "What liberties?"

The girl pressed her lips together so tightly that they almost disappeared. "As if you didn't know."

"I don't! What liberties?"

She turned away for a moment, and the expression on her face when she looked at him again reminded him of a picture of a Puritan preacher he'd once seen in a book. "That you have repeatedly, and with several different girls, taken the liberty of kissing them . . . on the mouth."

Miles clamped his tongue between his teeth, trying very hard not to burst into laughter at the scathing disapproval in her voice. "Good God, that *is* shocking, isn't it?"

"Indeed it is. Now, enough of this. I want you out of here. . . ."

By now Miles was enjoying himself so much that he was loathe to see the conversation with the high-spirited stable wench end. "Wait a minute," he interrupted, holding up a staying hand. "Before you throw me out answer one more question for me."

The girl let loose with a very unladylike snort and planted her hands on her slim hips. "Only if you promise to leave immediately if I do."

Miles forced a somber expression and drew an *X* with his index finger over his heart. "I promise."

The girl nodded her head in assent, then snapped, "What is it, then?"

"Of all these girls that I've supposedly been kissing, did any of them like it?"

She blinked in surprise at his question, then drew herself up and said haughtily, "I'm sure I wouldn't know that."

Miles's brows lowered in disappointment. "You mean not one of them has rated my kissing ability?"

"Not that I've heard."

"Then I guess that must mean that I'm not very good."

Jamming her hands into the pockets of her tight riding breeches, she gazed at him in smug derision. "Come to think of it, I guess it must."

Miles considered her for a moment. She was obviously throwing down the gauntlet, and after the last few minutes spent in her company he was more than ready to pick it up. Leaning down so his mouth nearly touched her ear, he whispered, "I'd like your opinion."

Her eyes widened and her expression lost a great deal of its bravado. "Mine?"

"Yes," he murmured, wrapping one arm around her shoulders and pulling her up against him. "Yours."

Before she could protest, he lowered his mouth to hers, catching her lips in a seductive caress. He could feel the jolt of tension that shot through her body as their mouths touched. Reflexively, he threaded his fingers into her hair, loosening her untidy chignon until her heavy dark curls poured over his arm like an ebony river. He massaged her scalp, all the while teasing her mouth with his until he felt her lips soften.

Surprised and delighted by her unexpected surrender, Miles redoubled his efforts, running his tongue provocatively along the seam of her lips.

She sighed; a soft, breathy sound that sent a streak of desire sizzling through him, making his loins tighten and his hands begin to shake.

Still, the kiss continued. Their mouths melded together, moving against each other in an erotic little dance so stimulating that Miles realized it could very quickly get out of control. Drawing on a wellspring of restraint he didn't even realize he possessed, he reluctantly lifted his head, running a thumb gently down the girl's cheek as he smiled at her.

She slowly opened her eyes, looking at him vaguely for a moment, her eyes dreamy and unfocused with the first blush of sexual awakening.

"What do you think?" he whispered.

At the sound of his voice, reality suddenly crashed down on her and with a sharply indrawn breath she took a lurching step backward, her eyes widening with horror. "Think?" she cried, her voice shrill with recrimination. "I'll tell you what I think! I think you are despicable. You're everything I expected you to be—an arrogant, mannerless . . . American!"

"*What?*" Miles gasped, his passion quickly flagging in the face of her rude attack. "Now, wait just a damn minute!" He reached out, intending to catch her by the arm, but she danced away and pointed a shaking finger at him.

"Don't you touch me! Don't you ever touch me again, do you understand? Get out of this barn . . . *now!*"

Miles's face darkened. "Now, look, lady, I don't know who you think you are, but . . ."

"Never mind who I am. Just get out of here before I scream for help. And don't you ever come near me again!"

"Don't worry about it!" Miles snarled, turning on his heel and stalking down the barn aisle toward the door. "I'd sooner take on a viper than come near you again!"

"Good!" she yelled as he walked out the door. Then, almost as an afterthought, she tore down the barn aisle after him. "Mr. Wellesley?"

He turned, his handsome face black with fury. "What?"

"Just so you know, I think you're a terrible kisser."

Chapter 3

John Pembroke pulled open the heavy oak door and beamed with pleasure. "Ah, Mr. Wellesley, welcome! We were beginning to think you weren't going to make it in time for dinner. Come in, my boy, come in."

Miles smiled and stepped into the marble foyer of Pembroke House. "I'm sorry I'm late, Sir John. I got a bit . . . sidetracked on my way over."

John's smile faded. "No trouble on the road, I hope."

"No," Miles assured him. "None at all. Just a personal matter that took more time than I had anticipated."

A young maid suddenly tore around the corner, patting her unruly red hair and straightening her apron as she sped across the shiny floor toward them. "I'm so sorry, Sir John," she gasped, skidding to a halt and dropping into a flustered curtsy. "I was upstairs helping Miss Carolina dress for dinner and I didn't realize anyone was at the door. Please forgive me."

"I understand, Rebecca," Sir John said benevolently, "and rest assured, I'm not so arthritic that I can't answer the door once in a while, especially to admit such an esteemed guest."

The little maid smiled with relief, then reached for Miles's coat and satchel. "I'll take these for you, sir."

"That's not necessary," Miles protested, taking pity on the poor girl's harried state. "I can carry my own bag, if you'll just show me where to put it."

Rebecca glanced at Sir John, who gave his head a quick, negative shake. "Oh, no, sir," she protested, turning back to Miles, "I'll do it. I'd be happy to, really."

Miles turned a bewildered look at Sir John. "Butler's day off?"

John cleared his throat uncomfortably. "Something like that. Just take the bag, Rebecca. I'm sure it's not so heavy as to give you any problem."

"Yes, sir," she replied, bobbing again and plucking the bag off the floor.

"The blue bedroom at the end of the hall," Sir John directed as she hurried off toward a sweeping staircase.

Without turning, the girl nodded and raced headlong up the long flight of stairs.

John chuckled a bit nervously. "I'm afraid the poor dear has had her hands full today, what with helping prepare all four ladies for your arrival."

Miles's eyebrows furrowed as he pondered this statement. Could it be that in a household of this size, there was only one lady's maid? The rumors regarding the desperate state of the Pembroke family finances must be true.

As he and John sauntered through the imposing foyer toward a set of double doors, everything Miles saw confirmed his suspicions. Light patches on the fading silk wallpaper betrayed the absence of pictures that had once hung there, and the Aubusson carpet gracing the center of the large hall showed signs of careful patching. Still, despite its rundown state, Pembroke House was a grand old mansion, and Miles couldn't help but be impressed by its lofty ceilings and intricately carved columns.

"Lovely home you have here, Sir John," he remarked.

John Pembroke gazed around, his expression slightly wistful.

"Yes, it is, isn't it? Been in my family for generations, you know. It was a gift from one of the Stuart kings to my great-grandfather over a century ago. My daughters are the fourth generation of Pembrokes to be born under its roof."

"That's a wonderful legacy."

"Yes," John nodded, "and one I hope will continue."

Miles looked at him curiously.

"By tradition, the house and lands go to the eldest son," John explained, "or, in a case like mine, where there are no sons, the eldest daughter and her husband. However, since Victoria is my oldest and shows no sign of ever marrying, the house, by rights, will undoubtedly go to Georgia or Carolina. The problem is, since they're twins, which one?"

"That *is* a bit of a problem," Miles chuckled. "I suppose it will depend on which of them marries first."

John sighed. "Yes, I suppose so. But knowing those two, and their penchant for doing everything together, it will be just my luck that they'll decide to marry on the same day in a double wedding!"

Miles laughed at Sir John's quip, liking the big, bluff man more with each passing minute. They walked into the library, and Miles looked around appreciatively. The room was bordered on all four walls by floor-to-ceiling bookcases of dark oak. The furniture, although somewhat worn, was large and comfortable, and the massive fireplace on the north wall added to the feeling of cozy warmth and welcome. Settling himself in an overstuffed chair, Miles accepted the snifter of brandy his host handed him.

"Tell me," John said, lowering his heavy frame into an identical chair on the opposite side of a small lamp table, "what kind of horseflesh are you looking for?"

"A good stallion, mainly," Miles responded. "I already have an excellent herd of mares. They're strong and sound—good breeding stock—but they lack the confirmation to produce quality riding horses. I think that by introducing some Thoroughbred traits into the line, I can breed a horse that has it all."

"Possibly," John mused, twirling the stem of his snifter between his fingers. "It certainly is a novel approach to breeding a working animal."

"Oh, I don't know." Miles shrugged. "Look at your really good hunters. They have a little bit of everything mixed into them. It's that kind of outcrossing that I want to try."

Silence fell between the two men as Sir John pondered Miles's rather unorthodox ideas. Finally, he spoke, careful to keep his tone casual. "I have a couple of studs out in the barn that may interest you."

Miles swallowed, trying to think of a nonchalant way to bring up the subject of King's Ransom. "I've heard about one of your stallions," he said casually. "I believe his name is King's Ransom. Do you think he'd fit into my program?"

"King's Ransom!" John blurted. "Heavens, no! He's a race horse, born and bred. We ran him in the Derby several years ago and he came in second. I have high hopes that one of his sons might take the prize some year."

Miles kept his expression carefully blank as he tried to conceal his disappointment. "He's definitely not for sale, then?"

John shook his head vehemently. "Definitely not. He's the best I have. Perhaps the best I'll ever have. I couldn't possibly put a price on him. Besides, even if I was willing to sell him, I couldn't; he belongs to my daughter. I gave him to her the day he was foaled—as a gift for her sixteenth birthday."

Miles's eyes widened at this startling news. "Do you mean your daughter owns him legally? That he's registered in her name?"

"Well, of course not!" John snorted, taking a long swallow of his brandy. "I'm the legal owner, but in every other way, Ransom is Victoria's horse."

Miles paused for a moment, then said slowly, "But, legally, you could sell him if you so desired."

"Well, yes, I suppose I could, but I wouldn't. In fact, I wouldn't let Victoria sell him either, even if she wanted to—which, I assure you, she doesn't."

"I see."

Sir John set down his glass and eyed Miles speculatively for a moment. "Why are you so interested in that particular horse? You haven't even seen him."

Miles cleared his throat, stalling for time while he came up with a plausible excuse for his inordinate interest in King's Ransom. "I've heard a lot about him."

"Really? From whom?"

"Oh, here and there," Miles answered evasively. "From people I've talked to. Everyone says he's quite remarkable. Naturally, I was intrigued."

John smiled broadly, his chest visibly puffing up with pride of ownership. "He *is* remarkable, and I'll be happy to show him to you tomorrow morning, even though he's not for sale."

"I'll look forward to that," Miles murmured, then cast about for a change of subject. Considering what he'd learned about the Pembroke family fortunes, he still believed it might be possible to strike a deal for the stallion, but he didn't want to seem overly eager at this early stage of the game. "Perhaps you can tell me a little about the studs you are considering selling."

It was all the encouragement Sir John needed, and for the next half hour he expounded on the virtues of two other horses, both of which Miles had seen in the stable and knew were clearly inferior to King's Ransom. Still, he listened politely, nodding and making small comments at appropriate intervals, while he tried to figure out how much money it would take to get the horse he really wanted.

Sir John's long-winded dissertation finally came to an abrupt end when a lovely blond woman in her late thirties swept into the room. "Here you are," she drawled, her soft voice betraying a hint of an American southern accent.

Miles quickly rose to his feet and gave the lady the brilliant smile for which he was famous.

Gliding over to Sir John's chair, Lady Fiona perched herself fetchingly on the arm, giving her husband's shoulder an affectionate little squeeze while, above his head, her sea green gaze subtly assessed Miles. "I have been waiting and waiting for you two to come out of hiding so that I might meet our guest," she said, pursing her mouth into a charming little pout.

Sir John looked up adoringly at his wife. "I'm so sorry, my dear. Please forgive me for my breach of manners." He rose heavily to his feet and turned toward Miles. "May I introduce Mr. Miles Wellesley. Mr. Wellesley, my wife, Lady Fiona Pembroke."

Miles stepped forward and bowed over Lady Fiona's perfectly manicured white hand. "A pleasure, my lady."

Fiona answered his very proper greeting with a nod and a saucy smile. "The pleasure is mine, I assure you, Mr. Wellesley."

"I didn't realize how long Mr. Wellesley and I had been in here," John blustered, still trying to make amends to his wife for losing track of time. "I hope we haven't inconvenienced you with our tardiness."

Lady Fiona looped her arm through his. "You haven't inconvenienced me in the least, darling, but Cook is absolutely apoplectic that her first course will be ruined if we don't dine immediately."

"Well, then, by all means, let's go straight in to dinner. Are the girls ready?"

"They're waiting in the dining room," Fiona assured him. The three of them proceeded through the library's double doors, traversing the foyer and entering the dining room, a huge, elegant hall furnished with a massive table flanked by twelve chairs and an ornate mahogany sideboard against one wall.

Georgia and Carolina were already standing side by side behind their chairs, their identical wide-skirted satin dresses of pink and blue belling gracefully around them.

"Mr. Wellesley!" the one in pink squealed excitedly. "You did make it, after all!"

"Lady Georgia?" Miles guessed hopefully.

"Yes!"

He breathed a sigh of relief at his good luck. "You look very lovely tonight." Looking at the girl in blue, he was careful to keep his eyes averted from the scandalous expanse of bosom her low-cut bodice revealed. "As do you, Lady Carolina."

"Thank you, sir," she cooed. "It's so kind of you to say so."

"Where's Victoria?" Sir John asked, seating his wife. Picking up his host's cue, Miles moved to do the same for the twins, saying a silent prayer that Carolina wouldn't be piqued by the fact that he pulled Georgia's chair out first.

"She's still dressing, I think," Carolina responded. "She got in late from riding, but I expect she'll be down directly."

"I'm right here," came a voice from just beyond the dining room doorway.

Miles's head jerked around in the direction of the familiar, melodic voice, his heart bounding into his throat. *It couldn't be . . .*

But, of course, it was.

The girl from the stable walked through the double doors and paused, her eyes lighting on Miles's astonished face, then quickly flicking away, as if to let him know that he was of no consequence whatsoever.

Except for her voice and her dark eyes, she was barely recognizable as the same girl whom he had kissed so passionately barely an hour before. Now, her luxurious dark hair was skinned back into a prim bun and her form-fitting breeches and light shirt had been replaced by a high-necked, long-sleeved dress of heavy gray satin. But despite her attempts to look the part of the forgotten spinster she was reputed to be, her natural beauty and grace were readily apparent to Miles's appreciative eye.

"Mr. Wellesley," John said hurriedly, "may I present my eldest daughter, Victoria."

"We've already met," Victoria said, throwing a look at Miles that dared him to deny it.

Sir John's expression clearly mirrored his surprise. "You have?"

"Yes, indeed." Turning toward Miles, she smiled—a haughty little smirk that let him know the game was up and his secret visit to the stables would be a secret no more. "It was . . ." She paused, giving him a look that told him she knew he was holding his breath. ". . . outside. When Mr. Wellesley first arrived this afternoon."

Miles's eyes widened in astonished disbelief at Victoria's vague response. She hadn't betrayed him. But why? Surely she knew exactly why he'd been in the barn and just as surely, she knew that his brazen comments about having her father's permission to be there were lies. He couldn't imagine why she hadn't blurted out the truth, but he was forever in her debt for not disgracing him in front of her entire family.

Perhaps it was because she didn't want to provoke any more questions from her father about their encounter—questions that might somehow reveal that she had allowed the bold stranger to kiss and fondle her as if she were a common street wench, or perhaps it was simply that she was as discreet a lady as his grandmother had said she was.

Whatever the reason for her unexpected discretion, Miles was extremely grateful, and as he pulled out her chair, he leaned close and whispered "Thank you" into her ear. Victoria didn't acknowledge his comment in any way, but he knew she had heard him when he saw her cheeks turn pink. Sitting down in the chair next to her, he threw her a quick smile. Again, she pretended not to notice.

One person at the table noticed everything, however. Lady Fiona, seated at the end, missed nothing of what had just passed between the handsome stranger and her stepdaughter. *He's interested in Victoria?* she thought. *How incredibly odd that he would be attracted to her when he knows Georgia and Carolina are unspoken for.*

Again her gaze drifted from her stepdaughter to the handsome man seated next to her. What she saw caused her to shake her head in bewildered disbelief. Miles still had not taken his eyes off Victoria, regardless of the fact that the girl was pointedly

ignoring him. Furthermore, the hungry expression in his blue
eyes was undeniable. The man was attracted ... very, very
attracted.

Fiona felt a wave of disappointment wash over her. Although
the twins had never lacked for suitors, Fiona had taken one
look at Miles Wellesley and determined that he was the *one*,
and if she had anything to say about it, one of her adored
daughters would be sporting his betrothal ring by the end of
the Season.

Miles was everything she could hope for in a son-in-law: tall,
blond, handsome, and the principle heir to the vast Wellesley
fortune. He was even American, which was more than she'd
ever dreamed of finding in this stuffy British shire where she'd
been forced to live for the past twenty years.

It had seemed like such a perfect opportunity to see at least
one of her daughters brilliantly mated. She even had the satisfaction of knowing that gaining the girls' compliance in this regard
would be no problem, since they were both so smitten by the
breathtakingly handsome Mr. Wellesley that they could barely
talk of anyone else.

But now, as she sat at the end of the table, seeing Miles
covertly watch Victoria, her dreams of visiting her home in
Virginia as a wealthy and influential member of the Wellesley
family floated away.

And the worst of it was that, try as she might, she couldn't
imagine what it was that Miles Wellesley saw in Victoria to so
pique his interest.

Although Fiona was very fond of Victoria and had been
heartbroken for her when three Seasons had not netted her a
single marriage proposal, she had not been surprised. Victoria
was so plain, with her unfashionably dark hair and cool,
assessing eyes, and to add to her physical drawbacks, she was
also far too independent to be appealing to men.

But regardless of how many times Fiona had gently reproved
Victoria about her outspokenness, reminding her that men did
not appreciate women who were headstrong and opinionated,

Victoria had refused to listen. And up until tonight Fiona had been convinced that her stepdaughter was going to be relegated to the lonely life of a spinster, albeit one beloved by her family for the very eccentricities that had caused her to remain unmarried in the first place.

But that was before she had seen the looks that Miles Wellesley was even now continuing to throw at the girl. There was no doubt as to the extent of the attraction he was feeling as he watched Victoria daintily eat her soup. Fiona had had enough experience with men to know that she was not misinterpreting what she saw.

With a small sigh of surrender, she resigned herself to abandoning her lofty plans for her daughters and letting nature take its course. After all, even if it was just her stepdaughter who married a Wellesley, Richmond society would certainly still consider her a close relative of the famous family, wouldn't they?

Fiona desperately hoped so, since it looked like that was going to be the only claim she could hope to have.

Chapter 4

"Tell us, Mr. Wellesley, do people in your part of America really live in tepees?"

Miles looked up from the huge serving of sweetmeats in front of him and sighed inwardly. "No, Lady Carolina, I don't know anyone who lives in a tepee."

"Oh," she said, sounding disappointed. "I'd heard that everyone west of the . . . Missa . . . Missa . . . oh, Mother, what is the name of that big river?"

"The Mississippi," Fiona supplied with an indulgent smile.

"Yes," Carolina nodded. "Of course. I don't know why I can never remember that." Fluttering her hands in feigned embarrassment, she turned her attention back to Miles. "Anyway, I had heard that everyone who lives west of the Miss . . . issippi either lives in houses made of dirt or in tepees like the savages."

"I'm afraid whoever told you that was misinformed," Miles responded patiently, "although some settlers do build sod huts until they have time to cut timber and construct a log house."

"I guess that just goes to show you that you can't believe everything you hear." Carolina giggled. "What about your house? Certainly it isn't made of logs, is it?"

Ah, thought Miles wryly, *now* we're getting down to the real reason for this little interrogation. "As a matter of fact, yes, it is. It's completely constructed of ponderosa pine." He could barely contain his smile when he saw the girl's face fall.

"But," she faltered, "it must have taken a tremendous amount of trees to build a house large enough for a family the size of yours. Didn't you say you have six younger brothers?"

Again he smiled. "Yes, but there's plenty of timber in Colorado."

Carolina looked at him expectantly, hoping that he'd say more about the size of his home, but Miles was of no mind to humor her and merely smiled benignly.

He looked down at his plate, wondering if he could force himself to eat one more of the rich confections still sitting on it. He felt as if he'd been eating forever, and still the meal dragged on.

Although Miles was well aware of the British tradition of multicourse evening feasts, he'd never seen anything like the dinner he was served tonight. It was no wonder Pembroke was hurting, he thought. The cost of this dinner alone would break a man of ordinary means.

The meal had started with two soups, one cream and one broth, followed by a fish course of poached turbot in mayonnaise, then roast mutton, turkey and veal cutlets, a haunch of venison, lobster salad, maraschino cherries and, finally, truffles with champagne and sweetmeats. Since a full twenty minutes was allotted for each course, it was now nearly eleven o'clock.

Miles had spent most of the evening answering an endless stream of questions from Fiona and the States. Early on, it seemed to him that the two girls possessed a truly remarkable talent for pointless chatter, but as the meal progressed, he realized that every inane and seemingly inconsequential question was actually calculated to provide some kernel of information about himself, his family or, most importantly, his wealth and social status.

By the time dessert was served Miles was sure that no team

of skilled lawyers could have dragged more information out of him than these three unlikely inquisitors had.

Only Victoria remained silent, offering polite but brief answers when a question or comment was directed to her, but otherwise spending her time bent over her plate as she delicately nibbled at her food.

Although Miles found her silence somewhat disconcerting, he was most bothered by the fact that she acted as if he was not even present at the table, refusing to so much as glance at him and quickly turning her head away if he did manage to catch her eye.

At long last, the beleaguered Rebecca came puffing through the kitchen door, her red corkscrew curls bouncing in every direction as she collected their plates. Miles breathed a sigh of relief, immensely grateful that the interminable meal was finally coming to an end. Perhaps now he'd have an opportunity to speak privately to Victoria.

Her cool attitude during dinner had made it abundantly clear that she was still angry about his behavior that afternoon, and he wanted to apologize. Not only was he embarrassed by his cavalier treatment of her in the barn, but he also knew that if he were to have the slightest chance of purchasing King's Ransom, he needed to ingratiate himself with her.

Unfortunately, luck was not with him.

"I know it is the custom for the gentlemen to remain in the dining room with their brandy and cigars," Fiona said as she rose gracefully from her chair, "but we ladies would be delighted if you would join us in the drawing room."

"Oh, yes, Mr. Wellesley, please do!" Georgia enjoined, batting her eyes hopefully at Miles. "Carolina and I don't mind the smell of cigars at all, and we have so many more things we still wish to ask you about. And if you like," she added coyly, "we could probably be coerced into a short piano and voice recital."

Oh, my God, no! Miles thought desperately.

"That would be lovely," he said aloud.

"Wonderful!" Georgia enthused, clapping her small, milky white hands together. "It's all settled then. Shall we retire to the drawing room?"

As the party began to move out of the dining room, Miles saw Victoria veer off to the left and head for the stairs. "You aren't joining us?" he asked.

She turned to look at him, her expression forbidding. "No, Mr. Wellesley, I'm not. I'm quite weary. I'm going directly to my room."

"I'm sorry to hear that."

Victoria gave him a look that said she didn't believe that for a minute, then turned again toward the stairs.

Miles followed, determined to talk to her before she disappeared into the shadows leading to the second floor. "Lady Victoria?" he called.

By this time Victoria was halfway up the stairs. She paused again, her shoulders stiffening, then turned and gave him an impatient look. "Yes, Mr. Wellesley?"

"Could I speak with you for a moment?" Without waiting for a response he quickly ascended the staircase after her. "I understand that you are a horse enthusiast, and I thought we might have a chance to talk tomorrow . . ."

"I don't think so."

Miles blinked with surprise. "I beg your pardon?"

Victoria clasped her hands tightly in front of her. "Let me see if I can put this more succinctly. I don't want to talk to you. Not about horses or anything else for that matter."

Miles backed down a step, gaping up at her in astonishment. "I see. But I just wanted to say . . ."

"I don't care what you wanted to say," she interrupted rudely. "I'm not interested. Now, if you'll excuse me . . ." Gathering up her skirts, she climbed another step.

Miles's jaw clenched angrily as he watched her haughty departure. "Just a minute," he called. "I have something to say to you and I'm going to say it, even if I have to follow you all the way up to your bedroom to do it." He quickly bolted up three more steps until he was close enough to her that no one could overhear them. "I just wanted to say that I'm sorry about what happened in the barn this afternoon. I didn't know who you were."

To his surprise, Victoria turned blazing eyes on him. "That should have made no difference, sir. Your behavior was abominable, regardless of who I was."

"You're right," he admitted, having the good grace to look abashed. "I shouldn't have talked to you the way I did, and I apologize."

She blew out a long breath. "All right, then; as far as it goes, your apology is accepted." She continued to glare down at him, as if waiting for him to say more. When Miles didn't reply immediately she added, "Isn't there something else you want to apologize to me for?"

He looked at her blankly; then, suddenly, her meaning hit him. "No," he smiled, shaking his head. "I've said all I have to say. Was there something else you thought I should apologize for?"

Victoria's eyes narrowed as she searched his face, trying to determine whether he was toying with her. "The kiss, Mr. Wellesley. Don't you think you should apologize for that?"

Miles bit his lip, trying to quell the laughter that threatened him. "I suppose I could," he mused, "but it really wouldn't seem right to do so."

"Why not?"

"Because I'm not sorry."

Victoria's quickly indrawn breath told him that he'd probably just made a grave error in judgment, but what he'd said was the truth and he wouldn't take it back now.

"Oh! You are truly odious," she hissed, glaring at him in open hostility. "I find it astonishing that anyone with the charm and grace of the Viscountess of Ashmont could possibly be related to you. I guess it must be true what they say about

Americans: No matter how distinguished their lineage, enough time spent in that barbaric land turns you all into savages."

Miles's smile faded and his voice lost its teasing tone. "You think American men are barbarians simply because we like to kiss pretty girls out in the sunshine on a spring afternoon?"

"No, Mr. Wellesley," she parried, staring down her nose at him with a glacial look, "I think American men are barbarians because they don't have the manners to find out if the girl wants to be kissed before they do it."

Miles raised his eyebrows challengingly. "If I'd asked you, you would have undoubtedly said no, and then we both would have missed a very pleasant moment. Don't you agree?"

"No, sir, I most certainly do not."

Miles cocked his head, gazing directly into her dark eyes, as if judging the truth of her response. "Can you honestly look me in the eye, Lady Pembroke, and tell me that you didn't enjoy my kiss?"

Victoria's eyes bored into his. "Absolutely, Mr. Wellesley. I did not invite your kiss, nor did I enjoy it." Steeling herself against the mocking smile that curved his lips, she tried desperately to hold his gaze. But the unflinching clarity of his sea blue eyes was so disconcerting that she finally looked away.

"You know, that's very discouraging." He sighed.

"What is? To find out that British ladies of quality don't enjoy being mauled by strangers?" Her mouth curved in a triumphant smile.

"No, not that. What's discouraging is to find that 'British ladies of quality' aren't above telling lies."

Victoria's smile evaporated and her face flushed angrily, but before she could think of a suitable set down Miles turned on his heel and clattered down the stairs, disappearing around the corner into the drawing room.

She was still staring after him when, a moment later, she heard her half-sisters' titters of delight as the incorrigible man returned to their midst.

* * *

It was nearly two hours later when Miles was finally able to extricate himself from the twins and go to bed.

As he sank wearily into the luxurious feather mattress, a vision of Georgia and Carolina in their low-cut evening dresses rose in his mind. The two of them really were beautiful, with their creamy skin and pale hair. Funny, then, that neither of them aroused any feelings of desire within him. Perhaps it was their overt coyness and well-rehearsed flirtatiousness that put him off, but the whole time he was with them he couldn't help but feel he was being carefully and calculatedly tantalized.

Unfortunately, he'd had the same feeling with just about every eligible girl he'd met since arriving in England. It was as if all of them had been taught from some textbook entitled *Ten Never Fail Steps Guaranteed to Snare the Husband of Your Choice.* And because they all studiously adhered to an identical set of rules, the age-old game of courtship had lost much of its spontaneity.

Miles sighed, wishing that just one of the girls he had met would realize how much more exciting it would be for everyone if they would offer a little challenge to the men they hoped to attract.

Unbidden, an image of Victoria as she had looked in the barn that afternoon swam before his eyes. Now *there* was a woman who would be a worthy opponent in the timeless game between men and women. He smiled as he thought about his first heady encounter with her—the startling jolt of desire he'd felt during their kiss, and the anger she'd provoked in him with her caustic words on the stairs. Despite her rudeness that evening, the very thought of her stirred his senses.

She was gorgeous, she was intelligent, and she had spirit. In fact, from what he'd seen of Lady Victoria Pembroke, she was just about everything he found attractive in a woman—except interested. That something she definitely was not.

And yet, he was convinced that beneath the thin veneer of

proper Victorian spinsterhood that she wore like a banner of
honor lay a tempestuous and passionate nature. Her heated
response to his bold kiss had been testament to that. And odds
were that all it would take was the right man to unleash that
passion.

"And this 'odious, arrogant American boor' is just the one
to take you on, sweetheart," he whispered, grinning into the
darkness. "Get ready, Lady Victoria, because tomorrow morning the game begins."

Little did Miles realize what a formidable foe he had just
decided to engage.

Chapter 5

"Good morning."

Victoria jerked the brush away from King's Ransom's sleek coat and wheeled around to see Miles Wellesley leaning casually against the stall door. "What are you doing here?"

Miles shrugged innocently. "That's a strange question. I thought you understood last night at dinner why I'm here."

Irritably, Victoria threw the brush into a bucket and planted her hands on her slim hips. "Mr. Wellesley . . ."

"Ah," Miles grinned, "so you *do* remember my name, after all."

"Of course I remember your name. Unfortunately, you are a difficult man to forget."

Miles conveniently ignored the first word of her sentence and responded glibly, "Why, thank you. I'm very flattered that you find me memorable."

"That's not what I said," Victoria sputtered, shaking her head in frustration at the man's deliberate twisting of her words.

"I know what you said," he laughed, "but, since it looks like we're spending the morning together, what say you we start over and see if we can get off on a better footing? Good morning, Lady Victoria. You're looking absolutely ravishing today."

Although Miles's tongue had been firmly planted in his cheek through most of this conversation, his last statement, at least, was heartfelt. Victoria *did* look ravishing, clad in a pair of tight-fitting riding breeches, high black boots and a loose linen shirt that clung provocatively to her generous breasts. Her hair, as it had been the day before, was caught up in a loose chignon at the back of her neck. Several wispy tendrils had already come loose and now delicately framed her face. The perfection of her warm-toned skin and her clear, dark eyes made her look more fetching than any artificial enhancements ever could have.

"Mr. Wellesley," she began again, her voice taking on a definite tone of impatience, "I'm far too busy to stand here and play inane word games, much less 'spend the morning' with you, as you seem to think I'm going to. But, before I say adieu, I'd appreciate it if you'd answer my question."

Miles smiled guilelessly. "What question was that?"

By this time, Victoria was so frustrated with the infuriating man that she wanted to throw a currycomb at him. "I want to know what you are doing here in the barn again—alone. It was my understanding that my father was going to show you the horses this morning. Am I to take it that you are so anxious to rob our stable of its most valuable residents that you couldn't even extend my father the courtesy of waiting for him to escort you? Or did you just decide to repeat yesterday afternoon's escapade and sneak down here like a common thief?"

Miles's teasing grin faded. "No, Lady Victoria, even I, barbaric American that you think I am, am not quite that rude. The fact is, your maid, Rebecca, told me this morning that your father is a bit under the weather and is resting in bed today. It was his suggestion that I come down to the stables and enlist your assistance in showing me the stock."

"My father is ill?" Victoria asked, her voice suddenly betraying a frightened tremor. "Did Rebecca say what's wrong?"

Miles shook his head, surprised how concerned she was over what had seemed to him to be a minor ailment of some kind. "No she didn't, but she also didn't seem to be overly concerned about it. Why? Is there a problem with your father's health?"

Victoria looked at him for a moment, as if debating whether to confide even a kernel of personal information to him, then said slowly, "He has a bad heart."

It was Miles's turn to look concerned. "Is it serious?"

"Any condition of the heart is serious."

"I understand that, but some are a great deal more serious than others."

Victoria looked away for a moment, running her hand absently over Ransom's coat. "He gets pains in his chest once in a while, and sometimes he has trouble catching his breath. The pains always pass, but still . . ."

Miles frowned. One of his father's closest friends in America had shown a pattern of similar symptoms and had ultimately suffered a massive heart attack and died. "Have you had a physician examine him?"

Victoria's hands clenched and she threw him a withering look. "Yes, Mr. Wellesley, we have."

"And what did he say?"

"Not much," she admitted, "but please, don't concern yourself. It's not your affair and there's no need for you to get involved."

Despite his vow to be charming with the prickly woman, Miles felt his jaw tighten. "I'm sorry, my lady. I didn't realize you would interpret a gesture of concern as interference."

Although his comment caused Victoria to secretly regret her uncalled for rudeness, she refused to apologize to him. Instead, she swept out of Ransom's stall, pulling the door closed behind her and brushing her hands together. "All right, then. If my father wants me to show you the horses that are for sale, let's get to it." Seeing Miles's gaze drift over to King's Ransom, she added tartly, "He's not one of them."

"So I've been told," Miles acknowledged, dragging his eyes away from the beautiful animal. "All right; which ones are?"

Victoria strode down the barn aisle while Miles trailed along in her wake, appreciatively eyeing the gentle sway of her hips in her tight breeches. Four stalls farther down the lane, she paused.

"This is one of Ransom's sons," she announced, clucking softly to the horse in the stall. "His name is The Highwayman, and although he's only three, he's an excellent prospect for stud."

Miles's eyes skimmed assessingly over the horse. "I think 'excellent' might be stretching it a bit."

"I beg your pardon?"

Miles shrugged. "He doesn't have the breadth of chest I'm looking for."

Victoria shot him a tight-lipped look. "Fine. If that's the way you feel, it's your loss. Follow me, please." She stalked off again, not stopping until she reached the end of the aisle. "Here's another possibility. Perhaps you'll find his chest more to your liking."

"Is this also a son of King's Ransom?" Miles asked, walking up beside her.

Victoria nodded.

Miles carefully scrutinized the horse, then turned to Victoria and shook his head. "I'm afraid not."

If possible, her expression became even more hostile. "Why not? He has a very deep chest."

"You're right, he does, but I don't like his hindquarters."

"His hindquarters? What's wrong with them?"

"He's cowhocked."

"He is not!"

"Yes, he is. Look at his hind legs; his knees almost touch. As you know, that's not good in a breeding stallion." Wiggling his eyebrows meaningfully, he added, "Got to have strong, straight hind legs to get the job done, you know."

Victoria reacted exactly as he knew she would, drawing in

a scandalized little breath. "I refuse to even dignify that crude comment with an answer," she snapped, "but I do take issue with your other statement. Pembroke Stables does not breed cowhocked horses!"

"Well, you did this time." Miles shrugged. "And if you'd quit glaring at me long enough to take a good look at him, you'd see I'm right."

"You're wrong," Victoria insisted. "You're just looking at him from a strange angle. Perhaps if I brought him out of his stall . . ."

"Don't bother," Miles said, holding up a hand. "That colt is cowhocked—at any angle—and I'm definitely not interested in him. Do you have any other studs for sale?"

"Only two-year-olds," she gritted. "Since they'll not be ready for . . . breeding for at least another year yet, I'm sure you wouldn't be interested in them."

"Probably not," Miles agreed, "but I'd like to see them anyway."

With a curt nod, Victoria gestured for him to follow her. Walking over to the next aisle, she showed him three young horses. This time Miles reserved judgment until he had seen all of them.

"Well, what do you think of those?" Victoria finally asked.

"I think they have the same problem as the others: shallow chests and poor rear conformation. Does Ransom have these problems? They're certainly not apparent to the casual observer."

"King's Ransom has no problems whatsoever," Victoria retorted. "His conformation is nearly flawless. After all, he came in second in the Derby, and a horse doesn't do that with a 'shallow chest' and 'poor rear conformation.' "

"I agree," Miles said, looking down the aisle again at the two-year-olds. "But I'll wager if all his sons look like these, you haven't come close to having a runner of his quality since, have you?"

Victoria shifted her weight uncomfortably. "No, but if you

knew anything at all about horse breeding, which I still doubt, you'd know that stables often go many years without producing a champion. It will happen for us again. It's only a matter of time."

Miles shook his head. "I don't think so, unless you make some major changes in your breeding program. Tell me this: Do you own the dams of these colts?"

"Yes."

"May I see them?"

"They're excellent mares," she bristled.

"I'm not saying they aren't, Victoria. I'd just like to see them."

Victoria noticed that Miles had dropped her title and addressed her far more casually than their relationship allowed, but she decided to forego chastising him for this latest breach of etiquette. Instead, she nodded stiffly and led him across the barn's main aisle into the section reserved for the female horses. Together, they strolled down the length of the stalls, pausing occasionally as she pointed out the dams of the colts she had shown him.

"I think the mares are your problem," Miles said when they finished their brief tour.

"We don't *have* a problem, Mr. Wellesley."

Miles sighed with resignation. "All right; then let me put it this way. I think that, perhaps, these mares aren't as strong as King's Ransom deserves. Do they all have similar pedigrees?"

"Well, yes."

Miles nodded knowingly. "Then there's your problem."

Victoria's eyes narrowed into a wrathful glare. "I will say this just once more, sir: We do *not* have a problem! Pembroke stock has been respected among British horsemen for generations."

"I understand that. I wouldn't be here if it weren't. All I'm saying is that King's Ransom is too good a horse to be siring cowhocked foals and that the problem might be alleviated by breeding mares to him with a different pedigree than those you've been using."

"You obviously don't have the slightest idea what you're talking about," Victoria snorted. "None of these mares is cowhocked."

Miles shrugged. "I'll admit the problem isn't nearly as pronounced in the mares as it is in their sons, but that doesn't mean it doesn't exist. All I'm suggesting is that since the mares are of the same lineage, perhaps you need to look back a few generations and see if there was a problem at one time that has suddenly reasserted itself. If you find there wasn't, then perhaps the problem lies in Ransom's ancestors."

"I have spent many an hour researching Ransom's pedigree, Mr. Wellesley, and I can assure you, there is not a cowhocked horse anywhere."

A satisfied little smile played about Miles's lips. "Then I rest my case. It must be the mares." Slowly, he sauntered down the long line of stalls, looking into one and then the next, until finally he stopped at a stall near the back of the barn.

"Now, here's a lady who is definitely worthy of your champion."

Victoria hastened over to him, glancing into the stall and then, suddenly, bursting into triumphant laughter. "Spring Daffodil? Oh, Mr. Wellesley, I'm afraid you have finally betrayed your true lack of knowledge about Thoroughbreds."

Miles looked over at her, his breath catching in his throat as he drank in her beauty. Dear God, but the woman was gorgeous when she smiled. If only she'd do it more often, and for some other reason than to ridicule him. "Why do you say that?" he asked nonchalantly.

"Because this 'worthy lady,' as you call her, is at least fourteen or fifteen years old. My father bought her for me when I was a child. In fact, she's the horse I learned to ride on. She's far past her useful years, but I was so attached to her when I was young that Papa has kept her out of sentimentality."

Miles again turned to look at the elderly horse. "You mean you've never bred this mare?"

"Well, yes, once or twice when she was much younger, but not for years and years."

"Then you're missing a bet," he said flatly. "Just look at her conformation. Beautiful head and neck, large eyes, deep chest, straight legs. She's a splendid old girl. Looks like she might be Black Prince breeding."

Despite her vow not to give an ounce of credit to this arrogant stranger, Victoria couldn't conceal the look of grudging admiration that came into her eyes. "Actually, she is. Black Prince was her sire."

"Her sire!" Miles blurted. "You have a Black Prince daughter and you don't breed her?"

"I told you, Mr. Wellesley, she's retired."

"Nonsense. There's no reason in the world why you can't breed a mare of this age, unless she has health problems. Does she?"

"Not that I know of," Victoria admitted reluctantly.

"Then what do you have to lose? Breed her and see what you get. You couldn't do worse than the colts you've just shown me, and I guarantee you won't get cowhocks."

Victoria flushed angrily at his autocratic tone. "May I remind you, sir, that you weren't invited here to plan a breeding program for this stable. We have been doing it very successfully for several generations and I can assure you, we will continue to do so for many more, despite your opinion to the contrary. Now, if you've seen nothing you're interested in purchasing among the horses I've shown you, I don't think we have anything else to discuss."

Miles gazed around one last time, then shook his head. "No, Lady Victoria, I'm afraid I don't see anything for sale here that interests me."

"Fine. If you'll excuse me, I really do have a great deal of work to do." Without waiting for a response, she turned sharply on her heel and marched off down the barn aisle.

Miles watched her angry departure for a moment, then turned and absently stroked Spring Daffodil's soft nose. "Guess I didn't do a very good job of ingratiating myself with the lady, did I?" He chuckled. "But regardless of how put out your mistress is with my opinions, the fact remains, you're the finest mare in this barn and definitely the one who should be bred to His Majesty."

Spring Daffodil pulled her head away from his stroking hand, then playfully reached out to nibble at a lock of his blond hair.

"Stop it!" Miles laughed, backing up. "I know it looks like hay, but it's not!" Giving the mare one last pat, he turned and strolled out into the yard.

From behind a post at the back of the barn, Victoria surreptitiously watched Miles leave, waiting until she saw him reenter the house before she hurried out of the back door and over to the stablemaster's quarters. "George?" she called softly.

A bandy-legged old man suddenly appeared in the doorway, grinning with unconcealed delight at his unexpected visitor. "Yes, miss? Can I do something for you? Is there a problem in the barn?"

"No, nothing like that," Victoria answered, smiling fondly at him as he stepped out into the sunshine. "I just have a question."

"Yes, ma'am?"

"Spring Daffodil: Is she still . . . breedable?" Never, in all her years had Victoria discussed such an intimate topic with the stablemaster, and she could feel her face flush with embarrassment.

George's squinty old eyes widened in astonishment. What in the world would make Lady Victoria ask him such a scandalous question? Although the Pembrokes had always made the bulk of their living by breeding and racing horses, none of the young ladies of the household had ever so much as hinted that they knew where all those frolicking foals in the paddocks actually came from. Scratching his bald head to cover his discomfiture, he wheezed, "I expect so, miss. No reason why she wouldn't be."

Victoria looked down, unable to meet his eye as she asked her next question. "You mean, everything is still . . . normal with her?"

"Normal, miss?"

If possible, Victoria's color rose even higher. "You know, *normal* in that way . . . for that purpose."

George's hand stopped in midscratch as he realized what she was asking. "Oh, yes, ma'am." He nodded. "She be fine. Just like a young filly."

"Good. Then the next time she . . . well . . . the next time, I want her bred to King's Ransom."

"King's Ransom, miss?" George blurted, clearly taken aback by her request.

"Yes. King's Ransom."

"As you say, miss. King's Ransom it is. I'll keep a close eye on the mare starting today."

"Good," Victoria answered, forcing herself to raise her eyes and smile. "Please keep me posted."

George nodded, his old eyes nearly popping out of his head. "I'll do that, miss."

With a fleeting wave, Victoria turned and fled down the path leading to the main drive, leaving the stablemaster to stare after her in bewilderment.

"Breed King's Ransom to Spring Daffodil?" he muttered to himself. "The girl must be daft."

Walking into the barn, he proceeded directly to the old mare's stall, squinting at her closely. With expert eyes, he assessed the breadth of her chest and the parallel contours of her hind legs. "On second thought," he murmured, "she may not be so daft after all. In fact, it might be a right good idea at that."

Smiling fondly at the mare, he said, "So, they're going to

put you back into service, old girl, and breed you to His Nibs, no less. What do you think of that?"

Again, his gaze settled on Spring Daffodil's hind legs.

"Who knows? Introducing some of your daddy's blood into the strain might just solve that cowhock problem that nobody will admit to."

Chapter 6

Victoria was standing in front of a large pier glass, pinning her hair into a tight bun in preparation for a party Fiona had planned in Miles Wellesley's honor when, suddenly, Georgia raced into her bedroom, her face flushed and her eyes wide with incredulity. "Is it true, Tory?" she demanded breathlessly.

"Is what true?" Victoria asked, turning away from the mirror to look at her younger sister curiously.

"That you spent the whole morning with Mr. Wellesley!"

"It was hardly the whole morning," Victoria corrected, turning back to the mirror and patting an errant strand into place.

"But you were with him? Unchaperoned? In the barn?"

"Georgia, you know he came here to look at our horses. I merely showed him a few of the colts Papa has for sale. That's all there was to it."

Georgia flopped down on the edge of Victoria's bed, her mouth pursed in an envious little pout. "Oh, you're so lucky! I've been trying to figure out some way to spend time alone with Mr. Wellesley ever since he arrived and you, who don't even care, had the whole morning with him!"

Victoria leaned toward the mirror, pinching her cheeks to heighten their color. "It was nothing, Georgia. Nothing at all."

"It's just like you to say that," Georgia sighed. "But tell me truthfully, don't you think he's wonderful?"

"Wonderful?" Victoria laughed. "Hardly!"

"I don't understand you at all, Tory. I think Miles Wellesley is the most handsome, most charming, most *perfect* man I've ever met."

Victoria shrugged. "Everyone is entitled to their own opinion, I suppose."

"Are you saying you don't think he's handsome?"

"No, I'm not saying that, exactly. I suppose there are some women who would find him attractive, if they happened to like that grinning, toothy type."

"Toothy! You think he's toothy? Why, I think his smile is simply divine. And his hair . . . Don't you love his hair? It's exactly the same color as freshly churned butter."

"Oh, Georgia, really!" Victoria snorted. "What nonsense!"

"It's *not* nonsense. His hair is beautiful, and so is his smile. And those blue eyes, and that deep voice . . . Even with that unfortunate American accent, his voice is still wonderful."

Georgia stared off dreamily for a moment, then turned back to Victoria, studying her as if she were some curious specimen Georgia couldn't quite identify. "Do you know what I think your problem is, Tory?"

Victoria looked at her in exasperated amusement. "I didn't know you thought I had a problem."

"Well, maybe not a *problem,* exactly, but I think the reason you never show any interest in men is because you're not romantic. You're just so . . . so practical!"

"Georgia, you make being practical sound like a disease," Victoria protested. "Many people consider practicality a virtue."

Georgia threw her sister an apologetic look, then stood up and hurried over to lay a hand on her arm. "I'm sorry, my dear. I didn't mean to offend you. It's not that I think there's anything *wrong* with being practical. I just think that because you're so logical and unromantic, you don't see people the same way Carolina and I do."

Victoria quickly turned away, fearful that her face would betray how wrong Georgia's assessment was. If the truth be known, her impression of Miles Wellesley's magnificent physical attributes was not far different from her sisters'. She *had* noticed his golden hair, his lazy smile, his deep, rich voice. In fact, that morning, when they'd been standing next to each other outside Spring Daffodil's stall, she'd been hard pressed to keep herself from gaping at him in awe.

The man was incredibly handsome; there was no denying it. But he was also cocky, arrogant, autocratic and egotistical in the extreme. And Victoria was very glad that the "logical, unromantic" side of her nature afforded her the ability to see through his seemingly perfect facade.

Her younger sisters, with their naive, romantic notions about men and marriage, fell in love with nearly every male who looked their way and, consequently, there was hardly a time that at least one of them wasn't nursing a broken heart.

But Victoria was different, and more than once she had thanked the fates that had bestowed on her a level head and a sense of caution. Never, during her three Seasons on the marriage market, had she ever truly believed the honey-tongued young swains who had plied her with syrupy compliments or filled her head with empty promises in order to gain their own ends—be it her virtue or her fortune.

Fiona had frequently chastised her about her acerbic tongue and her innate wariness, insisting that it was these "unfeminine" characteristics that had prevented her from catching a husband.

But a husband had never been important to Victoria. In fact, as far as she could tell, most of her friends who had married were now little more than broodmares and personal servants to the men whom had once seemed to dote on them so expansively. Even those few who professed to be blissfully happy in their marriages stirred no envy within her.

She was perfectly content to be "on the shelf," as long as it meant she could come and go as she pleased and not have to answer to some overbearing, pompous jackass who felt he owned her, body and soul, just because he'd put a ring on her finger. And Miles Wellesley was no different than any of the others—except, perhaps, that he was a little smoother in his approach.

"Just remember, Georgia," Victoria said, holding up a warning finger as she turned back to face her sister, "there's much more to a man than his looks and his voice. You and Carrie would be wise to keep that in mind before you let yourselves fall in love with Mr. Wellesley."

"Oh, we know that." Georgia giggled, nudging Victoria aside and stepping in front of the pier glass to make one last check of her coiffure. "There's also wealth, social status and manners to consider. But Miles Wellesley has them all."

Victoria shot her a jaundiced look. "Wealth and social status, perhaps, but manners? You obviously haven't spent much time with him."

Georgia paused in her primping and looked at her sister in surprise. "Why do you say that? He wasn't rude to you, was he?"

A vision of Miles's seductive mouth just before it had settled on her lips swam up in Victoria's mind. "Not really rude," she murmured, "but he's . . . oh I don't know, too bold, I guess."

"Bold!" Georgia squealed, shivering deliciously. "I don't find anything objectionable about 'bold'—as long as it's not *that* way, of course."

"What way?"

Georgia blushed prettily. "Oh, you know. That man woman way." She paused, scrutinizing her sister carefully. "That's not what you mean, is it? He didn't try to take . . . liberties with you, did he?"

Victoria's breath caught in her throat. "Of course not," she said quickly. "Whatever would make you think that?"

"Because I've heard gossip about him," Georgia confided.

"Oh, I've heard all of that nonsense, too. And that's just what it is . . . idle gossip."

Georgia looked around surreptitiously, as if making sure that no one was lurking inside one of the wardrobes. Then, in a conspiratorial whisper, she hissed, "Not all of it. I know for a fact that at least some of what everyone is saying about him is true because I had it from Cynthia Highcroft herself that he tried to kiss her in an alcove at the Huntfords' ball."

Victoria's eyebrows shot up before she could stop them, but by the time she spoke she had regained her composure and her voice was reproachful, betraying none of her surprise. "You shouldn't believe everything you hear. Everyone knows that Cynthia Highcroft exaggerates about everything."

"I know," Georgia admitted, "but I heard the same thing from Elizabeth Hanford. She swears that Mr. Wellesley tried to kiss her at the Kingstons' post-hunt breakfast. So, you see, what they're saying about him being a rounder is true. But, surely he wouldn't have tried anything like that with you!"

For some reason Victoria couldn't identify she found Georgia's confidence that Miles Wellesley wouldn't try to take liberties with her incredibly insulting. "Why wouldn't he?" she asked peevishly.

"You mean he did?"

"I didn't say that. I just wondered why you seem so sure he wouldn't."

"I don't know," Georgia faltered, not fully understanding why her usually unflappable older sister suddenly seemed to be so put out with her. "You're just not the kind of woman . . ."

". . . that men want to take liberties with?" Victoria finished.

"Why, Tory, you're angry!"

"No, I'm not," Victoria said quickly. "It's just that sometimes . . ."

Georgia's eyes widened into huge blue saucers of disbelief. "Are you saying that you *wish* Mr. Wellesley had taken liberties with you? Tory, I'm shocked that you'd even *think* something like that, much less say it out loud! My word, what would Mother say if she heard you?"

"I'm *not* saying that!" Victoria snapped, snatching a lacy fan off her dresser, even though the night had turned cold and rainy. "I'm not saying anything except to warn you and Carolina to be careful around Mr. Wellesley. Remember, he's American, not British, and American men are . . . well, different than our gentlemen."

"I know that," Georgia giggled. "That's what makes them so exciting!"

Victoria looked at her sister and sighed. There was just no reasoning with either of the twins when it came to the subject of men. "I give up," she chuckled, shaking her head in surrender. "Come along, we had better go downstairs. Fiona said Papa still isn't feeling well enough to attend the party tonight, and you know how annoyed she gets if she has to receive alone."

"I'm coming." Georgia nodded, giving her full lavender skirts a last satisfied pat. "But I still want to know why you said Mr. Wellesley is bold."

Victoria waved her fan in airy dismissal. "Never mind. It was just a bad choice of words."

Georgia looked at her sister with uncharacteristic shrewdness. "I don't think so, Tory. I think something happened while you two were alone together in the barn—and before the evening is over I mean to find out what!"

Miles stood at the perimeter of the Pembrokes' large ballroom and wearily watched the room begin to fill. Another party. Another five or six hours of being forced to smile, dance, flirt and mingle with dozens of women who had nothing more stimulating to talk about than the weather or the latest London rage in men's headwear—the ridiculous-looking bowler hat.

Didn't these people have anything better to do than attend parties? How did anyone ever get any business done in this country when mornings were spent sleeping off the previous night's excesses and afternoons were taken up preparing for the next night's revelries?

He was still shaking his head and frowning when his friend Alexander Shaw sauntered over with two glasses of brandy. "You're looking to be in fine fettle tonight, Wellesley," he greeted, offering Miles one of the drinks. "New frock coat?"

"Yes," Miles admitted, smiling a bit sheepishly. "When I first arrived my grandmother made it perfectly clear that she did not find my 'cowboy wardrobe' as she called it, suitable for polite company, and she insisted that I go to a tailor and have some 'proper' clothes made. What I'll do with all these embroidered waistcoats and silk cravats once I go home I can't imagine. They should give my younger brothers a good laugh, though."

"Ah, yes." Alex chuckled. "All those brothers. How is the Wellesley tribe?"

"Fine," Miles answered, his face taking on a fond expression. "Growing. Raising hell. Stu is at Harvard. Eric has announced that as soon as he's finished with school, he wants to move someplace where he can start a farm, of all things, and Geoff is still cutting down every tree he can find."

"Why?"

"Who knows why he does what he does? He's fifteen. He says he's collecting a sample of all the different species native to western Colorado. I don't know what he plans to do with the collection once he's completed it, but that's what he says he's doing."

"And the little ones? How are they?"

Miles smiled again. "Nate and Seth spend most of their time running horses into the ground, playing sheriff and outlaw, and the babies, Adam and Paula, just try to stay out of everybody's way so they don't get trampled."

"You know, I always love hearing about your family." Alex laughed. "Being an only child, it's absolutely fascinating to envision being brought up in a household with so many children."

"Tell you what, Shaw, you come visit sometime and you'll find out how fast fascination turns to frustration."

"Ah, come now, Wellesley, you know you adore them."

"Sure I do, and I miss them all like hell. But they still drive me crazy sometimes." He paused, looking around the increasingly crowded ballroom, then added, "But not as crazy as this does."

"You really don't care for British society, do you?"

"It's not that. I like a good party as much as the next man. But every night . . . the same people talking about the same things. Don't you ever get bored with it?"

Alex shrugged. "I guess when you're born into it you just come to accept that during the Season this is normal. Besides, how else are we going to meet our future wives? How do you meet girls in America?"

"Lots of ways. At parties, in church; sometimes through friends of our parents."

"That doesn't sound much different to me," Alex noted.

"I guess it's not," Miles conceded. "As I told you the other night, I think I'm just bored with all this because I'm in the market for a horse, not a wife."

"Ah yes. How did your tour of Pembroke's stables go today? Did you find anything you like?"

"Only one. And he's not for sale."

"You must mean King's Ransom."

Miles nodded ruefully. "That's the one."

"You might as well forget it," Alex advised. "Pembroke would be more apt to sell one of the States than he would that stud." He paused, a small smile quirking the corner of his mouth. "Now, there's an idea, Wellesley. Why don't you marry yourself into ownership?"

Miles looked at him as if he'd lost his mind. "No thanks. I don't want the stud *that* badly! Anyway, I was told the horse belongs to Lady Victoria. The twins have no claim to him."

"I've heard that, too," Alex nodded, "although I wasn't sure if it was really true."

"According to John Pembroke, it is."

Alex shook his head. "Well, then, old boy, I guess you're out of luck. God knows, no horse on earth would be worth spending your life trying to tame that little virago. Have you met her yet?"

Miles nodded. "As a matter of fact, I spent the morning with her. She's the one who showed me the horses, since her father wasn't feeling well."

"Is Sir John ill again?" Alex asked in surprise.

"Apparently."

"No wonder I didn't see him when I arrived. Poor man, he's really quite unwell, you know. Something to do with his heart."

"That's what Victoria said."

"Oh," Alex chortled. "So it's 'Victoria,' is it? I guess you two must have gotten along better than I expected."

"Not really," Miles denied, draining his glass and setting it on a passing maid's tray. "She was just as prickly as you said she would be. In fact, when I made a couple of negative comments on the quality of the stock she was showing me, she more or less told me to go to hell and walked away."

Alex's eyes widened. "She actually told you to go to hell?"

"Not in so many words. But close."

"Sounds just like her." Alex chuckled. "Now you know why she's twenty-three and still unmarried. She always . . ." His voice trailed off as his attention was suddenly drawn to a movement near the ballroom's huge double doors. "And speaking of the Ice Queen, here she comes now."

Following Alex's gaze, Miles watched Victoria enter the ballroom, flanked on either side by the smiling twins. As usual, the pretty blond girls were dressed in complementary pastels, while Victoria had again opted for gunmetal gray. As it had been the previous evening, her hair was tightly bound to the back of her head, without so much as a loose wisp to soften her austere presentation. Her lips were set in a stiff smile, but even from across the room Miles could see that the expression didn't reach her dark eyes.

She doesn't enjoy this sort of thing any more than I do, he thought.

"She really loves to play the part of the spinster older sister, doesn't she?" Alex commented.

Miles nodded. "I wonder why."

"Probably because she's resigned herself to the fact that that's what she is."

"I don't think so," Miles mused. "My guess is that she's not nearly as pleased at having been passed over as she'd like everyone to believe. In fact, I think that beneath that prudish exterior there's a passionate woman just aching to be set free."

"Oh, Wellesley, you've got to be joking," Alex snorted. "Why, I'd lay a wager that the girl has never even allowed herself to be kissed."

Miles turned to him, a grin lighting his handsome face. "Then you'd be wrong."

"How would you know that?"

"Because I kissed her myself. Yesterday. In the barn. Now, if you'll excuse me, I think I'll go ask the lady for a dance."

Abruptly, Miles walked away, leaving Alex to stare after him in stunned disbelief.

Chapter 7

Victoria saw Miles striding across the highly polished ballroom floor in her direction, but before she realized he was headed for her, he was already there.

"Good evening," he smiled, "and congratulations on a lovely party."

Quickly, Victoria glanced over her shoulder, hoping desperately that she might find someone standing behind her to whom Miles's attentions were directed.

He caught her furtive look and chuckled. "There's no one back there, Lady Victoria. I'm talking to you."

Biting the inside of her lip to prevent herself from commenting on the mocking laughter she saw dancing in his eyes, she said simply, "Thank you, Mr. Wellesley, for the compliment. Perhaps you'll want to share it with my stepmother; the party is her doing."

"I've already spoken to Lady Fiona," he assured her, "and to your sisters."

"Oh, I see. So, I'm the only one who's left?"

"Not at all," he returned smoothly. "I was just saving the best for last. Would you care to dance?"

Victoria cocked her head, assessing his unwavering smile for a moment. "You know, Mr. Wellesley, I don't understand you at all."

Miles stepped closer, intrigued by her unexpected comment. "What don't you understand, my lady?"

"Why you're trying to charm me. Surely it must be obvious to you that I am the one woman in my family who doesn't have any interest in you. Why don't you concentrate your efforts on my sisters? I'm sure you would have more luck with them, since your masculine charms are completely wasted on me."

Miles's smile evaporated and he used the excuse of plucking two champagne glasses off a passing maid's tray to regain his composure. "What's wrong with you?" he asked flatly as he handed her a flute of champagne.

"I beg your pardon?"

"You heard me. What's wrong with you that you're always so rude?"

Victoria shot him a haughty look. "Are you saying that you think there's something wrong with me because I'm not fawning all over you?"

"No, I'm not saying that at all. I'm just puzzled about why you're so hostile toward me. Is this the way you treat every man, or is it just me you don't like?"

Without a moment's hesitation, she responded, "Oh, it's definitely you."

Her frank answer took Miles aback and, for a moment, he wasn't sure whether he should be insulted or impressed by her candor. "Well, at least you're honest," he conceded. "But I still don't understand what I've done to cause such an intense dislike on your part."

Victoria took a sip of her champagne, her eyes meeting his over the rim of her glass. "I should think it would be obvious, sir. You wangle an invitation into my father's home, sneak into our barn like a common thief, then have the audacity to insult our stock and our breeding program."

"Not to mention my audacity in daring to touch the untouchable Victoria Pembroke," Miles concluded.

Victoria's steady gaze skittered away for a moment. "I would prefer if that unpleasant incident wasn't mentioned again," she murmured.

Miles stared at her for a long moment, then drained his glass and set it on a nearby table. "Please forgive me for my many shortcomings, my lady. I won't bother you again." With a curt bow, he turned and stalked off, leaving Victoria openmouthed with surprise and, to her annoyance, feeling more than a little disappointed.

"I thought you were going to dance with the lady," Alex said as Miles walked up to him. Although Alex had not heard the conversation between the couple, he had closely watched the interplay of expressions as they'd talked. It hadn't taken a genius to see that Miles's encounter with the snippy Lady Victoria had not gone at all as he'd planned.

"She didn't want to dance," Miles said shortly.

Alex sighed dramatically and cast his friend a pitying look. "Well, don't take it too personally, Wellesley. Victoria Pembroke hasn't danced in years."

"Do you mean that literally or figuratively?"

Alex's look of sympathy dissolved into a grin. "Both."

The men stood together sipping their drinks; then Alex nudged Miles in the ribs and gestured over to a far corner of the ballroom. "Look over there. It appears that the lady under discussion is having a bit of a set-to with her stepmother."

Miles looked over in the direction Alex indicated to see Fiona obviously giving Victoria a dressing down about something. Although the women were careful to keep their voices low enough not to draw attention to themselves, Fiona's furious expression and Victoria's mutinous look betrayed the anger flaring between them.

"I think Lady Fiona is more than a little put out that Victoria refused to dance with you."

Miles watched the byplay between the two women for a moment, then shook his head. "As flattering as I might find that possibility, I doubt that whatever they're discussing has anything to do with me."

"I think you're wrong," Alex disagreed. "Fiona was all smiles before your little altercation with Victoria."

"Why should she care if Victoria dances with me or not?"

Alex looked at him in amusement. "Oh, come now, Wellesley. Surely you're not so provincial that you don't see what a good catch you'd be for one of the Pembroke girls. You're handsome, wealthy, come from a fine family and your grandmother's lands butt right up to their estate. I've told you before, Lady Fiona is no fool, and if she smells a potential match looming between you and one of her girls, she's going to do everything she can to promote it."

"But Victoria isn't one of her girls," Miles argued.

"She's a stepdaughter, and that's close enough. Anyway, everyone knows that Lady Fiona is very fond of Victoria, and if you aren't showing any interest in either of the States, I'm sure she's willing to settle for the next best thing."

Miles glanced over at Victoria and Fiona again, then shrugged. "It's a moot point. The lady made it perfectly clear that she didn't want to dance with me, and I'm not about to ask again."

"I'm sure that's exactly what Lady Fiona is chastising her about."

The men's conversation drifted on to other topics; then Alex excused himself to greet several acquaintances who had arrived late. Miles stood at the perimeter of the ballroom, sipping another glass of champagne. Finally, realizing that his grandmother would undoubtedly take him to task if he didn't show at least a modicum of interest in the party, he sauntered over to where Carolina Pembroke stood near a flower-bedecked punch bowl.

"Would you care to dance, my lady?" Miles asked, executing his best courtier's bow. He wasn't surprised when she, unlike her prickly sister, enthusiastically agreed.

"I'm so glad you asked me to dance, Mr. Wellesley," Carolina said as they dipped and swayed to the strains of a Strauss waltz. "I had heard from several of my friends that you are a wonderful dancer, and I see now that they were right."

Miles chuckled and Carolina's carefully plucked brows drew together in a charmingly perplexed expression. "Do you find my observation amusing, sir?"

Miles nodded. "Actually, I do, considering that most of the dancing I've done in my life has been in barns."

"Barns!"

"Yes. In Colorado that's where we do our dancing."

Carolina threw him a disbelieving look. "Surely you're not saying that you don't have a ballroom or a salon in your house in which to hold parties and dances."

"We have a big parlor and a huge dining room," Miles explained, noticing with amusement the furious glare Georgia shot her twin as she danced by. "But if there's going to be a big crowd and we're going to dance, we generally head for the barn."

Carolina shook her head. "I'll just never understand American ways. I'm so glad that even though Mama is American, she was sensible enough to realize how much more refined it is to live in England." Noting that Miles's expression had hardened at her unthinking slur, she quickly amended, "Actually, I'm sure if I ever had the chance to visit America, though, I'd love it. Mama assures me that it's beautiful and, in some areas, even reasonably civilized."

"In some places," Miles responded sarcastically.

Seemingly oblivious that she had just compounded one insult with another, Carolina careened off to another subject. "Look, there's Mama and Tory over there by the potted palm." Catching her mother's eye, she waved gaily. "You know, I can't imagine what they've had their heads together about for so long. They've been discussing something over there in that corner ever since we started to dance." Miles followed the direction of her gaze, confirming that Fiona and Victoria were indeed still embroiled in heated conversation, despite the frozen smiles they were carefully maintaining.

"I can't imagine either," he murmured. "Do you want to join them?"

"Oh, no!" Carolina said quickly, turning her attention back to him and gracing him with a dimpled smile. "I can talk to them anytime." She looked up at Miles flirtatiously, then cast her eyes downward in a calculated gesture of maidenly modesty. "I'd much rather spend the entire evening dancing with you." Again she lifted her eyes to his. "Don't you just love to dance, Mr. Wellesley? Couldn't you just do it all night long?"

Miles was eternally grateful that before he was forced to answer that question the music stopped. "Thank you for the dance," he said graciously, taking her arm and herding her subtly off the dance floor.

Carolina threw him a stricken look as she suddenly found herself being deposited next to her mother, but before she could think of a way to ingratiate herself back into his arms for another dance, Miles had nodded his farewell and headed off across the floor toward Alex and his bachelor friends.

"Oh, Mr. Wellesley?"

Miles slowed his step, cursing softly under his breath when he heard Fiona's husky voice beckoning him back. Sighing with resignation that a dance with the empty-headed Georgia was most certainly looming in his immediate future, he turned. "Yes, my lady?"

"I wonder if you would ask Lord Brooks to attend me for a moment."

Miles's mental sigh of relief was almost audible. "Certainly, ma'am." Joining the small knot of men, he grinned and said, "Oh, Marcus, Lady Fiona wishes for you to attend her for a moment."

A low rumble of laughter echoed across the group as Marcus sent them a perplexed smile and hurried off toward their hostess.

"And how was your dance with the beauteous Lady Carolina?"

Miles threw Alexander a jaundiced look. "Very flattering. She told me she wishes we could dance all night long."

A young sandy-haired man named Livingston Haworth stepped up to Miles and handed him a fresh glass of champagne. "I have to hand it to you, Wellesley; you really do have a way with the ladies."

"With all of them except the one he wants," Alex qualified.

Livingston's eyebrows raised with interest. "And who might that be?"

"Shaw . . ." Miles warned.

But Alexander was too far into his cups to heed Miles's softly voiced threat and plunged on. "Why, Victoria the Unapproachable; who else?"

Livingston whirled on Miles, his jaw dropping with astonishment. "Victoria Pembroke? Why in the world would you be interested in that old maid when you can have your pick of any of the debs in the room?"

"He even asked her to dance," Alex added, poking Livingston in the ribs good-naturedly. "But of course she turned him down."

"Of course." Livingston laughed. "Oh, Wellesley, you really should have talked to us first and saved yourself the trouble. We could have told you that Lady Victoria never dances with anyone. Why, that nose of hers is so far up in the air that I don't think she could see to dance even if she wanted to!"

Miles turned a furious look on the laughing men. "All right, that's enough. If I hear one more word about Lady Victoria from either one of you, I'm going to be forced to ask you to step outside."

Alexander and Livingston sobered immediately. "Sorry, Wellesley," Livingston mumbled contritely. "I had no idea you were serious about the girl."

"I'm not *serious* about anybody," Miles retorted hotly. "I

simply asked the lady to dance. It's only common courtesy when she's our host's daughter."

Alex leaned toward Livingston and whispered loudly, "Notice, however, that he hasn't asked Georgia to dance, and she's our host's daughter, too."

"A situation which I plan to remedy immediately," Miles shot back. Turning on his heel, he stalked off in the direction of Georgia Pembroke who, seeing him coming, broke into a blinding smile of welcome.

After enduring an endless waltz with the simpering, cooing girl Miles again returned to his friends. This time when he approached them, however, they were all staring at him with unconcealed respect. Looking from one face to the next, he said, "What? What is it?"

"Truly amazing," Alex muttered. "The man gets absolutely everything he wants."

"What in the hell are you talking about?" Miles demanded. "Why are you all gawking at me?"

Marcus Brooks sidled closer and bent his head toward Miles conspiratorially. "We're gawking, Wellesley, because you have managed to do the impossible."

"What are you talking about?"

"What Lady Fiona wanted when she called me over was to tell me that Lady Victoria very much regrets having turned down your invitation to dance. She has decided that she would love to dance with you, and her stepmother asked me if I might let you know that another invitation would be gladly accepted . . . if you are still interested, of course."

For a long moment, Miles just stared at Marcus. Then, with a shake of his head, he began to laugh. "You know, you British are crazy. Absolutely crazy!"

Marcus's smile disappeared and his brows drew together in a look of affront. "Crazy! Why would you say that?"

"Because you are," Miles said. "Lady Fiona asked me to have you attend her so she could tell you to tell me that Lady

Victoria would like me to ask her to dance. Think about it, Marcus. It's absurd!"

Marcus threw Miles a haughty look. "Oh, and I suppose you Americans would have handled the whole situation more expediently?"

"Far more," Miles confirmed. "In America the girl would simply come up to the man, apologize for turning him down the first time and tell him she'd like to dance. Then the couple would dance and that would be the end of it."

Marcus cast off this scenario with an impatient gesture. "Sounds so simple as to be downright boring. At any rate, old man, no matter how the message was delivered, the important point is that the lady has changed her mind. Now the question remains, are you going to dance with her?"

"No," Miles answered, and setting his empty glass on a silver tray he bowed to his friends and walked out of the ballroom.

Chapter 8

Miles sat down on a stone bench on the balcony outside the ballroom and blew out a long, weary breath. He wanted to go home. Closing his eyes, he pictured the soaring peaks and verdant valleys of southwestern Colorado and his heart wrenched in his chest.

He'd had such high hopes when he'd set out on this trip. He and his father had spent much of the long, cold Colorado winter, talking about his plans to crossbreed the native American horses with the more sophisticated British breeds, ultimately producing an animal suited for both working and riding. When spring had finally come and he'd been able to take ship for England it had seemed like such a simple goal. He would travel to Britain, visit his beloved grandmother, find a few good stallions to suit his purposes and return home to begin his career.

What had gone wrong?

"Everything," Miles muttered irritably, leaning his head back against the cold stone wall behind him. "Everything has gone wrong."

He had wasted the whole first month of his stay fruitlessly searching for a stallion to suit his needs. Now, when he'd finally found King's Ransom, who was exactly what he was looking for, he couldn't coerce the horse's owner into selling—regardless of the fact that the man was so impoverished that he was selling the family portraits right off the walls. And those daughters of his . . . What annoying distractions they had turned out to be—two of them because they wouldn't let him out of their sight and the other because she couldn't stand to have him in hers.

Then there was his grandmother. Miles readily admitted that there was hardly a soul on earth whom he loved more than he loved Regina Wellesley, but even she had become trying, with her well-intentioned but futile attempts to pair him up with the first blue-blooded maiden he happened to glance at. He knew it was only Regina's great love for him that motivated her to so desperately want him to marry and settle in England, but she didn't seem to be able to understand that it was not going to happen.

At least his grandmother could comfort herself with the knowledge that Miles's lack of interest was not due to her lack of trying. From the number of parties he'd attended in the past month he was certain he must have met every unmarried woman within three shires. And no one had caught his eye . . . no one, that is, except Victoria Pembroke, and for the life of him, he couldn't imagine what it was about her that he found so intriguing. Probably just the fact that she was so outspoken in her dislike of him.

Miles shrugged, deciding that his brief infatuation with Victoria was not worth pondering further. After all, tomorrow morning he was returning to his grandmother's estate, and he'd probably never see her again.

At that moment the object of his musings strolled out onto the balcony and leaned over the railing, breathing deeply of the cool night air.

"A bit stuffy inside, isn't it?"

Victoria whirled around at the deep, rich sound of Miles's

voice, her hand flying to her throat. "Good Lord, Mr. Wellesley, you scared me to death. I didn't see you out here."

Miles smiled into the darkness, guessing astutely that if Victoria had known of his presence, she would quickly have retreated into the crowded ballroom rather than face a private moment with him on the deserted balcony.

Standing up, he sauntered over to stand next to her, draping his arms over the banister and gazing out over the flower gardens.

"Lovely night," Victoria murmured. "May is the month of the year I love most."

Miles's eyebrows rose with interest. "Why is that?"

Victoria ran her tongue across her lips, cursing her dry mouth and pounding heart. What was it about this man that every time he came near her she reacted like a blushing schoolgirl at her first dance? He was standing so close to her that she could feel the heat of him through the fabric of her dress, and she knew that if she turned her head in his direction, the wisps of hair escaping her tight bun would brush against his cheek.

"I love it when the flowers bud and the trees bloom," she said quietly.

"I know what you mean. At home at this time of year, the mountains are covered with spring grass and the first blooming of blue columbine. It makes the whole world look new and fresh."

Slowly, Victoria turned to gaze at him. He was so handsome. Even in the darkness, his hair shone with an ivory hue and the faint light pouring out from the ballroom cast mesmerizing shadows on his full, sensuous lips. For a moment she stared at his mouth, remembering what it had felt like when he had kissed her in the barn. Soft and warm, yet firm and sculpted, the sensation of Miles Wellesley's lips on hers was a memory she would hold close for the rest of her life.

"Would you like to dance?"

His voice was so low that had they not been standing right next to each other, Victoria might not have even heard him.

But she *had* heard him, and when she answered her tone was as soft as his had been.

"Here?"

"Yes."

With a slow nod, Victoria held out her hand.

Miles clasped her hand in his and even through her glove, Victoria felt a sizzle of electricity surge all the way up her arm. The feeling was exciting, almost frightening, and for a split second she almost drew away. Warily, she lifted her eyes to meet his, but the warmth she saw within those blue depths made her relax and step into his embrace. His arm circled her waist and they began to move in a graceful circle across the balcony.

A silent moment passed, the only sound the swish of Victoria's satin dress and the faraway splash of a fountain in the garden.

"You dance very well," she murmured.

"So do you," he returned.

He gathered her closer, wondering briefly if she would protest, but her body remained pliant, moving in time with his with an effortlessness that belied the fact that this was their first dance together.

The tempo of the music slowed and unconsciously, Miles accepted the violins' seductive invitation, moving his hand up Victoria's back and bending his head so that his warm breath stirred the soft hair at the nape of her neck.

Instinctively, she turned her face toward his beckoning lips, her eyes drooping languidly as she anticipated his kiss.

From inside the ballroom the final note of the waltz died away. It was the loudest silence Victoria had ever heard and, quickly she opened her eyes, pulling her head away.

The moment had passed.

Silently cursing the orchestra's bad timing, Miles stopped moving and, after an instant of frustrated hesitation, released Victoria from his embrace. He stepped back, looking down at her hungrily for a moment, then took her hand and led her back to the stone bench.

They sat down, each of them struggling to regain their composure as they stared intently out at the gardens. Finally, after an interminable silence, Miles spoke. "I'll be leaving tomorrow morning."

Victoria felt an unexpected little knot of disappointment twist deep inside her. "Oh?"

Miles held his breath, hoping she might say something, *anything,* to encourage him to stay longer. But she didn't, and after another strained moment he spoke again. "I'm hoping to speak to your father before I go. How is he feeling?"

Victoria shook her head . "Not well at all, I'm afraid."

"What does the doctor say?"

"That it's just another episode. The pains come; then, after a few days spent in bed, he feels better. Rest seems to help."

"But the pains eventually come back?"

Slowly, Victoria nodded. "Yes."

"Does the doctor have any idea what brings on the pains?"

Idly, Victoria plucked at a nonexistent piece of lint on her gray dress. "Different things. Stress or upset, usually."

"Is your father upset about something?"

She let out a trembling sigh and, for the first time since they'd begun this conversation, looked over at him. "More nervous than upset, I think."

Miles's look of concern faded to one of bewilderment. "Nervous? About what?"

"You."

"Me? What do I have to do with this?"

Pressing her lips together, Victoria turned and faced him squarely. "Papa was hoping you might find one of our stallions to your liking, but after his talk with you the other evening I think he realized you're only interested in Ransom, and he knows I won't sell him."

Miles's expression tensed. "You mean you'd sooner let your

father suffer heart pains than sell a horse? Don't you think that's a bit selfish of you?"

Victoria drew in a quick breath, shocked by his unexpected accusation. Jumping to her feet, she whirled on him. "How dare you speak to me like that? You don't understand anything, Mr. Wellesley, so I will thank you not to make judgments." With an outraged jerk of her chin she stalked off toward the French doors leading back into the ballroom.

"Good night, Lady Victoria. Thank you for the dance."

She did not return Miles's farewell.

Lady Fiona let out a long disappointed breath and leaned heavily against the ballroom wall. She had been standing in the concealing shadows near the balcony door for several minutes, shamelessly watching Miles and Victoria as they shared their private encounter.

At first she had been ecstatic, watching the couple dance together, moving ever closer until their lips were nearly touching. She had held her breath, waiting for the kiss she knew was coming; then she cursed under her breath when the music stopped and they moved apart.

Her hopes had soared again, however, as Miles had taken Victoria's hand and led her over to the secluded bench. Although Fiona couldn't hear what they were saying as they sat together, secluded from prying eyes, she was aware the moment the conversation turned from an intimate chat to an angry confrontation. The only thing she couldn't figure out was what had been said to so quickly change their attitudes toward each other.

Whatever it was, she was convinced it was Victoria's doing, since it was she who had stalked off in a rage. Damn the girl! Didn't she realize how much the family needed Miles Wellesley's goodwill? Fiona thought she'd made it perfectly clear to her earlier that evening when she'd confronted her about her refusal to dance with him, but obviously she'd failed to make her point.

Peering around the doorjamb, Fiona sneaked a peek at Miles. He was still seated on the bench, staring moodily out at the rose garden. She sighed, wishing for the hundredth time that it had been Georgia or Carolina whom he had been attracted to. Her own two girls were so much more conformable than the difficult and obstinate Victoria.

Still, Fiona was not about to give up on Miles Wellesley. She had seen the hotly charged looks that had passed between the couple while they had danced, and regardless of how stubbornly Victoria insisted that she felt nothing for the handsome American, Fiona knew better. No woman looked at a man as Victoria had looked at Miles unless she felt a great deal.

Fiona sighed, knowing that it was going to be up to her to make Victoria realize that she was attracted to the man, then figure out a way to bring the couple back together. After that she was convinced that nature would take its course.

Please God that she was right.

"Sir John will see you now, Mr. Wellesley."

Miles set his hat and gloves on top of his traveling valise and rose from the hard chair on which he was sitting. "Thank you, Rebecca." He smiled.

The pert little red-haired maid bobbed a curtsy, blushing profusely in response to the handsome man's smile. "Oh, you're welcome, sir, you certainly are." With a dramatic flourish she flung open the door to Sir John's bedchamber and waved Miles through. "Mind you don't keep him long, sir," she whispered loudly. "The master really ain't feelin' up to snuff this morning."

"I'll only stay a moment, I promise," Miles returned conspiratorially. Reaching out, he gave a playful tug to one of Rebecca's flaming corkscrew curls. "You have very pretty hair, Rebecca."

The little maid looked as if she might faint from pure pleasure, but before she could think of a worthy response to his unexpected compliment Miles had slipped through the bedroom door and closed it softly behind him.

At the sound of the door Sir John opened sunken, red-rimmed eyes and forced a wan smile. "Ah, Mr. Wellesley," he wheezed, his voice sounding raspy and breathless, "so sorry about this situation. Damned inconvenience."

Miles walked over to the bed, careful to conceal his distress at Sir John's rapidly failing condition. "Please don't concern yourself, sir. Unfortunately, there's never a convenient time to be ill."

Sir John nodded weakly and patted the mattress next to him. "Sit down, my boy, and let's have a chat. Fiona tells me you're leaving this morning."

Cautiously, Miles perched a hip on the edge of the large bed. "Yes, sir. I have to return to my grandmother's. I want you to know, though, how much I've appreciated the wonderful hospitality you and your family have shown me in the last few days."

Sir John managed another pained smile. "Glad you enjoyed yourself. My dear Fiona does know how to put on a party, doesn't she? I just wish you could have found a horse you liked. I was hoping to do some business with you."

Miles felt a rush of guilt course through him. It was obvious Sir John was far more ill than anyone was admitting, and it tore at him to think that his lack of interest in the man's horses had played any part in his current malaise. "I was hoping so too, sir, but I'm looking for a very specific type of stud and, unfortunately, I haven't found it yet."

"Except for King's Ransom." Sir John sighed.

Miles nodded slowly. "Except for King's Ransom. But I understand why you don't want to sell him. He's a magnificent animal and if he were mine, I wouldn't sell him either."

Sir John closed his eyes without answering, but just when Miles thought that he must have drifted off to sleep, he opened them again. "Well, you never know, my boy," he said, as if there had been no lull in the conversation, "we might do business yet."

Miles's brows drew together in bewilderment at the ambiguous statement, but he merely nodded. "That's always a possibility, sir."

Reaching over, Sir John patted Miles's hand warmly. "Keep in touch, my boy, and come back anytime to visit. I know the ladies would love to have you; as would I, of course."

Miles rose, aware that he was being dismissed. "Thank you, sir. I'll remember that."

Again, John Pembroke's eyes fluttered closed, and although Miles stood at his bedside for another full minute, this time the old man didn't open them again. Finally, Miles turned and walked quietly out of the room.

When he reached the hall he closed the bedroom door and leaned heavily against it. My God, how could anyone fail so much in so short a time? The man lying so pathetically in that bed bore almost no resemblance to the blustering, good-natured country squire who had greeted him at the door only two days before.

"Sad, ain't it?" Rebecca asked, seeming to appear out of nowhere. "Somehow I don't think the master is goin' to come out of this one. He looks too far gone to me."

Miles turned toward the maid, ready to give her a good dressing down for her impertinent comments, but when he saw the large, luminous tears welling in her sea-green eyes, he bit back his harsh words. "Take good care of him, Rebecca."

"Oh, we will, sir. You can be sure of that."

With a solemn nod, Miles picked up his valise and headed down the stairs to say his good-byes to the rest of the family.

As he turned on the landing, he spotted Fiona and the States waiting for him in the foyer, but a quick glance around confirmed that Victoria was conspicuously absent.

He had barely alighted from the bottom step when Georgia rushed up and laid a beseeching hand on his arm. "Oh, Mr. Wellesley, are you absolutely certain you have to leave so soon?"

"I'm afraid so, Lady Georgia, but I want to thank you for

your hospitality. I've enjoyed my stay at Pembroke House a great deal."

"Please come back soon," Carolina pleaded, hurrying over to join her sister. "There are so many things we wanted to do that we didn't have time for."

"I'll try," Miles promised. Turning to Fiona, he bowed over her extended hand. "Lady Fiona, my thanks."

"You're most welcome, Mr. Wellesley. I'm just sorry that you and my husband couldn't come to an agreement about any of our horses."

"Perhaps some other time," Miles responded. Straightening, he looked at Fiona and added, "Please express my thanks to Lady Victoria also."

Fiona's whiskey-colored eyes narrowed knowingly. "For anything in particular?"

Miles studied the shrewd woman closely for a moment, then smiled. "Yes. Thank her for the dance last night."

Fiona returned his smile, leaving Miles no doubt that she was aware of the intimate moments he and Victoria had spent on the balcony. "I shall, Mr. Wellesley. You can count on it."

Miles saw Georgia and Carolina exchange a curious look and quickly walked out the door before they could launch into a barrage of questions he had no wish to answer. "Thank you all again," he called, raising his hand in a final salute.

As his grandmother's carriage rumbled down the long drive, he peered anxiously out the side window toward the stables, hoping for a last glimpse of Victoria. To his disappointment she was nowhere to be seen.

With a sigh, he settled back into the luxurious squabs, shaking his head and smiling as he thought of the feisty little firebrand who, without even trying, had held him in thrall for three straight days.

Chapter 9

"John Pembroke is dead."

Miles looked up from the newspaper he was reading, his expression pained. "Oh, no."

His grandmother nodded, her eyes welling with tears. "I just received a message from Pembroke House. Sir John slipped into a coma late last night and just faded away. What a pity. He was such a nice man, always so friendly and good hearted."

Miles set aside his newspaper and rose to put his arms around Regina, who was now openly weeping. "At least he went peacefully," he murmured. "I knew he was quite ill when I saw him yesterday morning, but I didn't realize how grave his condition really was." Pulling a handkerchief out of his pocket, Miles offered it to his grandmother. "Here, darling, don't cry."

"I'm sorry," she sniffed. "I guess I didn't realize how much Sir John meant to me. He was a great admirer of your grandfather's, you know. He often sought Charles's advice after his own father died and John took over the running of the family estate. He and your father were friends, too. They knew each other when they were boys together at school. John always said he wished he'd met your mother before your father did. I think he was a little bit in love with Mary all his life."

Miles smiled and nodded. "He mentioned Mother the first time I met him, and I thought the same thing."

"And now the poor man is dead." Regina sighed. Turning away, she delicately blew her nose and sat down on the edge of the velvet settee. "The one I really feel sorry for in all of this is poor Victoria."

Miles's eyebrows lifted in surprise. "Oh? Why is that?"

Regina dabbed at her eyes with the handkerchief. "She's going to be left with all the responsibility. Heaven knows, that scatterbrained Fiona can't run an estate, and as for those two girls of hers . . . well, you know how I feel about them. What are their names again? Philadelphia and Denver?"

Despite his sorrow at the sad news of Sir John's passing, Miles could barely suppress the smile that threatened. "Georgia and Carolina."

Regina waved a dismissive hand. "Yes, well, I'm afraid they'll both be worthless when it comes to taking on any responsibility, so the whole lot is going to fall to Victoria."

"Well, if any woman can handle it, I'm sure she can," Miles said dryly.

"But that's just my point, Miles. I don't think any woman, even one as intelligent and resourceful as Victoria, could handle the running of an estate the size of Pembroke."

Miles considered his grandmother for a moment, shaking his head. "I'm surprised you'd say that, Grandmama. You're usually such a champion of your own sex."

"Gender has nothing to do with it," Regina said tartly, beginning to pace the length of the room. "The fact is, Victoria has no way of making the contacts necessary to run a successful horse breeding business. For that you need to be a man, or at least have one to help you. And without a brother or a husband, I fear for how long she'll be able to hang on to the Pembroke holdings, especially if there is any truth to the rumors about the family's current financial crisis."

"I'm afraid there is."

"Is what?"

"Truth to the rumors. I noticed a lot of telltale signs that the family was having financial trouble while I was staying there."

Regina nodded dismally. "The missing pictures?"

"Yes, and the worn carpets and the shabby upholstery on the furniture and . . ."

"Oh, don't go on," Regina pleaded, holding up her hands to stay his words. "I hate to think of those poor empty-headed women being put out on the street."

"So do I," Miles muttered, staring pensively out of the drawing room window. "Do you suppose there's anything we can do to help them?"

Regina stopped pacing and threw him a wry look. "I suppose you could marry one of them, so long as it's Victoria."

"Grandmother . . ."

"Well, you asked me," she said innocently. "Besides, Fiona told me that you and Victoria seemed to be getting along famously at the party the other night."

"I can't imagine what led her to think that," Miles bristled. "I asked Victoria to dance and she said no; then she finally consented to one waltz. That's all there was to it."

"Except that I heard that that one waltz took place out on a deserted balcony," Regina said slyly.

Miles looked at her in astonishment, wondering how she had found out that little tidbit so quickly. "Yes, it did," he admitted, "but did you also hear that it ended with Victoria stomping off in a huff?"

Regina's expression clearly betrayed the fact that she hadn't been apprised of that detail.

"And," Miles continued, "did you also hear that she did not even show me the courtesy of saying good-bye the next morning when I left?"

Regina's frown deepened.

"I didn't think so," Miles concluded. Touching a finger under his grandmother's chin, he tilted her face up to look at him.

"So, you see, my little matchmaker, there is absolutely nothing between Lady Victoria and myself. I'm afraid that if we are to find a way to help the Pembrokes, it will have to be through some means other than marriage."

Regina nodded and quickly turned away so that Miles would not see how truly crushed she was. She paced across the room again, finally turning back to face him. "You're absolutely sure you aren't attracted to the girl?"

"Absolutely," Miles affirmed, hoping desperately that she wouldn't be able to tell he was lying. "Actually, I find her ill-tempered and difficult in the extreme."

"But pretty . . ."

"All right, yes," he conceded. "She's pretty. Very pretty, in fact. But as far as I can tell, that's the only quality the lady has to commend her, and that's hardly enough to justify a romantic relationship."

To his surprise, Regina smiled. "You're right, my dear, it's not much." Walking over to a small writing desk, she sat down and pulled out a piece of paper. "I'm going to write Fiona a note and inquire about the funeral arrangements." Turning in her chair, she looked back at Miles. "Will you escort me to the service, or would you prefer not being thrown back into the midst of the Pembroke women?"

"Of course I'll escort you, but are you sure you're up to attending?"

"Yes," Regina answered, picking up a pen and beginning to write. "I'm fine."

"Good. Then, if you'll excuse me, I must go. I made plans to meet Alex Shaw at the club. I'll see you at dinner."

Regina nodded absently and continued to write, but as she heard Miles leave the room, she looked over her shoulder, gazing fondly at him as he disappeared down the hall. "You may be right that physical attraction alone is not much on which to base a relationship, but it's a start, my boy. It's definitely a start."

* * *

The church was full of people when Miles and Regina arrived to take their place in the second row of pews.

"What a lovely tribute to Sir John," Regina whispered as they settled themselves on the hard wooden bench. "Why, the place is fairly overflowing!"

Fiona, who was seated directly in front of them, turned around, her swollen, red-rimmed eyes barely visible behind her heavy black veil. "You're right, Lady Ashmont," she murmured. "John would have been so pleased to see how many people came to pay their respects."

Miles leaned forward, picking up Fiona's hand where it rested on the back of the pew and giving it a little squeeze. "May I offer my deepest condolences," he said sincerely. "Although I only knew your husband for a short time, I thought he was a fine man."

"Thank you," Fiona responded, her voice thick with tears. "He spoke very highly of you also, Mr. Wellesley."

At that moment the minister walked through a side door and proceeded slowly toward the pulpit. With a last nod of thanks to Miles for his comforting words, Fiona turned to face forward again.

The organ sounded a solemn note and the congregation rose to sing. Miles reached for a hymnal, his eyes running along the backs of the Pembroke family members in front of him. The twins, clad in identical black dresses and veils, stood next to their mother, while on their other side was Victoria, her elbow held firmly by a man Miles didn't recognize.

"Who is that with Victoria?" he whispered, leaning toward his grandmother.

Regina peered in the direction in which he was looking. "Harrison Guildford."

"Who is he?"

"An old and, I'd say, very persistent suitor."

Miles's head whipped around as he took another look at the

man standing with Victoria. He was astonished at the rush of annoyance that coursed through him as he viewed the couple. Obviously Victoria had meant it that night when she'd so flatly told him that it wasn't all men she disliked, it was just him. What he didn't understand was why he cared.

The angry, jealous expression on Miles's face was not lost on his grandmother, who eyed him surreptitiously. *So, there's absolutely nothing between you, hmm?* she thought, smiling inwardly. *Why, you're no better a liar than your father was when he swore to me that he didn't give a rap about your mother.*

With a satisfied nod, Regina returned to her hymnal.

As was the custom, a reception was held at Pembroke House after Sir John's burial in the family plot. Miles was barely through the front door before he was descended upon by Georgia and Carolina, weeping and clinging to him as if he were a long-lost brother. It was several minutes before he was able to extricate himself from the twins, and only then after promising to sit with them during the planned luncheon.

Miles had always wondered why society dictated that a party be given after a funeral. In his mind, it would be far more comforting for the bereaved to spend time with close family members in fond reminiscence of their lost loved one than to worry about feeding and entertaining neighbors or business acquaintances. Judging by the size of the crowd filling Pembroke House, however, Lady Fiona didn't agree.

For several minutes after escaping the twins Miles strolled nonchalantly through the drawing room and foyer, trying to spot Victoria among the milling throng of mourners. Finally he saw her standing in a corner of the dining room, Harrison Guildford still at her side.

"Lady Victoria," he said warmly, approaching the couple and holding out a hand. "Please accept my most heartfelt sympathy."

Victoria limply clasped his hand, murmuring a nearly inaudible response. Unlike her stepmother and sisters, she was not wearing a mourning veil, preferring to leave her dark, severely styled hair uncovered and her pale, drawn face exposed.

Miles gazed at her for a moment, impressed by her composure, yet intuitively sensing that the depth of her grief was probably far greater than that of her wailing sisters.

Turning to the man standing at Victoria's side, Miles again extended his hand and said, "I don't believe we've met. I'm Miles Wellesley."

Before the other man could respond, there was a little gasp of distress from Victoria, who immediately jumped into the conversation. "I'm sorry, gentlemen. My manners are sorely lacking today, I'm afraid. Harrison, may I present Miles Wellesley. Mr. Wellesley, Harrison Guildford."

Harrison shot a look at Miles that told him clearly that he had no intention of shaking his hand. In a cold, slightly nasal voice, he snapped, "Yes, I've heard of you, Mr. Wellesley. You're the American who's attempting to buy everyone's horses out from under them."

Victoria's eyes widened at this unexpected insult, and again she intervened. "Thank you for coming today, Mr. Wellesley. I know my father would have appreciated both you and your grandmother being here."

Miles, who had never taken his eyes off Harrison during the whole of Victoria's placating statement, now swung his gaze back to her. "I'm glad we could come," he said, the cold look in his blue eyes fading as his gaze caressed her pale face. "I hope that if there's anything I can do to help you through the next few weeks, you'll let me know."

"I'm sure that won't be necessary," Harrison interjected. "I've already assured Lady Victoria that I will make myself available to her night or day to offer any counsel she might require. My family owns a breeding establishment much like Pembroke, so I feel well qualified to advise the lady on any matters that might arise."

Miles's lips tightened with annoyance. "I'm sure that's very comforting to her, Guildford, but sometimes a person likes more than one opinion on a subject, especially when that subject involves horses."

Harrison let out a snort of derision, turning to Victoria and shaking his head. "I'm sure there's nothing that any American could tell an Englishwoman about horses that she wouldn't already know, except maybe how to use one as a pack mule."

Miles's fists clenched at his sides, but his expression remained impassive. "Indeed, and I would be the last person in the world to underestimate any English man or woman's knowledge of horses, but as you probably know, the Wellesley family has been breeding horses very successfully on both sides of the Atlantic for many years. I think that international experience serves us very well in giving us a depth of knowledge no mere domestic breeder could possibly obtain."

Harrison, who knew very well the Wellesleys' reputation for breeding some of the finest bloodstock in all of England, as well as America, knew he was bested and prudently remained silent.

Satisfied that he had put the rude and arrogant man in his place, Miles bowed over Victoria's hand. "My thoughts are with you, my lady," he said softly, "and my offer still stands." Brushing a light kiss across her knuckles, he took his leave.

A moment later, Miles cornered an unsuspecting Alexander Shaw in a corner of the drawing room. "Who exactly is that pompous jackass with Victoria?" he demanded.

Alex looked at him, amusement dancing in his bright blue eyes. "You must mean Harrison."

"I *do* mean Harrison," Miles confirmed, his sarcastic tone leaving no doubt as to his opinion of the man. "And I repeat, who exactly is he?"

Alex shrugged. "He's nobody, really. His family is minor nobility and they just happen to live in this shire; that's all."

"I don't care about his pedigree," Miles snorted. "What I want to know is, who is he to Victoria?"

"Not nearly as much as he'd like to be," Alex chuckled.

"He's been trying to court the lady for years, but she's never given him much encouragement that I know of."

"He's certainly dancing attendance on her today."

"Yes, well, he probably sees her father's death as a rare chance to ingratiate himself. You know, comfort the bereaved daughter and all that sort of thing."

"He's an obnoxious ass," Miles snarled.

Alex studied his friend closely for a moment, surprised at the depth of his anger. "I didn't realize you cared who danced attendance on Victoria Pembroke."

"I don't," Miles said quickly, "but Guildford's a boor, and I hate to see any woman fall for someone like that just because he happens to be around when she's going through a bad time."

Alex wasn't one bit fooled by Miles's hasty denial of his interest in Victoria Pembroke, but he said simply, "If the lady needs somebody right now and neither you nor I have any interest in filling the bill, then we can't fairly criticize someone who does."

"He's an idiot," Miles growled, "and whether I'm interested in the lady or not, her father was a good friend of my father's, and I'll not stand by and watch some overbearing, self-aggrandizing dandy annoy her."

Alex could stand it no longer and burst into a gusty laugh. "Overbearing and self-aggrandizing? My God, Wellesley, I didn't know you Americans even *knew* words like that, much less used them in casual conversation. Overbearing and self-aggrandizing ... I'll have to remember those and try my damnedest to get embroiled in a conversation where I can use them."

"Oh, shut up, Shaw," Miles growled. "You're not being funny and it's highly inappropriate to stand here braying like a jackass at a funeral reception."

Alex had the good grace to look chagrined. "You're right," he said, biting down hard on his lip. "I'm sorry; I shouldn't be laughing. But really, Wellesley, you and Guildford standing nose to nose, stamping and pawing the ground over who is going to comfort Lady Victoria is hardly appropriate either."

Now it was Miles's turn to appear chagrined. "I guess we both should be apologizing, shouldn't we?"

The mischievous smile that still lurked around Alex's mouth widened into a grin. "Ah, well, you're an American. No one expects you to know how to behave in polite company."

Miles threw his friend a killing glance but refused to take the bait. "I'm going to find my grandmother and get the hell out of here before I suffer any more insults from pompous Englishmen."

"Overbearing and self-aggrandizing." Alex winked. "That's us."

Miles threw Alex one last withering look and then walked away, leaving Alex to contemplate how amusing it was going to be to watch his obviously besotted friend try to melt the ice maiden's heart.

Chapter 10

"I had a most intriguing conversation with Lady Fiona this afternoon."

Miles looked across the carriage at his grandmother and assumed an expression of polite interest. "Oh? Intriguing in what way?"

"She asked if she might speak to me privately. Her manner was so clandestine that I couldn't imagine what she wanted."

Miles straightened up, his interest piqued. "And what *did* she want?"

Regina smiled smugly and made a great show of arranging the folds of her black velvet pelisse. "She wants to talk with me at Wellesley Manor tomorrow afternoon."

"Really? What about?"

"She didn't say, but I have my suspicions."

Miles waited for his grandmother to elaborate, but she remained conspicuously silent. Finally, with a resigned sigh, he capitulated and asked her the question he knew she was waiting to hear. "All right, Grandmama, enough games. What is it you think Lady Fiona wants to discuss with you?"

"I think she wants to sell me Pembroke."

Miles's jaw dropped. "You're joking."

"Not at all."

Miles continued to gape, shaking his head. "Whatever would make you think that?"

"Because, my dear, the unfortunate woman is destitute."

"I know that, but you told me just a few days ago that you thought she would try to hold on to the estate and have Victoria run it for her."

"I know I did," Regina admitted, "but I suppose Fiona is not quite as scatterbrained as I thought she was."

"And you're sure that's what she wants to discuss?"

"Reasonably."

Miles let out a long, frustrated breath, annoyed by his grand-mother's intentionally evasive answers.

"What did Lady Fiona say that made you believe she wants to sell Pembroke to you?"

"It wasn't so much what she said as what she intimated."

"And what was that?" Miles gritted out, by now completely exasperated with the whole discussion.

"She was very insistent that we have this meeting immediately. She said that she and—what are their names?—Minneapolis and St. Paul . . ."

"Georgia and Carolina," Miles muttered.

"Well, she and the two girls are leaving on a trip as soon as possible and Lady Fiona said it is critical that she and I speak before then. I assume her insistence is because she wants to strike a deal on the estate before the family departs for wherever it is they're going."

"I have to admit, it sounds plausible," Miles conceded. "Are you interested?"

"In acquiring Pembroke? I don't think so."

Miles looked at her in surprise. "Why not?"

"I don't need more land." Regina shrugged. "I have more now than I know what to do with. Your father and your uncles have all gone their own ways and none of them show any propensity to be farmers or horse breeders, so why do I need another estate? Unless, of course," she added slyly, "you want it."

"Me?" Miles laughed. "No thanks, Grandmother. I definitely do not need an estate in England when I live in America."

Regina looked out the carriage's side window, careful to keep her voice nonchalant. "You don't *have* to live in America, Miles."

"It's my home," Miles reminded her firmly. "It's where I live. Where I *want* to live."

Regina sighed dramatically. "Well, then, in that case, I expect my conference with Lady Fiona will be extremely brief."

"Would you like me to sit in with you?"

Regina shook her head. "I don't think that's a good idea, dear. If my suspicions about Fiona's purpose are correct, I wouldn't want to exacerbate her embarrassment by forcing her to admit to her destitution in front of you."

"But you will tell me about the meeting after it's over?"

Regina looked at Miles shrewdly. "Certainly, if you like. But as you're not interested in the transaction, . . ."

"Well," Miles stammered, "I just thought . . . you know, since I stayed with the Pembrokes and all . . . I do have an interest because . . ."

"I'll tell you everything, my dear," Regina chuckled, "including where Lady Victoria fits into all of this. Fiona didn't mention that Victoria was going along on this proposed journey."

"Grandmother, I wish I could convince you that I really don't care where Lady Victoria—"

"I know you don't care," Regina sighed, holding up her hand to stop the torrent of denials she could foresee coming, "but I'll tell you anyway."

Miles shot her a lopsided grin. "Somehow I knew you would."

At promptly three o'clock the following afternoon, Fiona Pembroke walked up to the front door of Wellesley Manor.

Taking a deep, bracing breath, she knocked twice, then forced a determined smile as the door swung open and the Wellesleys' butler, Cedric, greeted her.

"I'm here to see the viscountess," Fiona announced. "I believe she's expecting me."

"Indeed she is," Cedric confirmed. "Her ladyship is awaiting you in the drawing room."

Fiona handed the impeccably dressed old man her cloak, careful to conceal the worn seams as she folded it over his arm. After a quick pat to her hair she nodded her readiness, then followed Cedric through the magnificent marble foyer, looking around with wistful envy at the priceless works of art that adorned the high walls.

The butler ushered her into the drawing room, then discreetly disappeared, closing the double doors behind him.

Regina rose from the velvet settee and brushed a kiss against each of Fiona's cheeks. "How are you, my dear?" she asked graciously as she gestured Fiona into a plush chair.

"Very tired," Fiona admitted.

"I'm sure you must be. Will you have some tea? I know that no matter what crisis I'm facing, a cup of tea always helps."

"I'd love some, thank you."

Regina dispatched her hostess duties, then sat back, slowly stirring milk into the steaming cup of liquid she held. "Now, why don't you tell me what you wanted to see me about."

Fiona emitted a long, tremulous sigh. "It's all so complicated, Lady Ashmont, that I hardly know where to begin."

"You said you and your daughters are planning to take a trip . . ." Regina prompted helpfully. "Does our meeting today have anything to do with that?"

"Indirectly, yes," Fiona acknowledged. "Georgia, Carolina and I are planning an extended trip back to my home in Virginia. In fact, we may very well take up residence there permanently."

Regina's eyebrows rose. "Really? Leave England for good?"

Fiona smiled wanly. "Lady Ashmont, you and I both know

that I've never truly been accepted here. I always felt that I was merely tolerated because I was Sir John Pembroke's wife."

Regina opened her mouth to protest her words, but Fiona cut her off with a raised hand. "No, don't bother defending your countrymen. I'm not complaining. I knew how it would be before I ever came to England to live. And please, don't misunderstand me. I've grown very fond of many of the people whom I've met here. But the fact is, I'm American through and through, and now that my John is gone, I really don't see any reason why I shouldn't return to my homeland."

"But what about your daughters? They're British citizens."

Fiona waved a hand dismissively. "I'm not worried about them. Georgia and Carolina have temperaments that will stand them in good stead no matter where they are. Besides, they're both very close to marrying age, and there are far more men in Virginia who would be proud to have half-English wives than there are men in England who appreciate half-American brides. My girls will be fine."

"And you?" Regina asked. "Will you be fine also?"

Fiona placed her cup carefully on her saucer, making a valiant effort to remain composed. "Yes, I will. You know, my lady, despite his weaknesses, I loved John Pembroke with all my heart. But now that he's gone, I want to go home. I have a brother and a sister in Richmond, and I feel that what I need most right now is the comfort of being in the bosom of my family. Can you understand that?"

"Of course." Regina smiled. "There is no greater comfort than family, especially in times of trouble or grief. So, it would appear that everyone has definite plans except Victoria."

Fiona set down her cup and inched forward until she was perched on the edge of her chair. "Exactly. And Victoria is the reason I'm here."

Regina's eyebrows shot up in surprise. "She is?"

"Yes, at least partially. I have a proposition that I would like to offer you, and Victoria is an integral part of it."

Regina set her cup down next to Fiona's and folded her hands in her lap. "I'm listening."

Fiona licked her lips nervously, knowing that her family's entire future hung on her powers of persuasion over the next few minutes. It was a daunting thought. "I'll come right to the point. I would like Miles to marry Victoria. And I would like for you and I to work together to facilitate that happening."

She paused to see how Regina would react to this outrageous suggestion, but the dowager remained silent, merely staring at her. Fiona took Regina's silence as a good omen and plunged on. "In exchange for Miles marrying Victoria, I am prepared to sell him—or you, if you prefer—the Pembroke estate in its entirety at a very attractive price."

Regina studied Fiona for another long moment, realizing that she had misjudged the woman all these years. She wasn't scatterbrained at all. In fact, she was shrewd to the point of being almost intimidating. "You know, my dear," Regina said, choosing her words very carefully, "when you asked me for this meeting today, I suspected that your motive was to offer to sell me Pembroke. However, it never occurred to me that Victoria would be part of the sale."

Fiona rose from her chair and walked over to the bay window, staring out pensively for a moment as she gathered her thoughts. Regina waited patiently until Fiona finally turned back to face her.

"I love my stepdaughter very much," Fiona stated quietly. "I know it is not common for stepmothers to feel true affection toward their stepchildren, but I do. After the twins and I agreed that we would return to America I asked Victoria—begged her, in fact—to come with us, but she would have none of it. I'm afraid that she believes she can stay on at Pembroke and that things are going to be just as they have always been. Unfortunately, what Victoria doesn't understand is that our current . . . ah . . . financial situation is such that that is impossible. Therefore, I have been trying desperately to think of an alternative plan for her—one that would allow her to retain Pembroke and have the security she needs."

"And my grandson is the key to that security."

"Well, yes," Fiona admitted, "but, lest you think me completely heartless, let me assure you that I would never dream of broaching this proposal if I were not truly convinced that Miles and Victoria are well suited and could be very happily wed."

"It's interesting that you would say that, since Miles has told me that there is absolutely nothing between him and Victoria, especially on Victoria's part. According to him, she was barely civil to him while he was visiting."

Fiona sighed heavily. "That's true. Victoria is a difficult girl. But I must disagree with Miles's assessment of her feelings toward him. I watched the two of them at some length while he was visiting, and Victoria was no more immune to Miles's charms than he was to hers."

Regina leaned her head against the settee's high back and chuckled. "I'll agree with you about Miles being smitten. He has been fairly mooning around here since he met Victoria. And, Lord knows, I would love to see a match between the two of them. But even if I agree to buy Pembroke on the stipulation that this marriage takes place, how do you see us getting the two of them to agree?"

"I'm afraid that is going to be a problem," Fiona admitted.

"I take it, then, that you are expecting resistance from Victoria?"

Fiona sighed heavily. "I expect resistance from Victoria when I tell her what is planned for dinner."

Regina chuckled at Fiona's unintentional witticism. "Oh, dear, she does sound like a problem. And if she's as difficult as you say she is, what makes you think you'll be able to coerce her into agreeing to this?"

"Simple." Fiona smiled. "I'm not going to tell her what we truly have in mind."

"You're not going to tell her!" Regina gasped. "How do you plan to keep it from her?"

"What I mean is that I'm not going to mention anything about a possible marriage. My plan is merely to say that Miles has requested permission to court her and that I've granted it."

"And you think she'll agree to that much?"

Fiona shrugged. "I don't know why she wouldn't. She allows Harrison Guildford to call on her occasionally, so why not Miles?"

"Why not, indeed?" Regina murmured, her expression pensive. "You know, there's one more aspect of this situation that we haven't discussed. Victoria is in mourning for her father and could very properly insist that she not be forced to participate in social events for a whole year."

Fiona shook her head. "No, she can't. Before he died, John expressly requested that none of us recognize a formal mourning period. John was a great believer that life should be celebrated, and that the passing of a life was not to be mourned, but remembered with laughter and warmth. As you can see," she added, pointing to her midnight blue morning dress, "even I am acceding to his wishes. If Victoria tried to use her father's death as an excuse not to allow Miles to court her, she would be ignoring his last request, and I do not think she would do that."

Regina smiled fondly. "I always held a great affection for your husband, and knowing that his last wish was to have his memory celebrated rather than mourned has only served to reinforce that feeling. He was an exceptionally kind person."

"Thank you," Fiona whispered, trying hard to hold back the tears that threatened. "He was, indeed."

Regina straightened in her chair, deciding that it would be best to get back to the business at hand before Fiona gave way to her emotions. "And what about Miles? What inducement are you offering to bring him along with this mad scheme, aside from the obvious one of receiving Victoria's hand in marriage."

Fiona drew a deep breath, knowing the time had come to

play her trump card. "When I told you that I was willing to sell Pembroke in its entirety that's exactly what I meant." She paused for effect, then said, "The sale will include the stables . . . and the horses."

"King's Ransom," Regina breathed. "You're buying Miles's agreement to this with King's Ransom."

Fiona swallowed hard but bravely held Regina's gaze. "As I said before, I think Miles and Victoria will grow to truly care for one another. But, yes, my lady, I will admit it: King's Ransom is a way to 'sweeten the pot,' so to speak."

Regina sat silently for a moment, contemplating all that Fiona had just proposed. From the myriad of expressions crossing her face, Fiona was sure the viscountess was ready to comply with her proposal. She was surprised and disappointed, then, when, instead of agreeing, Regina suddenly shot off a barrage of rapid-fire questions. "Has Sir John's will been read yet?"

"Yes."

"And did he leave the whole of the estate to you alone?"

"Yes. He trusted me to see that the girls receive their rightful shares."

"That makes sense." Regina nodded. "Any husband with a loving wife would. But it does put Victoria in a bit of a spot if you are forced to sell all your holdings to clear up Sir John's debts and there's nothing left for the girls to inherit."

"Yes, it does. But if I sell the estate to the man Victoria marries, then the twins can receive their shares in cash out of the proceeds, and Victoria can retain ownership—of the house, the lands, *and* her horse."

"But aren't you afraid that once you've explained the true state of the family finances, Victoria is likely to say that she doesn't care about her inheritance? Perhaps she'll decide to take King's Ransom and strike off on her own."

Fiona nodded. "She might very well want that, but where would she go? I suppose she could become a governess to some other family's children, but, after all, Victoria is of noble birth herself, and I can't imagine her being so stubborn or so foolish as to agree to a life of servitude just to prove a point. And even if she is willing to degrade herself by becoming someone's paid servant just to retain her independence, she would still lose King's Ransom. The horse is registered in John's name and is, therefore, my property now. Legally, she doesn't own him."

"Good point." Regina nodded. "And, like you, I can't feature Victoria being willing to settle for the life of a paid domestic, but it's hard to tell what young people today are going to do. Especially a young woman as intractable and strong-willed as Victoria."

Fiona sighed. "All we can do is try to make her see reason. The first step I feel we have to take—providing, of course, that we can reach an agreement between ourselves—is to solicit Miles's agreement."

"Oh, I don't think we'd get much argument from him about courting Victoria, but I'm not sure he'd actually agree to marry her, horse or no horse. All he talks about is how much he wants to finish his business here and return to Colorado."

Fiona shrugged. "I'm sure he and Victoria could work that out. After all, once they're married she'll have no choice but to go where he goes. Perhaps they'll be like so many Anglo-American couples these days, who live part of the year heie and part of the year there. There are any number of ways to solve that dilemma."

Regina nodded, but her expression was doubtful. "I hope you're right."

"So do I," Fiona replied. She paused, waiting for the dowager to give her stamp of approval to the plan. But again, the silence stretched on for so long that Fiona began to despair that she had convinced the old woman after all. She was about to launch into another argument in her favor when Regina looked up at her and smiled.

"All right, Fiona, I'll agree to assist you in making your match. After all, what do we have to lose? You want your daughter married; I want my grandson near me. Let's make our plans."

Chapter 11

Miles leaned back in an overstuffed leather chair and stared moodily at his snifter of brandy. "So there you have it, Shaw. Can you believe that my grandmother actually approached me with the idea of an arranged marriage? And she was serious, too!"

Alex Shaw swirled the amber liquid in his glass and shrugged languidly. The two men had spent the afternoon at Alex's club, and after several drinks and an excellent port at lunch, Alex was suffused with a feeling of well being. Even Miles's prolonged ranting about his grandmother's proposal that he marry Victoria Pembroke had not altered his mellow mood.

"I don't know, Wellesley, old man; I don't think it's such a bad idea, actually. Arranged marriages have quite a tradition."

"I know that," Miles grumbled, "but I thought it had been abandoned sometime in the last century. Think about it, Alex! It's 1858, for God's sake. Men and women don't need to rely on their families to choose mates for them. They do it themselves. Otherwise, why would you all waste so much time going to those bloody parties?"

"It's true that the concept isn't as popular as it once was, but it's hardly unheard of. Arranged marriages take place every day. And sometimes, in situations like this one, they can be damned advantageous."

"Advantageous!" Miles barked. "Just how do you figure that?"

"Simple. Victoria wants the money you have, you want the horse she has, not to mention the fact that you'd also receive the whole of Pembroke Estate. All in all, I'd say it's not a bad plan. And besides, Victoria would make a stimulating wife, once you made it clear to her who was going to be the head of the household."

"As if that would be any easy feat," Miles grunted.

"Well, it might take a little doing, but look what the rewards would be. She's accomplished, bright and beautiful as hell. What more could any man want? God's nightgown, Miles, the honeymoon alone would make the deal worth it to me."

"Fine," Miles snorted. "Then you marry her."

Alex wagged a lazy finger in Miles's face. "Would that I could, but she didn't ask me."

"She didn't ask me either! Her stepmother asked my grandmother, for God's sake. I still can't get over the sheer medievalism of this whole absurd situation!"

"This is England," Alex chuckled, "and old traditions die hard."

"Well, as far as I'm concerned, this one should have died a long time ago."

Alex sighed and took another sip of his brandy. "Sometimes I don't know about you, Wellesley. There are times when you're just so damned American."

"I'll take that as a compliment."

Alex shrugged, refusing to be disturbed by his friend's ill humor. "It wasn't meant to be, but I suppose you can take it any way you wish. Now the question remains: What are you going to do?"

"What do you think I'm going to do? I'm going to tell my grandmother that I'm not interested."

"You mean you didn't tell her that already?"

"Well, not in so many words," Miles said sheepishly. "I told her I'd think about her proposal, but I was just buying time to try to figure out a way to let the old girl down gently. You know I wouldn't hurt her for the world."

"No, of course you wouldn't. You're really going to let all those Pembroke horses slip through your fingers, are you?"

"All those horses!" Miles chortled. "Why, there aren't enough horses in those barns to be of any consequence whatsoever. And besides, I wouldn't care if there were fifty horses at stake."

"Fifty!" Alex hiccoughed. "There are probably two hundred head over at Pembroke."

"You're mad. Victoria showed me around just last week, and there weren't more than a dozen. Sir John must have sold the rest to try to keep the family afloat."

"Did Victoria show you the pastures, too?"

Miles shook his head. "Just the barns. She didn't mention anything about there being horses in the pastures. But I saw the pastures and they were empty."

Alex started to laugh, a low rumbling sound that gradually built into a full-fledged guffaw. "If they were, Victoria undoubtedly made sure of it."

Miles's eyes narrowed angrily. "I take it there is some good stock hidden about the place?"

"Some of the best in England."

"But she showed me several two- and three-year-olds in the barn. She said they were the only ones the family had for sale."

"To *you*, maybe. For the rest of the world there are dozens of good prospects out in the far fields and paddocks."

Miles's face darkened with anger. "Why, that little . . ."

"Temper, my boy, temper! Remember, the lady didn't want to sell to you and then be forced to watch her precious babies be shipped over to the Colonies to be used as—what did Guildford call them? Pack mules?"

"Yes," Miles snarled. "Pack mules."

"So, now how do you feel about Lady Fiona's offer?"

The furious bunching of a muscle in Miles's cheek betrayed how angry he was, but when he spoke his voice was calm and controlled. "It doesn't change anything. In fact, now that I've heard this little bit of news, I wouldn't marry the girl even if I had been charged with the responsibility of saving the human race from extinction and she were the last woman on earth!"

"Fiona, I wouldn't allow Miles Wellesley to court me if he was the last man on earth, so you might as well save your breath."

Fiona set down her teacup and let out a long, frustrated breath. "Victoria, you don't seem to understand. The Wellesleys are our only hope."

"Our only hope? What are you talking about? Our only hope for what?"

"Financial salvation," Fiona muttered.

Victoria shook her head, her face a mask of confusion. "Fiona, I don't understand a word of what you're saying. Why do we need the Wellesleys for financial salvation? In fact, why do we need financial salvation at all?"

Fiona looked down the length of the vast dining-room table, knowing she was going to have to reveal several hard truths to her stepdaughter that she'd originally hoped to keep secret. And even though it was Victoria's stubbornness that was forcing her to confide the unpleasant realities of their situation, her heart still wrenched at the pain she knew she was about to inflict. "Tory," she began softly, "there are a lot of things about your father that you didn't know."

Victoria's mouth tightened warily. "What things?"

Fiona picked up her teaspoon and began tracing patterns in the tablecloth with the handle, a transgression of manners for which all three girls had had their knuckles rapped repeatedly as children. From this small gesture alone Victoria knew that whatever Fiona was about to tell her was something she wasn't going to enjoy hearing.

"Fiona? What about Papa?"

Fiona set down the spoon and looked at Victoria squarely. "Your father never had much of a head for business and, consequently, he squandered away most of the Pembroke fortune. We are drowning in debt, and now that your father is gone our creditors are demanding payment—in full and immediately."

Victoria breathed a huge sigh of relief. Thank God, the only problem was a few debts. She had been afraid that Fiona was about to tell her something really terrible—that her father was a bigamist or a highwayman or something. Money problems could, at least, be solved with no long-term adverse effect on the family name.

"We shall sell some of the horses." Victoria shrugged. "I knew we were having some financial difficulties. Why else would Papa have sold off so much of the art? But surely if we liquidate the two- and three-year-olds, that's bound to be more than enough to cover any debts he might have incurred."

"Revenue from the two- and three-year-olds wouldn't even touch it, dear," Fiona mumbled.

Victoria's eyes widened. "Wouldn't touch it?"

Fiona shook her head sadly.

"Lord above, Fiona, how much did Papa owe?"

"In excess of two hundred thousand pounds."

Victoria's breath came out in a rush. "That's not possible. How could he have spent that kind of money?"

"As I said before, he made some disastrous investments. He also loved to gamble. You know how much he enjoyed playing cards at the club and betting on the races. And then there was his misguided notion that you girls and I had to be dressed better than Queen Victoria herself. There were the balls, the house parties, the trips to the Continent, educating the three of you, including sending the twins to France for finishing school, bringing you all out properly—well, the list goes on and on. After years of this kind of mismanagement the debts finally became overwhelming. Your father started borrowing at horrendous interest rates and that, of course, served to make matters even worse."

Victoria jumped up from her chair, nearly knocking it over in her agitation. "If you knew about this, why didn't you stop him?" she accused.

Fiona sighed wearily. "Stop John Pembroke? How?"

"Surely you could have at least tried! You could have told him to stop spending so wildly. Said no when he suggested a trip to the Continent or a weekend house party for every family in the shire. You could have convinced him that the twins didn't need new ball gowns for every single party, or insisted that they finish school here in England instead of France. Oh, I don't know, Fiona. Surely, *surely,* there must have been something you could have done!"

Fiona hung her head, mortified by Victoria's unexpected attack. "You're probably right, dear. I should have done more to try to rein John in. I realize that much of this disaster is my fault, and that's why I'm trying so desperately to put the situation to rights. Unfortunately, the only way I can think to do that is to sell Pembroke. And the only people in the shire with enough money to give us a high enough price to pay off our debts and leave all four of us with something to live on are the Wellesleys. Somehow we have to induce them to buy."

Victoria lifted her chin and glared furiously at her stepmother. "And you intend to do that by having me play the coquette with Miles? What else do you expect, Fiona? That I'll take him to my bed in order to settle your accounts?"

Fiona rose to her full diminutive height and slammed a lily-white fist down on the table. "Victoria! That is quite enough!"

Victoria's eyes widened with astonishment at her soft-spoken stepmother's angry outburst. Then she let out a ragged breath and sagged into one of the side chairs, burying her head in her hands. "I'm sorry, Fiona. I shouldn't have said those things to you. I know how Papa was, and there probably wouldn't have been anything you could have done to change his ways, even if you had tried."

Slowly, Fiona lowered herself back into her own chair. "I'm sorry, too," she whispered. "The last thing I want to do is argue with you, dear. But can't you see what a desperate situation we're in?"

"Yes, I can," Victoria admitted, "and as much as it pains me to think of losing Pembroke, I understand that it's probably the only way out of this debacle. But I still don't think I'm the answer. Let Miles court one of the twins. They're both dotty over him."

"I know." Fiona sighed. "But unfortunately he's not dotty over them. It's you he wants to see." She quickly looked away, hoping desperately that her face wouldn't betray her lie. It was imperative that Victoria believe that Miles actually had asked to court her, or she'd never, ever agree.

Victoria shook her head dismally. "I can't believe that the Wellesleys are the only family who would be interested in buying Pembroke. Can't you at least *try* to find some other prospect?"

"Who?" Fiona cried, throwing her arms wide. "There aren't any other families for which Pembroke would hold the same value as it would for the Wellesleys. The fact that our land abuts theirs makes it far more valuable to them than to anyone else. And even if I could find another buyer, we'd never be able to command as high a price. We'd be forced to sell the horses to make up the difference."

"Sell the horses." Victoria shrugged. "If we don't have the estate anymore, we're not going to be able to keep them anyway."

A thought suddenly flashed through Fiona's mind—one so brilliant that she almost laughed out loud with sheer delight. The horses! Why hadn't she thought of this before? Slowly she raised her eyes to Victoria and said dramatically, "I'm surprised you'd say that, dear. I never thought you'd be willing to part with King's Ransom."

Victoria's jaw dropped. "King's Ransom? What does he have to do with this?"

Fiona forced a look of pained regret. "That's just what I've been trying to explain to you. If the viscountess won't buy the estate, we'll be forced to liquidate it and everything else we own to get the money we need. That includes the horses. *All* of the horses."

"No," Victoria said flatly. "It doesn't include King's Ransom. He's not Papa's property; he's mine. Therefore, he can't be considered part of the estate."

"You're wrong, Tory. King's Ransom is legally registered to your father, not you. He *is* part of the estate, and he will have to be sold along with the rest of the stock."

Victoria shook her head so adamantly that her tight bun shook loose, cascading a river of silky dark hair down her back. "No, Fiona! They can take everything else, but not him!"

"Victoria," Fiona pleaded, leaning forward and grasping the girl's shaking hands in her own, "listen to what I'm saying. We only have two choices. We either sell the estate to the viscountess for top money, or we sell it to someone else for less, and include the horses. At this point the choice is yours. If you want to keep your horse, you had better not insult the viscountess by turning down her favorite grandson's request to court you."

For a long moment Victoria sat staring at her stepmother, a stony expression on her face, despite the fact that her mind was racing madly. "All right," she said suddenly. "I will allow Miles to court me until you can consummate the sale of Pembroke with the viscountess."

Fiona breathed a huge sigh of relief. "Do you really mean that, Tory? And you'll accept the man's attentions . . . amicably?"

"Yes," Victoria nodded absently, her mind ticking off a list of possessions she might be able to sell quickly.

"Thank you," Fiona whispered, rising and coming over to give Victoria a hug. "You're a wonderful daughter."

Victoria hugged her stepmother back, a little ripple of guilt coursing through her. If Fiona knew what she was really planning, she doubted that "a wonderful daughter" would be the phrase her stepmother would use to describe her.

Less than an hour later, as Victoria sat at the small writing desk in her bedroom, there was a soft knock on the door.

"Who is it?" she called, looking up with an irritated expression.

"It's me; Georgia."

Quickly putting away the notes she was making, Victoria picked up a lace handkerchief and energetically dabbed at the ink staining her fingers. "Come in, dear."

Georgia swept into the room in a flurry of petticoats and bobbing blond ringlets. "Oh, Tory, I'm so excited for you!" she cried, rushing over and embracing her older sister. "I heard part of your discussion with Mama—not that I was eavesdropping, mind you—but you could hardly *not* hear the two of you, you were talking so loudly."

Victoria looked at her sister knowingly, and Georgia tittered with embarrassment. "Anyway, I'm just thrilled that you're going to allow that handsome Mr. Wellesley to call on you. Of course, I do wish it was me," she sighed, "but I'm almost as excited as if it was, just knowing that at least he set his cap for one of us."

Victoria tried mightily to conjure up a smile, so tired was she of the topic of Miles Wellesley that she wished she never had to hear his hated name again. "Thank you, dear."

"There's just one thing I don't understand," Georgia continued, perching daintily on the edge of Victoria's bed and crossing her slim ankles. "I thought you said you didn't like him when he was here."

"I didn't."

Georgia's mouth pursed into a little moue of surprise. "Then why did you agree to let him court you?"

"It just seemed like the most prudent thing to do," Victoria said evasively. Putting her arm around Georgia's shoulders, she ushered her off the bed and toward the door. "Now, if you don't mind, darling, I must get some letters written."

"Of course," Georgia agreed. "I didn't mean to interrupt you." She stepped out into the hall, then turned back, looking at Victoria as if something she'd heard had just sunk in. "The most *prudent* thing to do?"

"Yes." Victoria nodded and softly closed the door. Leaning against it, she muttered, "At least the most prudent thing to do when one's goal is to buy some time."

Chapter 12

"So, even though she wasn't thrilled with the idea, I did manage to get Victoria to agree to allow Miles to court her." Nervously, Fiona picked up her teacup, darting a glance at Regina Wellesley over the rim.

"Well, you've done better than I, my dear." Regina sighed. "I couldn't even elicit that much of a commitment from that young whipper snapper I call a grandson."

Fiona's eyes widened at this unexpected piece of news. "You couldn't?"

Regina shook her head sadly. "No, but he'll come around."

"You sound very confident of that, my lady."

"I am."

"Any particular reason?" Fiona held her breath, hoping the venerable old dowager wouldn't take exception to her prying.

"I always have a reason for every statement I make," Regina said imperiously, "and this is no exception."

Fiona edged closer, waiting in great anticipation for whatever it was the viscountess was about to confide.

Regina waited a long moment, until her rapt guest was nearly squirming with anticipation. Finally she relented and said, "I wired his father and told him what we were about."

"Really . . ." Fiona breathed, not sure what good it would do to notify Miles's father of their plans, but hoping the viscountess would elaborate. She didn't have to wait long.

"They are coming."

Fiona looked at her blankly. "Who is coming?"

"James and Mary," Regina said, her expression mirroring her impatience at the other woman's slow-wittedness.

"Your son and his wife?"

"Yes, and they're bringing their children."

Fiona sat back and stared at Regina in astonishment. "All of them?"

"Yes." Regina laughed, clapping her hands together in unabashed delight. "Well, almost all of them. Stuart isn't coming."

"Stuart." Fiona looked at Regina and shook her head. "I'm not sure which one . . ."

"He's second in age to Miles," Regina supplied. "He's at university in Boston and can't leave his studies, but the rest of the children are coming. They should all be here in a few weeks."

Fiona blinked several times, trying to find the piece to this puzzle that she was obviously missing. Finally she gave up and said, "I'm sorry, my lady, but I don't understand what your son and his children coming to visit has to do with Miles and Victoria courting."

"Several things," Regina said smugly. "First of all, it ensures that Miles will not hightail it back to America any time soon. Secondly, if his parents are in favor of this match—and I'm convinced they will be—then we are almost assured success."

"Because . . ." Fiona prodded.

"Because James and Mary's opinion means a great deal to the boy. If his parents wish for him to marry Victoria, in addition to my wishing it, he can't possibly say no."

Fiona sat back, trying hard to look more enthusiastic than

she felt and desperately hoping that Regina Wellesley knew her grandson as well as she obviously thought she did.

. Miles stayed home that night to have dinner with his grandmother, hoping that, given a quiet evening alone, he would have the chance to clear the air about Victoria once and for all.

They dined on a light repast of poached salmon, popovers and asparagus spears, then retired to his grandmother's sitting room for after-dinner brandy and truffles.

"So, Miles," Regina said, settling herself in her favorite chair and delicately nibbling a bit of chocolate, "what do you want to talk to me about?"

Miles replaced the stopper in a cut-glass decanter of brandy and looked over his shoulder, smiling. "What makes you think I want to talk to you about anything special?"

"Of course you do. Why else would you forego the company of your young friends to spend a dull evening with an old woman?"

"I can't think of anyone's company whom I find less dull than yours," Miles said honestly. Pulling up a chair opposite his grandmother's, he sat down, rolling his brandy snifter idly between his fingers. "But you're right; I do want to talk to you, and I'm sure you know why."

"Lady Victoria?"

"Exactly. I don't know how to say this without upsetting you, Grandmother, so I'll just be frank."

"Please do."

"I am not going to marry her or even court her, for that matter." Seeing Regina immediately draw in a breath to start arguing, he held up his hand. "Please, let me speak my mind."

With a brief nod, she sat back, waiting.

"I will admit to you, I do find the lady intriguing. I don't know why, since she and I have barely exchanged a civil word, but I do."

Unable to help herself, Regina interjected, "Probably because she's the only female in the entire county who isn't throwing herself at you. That in itself is intriguing."

"You may be right," Miles shrugged, "but, regardless, there isn't going to be anything more between us."

Regina's beaming smile quickly faded to a frown of perplexed disappointment. "Why not?"

"Because I'm leaving next week." *There, he'd said it.*

"I see," Regina said slowly. "Then you've already made definite plans in this regard?"

"Yes. I booked passage today. I haven't found any horses here that meet my needs, so I've decided I might as well return home and continue my search there. I hope you're not too disappointed. I know you were hoping that I would pursue a relationship with Victoria."

Regina studied him closely for a moment. "Tell me something, Miles: If you knew that you were going to stay in England for, say, another three or four months, would you 'pursue' her then?"

Miles wondered briefly why his grandmother would be asking such a hypothetical question but decided there was no harm in humoring the old lady by giving her the answer he knew she wanted to hear. "Yes, I'm sure I would." Regina's satisfied smile was his first clue that he had probably just made a grave mistake.

"Well, then, my boy, dust off your courting togs because I think you're going to want to cancel that sailing ticket."

"I am?" he asked warily. "Why would I want to do that?"

Regina's face broke out in a beatific smile. "Because your family is coming to visit. They're on their way even as we speak."

The brandy glass suddenly came to an abrupt halt halfway to Miles's mouth. "They are?"

Regina rose from her chair and walked to her desk, returning a moment later with a slip of paper. "Yes, indeed. I received this wire today."

Miles quickly scanned the short missive, then read it again more slowly before handing it back. "They're all coming? The kids too?"

"I believe that's what it says."

"But why?"

Regina shrugged innocently. "Why not? Your parents haven't been home to visit in years."

"Well," Miles muttered, "I guess this does change my plans a bit."

Regina chuckled with unconcealed delight. "I knew you'd be pleased. I am, too. I will have the pleasure of having my family with me for the summer, and you will have the opportunity to really get to know Victoria, after all."

Miles opened his mouth, preparing to take back his rash words about courting Victoria, but promptly closed it again. He leaned back in his chair, his eyes seeming to focus on something far off in the distance.

Why not court her? After all, he'd been considering it for weeks now, and it could prove to be a pleasant diversion, since he was going to be staying on for awhile. Besides, it would give him no end of satisfaction to prove to Alexander Shaw that he could, indeed, break through the wall of ice around Victoria Pembroke's heart if he set his mind to it.

Turning his gaze on Regina, he said, "I just want to make one thing perfectly clear."

Regina looked at him expectantly. "Yes, dear?"

"If I do decide to call on Lady Victoria, I want you to understand that it doesn't mean that I'm going to marry her."

"Of course not." Regina smiled, brushing away his words with a wave of her bejeweled hand. "You'll receive no argument from me on that point. I'm a great believer in letting nature take its course."

Miles chuckled and rose from his chair to plant an affectionate kiss on Regina's forehead. "Sure you are, you old mixer. You'll let nature take its course as long as nature behaves exactly as you think it should."

* * *

"Lady Victoria, Lord Wellesley is here to see you."

Victoria looked up in astonishment at Rebecca, who hovered uncertainly near the parlor door. "He's here? Now?"

"Yes, ma'am."

"Who's Lord Wellesley?"

Victoria looked at Harrison Guildford, who sat next to her on the settee, a plate of scones in his lap. "She means Miles Wellesley."

Harrison's mouth thinned with annoyance. "Since when did he start sporting a title?"

"He didn't," Victoria assured him. "Rebecca just assumes everyone who comes to call has one."

"Well, at least she's correct *some* of the time."

Victoria rolled her eyes at Harrison's pompous remark, then turned her attention back to the maid. "Rebecca, please tell Mr. Wellesley that I am unable to receive him and that in the future I would appreciate his sending his card first, rather than just appearing at the door."

"Oh, ma'am," Rebecca pleaded, taking several steps into the room and wringing her hands nervously, "I can't say that to the gentleman. It would seem rude coming from the likes of me. Wouldn't it be all right if I just told him you can't receive him right now and to come back a little later?"

Victoria shook her head. "No, it wouldn't. I want Mr. Wellesley to know that regardless of what customs are acceptable for visiting in America, here in England, uninvited guests are not received."

"I don't need to be received," came a deep voice from the doorway. "I was just passing by and thought I'd stop to extend an invitation."

Everyone's gaze flew to the handsome blond man lounging nonchalantly against the portal. Miles's eyes swept across the three faces, amusedly noting delight on Rebecca's, astonishment on Victoria's and just plain fury on Harrison's.

"Now, see here, Wellesley," Harrison cried, leaping to his feet like an avenging warrior. "Just who do you think you are, barging in here like this?"

"Good afternoon to you, too, Guildford," Miles said pleasantly. He swung his gaze to Victoria, his actions making it blatantly clear that he didn't find Harrison Guildford's question worthy of an answer. "If I could just have one moment of your time, my lady, I promise I'll be on my way."

Victoria frowned in obvious irritation, but rather than take a chance of escalating the hostility she could sense radiating from Harrison, she nodded. Hurrying across the room, she extended her arm and ushered Miles back toward the foyer.

"This really is too much to be borne, Mr. Wellesley," she admonished as she rushed him through the main hall. "Surely even Americans must teach their children some sense of decorum; enough at least for them to know that it is inappropriate to burst into other people's homes uninvited."

"They do, indeed, and I'm sorry," Miles said. Although his words were contrite, his laughing expression made it very clear that he wasn't sorry at all that he'd broken up Victoria and Harrison's little visit. "I just stopped by to ask you if you'd like to go riding tomorrow morning."

Victoria eyed him speculatively for a moment. "If I ask you a question, will you tell me the truth for a change?"

"Why, Miss Pembroke, you wound me. When have I ever been anything but honest with you?"

"Oh, please," Victoria groaned, "don't . . ."

Miles grinned unrepentantly, then swept a courtly bow and said, "I assure you my lady, you'll get nothing but the truth from these lips, no matter how personal your question."

"Good. Then tell me this: Are you here because your grandmother made you come, or do you really want to go riding with me?"

All traces of amusement disappeared from Miles's face. "Let's get something perfectly clear between us, Victoria. I love my grandmother very much and I would do a great deal to please her, but no one, and I mean *no one* 'makes' me do anything. If I didn't want to be here, I wouldn't be, and if I didn't want to go riding with you, I wouldn't ask."

Victoria looked up into Miles's face, her breath catching in her throat. He was even more handsome when he was being serious than when he was laughing. She wouldn't have thought that was possible, but seeing him as he was this moment, his jaw set and his blue eyes devoid of their usual mockery, made her feel flushed all over. "All right, Mr. Wellesley, I'll be happy to go riding with you."

She expected Miles to smile and relax after she accepted his invitation and was surprised when his only response was, "Now you tell me something, my lady: Are you saying yes because your stepmother is forcing you to, or because you actually want to go riding with me?"

Victoria didn't quite know how to answer him since neither choice was exactly the truth. Prudently, she skirted the issue. "Like you, sir, I'm not easily forced either."

To her extreme relief, Miles seemed to be satisfied with her evasive response. "All right, then," he said, flashing a heart-melting grin, "I'll call for you at ten."

Despite her previous annoyance with him, Victoria found his smile too much to resist and she smiled back. "I'll be ready."

Opening the front door, she saw him out. As he started down the steps, she lifted her hand to wave. "Till tomorrow then."

As if he could see her even with his back turned, Miles raised a hand in a return salute and continued down the steps. He heard Victoria close the door behind him, then turned his attention to Harrison's horse, which was tied to a hitching post in front of the house.

Stepping close to the dozing animal, he reached up and unhooked the buckles on the flat saddle. "Dear, dear," he clucked, deftly loosening the girth by two holes, "Guildford really should be more careful about how tight his saddle is cinched. He could take a nasty fall trying to mount when one is as loose as this one."

With a devilish grin, Miles sprinted over to his own horse and mounted, cantering off down the driveway, the sound of his laughter trailing in his wake.

Chapter 13

"What did *he* want?"

Victoria eyes widened with surprise at Harrison's gritted demand. Walking over to the settee, she sat down next to him. "He wanted me to go riding with him tomorrow morning."

"I assume you declined."

Victoria's smile faded. "Actually, I told him I'd be happy to."

Harrison shot to his feet, the plate of scones on his lap hitting the floor with a crash. "What do you mean, you'd be happy to? How dare you make a fool of me by cavorting around the countryside with that . . . that backwoods American hick!"

Victoria also jumped up, her dark eyes blazing with indignation. "I beg your pardon, Harrison, but you have no claim on me. If I elect to go riding with Miles Wellesley, or anyone else for that matter, it's my business and has nothing whatsoever to do with you. Now I think, perhaps, you'd better leave."

Harrison realized that he had made a grave error in losing his temper in front of Victoria and immediately sought to make amends. "I'm sorry, Victoria. I'm afraid my emotions got the best of me for a moment there. Let's sit down and talk about this."

"There is nothing to talk about," Victoria said coldly. "Now, please, I asked you to leave."

Harrison's temper again ignited at Victoria's high-handed tone. "My, my, you're suddenly in a rush to get rid of me. What's the matter? Is your American hiding around the side of the house, waiting till I leave before he sneaks up to your room?"

Victoria was shocked to the core by Harrison's crude innuendo, but when she spoke again her voice was deadly calm. "We have been friends a long time, Harrison, and because of that I'm going to try to forget your last remark. Now, I'll ask you once more: Will you leave my home like the gentleman I've always thought you to be, or do I have to call for assistance and have you thrown out bodily?"

Harrison snatched his hat and gloves off a side table by the parlor door, then whirled on Victoria, his face black with fury. "No, my lady, you don't have to call for assistance; not that there's anyone in your household with a prayer of being able to throw me out. But, as you say, for the sake of our long friendship, I, too, am willing to forgive your abominable behavior this morning and take my leave as you request."

"My behavior!" Victoria gasped. "What in the world are you talking about?"

"You know very well what I'm talking about! You and I are very nearly betrothed. Now that your father is dead and you no longer have any reason to stay at Pembroke, everyone in the shire is waiting for an announcement of our engagement."

"Well, they're going to have a very long wait," Victoria raged, "since I have no intention of marrying you or anyone else."

"Oh, you'll marry me, all right," Harrison said smugly. "It's been part of my plan for a very long time."

"Maybe you should have found out if it was part of *my* plan!"

Harrison elected to ignore this comment and continued on,

as if Victoria hadn't spoken. "And, furthermore, I will *not* tolerate you humiliating me by being seen in the company of that upstart American."

Victoria squared her shoulders and looked Harrison directly in the eye. "This conversation is over, Mr. Guildford. Good day." With a swish of her skirts, she neatly sidestepped the formidable man and swept out the door, traversing the foyer and flying up the stairs to her bedroom.

Closing and locking the door behind her, she raised shaking fingers to her lips, her heart pounding with a combination of fear and anger. "How dare he talk to me as if he owned me!" she railed, pacing across the room and pulling back the lace curtain to see if Harrison had left yet.

She gasped and took a quick step backward when she saw him come charging out of the front door directly below her, but the breath she was holding suddenly came out in an explosion of laughter as she watched the man begin to mount his horse, only to suddenly end up lying ignominiously on his back in the dirt, one foot still dangling from a stirrup.

Covering her mouth with her hands, Victoria laughed until tears streamed down her face. For a moment she considered flinging open the window and asking the prostrate Guildford if he was all right, just so he'd know that she'd witnessed his embarrassment, but she thought better of it. After all, there was no sense in enraging him more than he already was. Staggering to her bed, Victoria fell on her back, still laughing uncontrollably. "Oh, that was rich," she guffawed. "A perfect comeuppance for the arrogant blighter. But how in the world did that saddle ever come loose? It's almost as if someone loosened it on purpose."

Her laughter abruptly subsided as she mulled over this possibility. Then she shook her head. "No," she murmured, "even he, 'upstart American' that he is, wouldn't dare do that!"

Then, again envisioning how Harrison had looked lying in the dirt, Victoria again erupted in another peal of laughter.

* * *

"Good morning, Rebecca. You're looking very fetching this morning."

The little maid blushed to the roots of her flaming hair, her freckled skin suffused with embarrassed color. "Oh, Lord Wellesley, the things you say! Do come in, please, sir. The mistress is all but ready."

"Not 'Lord,' Rebecca, just 'Mister,' " Miles corrected, winking at the pink-cheeked maid and stepping into the foyer.

"Would you like to take a seat in the parlor?" Rebecca offered. "I could bring you a spot of tea if you like, or perhaps a little cake or some scones or . . ."

"Nothing, thank you," Miles interjected before the girl reeled off the entire contents of the family larder. "And I'll just wait here in the hall if that's all right."

"Oh, yes, of course, sir. Make yourself comfortable and I'll tell Lady Victoria you're here."

"No hurry. I know I'm a few minutes early, so I certainly understand that the lady isn't ready." With another friendly smile, Miles took a seat in a hard chair set against the foyer wall, crossing one ankle over his other knee.

Unbeknownst to Miles, Victoria was indeed ready—and standing in the shadows at the top of the staircase. She put her fingers to her lips as Rebecca came charging up the steps, warning the maid not to give her presence away. Rebecca grinned conspiratorially as she reached the landing, leaning toward Victoria and whispering, "Isn't he the most dashing man you've ever seen, my lady?"

Victoria could only nod, barely able to take her eyes off the vision of masculine perfection awaiting her below. Miles was dressed in buff riding breeches and a dark brown serge jacket, a combination both elegant and masculine. His black riding boots were slightly scuffed at the toes, testament to the fact that they were actually used for the purpose intended, rather than kept in a closet and brought out only for show. "He *is* handsome, isn't he?" Victoria murmured.

"Oh, I think he's much more than handsome, my lady," Rebecca confided, "I think he's perfect. And so kind, too, even to the likes of me. Not like some of the other gentlemen who usually come to call."

Victoria looked at Rebecca aghast. "You think he's kind? My word, Rebecca, have you forgotten that his original intent in coming here was to fleece us of our best horses?"

"If you'll forgive me for saying so, ma'am, I don't think Lord Wellesley ever intended to fleece anyone. He came here to buy horses because Sir John, may God rest his soul, invited him. I think his intentions were entirely honorable."

Victoria looked at the little maid in astonishment. "You really mean that, don't you?"

"Oh, yes, ma'am, I do. And I also think you're the luckiest of ladies that he's obviously set his cap for you." Rebecca shivered deliciously. "What I wouldn't give . . ."

"All right, Rebecca," Victoria said suddenly. "You can return to your duties now."

Rebecca looked surprised by this abrupt dismissal, but scooted away before she inadvertently said something else to annoy her lady. Hurrying down the hall, she cast one last look over her shoulder at Victoria, mumbling, "Some people just don't know how lucky they really are. She should spend a few evenings in the company of the blokes from the stables. Then maybe she'd appreciate what a jewel Lord Wellesley is."

The "jewel" rose to his feet as Victoria descended the staircase, his eyes sweeping over her in unabashed appreciation. She was clad in a dove gray riding habit that fit her small waist and curved hips to perfection. Miles drew a deep breath as he felt a familiar surge of desire pulse through him. Fighting valiantly against the unexpected physical reaction Victoria's feminine beauty had elicited within him, he swallowed hard and managed a slightly strained smile. "Good morning, my lady. You look lovely."

Victoria glanced down at her plain gray habit. "Do you think so, Mr. Wellesley?"

"Yes," Miles answered honestly, "although the gray is a bit bland for my taste."

Victoria's eyebrows rose. "Really? And just what color would you prefer?"

Miles smiled beatifically. "On you, with your hair and eyes? There's only one color."

"Oh? And what's that?"

"Red."

"Red!" Victoria gasped, appalled. "You think I should wear red? Why, there's not an honorable single lady in all of England who would even consider . . ."

"You would be magnificent in red," Miles said firmly. "And someday I hope to have the pleasure of seeing you in it."

"I can assure you, sir, that will never happen."

Miles grinned like a mischievous school boy. "We'll see. Now, shall we ride?"

"By all means," Victoria said, pulling on her gloves. Taking his proffered arm, she allowed him to escort her down the front steps, all the while thinking that it was just like an American to think a proper English spinster would wear red. How am I ever going to tolerate having to spend whole days in his company while I put my plans into effect? she thought a bit desperately.

There was so much about Miles Wellesley that she didn't understand. He was too outspoken, too honest, too genuine in his reactions to those around him. Somehow, just being with him set her on edge. Maybe it was the sheer manliness of him. He was so much more overtly masculine than any other man she'd ever known. Briefly she wondered if all American men were like that but, somehow, she suspected that nationality had very little to do with it. Miles Wellesley would stand out in any group. He was so handsome, so big, so bold, that she felt breathless every time she was near him. He was what Fiona called "a man of overwhelming presence." Just the type of man who would think proper clothes were bland.

Casting him an arch look, Victoria nodded toward the waiting horses. "I hope you don't take exception to the fact that my horse is gray also. I don't have a red one handy."

Miles saw the challenge lurking deep within her dark eyes and blithely answered, "That *is* unfortunate. A nice strawberry roan would suit you to a *T*. Of course, it would be doubly stunning if you had a red riding habit to go along with it."

Victoria's smug smile evaporated as she realized that her little jibe had not gotten the best of him. "Where shall we ride?" she said quickly.

"How about west across the fields? I'd like to see some of the young horses I've heard you pasture back there."

Victoria slid him a quick, sideward glance, realizing that someone must have told him of the many excellent prospects she had neglected to show him during his initial visit. "As you wish, but I warn you, none of them is for sale." Mounting, she gave her horse a smart rap with her crop and took off at a spirited canter, hoping to leave the unsuspecting Miles in her dust.

No such luck. A horseman of exceptional skill, he easily caught up to her, then settled his long-legged gelding into a easy lope beside her.

They ate up several miles at their brisk pace; then Miles called, "You're going to run that little girl into the ground if you don't slow down pretty soon."

Victoria, realizing he was right, reined her mare into a sedate trot.

"Are those your horses?" Miles asked, pointing to a pasture ahead of them.

"Yes, they're yearlings."

"Let's stop and take a look."

Reluctantly, she nodded, and they walked their horses over to a perimeter fence and dismounted. Draping their arms over the top rail, they gazed at the herd of frolicking youngsters.

After a moment of viewing the horses from this vantage point Miles put his thumb and index finger against his teeth and let loose with a piercing whistle that nearly sent Victoria out of her boots. The young horses immediately raised their heads in the direction of the sound, then trotted over to greet the strangers, affording Miles a closer look at their confirmation.

"These are the same breeding as the ones you showed me before, aren't they?"

"For the most part, yes. Why do you ask?"

"Because they're cowhocked, too, just like the others."

"Mr. Wellesley," Victoria burst out, slamming her gloved hands to her hips, "if you say one more thing about the Pembroke horses being cowhocked, I'm going straight back to the house."

Miles looked at her and grinned. "You really are touchy about hearing unpleasant truths, aren't you?"

Victoria's response was to grab her mare's reins out of his hand. "I know one thing," she snapped, thrusting her left foot into the stirrup. "I've heard all I'm going to from you." She started to hoist herself into the saddle but found her efforts suddenly thwarted as Miles's hands circled her small waist and deftly lifted her back down.

"Don't leave," he murmured, bending so close that his nose nuzzled against her ear. "I promise I won't say anything more."

Victoria tried to twist out of his grasp, but his arms circling her waist were like steel bands. She struggled ineffectually for a moment, then relaxed against him, deciding to take another tack. "Mr. Wellesley, will you please let go of me?" she asked sweetly.

"Not yet," he whispered, his breath warm and soft against her neck. "I like the feeling of you against me."

"Mr. Wellesley! This is not at all proper. . . ."

"To hell with propriety," he muttered. "I've never been overly impressed with it. Besides, it wasn't proper when I kissed you in the barn that day either, but it sure was fun."

"Mr. Wellesley, please!"

"Miles."

"What?"

"Call me Miles. Mr. Wellesley is my father."

"All right, *Miles*," she amended, her voice trailing off lamely as she felt his lips against the nape of her neck. "We shouldn't . . ."

She never finished her protest since the next thing she knew, she was being turned in Miles's arms and her mouth was being covered by his soft, warm lips. She felt her hard riding hat being tugged off her head; then, as if by magic, her hair tumbled down her back.

Victoria wanted to pull away, knew she should pull away, but somehow she couldn't find the strength. It was as if she was using all the energy in her body just to stay conscious as Miles continued his sensual assault. Her lips tingled from the pressure of his mouth against hers and, for some reason she couldn't fathom, her breasts, crushed against the rock-hard planes of his chest, throbbed with an aching fullness she had never felt before.

She could feel his body against hers; hot, hard and demanding. His hands running up and down her spine made her squirm with delicious torment, his tongue—warm and wet and silky—traced the seams of her tightly closed lips, demanding with exquisite provocation that she open her mouth and allow him to invade the secret recesses of that warm, dark cavity.

Victoria heard a voice moan his name, then realized with a start that it was her own. He threaded his fingers through her hair, pulling gently until she arched backward over his arm. Suddenly she felt a waft of cool air hit her moist mouth as his lips left hers, but before she could protest the loss his tongue began trailing down the long alabaster column of her exposed throat, making her eyes droop languidly and her lips part with the first blush of ecstasy.

She knew she was going to faint, knew that if he didn't stop soon, her legs were going to buckle and she was going to collapse in a limp heap at his feet.

"Miles," she moaned, "you—have—to—stop. . . ."

To her surprise, he did. Immediately, he lifted his lips, although he still held her close enough that she could feel his breath coming fast and harsh against her forehead.

She opened her eyes, looking at him in bemusement. His usually clear blue eyes looked slightly glazed and he was breathing so hard that one would have thought he had just run a long race. Drawing a deep, calming breath of her own, Victoria straightened and stepped out of his embrace. This time he didn't try to hold her. "Are you all right?" she asked softly. "You look strange."

"I'll bet," Miles gasped, running a shaking hand across his mouth.

At Victoria's continued frown of concern, he closed his eyes for a moment. "I'm fine."

Victoria couldn't imagine what was wrong with him, but she was sure it had something to do with the kiss they had just shared. Suddenly she felt an overwhelming sense of guilty embarrassment. What must he think of her for allowing him such liberties? Why, after the way she'd just acted, he probably had no more respect for her than he would for some trollop from the streets.

Mortified by her wanton behavior, she set her features in what she hoped was a no-nonsense posture and said firmly, "Mr. Wellesley, I cannot continue to allow you to—"

Her words were abruptly cut off as Miles's eyes snapped open. Before she could guess his intent, he hauled her up against him and buried his lips in her hair. "Don't," he whispered raggedly. "Don't say anything to spoil it. Please."

"But, we shouldn't . . . it's not right."

"Don't say that! We didn't do anything wrong. We kissed, that's all, and there's nothing wrong with that." Pulling away so he could look at her squarely, he repeated, *"Nothing!"*

"Maybe not in America, but here in England, it just isn't done."

"Well, it must be done once in a while," he snorted, "or none of you Brits would be here!"

Victoria's eyes flared with genuine offense. "How dare you speak to me in such a base manner?" she cried. "You know, Mr. Wellesley, these crude tactics of yours might work with American women, but I can assure you that British ladies such as myself do not appreciate them."

"Ah, yes, now you've finally hit the nail on the head."

"Hit the nail on the head?" Victoria muttered. "Whatever are you talking about?"

"I'm talking about how you just very succinctly summed up the difference between British and American women."

Victoria looked completely nonplussed. "And that difference is . . ."

"That British women are only concerned with being 'ladies,' while American women concentrate on being just that."

"Just what?"

"Women!"

"Oh!" Victoria gasped in outrage. "So you're telling me that you prefer a 'woman' to a 'lady'?"

"Any day of the week, honey; any day of the week."

With great dignity, Victoria straightened her shoulders and looked Miles directly in the eye. "In my estimation, you, sir, are the very definition of the word *crass.*"

"And in my estimation, you, miss, are the very definition of the word *repressed.*"

"Repressed!" Victoria gasped. "You think I'm repressed? Why? Because I don't like being manhandled?"

"I don't know whether you like being 'manhandled' or not, since that's not what I was doing. What I do know is that you like being handled by a man very much, but you're too hypocritical to admit it. And, just to set the record straight, what you and I were doing a few minutes ago was kissing,

Lady Victoria. *Kissing.* There was no 'manhandling' involved. I pity you for not knowing the difference."

"Don't pity me, Mr. Wellesley," Victoria snarled, hurtling herself up into her saddle and reining her horse away from him. "And don't bother me again. Ever."

With that, she gave her mare a sound kick and took off across the pasture, her dark hair flying behind her like a black flag.

Miles stood staring after her, an enigmatic smile on his face. "We'll see, my lady," he murmured, cupping his hand over his eyes as he followed her frenzied flight. "After all, *ever* is a very long time."

Lady Victoria Abshire, whom Weston Wellington described,
I shudder to say, as "a buxom armful."

Chapter 14

Victoria stuck her head in the door of the parlor, looking around for Fiona. Spotting her stepmother sitting by the window, her embroidery frame in front of her, she said, "I'm going riding, Fiona. I'll be back in about an hour."

Fiona looked up from her tapestry and smiled. "Are you going with Miles Wellesley?"

"Hardly," Victoria snorted.

"Oh? I thought that since the two of you went riding yesterday . . ."

"Yes," Victoria interrupted, "I know what you thought, but after yesterday I never want to see Miles Wellesley again."

Fiona's needle dropped from suddenly nerveless fingers. "You don't?"

Victoria shook her head adamantly. "He's exactly as I said he was from the very beginning—arrogant, boorish and crass."

Fiona rose to her feet, quickly traversing the distance between herself and her stepdaughter. "He didn't try anything . . . untoward with you, did he?" she whispered hoarsely.

"As a matter of fact, he did."

Fiona's hand flew to her mouth in genuine horror. "Oh, my poor darling! Tell me, what did that cad do to you?"

Victoria looked at the floor, reluctant to discuss Miles's passionate caresses with her stepmother. "He . . . he kissed me."

Fiona waited, expecting to hear more, but when Victoria remained silent she finally said, "Kissed you? Is that all?"

Victoria's head jerked up and she pinned her stepmother with an offended look. "All! Yes, that's all, but I think it was highly improper, don't you agree?"

"Well, yes, of course, it's not altogether acceptable when you're not betrothed."

"I should say," Victoria huffed. "I told him I never want to see him again."

"Oh, Tory," Fiona moaned, "you didn't! Just because he kissed you? Oh, Tory, please reconsider. Just think of what we have to lose!"

"I don't care!" Victoria cried. "Miles Wellesley is an odious man, and I refuse to have any more to do with him." Seeing that her stepmother was still looking at her askance, she added, "Besides, he also said something very rude to me."

Fiona's eyebrows shot up. "He did? What?"

Victoria paused for a moment, trying to decide whether she could bring herself to repeat Miles's insult. Finally, she muttered, "He said that he thought I actually enjoyed his kisses, and that I was just too hypocritical to admit it."

Fiona had all she could do to keep a straight face. "And did you?"

"Did I what?"

"Enjoy his kisses?"

"Of course not!" Victoria's voice was filled with righteous indignation, but Fiona noticed that her eyes flicked away guiltily.

"So you did enjoy it."

"Well, maybe I did," Victoria said defensively. "For a moment, anyway, but that still gives him no right to call me

names and accuse me of being repressed when I told him never
to do it again!"

"He's a typical young man, Victoria. None of them like to
be rebuffed."

"Well, I don't care what he likes or doesn't like. The fact
is, I'm not going to see him again, and that's all there is to it.
I know I'm disappointing you, Fiona, but I simply can't abide
him."

"Tory," Fiona said quietly, trying her best to remain calm,
"you have to think of our future here. Every young, healthy
man is going to want to . . ."

"Oh, hang the future! I'm sorry, Fiona, but you're just going
to have to find another buyer for the house. As important as I
know the viscountess is to us, I refuse to spend one more minute
in Miles Wellesley's company!"

Fiona looked at Victoria miserably, but loathe to upset her
stepdaughter further, she said simply, "I understand, dear. You
go riding and don't worry about this anymore. I'll think of
something."

"Thank you," Victoria whispered, relieved that what she had
feared was going to become another confrontation with her
stepmother hadn't. Turning, she hurried out of the parlor, making good her escape before Fiona could think of any more
embarrassing questions to ask her.

It was a beautiful morning, and as Victoria cantered along
the road that ran between the Pembroke and Wellesley estates,
the fresh, cool breeze in her face did wonders for her mood.
Finally she could put Miles Wellesley behind her. Even Fiona
had seemed to agree to that.

Now the only problem she had to face was finding enough
money to set herself up *and* buy King's Ransom from Fiona.
But where could she get that kind of cash? She had thought to
sell the jewelry her mother had left her, but no one in the
village had any use for such valuable items, and she didn't

know anyone in London whom she could trust to sell them for her.

It had even crossed her mind to try to sell a few of the yearlings secretly. She didn't think Fiona had ever kept track of how many horses the family actually owned, so she probably wouldn't even miss them, but when she had approached George, the stablemaster, with the idea, he had again reminded her that all the registration certificates were in her father's name and would, therefore, have to be signed off by Fiona before any sales could take place.

At this point Victoria couldn't think of anything she personally owned that would come close to giving her the cash she needed.

Noticing that her little mare was tiring, she slowed her down to a leisurely walk, letting the horse amble down the path as she mulled over her situation. Perhaps she was going to have to take the line of last resort and hire herself out as a governess, or perhaps a companion to some elderly rich woman.

Maybe I can ask the viscountess if she needs a companion, Victoria thought whimsically. Wouldn't that be rich? She could just hear herself now: "So, you see, Lady Ashmont, since I cannot tolerate the thought of marrying that odious grandson of yours, I thought I'd come live with you instead." Victoria giggled just thinking about what Regina's reaction might be to that proposal.

Absently, she reached down and patted the gray mare's neck. "Ah, Laurel, what am I going to do?" She paused, almost as if she expected the horse to turn its head and give her an answer, but the mare just plodded placidly on. The only sound that broke the silence was the steady clip-clop of her hooves, followed by an unexpected nicker.

Victoria looked up from her daydreaming, knowing that the mare must have spotted another horse nearby. Sure enough, directly across the fence stood Miles Wellesley's big gelding, saddled but riderless.

Victoria felt an immediate knot of apprehension clench her

stomach. An untethered, riderless horse almost always portended an accident. Swinging her head around, she quickly scanned the immediate area, trying to spot Miles on the ground somewhere. He was nowhere to be seen.

Jumping down, Victoria tied Laurel to the fence, then climbed over the top rail, walking quickly toward the gelding. "Here, boy," she cooed, reaching for the trailing reins. "What are you doing out here alone? Where's your master?" She squatted down, deftly running her hands down the horse's legs, then over his shoulders and flanks. There didn't appear to be any injuries—at least not to the animal—but where was Miles?

Her concern building by the second, Victoria cupped her hands around her mouth and shouted Miles's name, then jumped with surprise when he immediately answered.

She looked around, still not seeing him. "Where are you?" she called.

"Up here. Above you."

Throwing her head back, Victoria peered up through the dense leaves of a nearby oak tree, drawing in a startled breath when she spotted Miles crawling along one of the upper branches.

"What in the world are you doing up there?" she gasped. "Are you crazy? You're going to kill yourself!"

"No, I'm not." He chuckled, inching farther out on the branch. "I've been climbing trees since I was old enough to walk."

Victoria planted her hands on her hips, angry now that he'd given her such a scare. "That may be," she retorted sarcastically, "but don't you think you're a bit old for it now?"

"As a rule I don't do it much anymore," he explained with a laugh, "but there's a bird's nest up here that must have gotten shaken loose by the wind. I saw it dangling from a branch and climbed up to anchor it before it fell. There are three eggs in it. Robins, I think."

"You're out of your mind!" Victoria snapped. "That branch you're on is too fragile to hold your weight."

"Naw, I'm fine," Miles assured her. "Anyway, I've almost

got it." Crawling another couple of inches out on the branch, he reached above him, carefully cupping the dangling nest in his hand and wedging it between two V-shaped twigs. "There!" he crowed, pleased with himself. "All done."

The words were hardly out of his mouth when Victoria heard a sharp cracking sound, followed by a harsh, guttural cry. The next thing she knew, Miles was lying on the ground next to her, his body still and his eyes closed.

"Oh, my God!" she shrieked, letting go of the gelding's reins and racing over to kneel next to the prostrate man. "Miles! Miles, are you all right?"

When her cry was met with silence she clapped her hand over her mouth and leaned down, gently placing her ear against his chest. "Oh, please God, don't let him be dead. Please!"

Her prayer died on her lips as she suddenly found herself being flipped over on her back, Miles's laughing face looming above her. "See?" He grinned. "You do care a little for me. You were upset when you thought I was dead!"

Suddenly realizing that he was playing a game with her, Victoria opened her mouth to tell him exactly what she thought of him. But before she could utter a word, Miles's lips covered her in a hot, lusty kiss. She started to pull away, but the sensation of his mouth on hers was like a drug, dulling her anger and causing a hot jolt of desire to sizzle through her. As if of their own accord, her arms circled his back, her fingers plunging deep into his flaxen hair. She could feel the heavy muscles of his chest pressing against her breasts, causing a tingling that traveled all the way down to the very core of her. As the kiss continued, he pulled her closer, throwing his leg over hers so she could feel his hard male arousal even through the heavy material of her riding habit.

With a soft groan, Victoria ran her hands down his back, unconsciously pressing the entire length of her body against his. Miles sensed her imminent surrender and redoubled his efforts. His hands were everywhere, tracing the delicate lines of her throat, then moving downward, where they insinuated themselves inside her riding jacket, cupping her full breasts and sweeping provocatively across her hardened nipples.

Victoria thought she was going to faint. Never, in all her life, had a man made her feel the way this one did. "We have to stop this," she rasped, her breathless tone taking much of the force out of her command.

"Oh, God, don't say that," Miles moaned, moving his hands up to cup her face. "Let me kiss you, Tory. Don't ask me to stop."

Again he lowered his lips to hers, his mouth devouring her with a driving passion that stole the very breath from her lungs. When he finally raised his head the unconcealed hunger in his blue eyes was so intense that it was almost frightening. Suddenly Victoria came to her senses, and with a swift lurching motion, she scrambled out from beneath his hot, hard body and sat up, her hands clapped against her flaming cheeks in mortification. "Why do you always do this to me?" she flung at him, her eyes huge and accusing.

It was a long moment before Miles could collect himself enough to answer. Finally he said simply, "Because you're beautiful and I love to kiss you. Why do you always get angry?"

The honest bewilderment in his words took Victoria so off guard that she had no response. For a long moment the two of them sat silently side by side in the tall grass, both of them breathing hard as they tried to calm their racing hearts and trembling bodies.

At last Victoria turned toward Miles, studying him through narrowed eyes. "You fell out of that tree on purpose, didn't you, just to make me think you'd been hurt, so you could get me into another . . . compromising position."

"I did not!" he retorted hotly. "You flatter yourself, my lady, if you think I'd risk breaking my neck just to get a kiss."

To his surprise, Victoria looked hurt by his comment. "Well, even if you didn't," she huffed, "you still kissed me again after I told you the other day that I didn't want you to."

Miles laughed sheepishly. "It just seemed like the natural

thing to do when I opened my eyes and saw you kneeling over me."

"Do you mean it was simply your first reaction?"

"Yes." Miles nodded. "It was indeed that." Prudently, he decided not to tell her exactly which part of him was having the reaction.

"Well, then," Victoria sighed, raising her hands to smooth her mussed hair, "I suppose I can forgive you—as long as you promise me that it was a one-time occurrence and will never happen again."

Miles looked over at her, careful to keep his expression serious. "I can't do that."

"Why not?"

"Because you never know when I might fall out of another tree and have another first reaction."

Victoria could see a mischievous light dancing deep within his eyes, but she decided to overlook it. For the first time in years she was actually enjoying being with a man, and she was loath to spoil the moment. "All right," she murmured, "since I doubt even you are foolish enough to fall out of trees with any regularity, I can accept that."

"Why, thank you," Miles said mockingly. "And I can assure you that I will do my very best to stay out of trees whenever you're around."

"I would appreciate that," Victoria responded, unable to contain the little bubble of laughter that rose up in her throat. Patting the grass surrounding them, she said, "Do you see any of my hairpins? I seem to be missing several."

"Don't bother with them," Miles answered softly, reaching over and running his hand down the length of her ebony mane. "You look wonderful with your hair down."

"Mr. Wellesley, please! No lady wears her hair down except . . ."

"Oh, God," Miles groaned, "are we back to 'Mr. Wellesley' again? Why is it that whenever I'm kissing you, you always call me Miles, but the rest of the time you insist on calling me Mr. Wellesley?"

Victoria gave him a shocked look, knowing that what he said was true and embarrassed that he'd noticed. Getting to her feet, she swept the grass off the back of her riding skirt. "I have to go now."

"You do? So soon?" At her emphatic nod, Miles also gained his feet, letting out a little grunt as a sharp pain ripped through his right knee.

"Are you all right?"

"Yes, but I think I twisted my knee when I fell."

"You're lucky that's all that's wrong. You really could have done yourself some serious harm, you know."

"Would you have cared?" Miles asked, trying hard not to let his voice betray how important her answer was to him.

"Of course," she answered, climbing nimbly over the fence and untying her mare's reins. "Think of what a loss it would be to the baby birds in the neighborhood if something happened to you." She mounted her horse, then turned to smile at him. "Good afternoon, Mr. Wellesley."

"Wait!" Miles called, hobbling over to the fence. "Will you have supper with me tonight?"

"Tonight? Why, I couldn't possibly on such short notice."

"Do you have other plans?"

"Well, not exactly, but one just doesn't decide during the afternoon to go to supper that very night."

"Why not?"

"It just isn't done. If you wish to have supper with me, you need to send a proper invitation, telling me exactly where and when; then you wait for my response."

"Sounds like a damned waste of time to me," Miles sighed, swatting his reins against his leg in frustration. "Tell me, Victoria, does anybody in this blasted country ever do anything spontaneously?"

"Spontaneously?"

"Yes. Do people ever do anything on the spur of the moment for no other reason than because it might be fun?"

Victoria thought seriously about this for a moment, then shook her head. "No one I know."

Miles took another couple of limping steps forward till he reached the fence. "Then why don't you be the first? Come on; have supper with me tonight. I'll come fetch you around seven and we'll go to the inn in the village."

"The inn!"

"Yes. They have a nice little private dining room."

Victoria looked at him aghast, then a sudden, knowing smile crossed her face. "You're having one off on me, aren't you?"

"What?"

"You're having one off on me. Come on; I'm not that thick. I do know when I'm being teased."

"Why do you think I'm teasing?"

Victoria laughed melodically. "Mr. Wellesley, no lady would go to a public inn with a man, unchaperoned, to have supper. Why, her reputation would be ruined forever!"

Miles sighed heavily, "You're right. But I'm going to be at the Dove and Hawk at eight o'clock tonight, having supper. If you just happen to be there, too, perhaps we'll run into each other and we can dine together."

Victoria shook her head. "I can't do that."

"You can't, or you won't?"

She hesitated, then said honestly, "I can't. Now I really do have to go."

Reining her mare around, she started off down the path toward Pembroke, but after only a few steps Miles's voice halted her. "Lady Victoria?"

Turning in the saddle, she looked back at him quizzically. "Yes, Mr. Wellesley?"

"I hope you never find your hairpins."

Chapter 15

Rebecca hurriedly climbed the stairs and flew down the second-floor hall, skidding to a halt in front of Victoria's room. She rapped once on the closed door, then called, "Lady Victoria, there's a message here for you from Lord Wellesley."

The door opened so quickly that Rebecca leaped back with a start. "Oh, my lady, you scared me!"

"I'm sorry." Victoria laughed, holding out her hand. "May I have the message, please; and it's *Mr.* Wellesley, not Lord Wellesley."

"Oh, yes, certainly, ma'am." Thrusting out her hand, Rebecca nearly tossed the heavy, cream-colored vellum envelope at Victoria. "I think it's an invitation," she said excitedly.

Victoria shot the maid a shaming look and purposely closed the door, letting Rebecca know what she thought of her prying. She looked down at the envelope, smiling at the sight of her name scrawled boldly across it.

She was just breaking the seal when her door flew open, revealing a breathless Carolina. "Oh, Tory, Rebecca says you've received some kind of invitation from Mr. Wellesley!"

"Sometimes Rebecca's mouth far outpaces her brain," Victoria said dryly.

Carolina's flawless forehead wrinkled with confusion. "It does? In what way?"

"Never mind." Victoria sighed. She pulled the single piece of stationery out of the envelope, then sank down on the edge of the bed, a small smile playing about her mouth as she read the few lines.

Carolina waited anxiously, but when Victoria merely refolded the letter and returned it to its envelope without so much as a word, her curiosity got the better of her. "What does he want you to do?" she cried.

"He wants to know if I'll attend Katharine Crawford's wedding with him."

"Oh!" Carolina squealed. "How romantic!"

"What's romantic?" Georgia asked, popping her head in the door.

"Miles Wellesley has asked Tory to Katie Crawford's wedding."

"No!" Georgia gasped. "Oh, Tory, he must be serious about you. No man asks a lady to accompany him to a wedding unless he has thoughts of marriage dancing inside his own head."

The thought of Miles Wellesley having anything "dancing inside his head" was so funny that Victoria burst out laughing. "You two are really over the top, do you know that? Miles's grandmother can't attend the wedding due to a prior engagement and he simply doesn't want to go alone. That's all there is to it."

"Oh, pooh," Carolina huffed. "He could have gone with Alexander Shaw or any of his other friends. He didn't have to ask you."

"That's right," Georgia concurred. "I don't know why you can't just admit that the man is attracted to you, Tory. Why, I'd be shouting it from the rooftops if he was smitten with me."

"The man definitely isn't attracted to me," Victoria denied, "nor is he smitten. He's just marking time until his family arrives, and for some reason he's decided he wants to mark it in my company. You wait and see; once his parents get here I'll never hear from him again—not that I care, mind you."

"I don't believe that's true," Georgia protested, "but even if it is, it's still exciting to be going to the Crawford wedding with him. Everyone says it's going to be *the* event of the season, and I can't imagine anything more thrilling than attending it with Mr. Wellesley. Besides, it's an evening wedding, so that makes it doubly romantic!"

"I wish he'd asked you, Georgia," Victoria said. "You'd enjoy it so much more than I. It's a real shame, since the 'thrill' as you call it, is wasted on me."

"But you are going, aren't you?" Carolina asked anxiously. "Surely you're not going to turn him down!"

Victoria thought briefly of Fiona and how upset she'd be if she didn't accept Miles's invitation. "No, I'm not going to turn him down."

"Well, I shouldn't think so!" Georgia gasped, her tone making it obvious that such a decision would be absolutely beyond consideration. "Come on, Carrie, let's go through the wardrobe and find something for Tory to wear that will absolutely send Mr. Wellesley over the edge. Who knows? With enough help from us, the next wedding in the shire might be hers!"

With a groan, Victoria flopped down on her bed and buried her head in her pillow.

Miles Wellesley looked so handsome that Rebecca nearly fainted when she opened the door. "Cor, but don't you look dashing," she gasped, her large green eyes roaming over his impeccably clad figure like a beggar at a banquet. "Wait till my lady gets a look at you!"

Miles smiled at the gaping girl, not sure whether to be flattered or embarrassed by her overt ogling. "May I come in?"

"Oh, yes." Rebecca blushed, stepping back and curtsying.

"By all means, of course you may. I'll just let Lady Victoria know you're here."

She dashed away so quickly that she forgot to take Miles's hat, leaving him to toss it on the hall table himself. Seating himself on his usual chair, he looked around absently, catching sight of himself in an oval mirror. *Lord,* he thought, *if Eric and Geoff could see me now, I'd never hear the end of it.* Thinking of his rough-and-tumble younger brothers, he smiled, trying to imagine what it would be like when the whole family arrived in England the following week. *Poor Grandmother; she has no idea what she has in store the next few weeks.* He smiled, envisioning the way the prune-faced Cedric might react the first time his baby brother, Adam, poured juice down his impeccably tailored black suit.

A slight sound at the top of the stairs drew Miles's eyes toward the landing. What he saw made all thoughts of little brothers instantly disappear.

Unaware of her suddenly awestruck suitor gaping up at her from below, Victoria began her descent. She was dressed in forest green satin, the off-the-shoulder sleeves and deep *V* décolletage modified somewhat by a matching stole, which she hugged around herself protectively. Holding up the full skirt slightly as she walked down the stairs, she inadvertently treated Miles to a delicious display of slender ankle and shapely calf. Nearing the bottom of the staircase, she looked up, sucking in a startled little breath as she saw her escort standing not three feet away from her.

"You look beautiful," he said softly, holding out his hand to assist her from the bottom step.

Victoria had to bite her tongue to keep from shouting, "So do you!" but somehow she managed to retain her composure. "Thank you very much."

Miles held out his arm to her, and together they descended the front steps. "You brought your grandmother's coach?" Victoria asked, looking in surprise at the huge conveyance standing in front of her house.

"Yes," Miles said. "I told Grandmother the brougham would do very nicely, but she insisted I take this monster."

Victoria smiled inwardly, pleased despite her protestations to her sisters, that not only was she going to arrive at Katharine's wedding in the most luxurious conveyance in the whole shire, but also with the most handsome man.

"I hope you don't find all these trappings as embarrassing as I do," Miles added.

Victoria shrugged and allowed him to help her into the coach. "I'm sure it's a very comfortable way to travel."

"It is, I suppose." Miles laughed, climbing in behind her. "But when you're only traveling two miles it seems a bit excessive."

Much to Victoria's regret, the two miles passed very quickly, and almost before she knew it they had arrived at the church where the wedding was being held.

They walked in, nodding to a small cluster of matrons, whom Victoria noticed immediately put their heads together to discuss her unexpected appearance with the much-sought-after Miles Wellesley. "They're all talking about you," Victoria whispered as they seated themselves in a back pew.

"Only because I'm with you," Miles returned.

Victoria knew that wasn't true, but she was still pleased that he'd said it. Looking around, she murmured, "I love summer weddings when the flowers are in bloom. I think they're so much prettier than winter weddings, when couples have to settle for simple evergreen bows."

"Then, by all means, when your turn comes you'll have to plan a summer wedding."

"Hardly. I have no intention of ever planning any wedding, summer or winter."

Miles was somewhat taken aback by this frank disclosure, but he said simply, "You really don't think you'll ever marry?"

Victoria shook her head adamantly. "No. I'm certain I never will."

"Why not?"

"Surely you must know, Mr. Wellesley, that I'm officially on the shelf."

Miles frowned. "Katharine Crawford is the same age as you are, if I'm not mistaken."

"There's a big difference, though. Katie always wanted to get married, so she kept herself on the marriage block until she finally got a proposal."

Miles grimaced. "The marriage block! What an awful expression that is. It makes me think of a slave auction."

"That's pretty much what it is, isn't it?"

"What?" he gasped. "Do you really think marriage is akin to being a slave?"

"Absolutely. At least for the woman it is."

"That's ridiculous!"

For the first time since they'd sat down, Victoria turned and looked Miles squarely in the eye. "Is it? Think about it: From the moment she marries, the only destiny a woman has is to please the man—to keep his house, entertain his guests, raise his children and . . ."

"Submit to his carnal appetites?" Miles supplied helpfully.

Victoria blushed and quickly turned away. "This is not an appropriate subject for us to be discussing."

Miles was about to say that in his estimation it was the first meaningful discussion they'd ever had, but his words were cut off by a sudden blast from the huge pipe organ at the front of the church. All conversation instantly ceased and, as one, the congregation turned toward the center aisle, awaiting the procession of the bridal party.

The ceremony was swiftly completed, and as the bride and groom came arm and arm back down the aisle, Miles couldn't resist whispering, "Now, just look at how happy Katharine looks. Do you really believe that she feels she's just been sold into slavery?"

"Ask her tomorrow morning how she feels," Victoria shot back. Then, realizing what she'd just implied, she turned away in mortification, but not before she saw Miles's wide grin.

* * *

The union of Katharine Crawford and James Bennington was one of the most prestigious the shire had seen in years, and the wedding reception at the family estate was a fitting celebration of the alliance. The ballroom was bedecked with spring flowers, including a bridal bower for the newly married couple to stand under as they received their guests. The wedding cake was towering, six layers of spun sugar and marzipan paste with fresh roses trailing from the tiny anniversary cake on top all the way down to the mammoth bottom layer.

"Isn't this lovely?" Victoria breathed as she and Miles walked into the ballroom.

Miles nodded, somewhat amazed by the ostentation at what was basically a country wedding. "I don't think I've ever seen so much food," he muttered, gazing around at the rows of tables covered by overflowing platters of meat, vegetables, breads and molded salads. "Guess we're going to eat."

"Don't you eat at wedding parties in America?"

Miles threw her a jaundiced look. "Of course we do, but the party usually only lasts one evening."

Victoria looked at him in confusion. "They only last one evening here, too."

"Really? From the amount of food on these tables, I thought perhaps they expected us to stay for two or three days."

Victoria chuckled at his comment, then gestured toward the twenty-piece orchestra warming up in a corner. "It looks as if there's going to be dancing, too."

"Good." Miles nodded. "I know you like to dance."

She cast him a smile, then allowed him to escort her to the receiving line.

The huge dinner passed without incident, although several times Miles saw Harrison Guildford glaring at him from far down the table. "I don't think your beau is at all pleased that I'm here with you," he noted as they ate tiny pieces of the rich, gooey cake.

The champagne she had imbibed had done much to lift Victoria's usual inhibitions. "He's not my beau, as you so quaintly put it," she giggled. "I told you before, I'm on the shelf and I don't have beaus."

"Stop saying you're on the shelf," Miles ordered. "No woman who looks like you do is on the shelf."

Victoria's eyes widened as she gazed at him over her champagne glass. "Why, Mr. Wellesley, I believe that is the first time you have ever given me a genuine compliment."

Miles eyed her closely for a moment, then took her glass out of her hand. "I think you've had enough champagne, my lady. Let's dance."

They were beginning their third waltz when Miles felt a finger stabbing into the back of his right shoulder. Abruptly, he stopped in midstep and turned in surprise, finding Harrison Guildford's set, angry face just inches from his own. "I beg your pardon," Miles snapped, annoyed by the man's rude gesture.

"I have been waiting patiently for a chance to ask Lady Victoria to dance," Harrison snarled, "but since it's obvious you're going to monopolize her for the entire evening, I have no choice but to cut in."

Miles stared at Harrison coldly for a moment, then turned back to Victoria. "Would you like to dance with Mr. Guildford?"

"It's *Lord* Guildford, if you don't mind," Harrison interrupted.

Miles's patronizing smile betrayed just how unimpressed he was with Guildford's title. "Of course; how forgetful of me." Again, he turned back to Victoria. "My lady?"

Victoria stole a quick look around, noticing the number of people who were beginning to stare at them. "Yes," she said quickly, "I'll be happy to dance with Lord Guildford."

Miles's lips thinned at her unexpected response, but he stepped back and placed Victoria's hand in Harrison's outstretched palm. "I'll be waiting for you when the dance is over," he murmured. He walked to the edge of the room and took up a position near a huge crystal bowl of champagne punch, picking up a stemmed glass and filling it.

Livingston Haworth had watched the little drama on the dance floor with great amusement. Now he sauntered over and stood next to Miles. "Insufferable bastard, isn't he?" he asked casually.

"Yes." Miles nodded, not even bothering to ask who Livingston was talking about. "He's a real ass."

Livingston watched Victoria and Harrison dance for a moment, then said, "You know, old Harry's been trying to court Lady Victoria for years, and she's never given him the time of day. Yet now, since Sir John's death, he seems to have redoubled his efforts, and she seems to be allowing it."

Miles nodded, remembering that Harrison had been at Pembroke House the day he'd stopped to ask Victoria to go riding. "Do you suppose she's seriously interested in him?" he asked, careful to keep his tone casual.

Livingston shrugged. "I can't imagine why, unless what they're saying about her family having serious financial difficulties is true."

"What does that have to do with anything? Does Guildford have that considerable a fortune?"

"Not really, but his family is comfortable. Actually, I think all the interest is on Harry's side. He's always wanted Victoria, and now that he knows she's alone and vulnerable he's pressing his suit." He turned to Miles and grinned. "So, Wellesley, if *you* want the lady, you'd better step up right away."

"Want her?" Miles snorted. "Where did you get that idea, Haworth? She and I are just friends, nothing more."

Livingston's grin remained firmly fixed on his plain face. "Really? As much as you two have been seen together lately, I thought perhaps there was a bit more to it than that."

"Well there isn't," Miles said firmly. "But I do think you're right about one thing: The lady *is* vulnerable right now, and I'd hate to see a pompous bastard like Guildford take advantage of that."

"It looks to me as if that's exactly what he's planning to do," Livingston noted, gesturing toward the couple. "In case you haven't noticed, the music has stopped, but he's obviously not planning to bring her back to you."

Miles's head jerked around toward the couple. Sure enough, as the orchestra struck up another waltz, Harrison put his hand on Victoria's waist and started dancing again. "I think you're right," Miles muttered angrily, "and I think I've been a gentleman long enough." Setting down his empty glass, he strode out onto the dance floor, waited until Harrison's back was to him, and then clamped his big hand down hard on the other man's shoulder. "Okay, you've had your dance, Guildford." Although his words were quiet, there was no mistaking the steely determination in his voice.

Harrison jerked his shoulder away from Miles's grasp, glaring at him menacingly. "Go away, Wellesley. This dance is mine."

Miles stood his ground. "No, Guildford, the last dance was yours. The rest of them are mine."

Victoria's eyes darted back and forth nervously between the two men. "Gentlemen, gentlemen," she murmured, her voice soft and placating, "please don't make a scene." Turning to Miles, she added, "Mr. Wellesley, why don't I just finish this dance with Lord Guildford and I'll rejoin you when it's over."

Miles's stormy eyes bore into her pleading ones for a moment; then, with a stiff nod, he turned away, stalking off the dance floor and stepping out through the French doors on to a balcony. A few minutes later he heard the music stop, but he didn't return to the ballroom, still too angry and humiliated at Victoria's rejection to face the crowd.

Finally he heard the soft rustle of a satin skirt behind him and turned to see her standing near the balcony door. "I couldn't find you," she said softly.

"I needed some air."

Slowly she walked over and stood next to him. "I think I'd like to go home now, if you don't mind."

Miles slammed his open palms against the balcony railing and turned toward her, his eyes cold and angry. "Fine. I'll get our wraps." Without another word, he walked away.

Ten minutes later they were again ensconced in the luxurious coach, but this time an uncomfortable silence stretched between them and the short ride seemed interminable.

Finally, just as they were turning into the drive at Pembroke House, Victoria said, "I don't understand what you're so angry about. I was only trying to prevent a scene in front of everyone at the party and, after all, it was just one dance."

"There still was a scene," Miles said bitterly, "only it was played out on me."

"It didn't have to be," Victoria flared, her own temper igniting. "If you had just walked away smiling, instead of stomping away like an irate child, no one would have thought anything about it."

Miles turned toward her, his eyes blazing. "You're wrong about that, my lady. You made your choice very clear by sending me away so you could have another dance with Guildford."

"Oh, that's ridiculous! I wasn't making any sort of choice at all."

"Really? Well, where I come from, a girl dances with the fellow she came with."

Victoria pressed her back hard against the luxurious squabs of the carriage seat and lifted her chin haughtily. "May I remind you yet again, sir, that this is not where you come from?"

"Oh, and it's so different here? Englishmen don't care if they're rejected by their lady in front of four hundred people?"

"I wasn't rejecting you!" Victoria railed, her voice now loud and shrill. "I was merely trying to . . ."

"Forget it!" Miles thundered, his shout deafening as the carriage came to a halt in front of the house. "It won't happen again."

"You're absolutely right about that!" Victoria cried, flinging open the carriage door and stepping out onto the drive. "Good night, Mr. Wellesley."

"Goddamn it!" Miles cursed as he lunged out of his seat and burst through the carriage door after her. In two long strides he caught up with her, holding on to her arm despite her angry attempts to wrench it from his grasp. "Quit it," he gritted, propelling her up the stairs. "Do you want Clement to see us? My God, the way coachmen talk, by tomorrow morning everyone in the shire will know we've had a quarrel."

Victoria slowed her angry pace. "I'm sure everyone in the shire already does, after the way you walked out at the party."

Miles remained silent until they reached the front door; then he took a deep, calming breath and slowly let it out. Placing a gentle finger against Victoria's cheek, he turned her face until she was looking up at him. "You're right, and I'm sorry. I was embarrassed and I acted like a jackass."

Victoria lowered her eyes, saying softly, "I didn't mean to embarrass you, Miles, and I really wasn't making any sort of choice, as you seem to think. Harrison Guildford and I have been friends since we were children, but that's all."

Miles cupped his hands on both sides of Victoria's face, again lifting her eyes to his. He lowered his head until she could feel his lips brushing hers. "And what about us?" he whispered. "Are we just friends, too?"

"I don't know," Victoria whispered back. "I don't know what we are." Her next words were lost as Miles's lips covered hers in a long, drugging kiss.

Clement, seated high atop the coach on the driver's seat, had not missed a word of the impassioned exchange between the couple. Now he sat back and smiled with satisfaction. Wouldn't the viscountess be pleased when she heard about this? He could hardly wait to get home and make a full report.

Chapter 16

"Lady Victoria, Lord Guildford is here to see you. He says it's important."

Victoria looked up from the book she was reading and groaned. "Did you already tell him I was in, Rebecca?"

The little red-haired maid winced. "Yes, I did, my lady, but I can tell him you're indisposed and not receiving. After all, when Lord Wellesley arrived unannounced the other day you said you wouldn't receive him."

Victoria shot Rebecca a withering look. "I'm quite aware of what I said, Rebecca, and it's *Mr.* Wellesley, not Lord Wellesley. I would appreciate it if you'd try to remember that in the future."

"Yes, my lady," Rebecca muttered.

Victoria put her book aside and stood up. "It's not like Lord Guildford to call without sending his card first, so his business, whatever it is, must be important. Tell him I'll see him here in the library."

"Yes, ma'am," Rebecca repeated, bobbing a curtsy.

The maid disappeared, returning a moment later accompanied by Harrison Guildford. Rebecca showed him into the room, then turned to Victoria. "Would you like the doors open or closed, my lady?"

"Closed," Harrison answered firmly.

Rebecca looked at him for a moment, then swung her eyes back to her mistress for confirmation. "Closed will be fine," Victoria nodded.

"Yes, my lady." Turning away, Rebecca marched out of the room, shaking her head in disapproval as she loudly closed the library's double doors.

"That girl should be sent packing," Harrison announced, frowning at Victoria. "I wouldn't accept that kind of insubordination from a servant for one minute."

"Oh, Rebecca's all right," Victoria said. "She occasionally forgets herself, but she was born here on the estate, and sometimes I believe she thinks of herself more as family than as an employee."

"That's still no excuse," Harrison opined. "You need to take her to task, Victoria. She's far too uppity for my liking."

Victoria sighed inwardly. The last thing she needed this morning was a lecture about servants. The previous night's altercation with Miles, followed by his passionate kisses at the front door, had conspired to give her a nearly sleepless night. It had been almost dawn before she had finally dozed off, and when Rebecca had come to awaken her at her usual rising time she'd felt as if she hadn't slept at all.

Hoping to head off a lengthy diatribe from Harrison regarding her inability to control her servants, she smiled sweetly and sat down on the settee, pouring him a cup of tea and holding it out to him. "Did you want to see me about something in particular?"

Harrison promptly set down the cup she handed him and moved next to her on the sofa. "Yes, Victoria, I do." Picking up both her hands, he looked at her, his expression intense. "I have come to ask for your hand in marriage."

Victoria felt herself blanch. She didn't know what she'd expected from Harrison's surprise visit, but it certainly wasn't a marriage proposal. She opened her mouth to respond, but before she could get a word out, he pressed a finger to her lips, effectively cutting off her words.

"Don't say anything until I'm finished."

Victoria quickly turned her face away to break the contact between her lips and his finger, but she nodded and sat back, waiting for him to continue.

He smiled, pleased with her apparent willingness to comply with his wishes. "You know that I've always said an alliance between our two families would be advantageous to everyone involved, and although I think you secretly agreed with me, you have always intimated that the time wasn't right. Well, now that your father has passed on, the time *is* right."

Again Victoria opened her mouth to voice an objection to this futile and embarrassing discourse, and again Harrison held up a hand. "Victoria, I asked you once to let me finish; now please show me the courtesy of doing so."

Victoria's eyes darkened to nearly black, a clear warning that her temper was rising, but Harrison was too wrapped up in his speech to notice.

"As I was saying," he continued pompously, "it has become very apparent since Sir John's death that the sharks are already circling, trying to get to you. Therefore, I think it's only prudent that before you get carried away with some ne'er do well and become involved in a situation that might well prevent me from being able to marry you, we should proceed with our plans."

"Stop!" Victoria cried, jumping up from the settee. "Don't say another word, Harrison, please!"

"Victoria," he said calmly, "I'm not finished. Now, please, sit down and hear me out."

"No," she stated flatly. "There's no point in your going on, and the longer I wait to tell you that, the more embarrassing it's going to be for both of us."

Harrison's lips thinned ominously. "Are you saying that you're rejecting my proposal before I'm even finished presenting it?"

Victoria let out a long, tremulous sigh. Why, oh why, on this of all mornings, when she was so tired and confused, did she have to deal with this nonsense?

Wearily, she sank back down on to the settee. "Harrison, I want you to know that I appreciate the great honor you've shown me this morning, but I cannot marry you."

Harrison's jaw clenched angrily and Victoria saw him dig his fingers into his palms, but when he spoke again his voice was calm and controlled. "Cannot, or will not?"

"Both, actually." When he continued to stare at her she added softly, "I don't love you and I won't marry a man I don't love. Furthermore, I would not do you the dishonor of marrying you when my feelings for you are not what a wife should feel for her husband."

Harrison lunged to his feet and turned his back to her, clenching his fists at his sides as he willed himself to hold on to his temper. When he finally turned around he was again under control, although the angry red flush suffusing his face betrayed his fury. "It's Wellesley, isn't it?"

"What?" Victoria asked in genuine surprise. "What are you talking about?"

"Don't deny it, Victoria. I know it's Wellesley. He's the reason you won't marry me. That arrogant, backwoods—"

"Harrison, please remember yourself!"

But Harrison was far too infuriated to be conscious of anything but the fact that penniless, spinsterish Victoria Pembroke had just turned down his offer of marriage.

"How dare you?" he snarled. "How dare you treat me like this? I warned you once before that I wouldn't put up with you cavorting around the neighborhood with that bastard, but you didn't listen, did you? You even went so far as to accompany him to Katharine Crawford's wedding! I was the laughingstock of every gossipy old prig there!"

With great dignity, Victoria rose to her feet. "Harrison, you are again forcing me to insist that you leave my house. And this time I must request that you not return."

"What? You're demanding that I leave? *I?* I'll wager you wouldn't ask Wellesley to leave if he were standing here offering marriage, would you?"

"Whether I would or wouldn't is none of your business," Victoria answered quietly. Walking over to the double doors leading to the hall, she opened one and stepped back.

For a long moment Harrison stood and stared at her in outraged disbelief. Then, with a snort of contempt, he strode past her into the hall, turning back to glare at her. "You've made a terrible mistake, Victoria—one you're going to regret immensely. I thought we could join our fortunes and estates amicably, but if you insist on continuing to play the grand lady when everyone in the shire knows you're destitute and about to be run out by your creditors, then remember this: I intend to get what I want from you. By the time I'm finished I'll have Pembroke, the horses, everything—and that includes you, if, after today, I reconsider and decide I still want you."

Victoria shook her head, a great sadness engulfing her as she looked at her old playmate. "Good-bye, Harrison," she whispered; then, very softly, she closed the library door.

It was more than an hour later when Rebecca entered the library to do the day's dusting and found her mistress still sitting on the settee, blankly staring off into space.

"Oh, my lady, I didn't know you were still in here!" she gasped. "Did Lord Guildford leave?"

"Yes," Victoria answered dully.

Rebecca waved her feather duster ineffectually at one of the top shelves of books. "And was his visit as important as you thought it would be?" she asked nonchalantly.

"He asked me to marry him."

The feather duster fell to the floor with a noisy clatter. "Oh, Lord, ma'am," Rebecca gasped, clapping her hands to her cheeks, "you didn't agree, did you?"

Victoria looked over at the distraught maid and shook her head. "No, Rebecca, I didn't agree."

Rebecca placed a hand to her chest and sighed with relief. "Oh, I'm so glad to hear you say that!" Bending over, she scooped the duster off the floor and began waving it at the bookshelves again. "I've been hoping and hoping that you and that handsome Lord—I mean, *Mister*—Wellesley would marry. I would hate to see you tied to that Lord Guildford. He has cold eyes, he does."

In spite of how upset Victoria was over the cruel barbs Harrison had flung at her, she couldn't help but smile. "Do you think so?"

"Oh, yes, my lady." Rebecca nodded, three or four of her tightly bound corkscrew curls springing free with the vehemence of her movements. "Very cold. My mum always said that you can tell a man's character by looking into his eyes. Now, take Mr. Wellesley, for instance. Those blue eyes of his say a lot to a girl—and none of the messages he sends are cold, if you get my meaning. Why, he winked at me one day when he was here to fetch you, and, I swear, I couldn't sleep all night for thinking about it!"

Victoria looked at the maid curiously. "Exactly what kind of messages do you think Mr. Wellesley's eyes send?"

"Oh, my lady," Rebecca tittered, "I couldn't be saying those things in front of you, but you just look at them real close sometime. You'll see what I mean. In fact, I'm surprised you haven't noticed already. Maybe if you just think about it a little, my meaning will come to you."

Victoria sighed wearily and lay her head back on the settee's cushions. "Honestly, Rebecca, I don't want to think about any man right now. At this moment I wish I never had to see or talk to another one again."

"Oh, Lady Victoria." Rebecca giggled. "The things you say. Why, if a girl didn't think about men, what would she think about?"

Victoria looked at Rebecca in amusement, wishing for just

a moment that she could trade places with the simple maid. At this point she couldn't think of anything she'd enjoy more than crawling off to a servant's pallet late at night to dream of a handsome man with blue eyes and hair the color of ripe wheat who'd done nothing more than wink at her that day.

Victoria was seated at the breakfast table the next morning, lingering over a last cup of tea, when George suddenly burst into the room, unannounced.

"Beggin' your pardon, my lady, but we have three mares who decided to foal this morning, and me and my boy can't handle all of 'em. Do you suppose you could come help?"

"Of course she cannot, George!" Fiona cried, looking at the stablemaster in horror. "Ladies do not tend horses in the barn. What is the matter with you?"

George threw Victoria an apologetic look. "I know it's improper askin' you to come, my lady, but all three of the mares are havin' their first babes, and they need someone to sit with them. Now that your father, God rest his soul, ain't here no more, I don't know who else to ask."

"I understand, George," Victoria said, looking down with dismay at the light lawn dress she was wearing. Miles had sent over a message the previous evening, asking if she'd accompany him on a shopping expedition in the village, and she'd accepted. She'd spent almost an hour dressing for the outing; still, she took one look at the distraught stablemaster's face and knew she had no choice. Rising from the table, she threw down her napkin and headed for the door. "I'll be there as soon as I change my clothes."

"Bless you, my lady," the old man wheezed. "Please hurry."

Victoria ran upstairs, unfastening buttons and untying ribbons as she went. She was just rounding the corner into her room when she met Rebecca, who was about to leave after making her bed. "Help me!" Victoria cried, grabbing the girl by her sleeve and hauling her back into the bedroom. "I have to change quickly."

"But, my lady," Rebecca stammered, "aren't you going shopping this morning with Mr. Wellesley?"

"Never mind about him," Victoria cried, dashing behind the dressing screen. "Just get me some old breeches and a blouse."

"But, my lady!" Rebecca protested.

"Don't argue, Rebecca; just do it!"

Less than five minutes later, Victoria was sprinting across the lawn, headed for the main barn. Bursting through the door, she looked around anxiously for the stablemaster but stopped in her tracks when she saw Miles hunkered down in a stall, his coat off and his spotless white cravat untied as he bent over a laboring mare.

"There's a good girl," Victoria heard him croon to the horse. "Just relax now. You're doing fine."

She tiptoed into the stall behind him. "Miles?"

He didn't turn his head but answered in the same crooning voice, "Come kneel here next to me and stroke her head. She's having a hard time of it and she's exhausted. I think a little comfort would go a long way in helping her."

"Is there something wrong?" Victoria asked apprehensively, dropping to her knees next to him.

"I don't think so. It's just slow going." Quietly, Miles moved down the mare's body, running his hands gently over her convulsing stomach. "Everything feels normal. Do you know, is this her first foal?"

Victoria looked more closely at the mare's head. "Berries and Cream," she murmured. "Yes, it's her first."

Miles nodded. "That's probably why it's taking so long, and why she's so frightened. I'm sure it's a pretty scary event for an animal who doesn't know what's happening to her."

Victoria chuckled softly. "I think it must be a frightening event even for women who *do* know what's happening to them."

"Have you ever helped deliver a foal before?"

"No," Victoria admitted. "Papa always came out to the barn

if there was a problem. He didn't feel it was appropriate for ladies to be present at such a time."

"It probably isn't," Miles agreed. "If you want to go back to the house, I'll stay with the mare."

"No," Victoria said adamantly. "I'm more or less in charge of the stables now, and if anyone should be here, it is I."

The mare let out a loud, guttural groan, raising her head and stiffening her legs.

Victoria's eyes widened fearfully. "There is something wrong, isn't there?"

"No, that was just a pain," Miles answered, stroking the horse gently. "She's coming along now."

Victoria nodded doubtfully. "What about you, Miles? Have you delivered a lot of foals?"

He smiled. "More than I can count. Of course, most of our horses foal on their own out in the pastures, but the riding horses in the barns are always attended."

Victoria looked worriedly at the laboring horse. "Have you ever . . . lost one?"

"Nope," Miles said firmly. "Not a one."

"Nope?" Victoria giggled, her anxiety making her almost giddy. "Is that cowboy talk?"

Miles smiled broadly, his eyes crinkling and his teeth flashing white against his bronzed skin. "Yup, cowboy talk. Gotta get back to talking like an American, you know. My brothers will never let me hear the end of it if they get here and find me talking like a Brit."

Their conversation was cut short when the mare emitted another loud grunt. Miles watched the horse's huge stomach contract, then nodded with satisfaction. "A couple more of those and we should have a baby here."

Events didn't go quite as smoothly as Miles had predicted, however, and the next few minutes had him more concerned than he cared to let on.

"Why doesn't something happen?" Victoria demanded when several more contractions passed with no progress.

"I think the problem is that the foal is very big. It's probably a colt, and they can sometimes be difficult for a young, inexperienced mare to deliver."

"Oh, dear! Perhaps I had better get George."

"That's not necessary," Miles assured her, positioning himself near the mare's hindquarters. "I'm just going to have to help her a little."

Victoria drew in a startled breath. "Are you sure you know what you're doing?"

She regretted her rash words the second she saw the offended look that crossed Miles's face. "Yes, I know what I'm doing," he said tersely, "but maybe you better leave. You might not want to watch this." Sitting back on his haunches, he rolled up his sleeves.

Turning away from him, Victoria swallowed hard, praying that she wouldn't lose her breakfast. "No, I'll stay," she mumbled. "You might need some help."

The mare stiffened again as another contraction racked her. "Good girl," Miles crooned. "Here comes the head. Come on now, my girl; give me another one of those so we can get these shoulders free."

As if she understood him, the mare pushed again. Miles braced himself against the stall wall and grabbed the foal's front legs, pulling steadily to assist the mare. Only a few seconds later, the mare gave another tremendous push and the foal slipped free.

"It's a fine bay colt," Miles announced, reaching over and grabbing a towel from a nearby stack. Deftly, he cleaned the foal, then got to his feet, wiping his hands and grinning down at the newborn animal. When he finally raised his eyes to meet Victoria's, he was astonished to see that they were filled with tears.

"Oh, Miles!" she cried, jumping to her feet and launching herself into his arms. "Thank you. Thank you so much!"

Miles barely had time to realize Victoria's intention before he found himself being hurtled backward into the corner of the stall. With a grunt of surprise, he landed on his back, Victoria on top of him. Under other circumstances he might have protested the painful jolt he'd just received, but at this particular moment he was far too involved with returning the kiss that Victoria was planting on his mouth to worry about such trivialities.

They kissed long and hotly, their caresses gradually becoming more intimate as Miles rolled Victoria over in the thick, fragrant straw. He threaded his fingers deep into her hair as he trailed his lips across her face and neck. He could feel the rapid rise and fall of her breasts beneath his lips, and the sound of her pounding heart beneath his ear did much to fuel his own excitement. Reaching for her mouth again, he kissed her deeply, greedily accepting her seductive invitation as she parted her lips. With a low moan, he tangled his tongue with hers, reveling in the erotic feast of the senses they were sharing.

"Well, isn't this common?"

With a startled gasp, Victoria pushed Miles away and lurched to a sitting position, throwing back her disheveled hair and staring up in horror at Harrison Guildford.

Miles, his body aflame with desire, took a little longer to return to reality. He looked around groggily for a moment before bracing himself on an elbow and glaring up at the smirking intruder. Finally realizing who it was looming over them, he jumped to his feet, turning on their uninvited guest in outrage. "What the hell are you doing here, Guildford?"

"I could say much the same about you, Wellesley," Harrison sneered, his eyes roaming rudely over Victoria's mussed clothes and wildly tossed hair. "Lady Victoria, I had no idea that you enjoyed a romp in the hay so much, or I would have suggested we carry on our visits in the barn instead of the drawing room."

Victoria's mortified gasp seemed to galvanize Miles. He launched himself so quickly at the leering Guildford that Harrison didn't even see Miles coming until he suddenly found himself on his back, his face being ruthlessly pummeled. "Get him off!" Harrison yelled, trying to cover his bleeding nose with his hands. "My God, he's going to break my nose!" Desperately, he pushed against Miles, trying to dislodge him from his straddled position by bucking his hips.

But Miles was by far the more accomplished pugilist, having had years of experience tussling with his brothers, and it wasn't until he felt Victoria grabbing at his shoulders and screaming at him to stop that he finally ceased his punishing blows and pinned Harrison's arms to the floor. "Apologize to the lady," he panted, his breath harsh and rasping from his exertions.

Guildford remained stubbornly silent.

Incensed, Miles gave him another quick cut to the jaw. "I said, apologize!"

Harrison let out a cry of pain and, fearful that he wouldn't have any teeth left if he didn't comply with the other man's demands, shouted, "All right, I apologize!"

"That's better," Miles said, releasing him and standing up. "Now, get out of here."

Harrison shakily got to his feet, grabbing the side of the stall for support. Despite his cuts and bruises, his face was terrifying in its rage. "You're going to be sorry for this, Wellesley," he snarled. "You both are going to be very, very sorry."

Clumsily, he unlocked the stall door, stumbling out into the barn aisle, then turning back to glare at the horror-stricken Victoria. "And you," he sneered, "who pretend to be so ladylike and proper. Why, you're no better than some common serving wench, rolling around in the dirt with a stablehand."

With another shout of fury, Miles lunged toward him again, but Harrison knew when he was outclassed and took off at a hobbling run toward the barn door.

"You'd better run, you bastard," Miles shouted, "before I kick you all the way back to Guildford Hall." He leaned out the stall door, watching Harrison's undignified retreat until he was out of sight.

Turning back to Victoria, Miles found her kneeling next to the newborn foal, tears streaming down her cheeks.

"What's wrong?" he asked, dropping to his knees beside her. "We didn't hurt the foal, did we?"

"No," she said, shaking her head. "The foal is fine. It is I who is ruined."

Miles reached out and put his arm around Victoria's shaking shoulders, ignoring her protests as he pulled her into his embrace. "You're not ruined, sweetheart. Harrison's not going to say anything about this; he'd have to admit that he'd been bested in a fight by that 'boorish American.'"

Victoria sniffed and looked at Miles from behind the veil of her tousled hair. "How do you know that's what he calls you?"

"Him?" Miles chuckled. "I heard that's what *you* call me!"

"Oh," Victoria moaned, even more embarrassed than she'd been a moment before. "Where did you hear that?"

"From everyone." Miles laughed, crooking a finger under her chin and nudging her head up until she was again looking into his eyes. "Are you all right?" he asked, his voice becoming serious.

"Yes." Victoria nodded, refusing to meet his eyes. "Just mortified, that's all."

"Why? Because Guildford found us kissing?"

"That's bad enough," she mumbled, "but the fact that we were doing exactly what he accused us of is even worse."

Miles frowned. "We're not going to go through that again, are we, Tory? So we were kissing. So what? There's nothing wrong with that."

Suddenly, Victoria pulled away from him, getting to her feet and racing toward the stall door. "You always say that, Miles, but you're wrong. No lady of quality would roll around in a stable with a man. And even if Harrison never tells a soul about what he saw us doing, I'll never be able to hold up my head in society again, knowing what I've become."

"What you've become!" Miles flared, jumping to his feet and following her out of the stall. "And what's that? A woman with feelings? A woman with emotions? A woman who responds with passion and joy to a man's kisses? You think that's something to be ashamed of?"

"Don't say those things!" Victoria shrieked, clapping her hands to her cheeks. "It's not right that you should talk to me about such things."

"This is exactly what we should talk about!"

"You just don't understand," Victoria cried.

"No, I don't," Miles shot back. "Why don't you see if you can explain it to me?"

Victoria shook her head wildly, her hair flying around her shoulders like a storm cloud. "I don't want to talk about it. I just want you to go. And this time please believe me when I tell you that I don't want you to come back."

Miles closed his eyes for a moment, feeling as if he was about to explode. The combination of unfulfilled sexual desire, the throbbing pain in his ribs where Guildford had landed a lucky blow, and now Victoria's unmerited rejection of him was almost more than his already strained emotions could bear.

"As you wish, my lady," he gritted, his hands balling into fists at his sides. "If you really prefer to wallow in guilt rather than work this out between us, then who am I to keep you from your pleasure?"

Tearing down the barn aisle, he disappeared out the door, his shouted curse of frustration reaching Victoria's ears from halfway across the pasture as he galloped away.

Chapter 17

Carolina rushed through the front door of Pembroke House and took the stairs two at a time. "Tory!" she yelled, running headlong down the second-floor hall. "Tory, where are you?"

Victoria rushed to the door of her room, gaping at her sister apprehensively. "I'm right here, Carrie. What's wrong?"

Carolina halted her flight so quickly that she had to throw out an arm to keep from mowing Victoria down. "Oh, Tory," she panted, bending over and gasping for breath, "I'm so glad you're here. Wait until you hear the outrageous story I have to tell you."

A wariness appeared in the depths of Victoria's eyes. "What outrageous story?"

"Just a minute; let me catch my breath." Pushing past Victoria, Carolina lurched into the room and flopped down on the bed.

Victoria stared at her sister's flushed face, a strange sense of foreboding gripping her. Closing the bedroom door, she sat down next to Carolina, patting her arm and saying, "All right now, tell me what you're so worked up about."

Carolina sat up and took a drink of water from a glass sitting on the nightstand. "You recollect I was invited to tea with Prudence Hathaway?"

Victoria nodded.

"Well, it was a very uncomfortable afternoon. All the ladies there kept staring at me as if I had a smudge of dirt on my cheek. Finally I retired to check and see what was wrong, but there was nothing. When I was walking back to the parlor I could hear them all talking, and yet, when I came into the room, everyone became very quiet. By then I was certain they were talking about me, so I just mustered up my British pluck and asked them, straight out, what they were whispering about."

Victoria closed her eyes and emitted a long, shaky breath, positive now that she knew what the women at the party had been whispering about. "What did they say?" she prodded, her nerves stretched so tight that she felt as if she was about to fly into a million pieces.

"They told me."

Victoria waited and waited, finally blurting, "What? What did they tell you?"

Carolina looked at her intently. "What they were gossiping about. And Tory, it didn't involve me at all. It was about you."

"Oh?" Victoria squeaked, losing her battle to sound nonchalant.

"Yes." Carolina nodded. "They said there is a rumor that you and Miles Wellesley were caught in a compromising position by Harrison Guildford. And in the stable, too!"

Victoria buried her head in her hands and groaned. "I knew it; I just knew Harrison would talk."

"Tory!" Carolina gasped. "Are you saying the rumor is true?" This last word came out in a near hysterical screech. "I can't believe it! You and Miles Wellesley? Oh, my, what is Mama going to say? And the viscountess! Oh, my dearest, whatever are you going to do? Why, everyone in the county knows about it and . . ."

"Hush!" Victoria cried, putting her hands over her ears to

block out her sister's strident voice. "Don't say anything more, Carrie. Please!"

Carolina stared openmouthed at her usually tranquil sister. "Why, Tory, you're *yelling* at me!"

Victoria threw her a stricken look. "I'm sorry, but I just can't stand to listen to you go on and on about what everyone is saying, or what everyone is going to say, or what I'm going to say, or what Miles Wellesley is going to say or . . . Oh, God, I wish I were dead!" Again, Victoria hid her face in her hands, and this time, Carolina could see her shoulders shaking as dry, shuddering sobs racked her body.

"Don't cry, Tory," Carolina begged, sympathetic tears filling her own eyes. "You'll think of something. You always do. Surely there's a simple explanation you can give to Mama."

"No," Victoria said, raising her tearstained face and gazing morosely at her sister. "There is no explanation for this."

Carolina got up off the bed and went to Victoria's bureau, pulling open a drawer and extracting a delicate linen handkerchief, which she held out to her sister. "Now, don't be rash, Tory. Perhaps we can think of something together that will explain all this. First of all, tell me, what exactly is a 'compromising position'? I know it's something wicked, but what exactly does it mean?"

"It means that I was caught doing something I shouldn't have been."

Carolina's eyes widened with excitement. "Doing something you shouldn't with Miles Wellesley?"

"Yes."

"Oh, how exciting! What exactly were you doing?"

"Kissing," Victoria answered, her voice muffled behind the handkerchief as she dabbed at her nose. "We were kissing in the barn."

Carolina rolled her eyes dreamily. "Oh, Tory, you lucky thing!"

"Lucky!" Victoria gasped. "How can you say that? Look at the mess I'm in. I'm a disgrace to the entire family."

"Oh, pooh," Carolina huffed, reseating herself next to Victoria. "You're not a disgrace. Just because of one little kiss? Why, I've had boys kiss me before. It's not so disgraceful. It's sort of tickly and strange, but not really disgraceful."

Victoria shot her a jaundiced look. Obviously Carolina had never been kissed by Miles Wellesley. There were lots of words she could use to describe his kisses, but *tickly* and *strange* were not among them.

"Probably the only reason people are talking," Carolina continued thoughtfully, "is because Mr. Wellesley was kissing you in the barn in the middle of the day and Lord Guildford saw you."

Victoria shook her head miserably. "No, the reason people are talking is because Mr. Wellesley and I were rolling around in the straw when Lord Guildford saw us."

Carolina's pretty face registered true, unmitigated shock. "Rolling around in the . . . in the straw?" she stammered. "You mean the two of you were lying down? Together?"

"Yes, yes, *yes!*" Victoria shrieked, jumping off the bed and running over to hide her face against the door. "We were lying in the straw, kissing, and Harrison walked in and found us."

"Oh, Tory," Carolina breathed, "I don't know how you're ever going to explain *that* to Mama."

Victoria whirled around, glaring at her sister. "I keep telling you, there is no way to explain it. It . . . just happened, that's all."

"What did you say when Lord Guildford found you?"

"I didn't say anything," Victoria muttered. "He and Miles got into a fight. I just stayed out of the way."

"They got into a fight?" Carolina cried. "I didn't hear that."

"Probably because Miles beat Harrison soundly. I'm sure that when Harrison is telling his tale, he doesn't want to admit to that part of it."

"They fought over you?" Carolina murmured, her eyes taking on a faraway, dreamy look. "You mean Mr. Wellesley fought Lord Guildford to save your honor?"

"My honor didn't have anything to do with it," Victoria snapped. "Miles beat Harrison because Harrison called us some rude names that Miles took exception to."

"Then he *was* avenging your honor. Oh, Tory, I think it's all scandalously romantic!"

"Well, I think it's the worst thing that's ever happened to me, and there's nothing romantic about it."

Carolina looked at her slyly. "Did Mr. Wellesley offer to marry you?"

"Marry me! Why would he offer to marry me?"

Carolina threw her arms wide. "Because you're ruined, of course." She was so caught up in her romantic musings that she didn't even notice Victoria's appalled expression at this last statement. "After all, now that Harrison has told everyone about it, what will people think? Mr. Wellesley *has* to offer to marry you. It's the only decent thing to do."

"That's preposterous. Miles Wellesley is not going to offer to marry me, and I wouldn't accept him even if he did."

Carolina's mouth dropped open in stunned amazement. "You wouldn't?"

"Of course not!"

Carolina smiled and waved a dismissive hand. "Mama will insist upon it, and the viscountess undoubtedly will, as well."

"They can insist all they want, but I'm not marrying Miles, even if he asks me, which he won't. I've told you and Georgia a hundred times that I don't ever plan to marry anyone, and especially not Miles Wellesley. I don't even like him."

"Oh, I see." Carolina giggled, hopping off the bed and skipping over to hug Victoria. "It's just his kisses you like, then."

"No!"

"You mean you don't like his kisses either?"

"No, I mean . . . Oh, I don't know *what* I mean. I'm very confused right now, Carrie. I need some time to think."

Carolina smiled sweetly. "I don't think it's so terrible, Tory. In fact, I can't imagine anything more romantic than being kissed by Miles Wellesley. I envy you."

"Well, don't. That man has caused me more problems in the month I've known him than anyone I've ever met in my entire life. I must find a way out of this with my reputation intact, because I think I finally made it clear to him that I never want to see him again. If I can just get past this debacle, perhaps I'll finally have Miles Wellesley out of my life and things will return to normal."

Carolina opened the bedroom door, grinning back at her sister over her shoulder. "Then I'll leave you alone to ponder how you're going to escape Mama's wrath and the viscountess's demands, because I'm sure you're going to be met with both—and very soon, too."

Miles stood before his frowning grandmother, a look of fury contorting his handsome face. "What do you mean, everyone knows?"

"Just what I said," Regina snapped. "Everyone knows; Harrison Guildford has made sure of that. And, unless I miss my guess, the story has been embellished through every telling, so that, by now, people are hearing that you and Victoria were fornicating on the barn floor in broad daylight!"

"That son of a bitch—"

"Miles! Remember yourself!"

Miles winced contritely. "I'm sorry, Grandmother, but this whole thing is insane. Nothing happened. We were kissing, that's all."

"I don't doubt you for a moment," Regina shrugged, "but the fact still remains, the girl's reputation is ruined and you're responsible. The only way you're going to save her name and ours is to marry her—immediately and quietly."

"I couldn't disagree more," Miles argued, smacking his palm on the mahogany desk behind which his grandmother sat. "If Victoria and I suddenly run off and get married, it's only going to lend credibility to this ludicrous story, and I refuse to give that goddamned Harrison Guildford the satisfaction of knowing that he was successful in sullying Victoria's good name."

"Miles, if you don't stop swearing in my presence, I'm going to get up and walk out of this room. Now sit down and stop acting like some hothead from the docks. We have important plans to make."

"Grandmother, are you listening to a single word I'm saying? Getting married is not the way to stop this gossip. Ignoring it is."

If possible, Regina's disapproving frown became even more pronounced. "I'm ashamed of you, Miles. Are you saying that you care so little for Victoria Pembroke that you would rather she live the rest of her life in disgrace than own up to your responsibilities and do the right thing by her?"

"I'm sorry, Grandmother, but I don't agree that it's 'doing the right thing' to force two people into a loveless marriage that neither of them wants."

Regina's eyes narrowed shrewdly. "So you're saying you don't love her?"

Miles hesitated a long moment, then said honestly, "I don't know what I feel for her. There are times when I believe I'm falling in love with her, but it seems that every time we're together, we end up having an argument. My God, she's ordered me off her property more times than I can remember."

"Then why do you keep going back?"

"You talked me into it once!"

"Yes, I did," Regina admitted, "but that was only once. What about all the other times?"

Miles plowed his fingers through his hair, shaking his head in complete frustration. "All right. I'll admit it, I'm attracted to the girl. And maybe, given the right time and circumstances, something might have developed between us that would eventually have led to marriage."

"So?" Regina interjected. "You have as much as admitted

that you're in love with the girl, and she certainly would make you a suitable wife. Believe me, Miles, many happy marriages, including my own, have begun with much less."

Miles sighed heavily and sank down in a chair. "Has anyone asked Victoria how she feels about all this?"

Regina nodded. "I believe Fiona is talking to her this afternoon. But if you think Victoria would refuse you, you're wrong. She is a well-bred, proper English girl who knows her responsibilities to her family's name and honor. She'll not refuse."

Miles balled his fists in his lap and squeezed his eyes shut. "I get so *damned* sick and tired of this endless prattle about what is and isn't proper and acceptable in England. To hear you people talk, you'd think all the rest of us were one step away from being barbarians!"

Regina's expression became stony. Regardless of how dearly she loved her grandson, she wasn't about to listen to anyone speak ill of England. "You'd be wise to remember that you come from a fine British heritage yourself, young man. There is no 'you people' about this. You are one of us, whether you want to admit it or not."

Miles held up his hands in surrender. "Let's not debate that issue right now. Forgive me for mentioning it. My point is that I don't believe in arranged marriages, I don't believe in forced marriages, and I don't believe in marriages of convenience. I believe that the only reason two people should marry is because they love each other and want to spend the rest of their lives together."

"A worthy sentiment," Regina said dryly, "but one you should have thought of before you threw Lady Victoria down in the hay and leapt on top of her."

"That's not the way it happened," Miles thundered. "In fact, if anything, it was quite the rever . . ." He halted his tirade in midsentence, realizing what he'd been about to divulge.

"Quite the reverse?" his grandmother finished, her eyebrows rising nearly to her hairline. "How very interesting."

"I shouldn't have said that," Miles muttered. "Please forget that I did."

To his surprise, Regina smiled. "Perhaps you're more chivalrous than I'm giving you credit for."

"Not chivalrous enough to agree to a forced marriage," Miles shot back.

"Miles," Regina sighed, "you have no choice. It doesn't matter who approached whom or what the circumstances of your encounter in the barn really were. Victoria Pembroke's reputation is in tatters and you are the only one who can rectify it."

Miles studied his grandmother for a long moment, his expression dark and accusatory. "You're enjoying this, aren't you? You've wanted me to marry Victoria ever since Lady Fiona approached you with the idea, and now you feel that you've got the leverage you need to force me to do it."

Regina ignored his surly tone. "I'll admit, I would love to see you and Victoria married. But if you think I'm enjoying having the Wellesley name associated with a tawdry little scandal like this, you're very wrong."

Miles blew out a long breath and stared down at his boots. "I don't know what to do," he admitted. "Even if I offered marriage and Victoria agreed, I think it would be for all the wrong reasons. I hate to think of the two of us being chained together for life if there's not enough love between us to sustain the relationship."

"You really don't think the girl's in love with you?"

"I don't know. The only thing I'm sure of is that there's an attraction between us. That much, at least, is reciprocal."

"Obviously."

Miles looked up, his eyes questioning. "Is attraction enough, Grandmama? Do you think it can lead to love? And what if it doesn't? Then we're both doomed to lives of unhappiness."

Regina looked at her grandson sympathetically. "Miles, you are the only one who can answer those questions. But when you're thinking about the decision you have to make, remember this: There can be no happiness without honor. You descend from a long line of honorable men—men who have always done the right thing when the situation demanded it. That's a proud heritage, and one I would think you'd want to uphold."

Miles nodded glumly. "I just wish I could talk to Father." Then, looking at his grandmother, he hastily added, "Not that I don't appreciate your counsel, of course."

"I understand." She smiled. "There are many things that men feel the need to discuss with other men, and this is certainly one of them. But, at least in that respect, I can give you one positive bit of news."

Miles looked at her hopefully.

"I received a wire today from your parents. They've landed at Liverpool and will arrive by Friday."

For the first time since their conversation had begun, Miles smiled with genuine happiness. "That's great. Can my decision wait at least that long?"

"I think so. But, please, for Fiona Pembroke's sake, make it one of the first things you discuss with your father . . . before horses and crops and the state of the fences at the ranch."

Miles grinned, promising he'd speak to his father the second he arrived. Rising from his chair, he leaned across the desk and gave Regina a quick kiss on the cheek, then hurriedly left the library, relieved that the confrontation with the venerable old dowager was over.

Regina watched her grandson's hasty departure, then leaned back in her chair, steepling her fingers in front of her.

If you think your father is going to give you permission to walk away from this, you're very wrong, my boy. I know my son. He may live in America now, but he's British to the core. And British men always do the right thing by their ladies.

Regina had no doubt that James would bring Miles around. She only hoped that Fiona was having the same success with Victoria.

* * *

"If you try to force me to marry him, I'll run away. I swear I will."

Fiona looked at Victoria's stubborn, set face and shook her head in despair. "Victoria, can't you see that's no answer? Where would you go? What would you do? We've been over and over this before. You must marry Miles; the family honor is at stake."

"Hang the family honor," Victoria spat. "I won't marry him. There's no sense in our continuing to argue about this, Fiona. I won't do it, and that's that."

"But what about all those terrible things Harrison Guildford is saying about you—about us? Are you willing to have the entire family disgraced because of your stubbornness?"

"Harrison Guildford isn't saying anything terrible about anyone but me, and if I don't give a rip what he's saying, I don't know why you're so concerned. Good heavens, you and the twins are leaving for America soon anyway. Why do you care what Harrison says? You'll probably never see the man again— or any of the people he's tattling to, for that matter."

"Victoria, I can't believe you'd say that! I care because I love you and want you to be happy. Do you really think I would leave for America and abandon you in the middle of a scandal?"

"I guess not," Victoria admitted, "and I'm sorry that I'm being difficult. But I just won't marry him, Fiona."

"Because you don't love him?" Fiona prodded.

Victoria hesitated, unable to admit that with any degree of truth. "I don't know. I'm not sure what I feel for him—something—but I'm not sure it's love. I think it's more attraction than anything else, and that frightens me."

"Frightens you? Why does it frighten you?"

Victoria fidgeted with the handkerchief she was holding, then muttered, "Because Miles makes me feel things that I don't think proper ladies are supposed to feel."

"But don't you see, Tory?" Fiona said, her face lighting with renewed hope, "there's nothing wrong with feeling that way. In fact, I think it's a wonderful beginning."

Victoria shook her head, the expression on her face almost sad. "I don't like the way Miles makes me feel. It's uncomfortable."

Fiona leaned forward until their foreheads were almost touching. "Exactly how *does* he make you feel?"

Victoria drew a shuddering breath. "Sort of hot and cold and shaky, all at the same time. It's not a feeling I enjoy."

Fiona smiled knowingly. "Believe me, Tory, it's a feeling that most women would give a great deal to experience."

"Well, I'm not 'most' women. And, besides, even if I did agree to marry Miles, how do you know that Miles would agree to marry me?"

"Of course he will," Fiona stated firmly. "He's a Wellesley. If there's anything that family prides itself on, it's their sense of honor. I know the viscountess is very adamant that Miles do the right thing by you. In fact, I believe she's talking to him this very afternoon."

"But don't you see?" Victoria wailed. "I don't want Miles to 'do the right thing' by me. If I ever marry, I want it to be because the man in question loves me, not because he feels obligated to do so. And I can assure you, Fiona, Miles Wellesley has never so much as intimated that he loves me."

"But, Victoria . . ."

"Please," Victoria said, holding up her hands to stay any further arguments, "don't say any more. I will think of something to rectify this situation I've gotten us all into, but marrying Miles is not the answer. As far as I'm concerned, the subject is closed."

With a final nod for emphasis, Victoria rose from her chair and marched out of the drawing room, leaving Fiona to stare after her morosely. "Such a difficult girl," she murmured, shaking her head.

Fiona sat back and took a sip from her ever-present cup of

tea. Despite what Victoria thought, the subject was not closed. Harrison Guildford's evil slander had firmly cemented the viscountess's resolve that this marriage would take place. And if Regina Wellesley was determined that her grandson was going to marry Victoria, Fiona had no doubt that the wedding would, indeed, take place.

Chapter 18

"Grandma, we're here!"

Ten-year-old Nathan Wellesley burst through the carved front doors of Wellesley Manor, his boots clumping noisily on the polished marble floor. "Grandma, where are you?"

Cedric, who had been rudely awakened from his midafternoon nap by the commotion in the front hall, rounded the corner into the foyer, frowning in furious disapproval. "Stop that yelling this instant, little boy! Who are you and what are you doing here?"

Nathan looked up at the stooped, old man and grinned. "My name is Nathan Buffington Wellesley, and I've come from America to visit my grandma. Where is she?"

Cedric closed his eyes, wishing desperately that when he opened them this young whipper snapper with the wheat-colored hair and the dirty boots would be gone. Unfortunately, he wasn't, and Cedric had no alternative but to face the fact that *they were here*. All of them. Young Master James's whole wild brood, come to stay for Lord knew how long. And, worst of all, they were a full day early! It was totally without precedent that guests would arrive twenty-four hours ahead of schedule, without so much as the courtesy of some sort of notification.

"You are tracking dirt all over the floor, young man," Cedric announced.

Nathan looked down at the black clods of dirt his boots were leaving and shrugged. "That always happens." Turning away from the frowning servant, he yelled, "Hey, Seth, come on in here and look at Grandma's house. She has a banister that looks even better for sliding than ours."

Almost immediately, another tow-headed boy, nearly identical in size and looks to the first, appeared in the doorway. "You're right, Nate!" he crowed, racing across the foyer and up the stairs. "Come on!" he yelled, gesturing wildly to his brother, "let's try it out!"

Just then, the viscountess appeared at the top of the staircase and said in an imperious voice, "That will be quite enough, boys. Go downstairs and wait for your parents to properly introduce you."

The two boys looked at each other out of identical sea blue eyes, then obediently tramped down the stairs, going to stand by the door with their hands folded in front of them.

"That's better." Regina nodded, and proceeded down the staircase. Inclining her head toward Cedric, she whispered, "You must always be firm, Cedric, but never cross. Surely you remember when my own boys were home."

Cedric shuddered discreetly, indeed remembering the viscountess's seven sons. Who could forget the chaos that had reigned for so many years when the young masters were growing up? And to think that now, all these years later, one had come back with seven rowdy offspring of his own. In Cedric's estimation, it was truly a cruel twist of fate that he was going to be forced to live again through an entire summer with children underfoot, getting in his way and dirtying his immaculate house. And at his age, too! What could the viscountess have been thinking when she invited the whole family to visit? It was really beyond all reason.

"Do you wish for me to prepare refreshments, my lady?" he asked resignedly.

"Yes, a bit of tea and some cakes and, oh yes, some juice for the children would be nice."

"I'll see to it immediately." He nodded, bowing and hurriedly taking his leave. Even helping Cook fix tea would be preferable to having to remain in the midst of the hoard swarming through the front door.

Regina had just entered the foyer when a tall, handsome man with thick, dark hair that was just beginning to gray at the temples stepped through the door. "Mother!" he cried, his deep voice warm with pleasure.

Regina turned at the sound and, seeing her youngest son standing in the doorway, let out a glad little cry and rushed into his open arms, moving at a speed that belied her seventy-odd years. "James! Oh, my darling, darling boy! I can hardly believe it's you!"

James Wellesley wrapped his arms around his mother and hugged her exuberantly. "Mother, how wonderful to see you. Can it really have been five years?" Holding the misty-eyed viscountess at arm's length, he flashed the signature Wellesley grin that every one of his handsome sons had been lucky enough to inherit. "You look magnificent!"

"Oh, you." Regina laughed, giving him a playful push. "I'm older than rocks and water, and you know it, but I love you for flattering me." Reaching up, she placed her hands on her son's cheeks and stared deep into his eyes. "The older you get, the more you look like your father, James. It's a balm to my heart to look into your face and see my Charles."

Regina gave her son one last quick kiss and turned to greet her daughter-in-law. "Mary, my dear. How are you?"

"I'm fine, Mother. A bit tired after the long journey, but very, very happy to be in England again."

"I'm happy to have you home again, too. I must say, dearest, you look as pretty and youthful as you did on your wedding day."

Mary smiled at her mother-in-law lovingly and shifted the toddler she held in her arms to a more comfortable position.

"And who have we here?" Regina cooed. "Could this be my granddaughter, whom I've waited so long to meet?"

"Yes." Mary smiled. "This is Paula."

Regina looked at the porcelain doll of a child, with her pink cheeks, blue eyes and blond hair and shook her head. "It took you two long enough to produce a daughter, but I must admit, when you finally did you certainly came up with an exquisite little beauty."

"An exquisite little beast, if the truth be known." Mary laughed, setting the child down. "Now don't touch anything, Paula. Do you hear Mama?"

The beautiful little girl nodded solemnly, then proceeded to pull a small silver tray used to hold calling cards off the hall table.

Regina smiled benignly as Mary hurried over to intervene, then turned back to the troop of boys clustered near the door. "And here are my grandsons," she beamed. "You've all grown so much since I last saw you, I'm not even sure I know who is who. I am sure that I've lost track of your ages, though, so you're going to have to enlighten me. But first I must ask your father about Stuart." Turning, she looked back at James. "How is he?"

"Wonderful." James smiled. "He's still at school in Boston, although he should be finished next spring. He says that when he graduates he wants to stay in Massachusetts and design ships."

"Really! That seems like a worthy aspiration. What kind of ships? Passenger or freight?"

"Passenger ships, eventually, but I'm afraid right now he's thinking more about warships." James lowered his voice and leaned confidentially toward his mother. "And what with all the unrest between the states that's festering in Congress, I fear he just might find a market for them."

Here's a special offer
for Zebra Historical
Romance Readers!

GET 4 FREE HISTORICAL ROMANCE NOVELS

A $19.96 Value!

Passion, adventure and hours of pleasure delivered right to your doorstep!

HERE'S A SPECIAL INVITATION TO ENJOY TODAY'S FINEST HISTORICAL ROMANCES— ABSOLUTELY FREE! *(a $19.96 value)*

Now you can enjoy the latest Zebra Lovegram Historical Romances without even leaving your home with our convenient Zebra Home Subscription Service. Zebra Home Subscription Service offers you the following benefits that you don't want to miss:

- 4 BRAND NEW bestselling Zebra Lovegram Historical Romances delivered to your doorstep each month (usually before they're available in the bookstores!)

- 20% off each title or a savings of almost $4.00 each month

- FREE home delivery

- A FREE monthly newsletter, *Zebra/Pinnacle Romance News* that features author profiles, contests, special member benefits, book previews and more

- No risks or obligations...in other words you can cancel whenever you wish with no questions asked

So join hundreds of thousands of readers who already belong to Zebra Home Subscription Service and enjoy the very best Historical Romances That Burn With The Fire of History!

And remember....there is no minimum purchase required. After you've enjoyed your initial FREE package of 4 books, you'll begin to receive monthly shipments of new Zebra titles. Each shipment will be yours to examine for 10 days and then if you decide to keep the books, you'll pay the preferred subscriber's price of just $4.00 per title. That's $16 for all 4 books with FREE home delivery! And if you want us to stop sending books, just say the word....it's that simple.

It's a no-lose proposition, so send for your 4 FREE books today!

4 FREE BOOKS

These books worth almost $20, are yours without cost or obligation when you fill out and mail this certificate.

(If the certificate is missing below, write to: Zebra Home Subscription Service, Inc., 120 Brighton Road, P.O. Box 5214, Clifton, New Jersey 07015-5214)

Complete and mail this card to receive 4 Free books!

YES! Please send me 4 Zebra Lovegram Historical Romances without cost or obligation. I understand that each month thereafter I will be able to preview 4 new Zebra Lovegram Historical Romances FREE for 10 days. Then if I decide to keep them, I will pay the money-saving preferred publisher's price of just $4.00 each...a total of $16. That's almost $4 less than the regular publisher's price, and there is never any additional charge for shipping and handling. I may return any shipment within 10 days and owe nothing, and I may cancel this subscription at any time. The 4 FREE books will be mine to keep in any case.

Name _____

Address _____ Apt. _____

City _____ State _____ Zip _____

Telephone ( ) _____

Signature _____

(If under 18, parent or guardian must sign.)

LF0596

Terms, offer and prices subject to change without notice. Subscription subject to acceptance by Zebra Home Subscription Service, Inc.. Zebra Home Subscription Service, Inc. reserves the right to reject any order or cancel any subscription.

A $19.96 value... absolutely FREE with no obligation to buy anything, ever!

ZEBRA HOME SUBSCRIPTION SERVICE, INC.
120 BRIGHTON ROAD
P.O. BOX 5214
CLIFTON, NEW JERSEY 07015-5214

AFFIX
STAMP
HERE

Regina's eyes clouded with concern. "We'll talk more about that later," she said softly.

Turning back to the boys, who were now lined up, waiting for their official introductions, she walked over to the tallest and said regally, "All right, young man, you may start. I assume that you're Eric."

"Yes, Grandmother, I am, and I'm seventeen."

"And a fine, tall boy you are, too. Another year or two and you're going to be taller than your father." Her prediction brought a pleased grin to the usually shy Eric's face.

Moving down the line, Regina stopped in front of the next boy, gazing curiously at his russet-colored hair and hazel eyes. "All I have to do is look at your hair to know that you're Geoffrey," she informed him, "although I've never understood where your parents came up with you. The whole lot of you is either blond like your mother, or dark like your father."

The auburn-haired boy grinned, his tawny skin taking on an embarrassed flush at his grandmother's teasing words.

"How old are you now, Geoffrey? From the looks of you, I'd guess about sixteen?"

Geoffrey beamed at his grandmother's incorrect guess. "No, ma'am." He laughed. "I'm fourteen."

"Fourteen!" the viscountess gasped. "Why, you're going to be as big as a tree when you're full grown."

"It's funny you should say that, Mother," James chuckled, "since trees are pretty much Geoff's life. We've a lumberjack in the making with this one."

"Well," Regina sighed, "I'm not sure whether that would have been my choice of profession for the boy, but I must admit he does have the build for it."

Patting Geoffrey on the cheek, she moved to her right again, this time bending over to cast a teasing glance at Nathan and Seth. "And I've already been reacquainted with these two," she said. Looking at Mary over her shoulder, she added, "They nearly ran poor Cedric down when they first came into the house. It will probably take him the better part of a week to recover."

Mary winced, causing Regina to laugh out loud. Turning back to the blond boys, she tapped her finger on her chin. "Are you sure you're not twins?"

"No, Grandma." Seth laughed. "We're a whole year apart! I'm still nine, but I'm stronger."

"You are not!" Nathan protested hotly, giving his younger brother a punch on the arm. "I can whip you any day!"

"Boys!" Mary cried, her tone hovering somewhere between embarrassment and amusement. "Mind your manners!"

"Pa says you have horses we can ride," Seth announced. "Me and Nate want to play sheriff and outlaw."

"Nate and I," Regina corrected. "Sheriff and outlaw, hmm? Well, why don't we wait until everyone is settled, and then perhaps I can introduce you to George, the stablemaster. I believe he might be able to come up with a couple of worthy mounts."

"Today?" Seth prodded.

"Tomorrow," his father answered firmly. "And that's the last we'll hear of it, young man."

Seth's face fell in disappointment, but he said only, "Yes, sir." Then, looking up again, he added, "But first thing tomorrow, right, Pa?"

James's stern countenance relaxed into an indulgent smile. "First thing, Seth."

Regina had finally worked her way down to the end of the line of children, and now stood in front of a small blond boy. "Here's a little man whom I've never had the pleasure of meeting." She beamed. "Is your name Adam?"

The little boy stuck his finger in his mouth and nodded.

"Does that finger taste good?"

Pulling it out of his mouth, Adam looked at it thoughtfully, then shook his head.

"That's what I thought," Regina said dryly. "Why don't you leave it out of your mouth, then?"

Adam looked at the aristocratic old woman, his blue eyes wide with curiosity, then nodded and stuck his hand into the pocket of his short trousers.

"He's absolutely adorable," Regina murmured, putting an affectionate arm around Mary's shoulders. "They all are." With a proud smile, she looked at James. "You two have done a wonderful job with your children and, believe me, I know what a challenge a large family is."

"Amen to that," Mary said.

"Tell me," Regina whispered, "Are there any more on the way?"

"Heavens, no!" Mary cried, heedless of the fact that most of the children were still within earshot. "James finally has his daughter and we are finished!"

"Do you agree with that, James?" Regina asked.

"Yes, indeed. I'm getting too old for fatherhood. It's time some of the boys took over that task."

"And speaking of that," Mary said, looking around the vast hall, "where is Miles? We're so anxious to see him."

"We didn't think you were going to be here until tomorrow," Regina explained, "so I'm afraid he's off with a group of his friends, undoubtedly getting up to no good."

"That's my boy." James grinned. "Actually, Mother, I'm glad he's not here. Mary and I wanted to have a chance to talk to you first, regarding the situation you wrote to me about."

"Ah, yes," Regina nodded, "and there is, indeed, a lot I need to tell you."

"Has anything changed since your letter?" Mary asked.

"A great deal," Regina said, "and not all of it pleasant, I'm afraid."

Mary threw a look of concern at her husband, then began herding the children together like a mother hen with a flock of chicks. "Let's get everyone settled," she said quietly. "Then we'll sit down and have a long talk."

Regina led the way up the stairs.

* * *

Miles poured two snifters of brandy and handed one to his father before seating himself in a chair in front of the library fire. "I'm so glad we finally have an opportunity to talk, Father. It's been so crazy since you arrived, I didn't think we were ever going to find a moment alone."

James chuckled and took a swallow of his drink, rolling the well-aged liquor across his tongue appreciatively. "The climate of a house does tend to change when you bring six children into its midst."

"That it does," Miles agreed. "It's wonderful to see everyone again. I hadn't realized how much I'd missed them."

"I think they feel the same way about you, considering the boys haven't left you alone for a minute."

"I don't mind. I enjoy every minute with them. I think Grandmother is enjoying them, too. I've never seen her so animated. She seems twenty years younger than she did yesterday."

James took another sip of his drink and smiled fondly. "Mother always did love children. If she hadn't, I doubt she would have survived raising the seven of us."

"Too bad Cedric doesn't feel the same way." Miles chuckled. "I'm not altogether sure he is going to survive your visit."

James laughed heartily. "Cedric's been the same since I was a boy. The most enjoyable moments of his life have been spent complaining about the evils of children. He'll manage. He always does."

They lapsed into silence, each of them dreading having to delve into the real reason for their private conference.

"Well," Miles sighed, "I suppose we might as well talk about it."

James nodded and lit a cheroot, a sure sign that he was anticipating a long session.

"I suppose Grandmother has told you the whole sordid story."

James shook out the match and tossed it in the tray on a small table next to his chair. "She has spoken to both your mother and me about the situation, yes. I, however, do not find anything sordid in what she recounted. Your behavior in the barn was a bit foolhardy, perhaps, but certainly not sordid."

Miles leaned forward, clasping his hands between his knees and dropping his head. "We were kissing, Father. That's all. Just kissing."

James smiled his understanding. "An enjoyable pastime to be sure, but, unfortunately, not one that should be conducted in front of a jealous competitor."

"Harrison Guildford is an ass," Miles gritted.

"Obviously. But he's an ass who must be dealt with."

Miles looked up and nodded gravely. "I know. What I don't know is, how."

James drew on his cigar, then blew out a stream of smoke thoughtfully. "The way I see it, Miles, you have three choices. You offer the lady marriage and see what she says, being aware that if she says 'yes,' you're going to have to go through with it. Or you simply go talk to the girl and ask her what she would like you to do, keeping in mind, again, that if she demands that you marry her, you're going to have to. There's always the chance, however, that Lady Victoria isn't any more interested in marrying you than you are in marrying her. Perhaps she has come up with a plan which will salvage her reputation without forcing the two of you to rush headlong into a marriage neither of you wants."

Miles nodded, listening intently to what his father was saying. "You said I have three choices. What's the third?"

"The third is that you ignore the whole situation and hope it goes away."

Miles shook his head. "I can't do that. Knowing as much about Guildford as I do, I don't think he's going to let it go away, and I can't expect Victoria to bear the brunt of the scandal alone."

James nodded approvingly and tipped his snifter in his son's direction. "Bravo, Miles. You're a credit to the family name."

Miles smiled, pleased with his father's praise. "Tell Grandmother that, will you? I think she believes I'm about to disgrace twenty generations of noble Wellesley men, who never did anything to discredit the family name."

"She's obviously forgotten my great-grandfather, who jilted his intended and ran away with the coachman's daughter on the eve of his wedding."

Miles looked at his father, aghast. "Really? Ran away with the coachman's daughter?"

"Yes, and they had twelve children and lived very happily to a ripe old age, although he never was forgiven by his parents."

Miles, who had never heard this particular bit of family history, grinned with delight. "Nice to know that there's been at least one other rapscallion in the family."

"Oh, Miles," James chuckled, getting up to refill their glasses, "there have been rapscallions in every generation of this family, and don't let anybody tell you any differently. You can't have a family as large and diverse as ours without having a few scoundrels and rounders. Your grandmother just prefers to forget that fact, especially when she's trying to make one of her children, or grandchildren as the case may be, come to heel. But back to the problem at hand. You have to make a decision and you have to make it soon. Maybe you should do what I do; whenever I have a difficult decision to make, it always helps me to ask myself pertinent questions."

"Such as?" Miles asked, leaning forward intently.

"First off and most importantly, do you love the girl? Can you picture yourself married to her?"

Miles thought for a long time, then said, "I honestly don't know. I think I could love her if she'd give me a chance. But Father, she's such a terror. I've never met such a strong-minded woman, and I don't know if I want to spend the rest of my life doing battle with her."

"But Miles, don't you think that perhaps her strong-mindedness is part of her charm? Part of what attracted you to her in the first place?"

Miles smiled in resignation. "I know very well that it is.

What I don't know is how we would get along if we were married. We haven't managed very well so far. And there's one other thing to consider here, too."

"What's that?"

"She's so . . . so *British,* and I don't want to live in England. I want to go home."

"Who says you have to live permanently in England?" James asked, blowing out another cloud of smoke. "If Victoria is your wife, she'll have to live where you choose. It's a wife's duty to follow her husband."

Miles laughed mirthlessly. "I can just hear what her reaction would be if I presented her with that edict!"

"All right then, compromise. Live part of the year here and part of the year in Colorado, or one year here and one year there. You can work it out if you both want to badly enough. Believe me, talking your mother into emigrating wasn't the easiest task I ever faced, but once we got settled in America she loved it. I don't think she'd come back to England to live, even if the opportunity presented itself. Once Victoria sees Colorado she may feel the same."

Miles rose and moved restlessly over to the bay window, bracing his palms on the wide sill. "You're saying you think I should offer marriage?"

James shook his head adamantly. "I'm not saying that at all. It's not for me to say what you should do."

Miles turned away from the window and faced James again. "But I'm asking you."

"All right, then, since you put it that way, I think you should talk to the girl. I think you owe that to her—and to yourself. And I think that once you do, the answers to all the other questions you're wrestling with will be obvious."

Miles nodded thoughtfully and turned back to stare out the window once again. "As usual, you're right, Father. We do need to talk."

James stubbed out his cigar and smiled with satisfaction. "Good. Then go write the lady a note requesting a meeting—

a private one. Take her on a picnic or something where you'll be assured of no interruptions or interference from anyone else."

Stretching, James yawned expansively. "As for me, I'm off to bed. I haven't had a moment alone with your mother in weeks, what with being on the ship and all. Maybe tonight, with any luck, Adam and Paula will sleep in their own beds instead of ours."

Miles threw his father a roguish grin. "Why, you old devil, you."

James wiggled his eyebrows meaningfully. "As I said, Miles, there's a rapscallion in every generation, and I'm proud to say that I have the distinction of being the uncontested title holder in mine. Now, I bid you good night." With a jaunty step, James walked toward the library doors, then paused and turned back again.

"Would you do me a favor?"

Miles looked at his father curiously. "Of course."

"If there's any way you can manage it, try to keep the children occupied until after nine tomorrow morning. Your mother and I have some catching up to do."

James disappeared through the library doors, leaving his son to stare after him in astonishment.

Chapter 19

Miles set down the heavy picnic basket and spread a large blanket on the grass. Kneeling down, he looked up at Victoria and smiled. "I really appreciate your seeing me today."

"Did you think I wouldn't?" she asked, settling herself next to him and carefully arranging her skirt so that not the slightest bit of ankle showed.

"I didn't really know, but I'm glad you did." Opening the basket his grandmother's cook had packed, he looked inside curiously. "Mmm, looks like we have chicken and a salad of some kind, and apples and a pie."

"What kind of pie?" Victoria asked.

Miles peered into the basket again. "I can't really tell, but let's pray it's not raisin. Grandmother's cook has a real penchant for raisin pie and I can hardly choke it down." Digging further down in the basket, he held up a bottle. "Ah ha; we also have wine!"

"I don't care for any of that," Victoria said primly.

Miles studied her set face for a moment, his own brow furrowing. "Why not? I've seen you drink wine before."

"Certainly not in the middle of the day! If you feel you'd like some, though, I have no objection."

Based on the prissy way Victoria was acting this afternoon, Miles not only felt that he'd like a glass of wine, he felt as if he *needed* one. "Well, thank you for your permission, my lady," he said dryly. Pulling a corkscrew out of the basket, he deftly opened the bottle and poured a liberal splash into one of the glasses the cook had packed. "Are you sure you won't have any? Just a taste?"

"No, thank you."

Miles blew out an irritated breath but forced himself to continue smiling. Why had Victoria agreed to see him today if she was going to act like this?

He'd been astounded by how glad he'd been to see her this afternoon. The mere sight of her, framed in the doorway, clad in a light pink dress with a matching hat and gloves, had made his heart—and other parts of him—stir warmly. But ever since he'd assisted her into the light phaeton and they'd started off for this lovely meadow on the far northern edge of the Wellesley estate, she'd hardly said a word. And when she had spoken there was a tone of starchy aloofness in her voice that had set his teeth on edge.

The words were out of his mouth before he could stop himself. "Why did you come today, Victoria? It's obvious you don't want to be here, so why did you agree?"

Because I wanted to see you! Because I haven't been able to think of anything but you since that day in the barn! Because I wanted to see if you really are as handsome and charming and exciting as you seemed that day, or if I've just conjured up a fantasy man who doesn't resemble the real you at all.

Miles would have been elated if he could have known the thoughts rushing through Victoria's mind, but all he heard was, "You said in your message that you thought we should talk, and I agree."

Miles nodded, his unwavering smile effectively hiding the fact that his spirits had sunk down to his boot tops at her brusk tone. "Why don't we eat first?" he suggested. "I find that decisions are always easier to make on a full stomach."

Victoria turned startled eyes on him. "Decisions? Is that why you asked me here today? To make decisions?"

Miles, who was just lifting a chicken leg to his mouth, promptly set it down again. "Yes. I think it's important that you and I agree how to fend off the ridiculous rumors your friend Harrison Guildford is spreading."

"He's not my friend!" Victoria snapped. "He may have been once, but he's not anymore."

Miles noticed how hard Victoria was struggling to remain composed, but deep in her eyes he could also see the pain she was trying so hard to conceal. "Tory," he murmured, reaching out to stroke her glossy dark hair, "I'm sorry about all this. I shouldn't have kissed you that day in the barn. Even my father, who's usually the epitome of understanding, said my behavior was foolhardy. The simple truth is, I got carried away, and even though I'm sure you consider that no excuse, it's the only one I have."

Victoria stared down at the plate of food sitting in front of her, unable to meet his gaze. "It's not entirely your fault, Miles, and I was wrong to place all the blame on you. I got carried away that day, too."

"So," he whispered, "what are we going to do about it?"

Victoria raised stricken eyes. "I don't know. I don't think there's anything we *can* do."

Miles stared at her for a long moment, his father's voice echoing in his mind. *Once you talk to her, the answers to all your other questions will be obvious.* "There is something we can do about it," he said, inching closer and picking up her hand. "We can get married."

Victoria drew in a startled breath and yanked her hand out of his grasp. "No!"

Miles sat back, blinking in offended surprise at her vehement denial of his proposal. Determined to conceal his disappointment, he shrugged nonchalantly and said, "All right; so much for that idea. Let's eat." Grabbing the chicken leg again, he savagely tore off a piece, chewing hard while he stared off into the distance.

"You . . . you don't want to marry me, Miles," Victoria stammered, her voice thick with unshed tears. "You may want my lands, my title, and my horses, but I know that deep down, you don't want me."

"You don't have any idea what I want," Miles growled, disappointment turning to anger. "As for your lands, I own far more land in America than your family ever thought of having here. I already have a title, if I care to use it, so I sure as hell don't need yours, and as far as your horses are concerned, the only one who holds any interest for me at all is King's Ransom, and even he isn't worth chaining myself to a woman I don't care about for the rest of my life. If I didn't want to marry you, my lady, I wouldn't have asked. Please give me credit for that at least."

Tears of remorse filled Victoria's eyes. "All right, then; perhaps you're asking because you feel beholden to me, but I assure you, you don't have to. I know my family and yours are pressuring you to do what they consider to be 'the right thing,' but it's really not necessary. I don't want any man to feel he has to marry me out of a sense of pity or obligation."

"It has never crossed my mind to pity you," Miles thundered, throwing down the bare bone from his chicken leg and glaring at her. "And I really wish you'd drop the 'forgotten spinster' role; it doesn't suit you. You're intelligent, stimulating and too beautiful for your own good, and I haven't been able to get you out of my mind since the first day we met in the barn."

Victoria didn't know whether to laugh or cry at his harsh, exciting words. Finally she just shook her head and said, "Barns have always been our downfall, haven't they?"

Miles picked up his wineglass and drained it in one swallow. "Yes. Maybe I should learn to stay out of them." Leaning forward, he crooked an arm around Victoria's neck and pulled her up hard against him, kissing her so soundly that she thought she might faint. When he finally lifted his mouth from hers he rasped, "Say you'll marry me, Tory. I'll make you happy. I swear I will."

"I can't," Victoria gasped, pushing against his shoulders in a feeble attempt to put some space between them.

Miles refused to let her break their embrace. "Why not?"

"We don't love each other," she protested lamely, knowing that her oft-repeated excuse was, at least on her part, a lie.

"That'll come."

"What makes you think so?"

"Because," Miles drawled, his hot gaze roaming all over her, "you take my breath away."

This time she gave him a hard enough shove to allow herself to escape. She scooted over to the far side of the blanket, better able to think rationally from a distance. "I can't marry you, Miles. I appreciate the offer, I really do, but I can't."

Miles frowned in frustration, realizing that now that he'd actually proposed, he wanted very much for Victoria to accept—and that his reasons didn't have anything to do with land, titles or horses. Shaking his head, he said quietly, "I won't buy that, Victoria, unless you can give me at least one concrete reason why not."

"Because," she stammered, "because I wouldn't . . . make you a good wife."

His frown dissolved into a look of consternation. "Why do you say that?"

Victoria blushed to the roots of her hair, desperately wishing that he would simply take her at her word. Obviously, though, he wasn't going to. Averting her eyes, she idly plucked at a blade of grass, her voice so low when she spoke that Miles had to lean forward to hear her. "There are . . . certain aspects of marriage that I believe I would find most difficult . . . to adjust to."

"I don't know why," Miles argued. "I don't think marriage to me would be far different from the life you're used to. You already know how to run a household, and I can certainly afford any domestic help you might need."

"That's not . . . what I mean," Victoria mumbled, still studying the blade.

"What? I didn't hear you."

She forced herself to look up, meeting his puzzled blue eyes for a split second before looking away again. "I said, that's not what I mean."

Her meaning finally dawned on him and he nodded slowly. "You're talking about sex, aren't you? You don't want to get married because you're scared of sex."

Victoria gasped, shocked to the core that Miles would use that word in front of her. No one, *no one,* ever said that word out loud, and especially not in front of a single lady. She was so stunned by his frankness that for a moment she was completely speechless. When she finally did find her voice, her tone was as reproving as a school mistress's to a recalcitrant student. "Mr. Wellesley! It is totally inappropriate for you to . . ."

"Oh, will you stop?" Miles flared, his patience with her prudishness coming to an end. "What's inappropriate is your insistence on calling me 'Mr. Wellesley' when we're discussing something as intimate as marriage. And don't tell me that you've never heard the word 'sex' before, because no one can live to be twenty-three years old without hearing it at least a few times."

"How do you know I'm twenty-three?" Victoria demanded, her modesty temporarily forgotten in the face of her mortification that Miles would be aware of her advanced age.

"I don't know how I know," he answered, annoyed that she was moving away from the subject at hand. "Somebody must have told me at some point. But your age isn't what's important here." Sliding across the blanket toward her, he picked up her hand and kissed it gently. "Are you afraid of lovemaking, Tory?"

Victoria yanked her hand out of his and jumped to her feet. "I don't want to talk about this!" Turning, she stumbled a few steps away, covering her mouth with her hands as she tried to calm her pounding heart.

But Miles was not about to be gainsaid and, getting to his feet, he followed her, gently placing his hands on her shaking shoulders. "I don't know what kind of horror stories you've heard . . ."

"I don't want to talk about it!" Victoria repeated, interrupting him before he could say something to further embarrass her. "Please, Miles!"

In truth, Victoria had, indeed, heard horror stories from her married friends about the pain and humiliation a woman suffered when normally pleasant, polite husbands allowed their base instincts to surface. Most of her friends told her that the only way they could tolerate the demoralizing activities that took place late at night in their bedrooms was to think about the rewards of children and the necessity of producing another generation of men for the good of Britain.

And it seemed that no married woman was exempt, regardless of how illustrious. Why, even their beloved Queen Victoria, a woman well known to be the very soul of propriety, was obviously forced to submit to her husband's lust, since her brood of children expanded by one nearly every year.

Miles gritted his teeth at Victoria's obvious refusal to hear him out. "Don't think that saying, 'please, Miles,' is going to shut me up, Victoria. We need to discuss this. Will you at least listen to what I have to say?"

A little shiver ran through Victoria, and she found that she couldn't bring herself to look at him, but she did nod her head. "Yes, I'll listen."

"Good." Leading her back to the blanket, they again sat down. Miles drew a deep breath, hoping he could find the right words for what he needed to say. He was aware that the next few minutes could be some of the most important of his life, and he didn't want something as insignificant as the wrong choice of words to ruin it.

Finally he swallowed and said, "There are a lot of aspects

to marriage, Victoria, and the intimacy between a man and his wife is only one of them. A big one, I'll grant you, but still only one. I assure you . . ." He paused, waiting until she finally looked up at him. ". . . that I'll never hurt you and I'll never force you."

Victoria's eyes widened hopefully. "Do you mean that you'd marry me even if I told you that I never want to . . . to be intimate with you?"

"No!" Miles barked, his voice louder than he'd intended. "I'm not saying that and I wouldn't agree to it. If you become my wife, I expect it to be in every way. What I am saying is that I'll never force you or demand more than you want to give. When you come to me it will be of your own free will."

"That will never happen," Victoria said positively, "and that's why I can't marry you. It wouldn't be fair to leave you pining for something that is never going to be."

Miles's mouth turned down sardonically. "You think a lot of yourself, don't you?" he muttered.

Victoria's brow furrowed with bewilderment. "I don't know what you mean."

"Never mind. But think about this for a minute: Every time we've kissed you've enjoyed it, haven't you?"

"I don't know if *enjoyed* is the word I'd use."

Miles tried hard not to let her see how deeply that comment stung. He could hardly believe that he was even having this conversation. To think that two hours ago he wasn't even sure that he wanted to marry the girl, and now he was finding himself cut to the quick by every argument she gave him.

Who would believe that this tight-lipped, prissy little woman could affect him so deeply? He, who had enjoyed the favors of just about every girl he'd ever cast his blue eyes upon. His brother Stuart always joked that the only reason Miles had gone to school in England was because he'd already sampled every available maiden in America and, therefore, had been forced to move on to a new continent.

And now here he was, practically begging a penniless,

passed-over and half-forgotten spinster to marry him, and losing the battle! God forbid his friends should ever hear about this. Seized by a rush of righteous indignation, he stood up and began throwing the uneaten food back into the picnic basket.

"What are you doing?"

"Leaving. You've made your feelings perfectly clear, and I see no reason why I should burden you with my company any longer." Squatting down, he grabbed the edge of the blanket. "If you'll get up, I'll fold the blanket."

Silently, Victoria got to her feet, wondering what she'd said to put him into such a fit of temper. "Miles," she said softly, placing a hand on his sleeve, "I'm sorry if I offended you. I thought you wanted me to be honest."

"I did, and you were," he retorted, shaking her hand off and whipping the blanket up off the ground. "I just think it's time we put an end to this. I'll go talk to Harrison Guildford and see if I can coerce him into ceasing his slander against you. Even if he won't cooperate, though, I'm sure that once you let everyone know that I proposed and you rejected me, the gossip will die down pretty quickly. And if that doesn't do it, my departure should. After all, it's no fun to gossip about somebody who isn't around to be hurt by it."

"Departure?" Victoria asked, feeling more miserable than she ever had in her life. "Are you leaving?"

"As soon as I can."

"But your family has just arrived."

Miles shrugged. "I'm sure they'll enjoy their holiday even without me. After all, I'll be home when they get back."

Victoria nodded dismally and followed him to the carriage. Miles handed her into the conveyance, then set the picnic basket on the floor and climbed in himself. Picking up the reins, he flicked them over the horse's back and started down the road toward Pembroke House.

The ride was silent and strained. Several times Victoria glanced surreptitiously in Miles's direction, feeling as if she should say something to ease the hurt she could see etched between his brows but unable to think of a single word.

Somehow looking at him always made her feel that way. Even now, despite his frowning expression, he still looked devastatingly handsome with the breeze riffling his blond hair and the sun shining on his bronzed skin. As she gazed at him, Victoria clasped her hands in her lap, fighting back a nearly irresistible urge to brush his tousled hair back from his forehead. Her throat clogged with tears of regret that she had hurt this handsome, laughing man when he had done nothing more than try to solve her problems by offering marriage.

Why didn't she accept his proposal? After all, as the twins and Fiona kept pointing out to her, he *was* everything any woman could want in a husband—intelligent, kind, witty, compassionate, not to mention handsome, wealthy and charming. Was she crazy to turn down a man of his ilk, preferring instead to spend her life in lonely servitude to some other woman's children? A little voice deep within her screamed a resounding "Yes!"

But there was that other aspect of marriage to consider, she argued silently. Could she somehow learn to tolerate his physical advances—submitting to his lust night after night in the deep darkness of his bedchamber?

Other women did, she answered herself, thousands and thousands of them. And most of the married women she knew seemed quite content with their lot, enjoying the love and fulfillment of children and motherhood as compensation for this one great sacrifice.

You liked his kisses, the little voice reminded her. *Could the rest of it be that bad?*

Before she could lose her nerve, she drew a deep breath and blurted, "Miles, I've decided I'll marry you."

The last thing she expected was the furious glare he turned on her. "You have, have you?"

"Yes." She nodded, her smile becoming increasingly tentative.

Guiding the horse over to the side of the road, Miles stopped the carriage and turned toward her, his expression dark and intimidating. "What makes you think that after everything you've said to me in the last hour I still want to marry you?"

Victoria's mouth dropped in astonishment. "It hardly seems possible you could have changed your mind that quickly."

"Oh? You don't think so? I propose to a girl and she responds by telling me that she can't marry me because she finds my touch too odious to bear and you think that's not enough to change my mind? You really know nothing about men, Victoria."

"But I've changed my mind about that," Victoria mumbled, staring at the carriage floor in abject embarrassment. "I may know very little about men, but I am aware how . . . important that part of marriage is to them, and I will agree to . . . submit to you . . . in that way . . . if you insist."

"If I insist!" Miles bellowed. "Please, madam, don't feel you need to do me any favors! I'm not that needy, I assure you. There are plenty of women who . . ." His voice trailed off in midsentence as he realized what he'd been about to tell her. Closing his eyes for a moment, he exhaled a long, calming breath. "Victoria," he said quietly, "no marriage is going to be successful if a man feels that the only way his wife will accept his attentions is if he 'insists.' A man wants his wife to feel the same passion and desire for him that he feels for her. Anything less . . ."

"None of my friends feel that!" Victoria interrupted recklessly. "Every married lady I know says that . . . what happens between a man and his wife is something that has to be borne . . . with dignity and fortitude."

"Well, I don't want 'dignity and fortitude,' " Miles thundered. "And if that's all your friends give to their husbands, then I pity the poor fools they're married to."

"I think it's all women can give," Victoria protested, hardly able to believe that she was participating in this scandalous conversation but determined not to let Miles have the last word.

"No," he snapped. "It's all they're *willing* to give. And if the husbands of these friends of yours are content to live with that, then bully for them. Call me greedy, but I want more."

"I think," Victoria began, swallowing hard as she forced herself to continue, "I think you don't understand that there are differences between men and women—in their attitudes toward this particular subject."

"I understand that there are differences of attitude between men and women on almost every subject. I also know that women are capable of feeling just as much desire as men, if they just let themselves."

"How could you know that?"

Miles was not about to admit to her how he *really* knew that was so; instead, he said simply, "All I have to do is kiss you."

Victoria's eyes immediately fled from his knowing gaze. "That's not true."

"Yes, it is true, and if you'd just admit it, there might be a chance for us. You're a beautiful woman, Victoria, full of fire and passion, but you've listened so long to other women telling you that 'real ladies' should never feel those emotions that you refuse to admit, even to yourself, that you do."

Victoria buried her head in her hands, moaning, "This is a completely inappropriate conversation."

"According to you," Miles snorted rudely, "every conversation that deals with relationships between men and women is inappropriate."

His insulting words caused Victoria to lift her head, her expression the very picture of righteous indignation. "You talk about private matters far too often."

"And you, my lady, talk about them far too little. Maybe, if you'd try being a little more candid, you'd get over your fears."

"I'm not afraid!"

"Prove it," Miles challenged. "Kiss me. And I mean *really* kiss me."

"All right, I will!"

Placing her hands on either side of Miles's lean cheeks,

Victoria drew his head down and pressed her soft lips against his. Miles responded by curling his arms around her shoulders, pulling her across the padded leather seat until she was nearly sitting on his lap.

Victoria parted her lips, shyly dipping her tongue into the warm recesses of his mouth. The kiss deepened and their tongues tangled in an erotic little game of tag as their breath came faster and their heartbeats increased.

Finally it was Miles who broke the sensuous caress. As he straightened, Victoria noticed that the challenging smile had faded from his mouth and he was looking at her with a rare solemnity. "Did you mean that, or were you just answering my dare?"

Victoria returned his serious look, suddenly realizing that the passion in her carnal kiss had been genuine. So genuine that she had never wanted it to end. "I meant it," she whispered.

"Well, hallelujah!" Miles crowed, pulling her back into his embrace. "Then let's do it again." Lowering his mouth to hers, he kissed her lustily.

Their second kiss went on so long that when Miles finally raised his head, Victoria had to grab his shoulders for support. "I think you like to kiss more than any man on earth," she said shakily, putting a hand to her forehead as she tried to right her suddenly reeling world.

"Yes, I do," he admitted happily. *There are a whole lot of other things I like to do too, lady, and I can hardly wait to show you what they are.* "Come on; let's go tell our families the news and then break open a bottle of my grandmother's French champagne."

Picking up the reins, he clucked to the horse and moved the carriage back onto the road. They rode in silence for a moment, but when he sneaked a look in Victoria's direction, he caught her looking at him strangely. "All right, I can tell you want to say something." He sighed. "What is it?"

"Oh!" Victoria gasped, embarrassed that he had read her so easily. "It's . . . nothing."

"Come on; what?"

"I was just wondering . . ." She cleared her throat and plucked a stray blade of grass off her skirt. ". . . if I'm all right at it."

Miles bit his lip to hold back the laughter that rose in his chest. "Are you asking me if you're a good kisser, Lady Victoria?"

Victoria blushed crimson. "Well, yes, I suppose I am."

Miles smiled at her wryly. "You'll do. For a beginner, at least."

Victoria's face lit in a pleased smile. "Really?"

"Yes, really." As they pulled up in front of Pembroke House, Miles glanced covertly at the erection that throbbed lustily just beneath his coat.

Thank God you're only a beginner, my lady, or I wouldn't be able to get down off this carriage seat!

Chapter 20

"Master James, I simply have to insist once again that you speak to your children about their behavior. I know the viscountess will not say anything to you about them, so I feel I must."

James Wellesley lowered the newspaper he was reading and looked at the outraged butler. "Who has done what this time, Cedric?"

Cedric pursed his mouth indignantly. "After the fiasco yesterday with young Master Eric digging up the viscountess's rose bushes . . ."

"It was one rose bush," James interrupted, "and Eric explained that he merely wanted to take a look at the root system. I thought you understood when I told you that Eric is very interested in all types of growing things and he's fascinated with his grandmother's roses since he's never seen plants of such quality in America. He's merely trying to determine whether the difference might be the soil or the roots or the fertilizer."

"Yes, sir, I know what you said, although I still cannot believe that the boy willfully dug up an irreplaceable plant without so much as asking permission."

"That was yesterday." James sighed. "What seems to be the problem today? Is it Eric again?"

Cedric shook his bald head. "No, sir, this time it's young Master Geoffrey, and I must warn you, his misdeed is even more unforgivable than his brother's."

James rolled his eyes. "What did he do?"

"He chopped down a tree!"

"He did what?" James gasped.

Cedric smiled in satisfaction, having finally gotten the reaction he was hoping for. "Yes, indeed. An apple tree. He took an ax, went out in the orchard and chopped it down."

James threw down his newspaper, shaking his head. "Where is the boy now?"

"I believe he's still in the orchard."

"Then I guess I'd better go have a little chat with him."

James walked out of the library, passing the open doors of the small parlor without even noticing Victoria and Mary sitting inside. Mary looked at her prospective daughter-in-law and chuckled. "Sons . . . I tell you, my dear, seven of them are almost too much for any one set of parents to handle successfully."

Picking up a silver teapot, she refilled Victoria's cup. "You know, I drink more tea when I'm in England than I do at home. Somehow it always tastes better here."

Victoria forced a smile, shocked by all she had just overheard about the wild Wellesley boys and even more amazed by James and Mary Wellesley's seeming nonchalance about their sons' behavior.

"How many children do you think one set of parents can handle successfully?" she asked.

Mary waved her hand airily. "Oh, I was just teasing when I said that. In all honesty, we've never had a moment of trouble from the boys. They're just high-spirited and exuberant, and sometimes it gets them into a spot of trouble. Basically they're good boys—overly curious occasionally, but good boys. Cedric has just forgotten what it's like to have children in the house, and after the incident with Seth and Nathan almost running those horses into the ground playing sheriff and outlaw, and then Paula spilling that entire glass of milk on the Aubusson, well, I'm afraid he's feeling a bit overwhelmed. Everything will be all right, though. James will speak to Geoffrey, and I'm sure the boy will apologize to his grandmother if James feels the situation warrants it."

Victoria couldn't believe how calm Mary Wellesley was as she casually recounted her children's many misdeeds. She didn't, of course, dare tell her that she felt much the same as Cedric about the children's rowdy play. Instead she said, "I take it you don't believe in the adage, 'Children should be seen and not heard.'"

Mary bit into a piece of shortbread and closed her eyes in grateful appreciation of the rich, buttery taste. "Oh, heavens no! If you don't allow children to speak out and to question, how are they ever going to learn anything, and how are you, as a mother, ever going to know how they're feeling about circumstances affecting them? I believe that talking to our children is of the utmost importance, and both James and I have always encouraged them to talk to us, too."

Victoria was appalled. Imagine inviting children to voice their opinions in the company of adults! Why, such a thing was unheard of in England. Cedric was right: These Americans were a queer lot.

Mary noticed Victoria's shocked expression, despite the girl's obvious attempt to remain impassive. "I can see that you are scandalized by my theories on raising children." She laughed. "But when I see what a fine man Miles has become and I look at how Stuart is following right along behind him, showing equal potential, I truly feel that James and I have done something right, even if our methods are a bit unorthodox."

"Oh, I'm sure you have," Victoria said quickly, embarrassed that Mary had read her thoughts so easily. "I've just never heard of parents encouraging their children to speak their minds in public."

"Well, of course, it is important that their privilege be tempered with a proper dose of manners and decorum when in company, but that's not hard to teach, either. Children emulate what they see at home. If their parents are happy, congenial and polite, they will follow suit. It only makes sense, don't you think?"

"I suppose so." Victoria nodded, still trying to imagine any of her married friends encouraging their children to speak out on any subject they chose. "It must be very difficult to raise so many children, though."

Mary nodded. "Indeed. Raising children, be it one or a dozen, is a never-ending challenge." She paused, smiling lovingly. "But the rewards are enormous."

Seeing Victoria's doubtful look, she added, "Just remember, dear, you only start with one. It's not as if you'll have eight of them dropped in your lap all at once."

"Of course, there's always the possibility of not having any at all," Victoria said cautiously. "I'm sure that childless couples can also lead happy lives."

Mary studied her future daughter-in-law closely for a moment, then said, "Of course there are couples who are unable to have children, and I'm sure they find a certain happiness without them. But I doubt very much that you'll have to worry about that, Victoria. Every generation of Wellesleys has always seemed to produce children with very little effort. I can't imagine why you and Miles would be any different."

Victoria bit her lip, wondering if she dare clarify her comment any further. Then, with a mental shrug, she plunged on. "I'm not talking specifically about couples who *can't* have children. I'm talking about couples who decide, for one reason or another, that they don't want them."

Mary's eyebrows shot up in alarm. "Are you saying you don't want a family, Victoria?"

"No," Victoria hedged, "I'm not saying that. But I do think a couple could live very happily without them, don't you?"

Mary Wellesley was a shrewd woman, and the real meaning

behind Victoria's words was perfectly clear to her. "Have you talked to Miles about this?"

"About what?" Victoria asked innocently.

"About the fact that you're not sure you want children. It's a very important decision, Victoria, and one that the two of you should settle before marriage. It would be grossly unfair to Miles if you waited until after you were married to tell him your feelings on the subject."

"I don't honestly *know* my feelings on the subject."

Astutely, Mary grasped Victoria's real problem and took a moment to carefully phrase her next question. "Do you like children, Victoria? Have you been around them much?"

"No, not much, except for my half-sisters, of course. They're six years younger than I am, so I do remember them when they were quite small."

"And how did you feel about them?"

"I thought they were a terrible nuisance," Victoria answered truthfully.

To her surprise, Mary laughed. "Of course they were! There isn't a normal twelve-year-old in the world who wouldn't think her six-year-old sisters were a nuisance." Her laughter faded and she gazed at Victoria solemnly. "But you're not twelve anymore, dear, and the relationship a mother has with her children is altogether different than that of an older sister. Motherhood is a unique experience, as is being a wife. Both of them take some getting used to, but I can assure you, they're well worth the effort. Perhaps you should talk to Fiona about your doubts. You and she seem very close."

"We are, although Fiona was so devoted to Papa that I'm sure she never had any doubts."

"But you do," Mary confirmed gently.

Victoria raised guilty eyes. "You must think I'm terrible."

"Not at all. Many girls have doubts about marriage and, as I'm sure you're aware, there are some aspects of the institution that almost every unmarried girl feels anxious about."

"Did you, Mrs. Wellesley?"

Mary's smile was wistful. "Absolutely. I dreaded my wedding night like the pox." She hesitated a moment, as if considering her next words, then said, "I'm going to tell you something now that you might find a bit scandalous, but I think it's important that it is said."

Victoria looked at Mary curiously, astounded, as always, by the forthrightness that seemed to be a trait of the Wellesleys, both male and female. "Yes?"

Mary leaned forward and picked up Victoria's icy hand. "If Miles is anything like his father—and from what I know of my son I think he is—you have nothing to worry about. In fact, if you're anything like I was, the biggest challenge you'll have to face the morning after your wedding is trying to hide the cat-who-got-the-cream smile you're sure to be wearing, so that you won't embarrass yourself in front of your family and friends at the wedding breakfast."

Victoria blushed and averted her eyes.

"Oh, now I've embarrassed you, and I didn't mean to."

"No, you haven't embarrassed me," Victoria whispered, rising. "I appreciate everything you've told me. It has given me some things to think about."

Mary stood up, too, reaching out and giving Victoria a warm hug. "Then I'm glad we had this little talk. Give Miles's love a chance, dear. It will bring you more joy than anything you could ever imagine."

With a last encouraging smile, Mary walked away, heading off to the fruit orchard to try to ascertain what possessed her fourth son to chop down his grandmother's apple tree.

Parties, parties, parties.

Victoria sat in a throne-shaped chair in the middle of Mary Ann Parks's parlor, holding a glass of tasteless punch and wondering how many more prenuptial parties she could endure before she completely lost her mind.

Today's tea was the fourth such event this week, all of them hosted by well-meaning friends determined to fill her already teeming wardrobe to overflowing. Thankfully, this one was finally ending.

As the smiling matrons said their good-byes, pressing her hand and kissing her cheek, Victoria smiled and thanked them so graciously that they never would have guessed what she was really thinking about.

Escape. Escape from Fiona with her never-ending schedules and lists. Escape from her friends, who insisted that they "would be absolutely devastated" if she didn't allow them to throw at least a "tiny little tea" in her honor. Most of all, she wanted to escape from Miles, who seemed to be suffering none of her misgivings. Rather, he had energetically thrown himself into the endless round of festivities, his smile never slipping, his charm never flagging.

If only she felt as sure about everything as he seemed to. But, despite her encouraging talk with Mary Wellesley and its inevitable follow-up from Fiona, she was still filled with trepidation.

Because of her ongoing doubts, she had asked Mary Ann if she could stay after the party was over and talk to her privately. Now, as her recently married friend closed the door on the last of her guests, the moment had finally arrived.

"Just look at all these gifts!" Mary Ann laughed, clapping her well-manicured hands to her cheeks and gazing around the ribbon-strewn room. "Why, you have enough items for your toilette to last you till your fifth wedding anniversary!"

Seating herself in a chair across a low table from Victoria, she reached out and clasped her hands. "Isn't getting married fun, Tory? It's just too bad that we only get to do it once. Why, if I had my way, I'd have a wedding every five years, just for the parties alone."

Victoria smiled thinly. "It was a lovely tea, Mary Ann. I don't know how to thank you."

Mary Ann beamed at the compliment. "I was delighted to do it. I'm just so thrilled for you, Victoria. It's going to be so much fun once you're married and living at Wellesley Manor. Why, you'll only be a fifteen-minute carriage ride away from me. Think of what a wonderful time we'll have, sharing recipes and gossiping about our servant problems . . . and our husbands." She raised a hand to her mouth to cover the giggle that bubbled up. "Oh, Tory, it will be so wonderful to have someone to confide in. I just can't wait!"

Now! Now's your chance! "I feel exactly the same way," Victoria agreed. "In fact, there's something I'd like to talk to you about right now, if it's all right."

Mary Ann sobered. "Of course, dear. Is something wrong? Did you and Miles have a lovers' quarrel?"

"No," Victoria said hastily. "It's nothing like that. There are just a few questions I need answered. Questions that are, well, *delicate.*"

Mary Ann looked at her understandingly. "I know what they are."

"You do?"

"Yes. They're the same questions all brides have, and few of us have anyone we can ask."

Victoria looked down at her tightly clasped hands. "Tell me—is it . . . awful?"

Mary Ann took so long to answer that Victoria finally raised her eyes. "It is, isn't it?"

"I don't know if *awful* is the word I'd use," Mary Ann said slowly. "It's . . . bearable, especially once you know what to expect."

"What to expect?"

"Well, yes. I know now that I can expect it every Saturday night." She paused, sighing with resignation. "*Every* Saturday night. So now, when Saturday comes, I just tell myself to buck up and do my duty. If I keep telling myself that all day, then it's not so bad."

"Oh Lord, Mary Ann," Victoria moaned, burying her head in her hands. "You have to tell yourself to 'buck up' just to get through it? And you even love Tom!"

"Tory! Are you saying that you don't love Miles?"

"Who knows? I suppose I should *say* I love him, since we're to be married in two weeks, but the truth is, I don't know! What I do know is that I can hardly bear thinking about facing fifty years of Saturday nights."

"Oh, you won't have to," Mary Ann said brightly. "Mama told me that once you give your husband an heir or two, he generally will respect your feelings and find himself a . . . well, you know."

Victoria's eyes widened to the size of saucers. "You mean a paramour?"

Mary Ann nodded conspiratorially. "Yes. Mama assures me it's very common, even gentlemanly."

"Did your father do that?" Victoria gasped.

"So Mama says."

"And it doesn't bother her to know that your father is . . . with another woman?"

Mary Ann laughed melodically. "Oh, heavens no. Mama says it's actually a blessing, because once Papa found a lady with whom to pass his Saturday evenings, he stopped making demands of that nature on her. And they've lived together very happily for almost twenty-five years. So, you see? We probably only have to face this . . . duty for five years or so; then the rest of our lives can be spent raising our children and having tea with our friends."

Victoria shook her head dubiously. "I don't know, Mary Ann. Miles's parents have eight children and there is twenty years between the oldest and the youngest, so they must still . . ."

"Well, I suppose there are always exceptions to every rule." Mary Ann shrugged. "Besides, they're American. I'm sure in such a primitive country their ways are different. Don't they live somewhere out in the wilderness?"

"Yes, in a place called Colorado. Miles says there are mountains as far as the eye can see, and almost no people."

Mary Ann nodded knowingly. "There, you see? There's your answer."

Victoria looked at her blankly. "What answer?"

"The reason why Mr. Wellesley still insists on Mrs. Wellesley's, um, *companionship* is undoubtedly because there are no
other women for him to take up company with. You and Miles,
on the other hand, will be living here in England, so he won't
have that problem. I'm telling you, Tory, Mama assures me
that as soon as I give Tom two children, so long as one is a
son, my duty will be done and I can simply tell him that I
expect to be left in peace from that time on."

Victoria bit her lip, trying to picture herself telling Miles
Wellesley that he was to leave her in peace and seek feminine
companionship elsewhere. Somehow, try as she might, she
couldn't envision that scene.

Looking again at her friend, she said, "Could I ask you one
more question?"

"Of course. Anything."

Victoria smiled, grateful that Mary Ann was willing to be
so candid. "Does Tom expect you to sleep in his bedroom with
him?"

"Oh, heaven forbid, no! I have my own suite, which adjoins
his. There's a lock on the connecting door, although I rarely
use it . . . unless, of course, I'm angry with him. But Tom would
never think of entering my room without knocking, so the lock
isn't really necessary."

"But what about on Saturday nights? I mean, do you go to
him or does he come to you?"

"It's just as I said. He comes to me, but he always knocks
first to make sure I'm ready to receive him."

Victoria studied her friend for a moment, then finally asked
the question foremost in her mind. "Do you ever turn him
away?"

Mary Ann lowered her eyes demurely. "Well, obviously
there's one Saturday night every month when I *can't* receive
him, but I usually drop little hints in advance so he doesn't,
ah, expect anything."

Victoria grimaced, imagining how embarrassing that would be.

"Other than that, though," Mary Ann continued, "I don't turn him away. After all, it is my duty as his wife to accept his attentions, and I do want children, so I just close my eyes and think of other things. Planning my next day's schedule works well for me. Besides, it doesn't last more than fifteen or twenty minutes; then Tom generally goes back to his room and it's over. Unless, of course, he falls asleep before he gets around to leaving. Sometimes that happens, but not very often."

"Do you mind that? Having him in bed with you?"

"Oh, no. In fact, I rather enjoy it. He's big and warm and it's rather nice to wake up in the morning and find him there." She hesitated a moment, then added, "I must warn you, though, that waking up together can sometimes lead to the man wanting . . ."

"No!" Victoria gasped, shocked to the core by what Mary Ann was implying. "Surely you're not saying that Tom expects you to . . . in the daylight?"

"I think he would like me to, but I've just made it very clear to him that I won't agree to that."

"And he's never pressed you?"

"I know that Tom was a bit put out with me when I refused him, so now I make sure I wake up first. That way, I can quickly slip out of bed, and by the time he wakes up I'm already dressed and ready for church."

Victoria nodded. "And I suppose that once he sees you're up and dressed, he doesn't pursue it."

"No, he doesn't." Mary Ann grinned. "It has worked out very nicely, although I never get much sleep on those nights. I'm always afraid that if I let myself really go to sleep, Tom might wake up first and then I'd be stuck."

Victoria nodded again, carefully cataloging everything her friend was telling her. "Have you any sign of a baby yet?" she asked.

"Not yet, but it's only been three months. Mama says sometimes the first one takes awhile. I wish it would hurry up."

"You're looking forward to a child, then?"

"Oh, yes. Besides, Mama said men rarely expect their wives to accommodate them while they're in the family way. She says that once you let your husband know that you're expecting, he'll generally not bother you again until after the baby is born."

Victoria raised her eyebrows thoughtfully. "Maybe that's why Mrs. Wellesley had so many children. Maybe that was the only way she could escape her husband's demands."

Victoria stared off in the distance, thinking about all that Mary Ann had told her. *She's right. Certainly I can stand Miles's attentions long enough to get with child. No matter how unpleasant and humiliating it is, certainly I can stand anything that long.*

Chapter 21

Victoria's wedding day dawned gray and dreary. *Just like my mood,* she thought as she lay in bed, gazing morosely out the window.

How in the world was she ever going to get through the day? Hours of smiling, accepting congratulations and kisses from her friends and family, and pretending to be ecstatically happy, when all she really wanted to do was run, run, run! How was she ever going to manage such a charade?

And if the prospect of the impossible day wasn't enough, there was also tonight to worry about. Tonight! The one night in her married life that she absolutely, positively could not say "No" to her husband. Victoria shivered, trying to block out the vision of Miles's big, hard body looming over her cowering one in the depths of the ancient tester bed that Mary Wellesley had confided had served as the nuptial nest for five generations of Wellesley men.

The previous afternoon, Fiona had called her into her sitting room to give her a quick and somewhat stilted little talk about "what she should expect" while in that bed. But Victoria knew what to expect; she had seen enough stallions and mares to know how the act was performed. And what information she had lacked about the differences between the way four-legged creatures and two-legged ones performed the deed had been supplied by Mary Ann Parks the day of her prenuptial tea.

Despite the fact that both Fiona and Mary Ann had tried to describe the absurd act in a reasonably positive manner, Victoria still found the whole idea grotesque—almost comically so. And tonight all her mental conjuring would become reality. Tonight she would not only have to think about it, she would actually be expected to *do* it!

With a groan, Victoria turned over on her stomach, burying her head in her pillow and letting the tears she'd held back for so many weeks flow. Who cared if her eyes were red at the wedding? Perhaps if her face was tear-streaked and swollen, Miles would find her so unattractive that he wouldn't demand his conjugal rights tonight. Victoria's shoulders shook with mirthless laughter, knowing that was far too much to hope for. Besides, Fiona and Mary Ann had both assured her that the act was always performed in total darkness, so what did it matter what her face looked like? Miles wouldn't be able to see her anyway.

No, Victoria sighed, flopping onto her back again, there was no way of avoiding it. She could only pray that he would be quick. Mary Ann had said it took less than twenty minutes. Hopefully, Miles's lust would be on the same time schedule as Tom Parks's. That way, at least her humiliation would be brief.

Her morose thoughts were suddenly shattered by a sharp knock on her door, followed by Rebecca's voice calling, "My lady, are you awake? You must get up now. There's much to do before the ceremony."

Like a martyred saint walking fearlessly to her doom, Victoria swung her legs over the side of the bed and forced her exhausted body to a standing position. She had barely slept all night, and now that she was on her feet, her head ached and her limbs felt heavy as lead. Still, she lifted her chin and walked purposely to the door, pulling it open and admitting the pink-cheeked and, as always, frazzled maid.

Rebecca's arms were full of brushes, combs, ribbons and pearl-studded hairpins, all of which she dumped unceremoniously on the dressing table. "Mrs. Wellesley has sent two of the viscountess's fancy maids over here this morning to attend you," she said breathlessly, "but I told them girls they could just bring up your tub and fill it. *I* will help you with the dressing."

Despite her trepidation about all that was to come that day, Victoria couldn't help but smile at Rebecca's indignant statement. "And what did the viscountess's maids say about that?"

"They said their lady told them they was to help you. But I told them that you were *my* lady, and no one was going to get you ready for the most important day of your life but me."

"And did they accept that?"

Rebecca grinned. "Yes, my lady. They didn't like it much, but they accepted it. They should be along with the tub any minute."

Victoria chuckled at the little maid's audacity and settled herself on a small round stool set in front of the dressing table. Rebecca came up behind her, running her hands gently over the dark cloud of Victoria's hair. "I'm glad we washed your hair yesterday. It'll make it easier to put up today."

"I've decided I don't want it up," Victoria said softly, surprising even herself with this spontaneous decision.

"My lady!" Rebecca gasped. "You're wearing your hair down for your wedding?"

"Yes."

"But, I thought . . . I mean, we discussed . . ."

"I know," Victoria interrupted, "but I changed my mind. I'm wearing it down."

Rebecca looked as if she might cry. "But the crown of your veil, my lady! I don't think it will fit without a coronet of hair to hold it."

"I'm sure you can make it work, Rebecca. You're so talented with hair."

"I don't know . . ."

"Well, then," Victoria said slyly, "perhaps I should ask the maids the viscountess sent over to help me. Maybe one of them could anchor my veil with my hair down."

Rebecca's green eyes narrowed in offense. "There's no need to do that, Lady Victoria. I will fix your hair and the veil will work just fine. I'll see to it."

Victoria smiled, having won at least one small victory today. "Thank you, Rebecca. I knew I could count on you."

Three hours later, Victoria stood in front of the pier glass, staring at the resplendent woman reflected back at her. Her wedding dress was a vision of white satin, draped with Brussels lace and trimmed with silk orange blossoms. The long tulle veil that Rebecca had fussed over so laboriously was firmly anchored to her long, loose hair, its spectacular crown, an intricate twining of tiny diamonds and fresh rosebuds, a gift from the viscountess.

"Oh, my lady," Rebecca breathed, staring at Victoria in awe, "you look magnificent! Just wait till Mr. Wellesley sees you. He'll probably be too dumbfounded by your beauty to remember his vows."

If only I would be that lucky, Victoria thought. She turned this way and that, viewing herself from all angles. What she saw made her sigh wistfully.

How often, when she'd still been a starry-eyed girl, had she thought about this day—how often had she dreamed of standing in front of a mirror in her wedding dress, feeling like the most beautiful and luckiest woman in the world.

But now that her wedding was a reality she didn't feel particularly beautiful, and she certainly wasn't lucky. In those girlhood dreams she'd always envisioned herself walking down the aisle and into the arms of a handsome suitor who loved her beyond all measure. A man who thought she was so ideal that he had chosen her above all other women in the world. A man whom she so adored that she could hardly wait to reach the altar and become his.

Never, ever, had she envisioned the situation in which she found herself today—marrying a man who neither loved her nor thought she was anywhere near ideal. A man who was marrying her not because he had chosen her above all other women in the world, but because he had been caught in a highly compromising position with her. A man whose family had so much dignity and pride that they would not allow common gossip to be spread about one of their own and was, therefore, forcing him to do the honorable thing by her.

Victoria sighed again, looking dismally at the vision in the mirror. Regardless of how lovely she looked in her finery, this was definitely not the wedding day of which she had dreamed.

Her unhappy musings were brought to an abrupt end by the sudden invasion of Fiona and the twins. They, too, were dressed in their wedding clothes, and as they crowded into her room, the space was suddenly so full of hoops and lace and layers of flounces that there was barely room for the four of them to stand without crushing each other's skirts.

"Oh, Tory," Georgia gasped, clapping her hands together rapturously, "you look like a princess!"

"Not just a princess, a queen!" Carolina cried, determined, as always, to do her sister one better.

Victoria smiled wanly at her sisters' effusive compliments. "You two are the ones who look like princesses," she remarked honestly.

The twins, clad in identical silk dresses, one pink, one buttercup yellow, did indeed look as if they had just stepped out of a fairy tale. The pastel dresses highlighted their blond hair, blue eyes and pink cheeks so perfectly that they reminded her of identical porcelain dolls. As Victoria gazed fondly at her sisters, she couldn't help but feel that it should have been one of them standing here today, wearing a bridal dress. Blinking back a fresh rush of tears, she turned quickly to Fiona. "Is everyone here?" she asked, her voice barely audible.

Fiona nodded. "Yes, packed in downstairs like sardines in a tin. Thank heavens it's a cool day, or I'm sure the ladies would faint dead away from the press. I will never understand why you insisted on having the wedding here at the house, Victoria, instead of at the cathedral, where it should be."

Victoria frowned, refusing to embark upon another pointless argument on that subject. The truth was, she couldn't bring herself to be married in a holy place when the union into which she was entering was anything but sacred. "Never mind about that now," she muttered, pulling on a pair of white kid gloves. "Is Uncle Harold here?"

"Of course." Fiona smiled. "He's waiting right outside to signal the orchestra when to begin."

"Miles is here, too," Carolina volunteered unnecessarily. "And, oh, Tory, wait till you see how handsome he looks. Why, he actually took my breath away when I saw him come in the front door."

I want to marry you because you take my breath away. For some reason the words Miles had murmured to Victoria the day of their betrothal raced through her mind, and for the first time all day, a genuine smile graced her beautiful face. Walking to her bureau, she picked up her lavish bouquet of white roses and heather. "All right, then; I'm ready."

"Wait a moment," Fiona directed, walking up behind Victoria and reaching around to place a string of perfectly matched pearls around her neck. "These were your grandmother Pembroke's," she announced, clasping them securely. "Your father asked me to be sure to give them to the first of his daughters to be married."

The mention of their father brought a wave of unexpected sadness crashing over all three girls, and the sudden silence in the bedroom stretched on for several seconds. Finally Georgia stepped forward, dashing away a tear that clung to her long lashes. "Carrie and I were asked to give you these." Holding out her hand, she smiled tremulously and presented Victoria with a rare and expensive sprig of orange blossoms.

"Oh!" Victoria gasped. "Wherever did you get these?"

"We promised to keep secret who they're from," Carolina said excitedly, "but he had to go all the way to London to get them!"

Victoria stared down at the tiny bouquet in wonder. For centuries orange blossoms had been intertwined in bridal bouquets, signifying the purity of the bride and offering good luck to the newly married couple. In recent years, however, the rare, fragrant little flowers had become so expensive that only the very wealthiest of brides had fresh ones. Most English girls had to settle for imitation blossoms made of silk or wax.

"Did Miles send me these?" Victoria asked softly, still staring at the delicate blooms.

"Oh, Carrie!" Georgia cried. "Now she knows, and you promised him you wouldn't tell!"

"I didn't tell! I just said that he went all the way to London to get them."

"So, that's where he's been the last couple of days," Victoria murmured.

"Did you think he'd abandoned you?" Fiona teased.

Victoria looked up at her, a guilty smile lurking about the corners of her mouth. "Actually, I wouldn't have blamed him if he had."

"Well, I can assure you he hasn't; at least not yet. He's very much in attendance, and that entire, huge family is with him. However, he just might give up waiting and leave if you don't join him at once."

Victoria nodded and took a deep breath, stepping toward the door. The four women gathered in the hallway, Fiona going ahead down the stairs to alert the gathering that the ceremony was about to begin, and to take her seat of honor.

From where she stood behind her two sisters, Victoria heard the first strains of *The Wedding March,* then watched as Eric and Geoffrey Wellesley hurried up the stairs to escort Georgia and Carolina. The boys were impeccably dressed in matching black suits with starched shirtfronts, stand-up collars and bowties. With their hair brushed and their faces scrubbed, Victoria was treated to her first glimpse of the handsome men they would someday both become.

They approached the waiting girls wearing serious expressions, formally offering their arms and taking up positions next to them. The twins blew a last kiss to the bride, then started down the flower-bedecked stairs with their escorts.

Victoria waited until Georgia had descended three steps, then turned to her late father's brother, who stood next to her. "Well, Uncle Harold, I guess it's our turn."

Harold, who had always been as quiet as his older brother had been effusive, nodded solemnly and held out his arm. "I wish John could be here today," he said softly. "He would be so proud."

Victoria smiled poignantly and, as the sound of the organ swelled, started down the stairs, taking her first step toward becoming Mrs. Miles Wellesley.

Chapter 22

As Victoria reached the bottom of the stairs, her eyes scanned the throng spread out before her. The main parlor was a sea of faces—old, young, male, female—all smiling and all looking in her direction.

But she only saw one: *his.*

Tall, handsome and standing militarily erect, Miles stood at the end of the room near the fireplace, looking back at Victoria as she proceeded down the narrow gauntlet, her hand grasping her uncle's arm in an almost desperate grip.

His eyes locked with hers—searching, questioning—as if he still wondered, even at this late date, whether she was really going to go through with this improbable marriage. She held his rapt gaze for a moment, then delicately dipped her nose into the enormous bouquet of flowers she carried, silently thanking him for the gift of the rare and cherished orange blossoms.

Miles blinked slowly and the slightest hint of a smile teased his mouth. It was obvious to Victoria that he was pleased with her acknowledgment of his gift, but the subtlety of his response made her realize how intensely personal he considered it.

Glancing down briefly at the magnificent betrothal ring on

the third finger of her left hand, Victoria suddenly understood that Miles considered the flowers a far more intimate sign of his feelings for her than this overt sign of his intentions. She smiled inwardly, realizing how much it meant to her that he, himself, had ridden all the way to London to bring her the flowers, making such an affirming statement of his hopes for their marriage's success.

By the time Victoria reached the bridal bower, so many silent messages had passed between them that she felt breathless and slightly light-headed. She dropped her uncle's arm and took a final step forward so that she stood at Miles's side. Lifting her dark eyes to his, she was surprised to see none of the sardonic amusement she expected, but rather a look of promise and sincerity that made a little shiver of pleasure ripple through her.

Standing so close to him, she could feel the heat emanating from his tall, strong body. He was so handsome, so muscular, so male. Her smile froze as that last word stalled her pleasant thoughts.

So male!

Her breath caught in her throat and the momentary pleasure she'd felt as she'd proceeded down the aisle toward her handsome groom faded. Even the solemn words Reverend Smythe intoned gave credence to the sudden sense of dread sweeping over her. They were standing here together in front of hundreds of witnesses for one reason and one reason only: *to join this man and this woman* . . .

To *join* them—spiritually this morning, physically tonight. The whole reason for this elaborate ceremony was to legitimize in the eyes of God and the law the much more earthy ceremony that would inevitably take place in Wellesley Manor's master suite this evening. That was what this was really all about . . . to *join* this man and this woman. And no amount of fragrant flowers or sweet cakes or lacy dresses could subdue the rising panic Victoria felt as she listened to the minister charge her to "love and cherish, honor and obey" the man standing beside her.

Victoria's mind whirled off in a thousand directions as she thought about what that vow meant. *Obey.* By saying the words "I do," she was giving her solemn promise to obey Miles Wellesley, regardless of what he might demand of her. To *obey* him if he dictated who her friends might be, to *obey* him if he directed which of her horses were to be bought and sold, to *obey* him when he demanded that she submit to his lust.

So lost in her dismal reverie was she that she didn't even notice the sudden silence as the minister waited for her answer to his questions.

"Victoria Ann?" he said softly, clearing his throat.

Victoria's head jerked up. "Yes?"

"Did you hear what I asked you?"

Victoria was aware only of Miles's sharp glance in her direction and the embarrassed titter running through the assembled congregation. "I'm sorry," she stammered. "Yes, I heard you."

"Then say 'I do,' please," the reverend hissed.

Victoria shot a glance at Miles, whose mouth was now pressed into a thin, angry line. *Oh, God, I've humiliated him in front of all these people!*

Pulling her distraught gaze away from his stony one, she lowered her head and quickly mumbled, "I do," cringing inwardly when she heard the collective sigh of relief from the assemblage.

The reverend nodded approvingly and, turning his benign gaze on Miles, asked the same questions of him. Miles's answer was clear and immediate, although his voice was cold and devoid of any feeling. After a terse, "I do," he reached over and plucked a gold wedding band from Geoffrey's outstretched hand, sliding it dispassionately onto Victoria's finger.

She threw him a quick, pleading look that he ignored, instead turning back to the minister and sinking to his knees for the blessing. Victoria immediately followed suit, mortified that she had embarrassed both of them in front of their guests but having no idea how to make amends.

As the final prayer ended, Victoria got to her feet, closing her eyes as she heard, "I now pronounce you man and wife. You may kiss the bride."

Miles hesitated for a split second, making Victoria wonder if he was so angry that he was going to refuse to kiss her. She drew in a shuddering breath, then let it out in an audible sign of relief when he finally turned toward her, lifting her veil and pressing hard, unyielding lips momentarily to hers. Turning toward the crowd, he hooked his arm through hers and muttered, "Smile, for Christ's sake. Do you want everyone to know how much you hate me?"

Victoria opened her mouth to protest his bitter statement, but, seeing the icy look in his eyes, closed it and silently allowed him to escort her back up the aisle.

They moved past the congregation, escaping through the parlor's double doors and into the empty foyer. Miles could see the crowd following them and seized upon the few seconds of privacy to whisper furiously, "How could you have done that to me?"

"Miles," Victoria began, her voice heavy with remorse, "I didn't mean . . ."

"Never mind! We'll talk about it later. Now smile, because here they come."

With a supreme effort, Victoria turned toward the oncoming crowd, planting a dazzling smile on her face and offering no resistance as Miles picked up her hand and thrust their arms over their heads in an age-old gesture of triumph.

The guests swirled around them, Victoria's many friends pulling her away from her new husband to exclaim over her dress and give her powdery kisses of congratulations. Several times she caught Miles's eye from where he stood across the room, surrounded by his best man, Alex Shaw, and several other friends, but each time she did he hurriedly looked away, maintaining his carefully calculated smile.

James and Mary Wellesley approached her and Victoria held her breath, terrified that Miles's parents might make some comment about her behavior during the ceremony. To her profound relief, they both kissed her graciously, welcoming her to the family and lavishing her with compliments on the beauty of her dress and veil.

The viscountess stood a little apart from the milling throng, carefully watching the looks being passed between her grandson and his new bride. Finally, as the crowd began to move into the dining room for dinner, she walked up to Miles and kissed him on the cheek. "Stop glaring at her," she whispered as she hugged him. "She was nervous, that's all. I did much the same thing at my wedding."

Miles studied the wise old lady for a long moment, then nodded. "You don't miss anything, do you?"

"Not much." Regina chuckled softly. "Now, make me proud and act the loving bridegroom during the reception. You two can work out this silly misunderstanding later."

Miles nodded, and Regina started to move away. She'd only gone a few steps, however, when she turned back and added, "Don't bring it up till tomorrow. Tonight she needs every bit of tenderness you can offer."

Miles smiled and gazed at the regal old dowager fondly. "I love you, Grandmama."

Regina cast him an arch look, then answered his smile with one of her own. "Be gentle with her, Miles. She's far more fragile than she wants you to know."

Miles nodded once in silent agreement, then turned again to his friends, surreptitiously watching Victoria as she wove her way toward him.

"Shall we go in to the dining room so everyone can start eating?" she asked, coming up beside him and casting him a hopeful look.

He nodded, then bent his head, giving her a soft, warm kiss on the lips. "Thank you for carrying my flowers," he whispered.

Victoria blushed, pleased that he had obviously forgiven her. "Thank you for sending them," she returned. "I love them."

"I'm glad." Placing his hand against the small of her back, he guided her toward the dining room. Victoria would have been astounded if she had known that, as they entered the crowded room, Miles was wondering what it would be like to hear her say that she loved *him* as well as the tiny orange flowers he'd given her.

The banquet was enormous and lavish, with the wedding party seated at a long table set on a raised dais. As tradition dictated, Miles and Victoria sat at the center of the table, with the adult members of Miles's family fanned out to his right and Victoria's to her left. The bulk of the Wellesley children were seated at a round table just beneath their mother's watchful eye and chaperoned closely by several of Mary Wellesley's sisters, who had come down from London for the festivities.

The feast consisted of a full six courses, beginning with fish soup and continuing on through cookies and bonbons, with huge platters of beef and fowl, bowls of lobster salad and plates of pâtés and cheeses served in between.

Sauterne and Madeira wines were provided with various courses, but it was when each guest was offered a flute of champagne to accompany the huge bowls of fresh strawberries that were set in the middle of the tables that Victoria finally gasped in dismay.

"What is it?" Miles asked solicitously, turning toward her.

"The cost," she whispered. "I don't know how Fiona is ever going to manage to pay for all this."

"Don't worry about the cost," Miles advised softly. "Just enjoy yourself."

"But my dress, all these flowers, this food and wine . . ."

Miles shook his head and placed his index finger over her lips. "Tory, it's all taken care of."

Victoria's eyes widened. "Do you mean your parents

paid for everything? Oh, but Miles! It's the bride's family's duty . . ."

"And if the bride's father is deceased and the bride's step-mother cannot afford the wedding she wants her husband's eldest child to have, then the groom's family should help, especially if they're well able."

"I had no idea," Victoria moaned. "If I'd known our wedding was going to become a financial burden to your parents, I would have cut back the guest list, simplified the meal, ordered fewer flowers, something!"

She was astonished when Miles broke out in a hearty guffaw. "A financial burden? Sweetheart, my parents could afford to throw a wedding for Queen Victoria's daughter and it wouldn't be a burden. Now, please, stop worrying about money. You're a Wellesley now and, I assure you, you need never worry about money again. Here, pick up your champagne glass. Alex is about to propose a toast."

Victoria picked up her glass and held it aloft as Alexander Shaw proposed a toast, but she didn't hear a word the exuberant man said.

"You're a Wellesley now . . ." Miles's casual words echoed through her brain like a litany. *A Wellesley!* Through all the recent weeks of doubt and tribulation, Victoria had never really thought about what it meant to marry Miles. Now she realized that, with only a few words spoken by Reverend Smythe, she had suddenly become a member of one of the most elite and illustrious families in the country. And even though her groom might have been reluctant to wed her, now that the deed was done he obviously was not adverse to claiming her as one of their own.

Mrs. Wellesley. Victoria Wellesley. How strange it seemed to hear her name paired with his. To Victoria's surprise, how-ever, the mental voicing of her married name was not altogether unpleasant. Different, but not unpleasant.

As the nuptial toasts continued, Victoria looked down the length of the long table, amused to see that the irrepressible

Georgia was honing her feminine wiles on the shy and reserved Eric. A little ripple of laughter escaped her as she watched Eric's embarrassed but flattered expression as Georgia coquettishly tapped his arm with her fan.

"I think your sister has made a conquest," Miles whispered, his eyes following the direction in which hers had strayed. "Poor Eric doesn't stand a chance against a girl of Georgia's talents."

"I suppose now that you're taken, Georgia has decided to move on to your brother."

"Hopefully he'll be more lucky than I," Miles muttered, a trace of bitterness creeping into his voice. "Maybe he'll actually marry a girl who cares for him."

Catching the stricken look in Victoria's eyes, he immediately regretted his rash words. "Too bad Stuart isn't here," he added quickly. "He'd be much more of an equal match for Georgia. Eric's far too young."

"Eric and Georgia are the same age," Victoria corrected.

Miles chuckled dryly. "In years, maybe, but that's all."

Another toast concluded and again the nuptial couple linked arms and drank.

"Watch how much of that you're drinking," Miles warned her softly as they held up their glasses to be refilled. "I know your limits."

Victoria shot him a challenging look and deliberately raised her glass to her lips, taking a long swallow of the bubbly amber liquid even though no one was currently offering a toast.

"You *are* a feisty one, aren't you?" Miles muttered. "Well, just remember, if your head is aching when we wake up tomorrow morning, don't turn to me for sympathy."

His casual reference to waking up together the following morning made Victoria blanch. Quickly, she put her glass down. "When is the dancing going to start?"

"I suppose right after we cut the cake."

As if on cue, the kitchen doors banged open and the Pembroke and Wellesley cooks marched in side by side, wheeling a cart containing a giant six-layer wedding cake trimmed with embracing marzipan cupids clad only in trailing ribbons tied in lovers' knots.

As the crowd applauded in stunned amazement at the size and intricacy of the cake, Miles took Victoria's hand and stepped down from the dais, leading her to the immense confection. He picked up a sterling silver knife and handed it to his bride, then placed his hand over hers. Together, they sliced the first piece, then cut it in two and fed it to each other. Again the guests applauded, laughing merrily when they saw that Miles had smeared a bit of frosting on Victoria's nose.

While the cake was being cut and served, the bridal couple strolled among the tables, stopping to receive felicitations and good wishes from their many friends. As they meandered through the crowded room, Cedric approached with two fresh glasses of champagne, holding them out.

"Mrs. Wellesley doesn't want any more champagne just now," Miles announced, pushing the proffered glass away just as Victoria was reaching for it.

"I most certainly do!" she countered, throwing him a look that dared him to naysay her.

Miles shrugged and gestured to Cedric to give Victoria the glass, but as the butler walked away, he whispered, "I swear, Victoria, if you get potted, I am going to be very upset."

"I am not going to get 'potted,' as you so crudely put it, and I wish you'd give me a little credit for being a responsible adult."

"Oh, I'm not doubting that you're a responsible adult," Miles retorted. "I'm just not sure about how responsible a wife you are."

Victoria's eyes flared at his obvious allusion to the night ahead and she quickly turned away. Seeing Mary Ann Parks sitting at a nearby table, she hurried over to speak to her.

"Are you all right?" Mary Ann asked, her expression filled with concern.

"Of course. Why?"

"Well, after your little faux pas at the ceremony, I thought perhaps . . ."

"Oh, that. I was just daydreaming."

Mary Ann nodded doubtfully, wondering how any bride could be woolgathering during her wedding ceremony. Nodding toward Victoria's champagne glass, she whispered, "That's a good idea."

"What is?"

"Having a few glasses of wine. It will help relax you and make things easier . . . later."

"My thoughts exactly." Victoria giggled. Lifting the glass, she again drained it, then turned and scanned the room for Cedric. "Oh, where is that man?" she muttered irritably when she didn't immediately spot him. "The next time I find him, I'm just going to take the whole bottle!"

The dancing began, although the traditional first waltz between the bride and her father was dispensed with out of respect for John Pembroke's recent passing. Instead, Miles stepped up to Victoria as the orchestra lifted their instruments and led her onto the dance floor.

"I'm always impressed by what a wonderful dancer you are," Victoria murmured as they dipped and swayed before their guests.

"I've always felt the same about you," Miles returned, "although you're not quite yourself tonight."

"I'm not?"

He shook his head, careful despite his annoyance to keep his smile firmly in place. "No. I think the six glasses of champagne I've watched you down since dinner are starting to take their toll. What are you trying to do? Work up your courage to face what's going to happen tonight, or get yourself so pie-eyed that you won't be able to feel it?"

Victoria gasped, shocked by Miles's crude words. "I can't *believe* you'd discuss such a thing with me in public!"

Miles shrugged, bending her in a graceful dip as they passed his grandmother's chair. "I thought I'd better say something now while you're still semicoherent."

"I assure you, I am far more than 'semicoherent,'" she snapped haughtily.

"Maybe, but you won't be for long if you don't stop swilling the wine."

Victoria made a quick movement, as if to try to break away from him, but Miles held her fast. "Don't you dare make a scene, Victoria. You don't want to have to answer the endless questions you'll get if you bolt in the middle of our nuptial dance. You're going to be busy enough trying to explain to everybody, including me, why you almost backed out on saying your vows at the wedding."

"I didn't almost back out!" Victoria cried.

"Keep your voice down!"

"I didn't almost back out," she repeated more softly. "My mind just wandered for a moment, and I didn't hear Reverend Smythe say my name."

"Sure." Miles snorted. "Three times you didn't hear him say your name."

"Three times!"

"Yes, three times."

Victoria dropped her gaze, unable to meet his angry eyes. "I'm sorry, Miles. I really am."

She didn't realize how much tension he was holding in his shoulders until she felt them relax beneath her hand.

"All right," he sighed. "We won't talk about it anymore."

Much chagrined, Victoria nodded. The music stopped and they walked off the dance floor, smiling and responding to well-wishes as they went. When they reached the edge of the room Miles planted a distracted kiss on her hand and said, "You're going to have to excuse me for a few minutes. I've had quite a bit of wine myself."

Victoria blushed, wondering if all husbands were as unembarrassed talking about bodily functions as Miles seemed to be. "Certainly," she said quietly. "I'll wait for you here."

"Good. And don't drink any more champagne while I'm gone."

Victoria watched him through narrowed eyes as he headed out the parlor door, then turned and made a beeline to a strolling waiter, greedily grabbing a glass of champagne off the surprised servant's tray and downing it in one swallow.

Chapter 23

By ten o'clock Victoria had drunk so much champagne that she could barely stand up. When Fiona approached her where she stood, chatting with several of her friends, and discreetly whispered that perhaps she would like to go upstairs and change her clothes in preparation for her departure for Wellesley Manor, Victoria turned and looked at her in bewilderment. "Already?" she slurred. "But everyone is still here. A hostess should never go to bed before her guests leave."

Fiona looked at her stepdaughter with startled eyes, immediately recognizing the state she was in. "This case is an exception," she said cheerily, hoping that no one else had noticed Victoria's inebriated state. "Come along, dear. I'll escort you to your room and help you change."

Victoria nodded agreeably and allowed Fiona to herd her toward the stairs. It took some doing, but they finally reached the second floor. Bracing the reeling Victoria against the wall, Fiona looked around wildly, trying to spot Rebecca. Spying the maid hanging over the banister at the far end of the hall, she softly called, "Rebecca! Come help me with Lady Victoria."

"Oh, dear!" Rebecca gasped, taking one look at the simple

smile on her mistress's face and biting her lip in vexation. "What's wrong with her?"

"Too much champagne, I'm afraid," Fiona whispered, pushing both girls into Victoria's bedroom and quietly closing the door. "Go ask Cook to make some coffee. Strong and black."

"Coffee!" Rebecca gasped. "Do we even have any of that nasty stuff in the house?"

"Let's pray we do," Fiona snapped. "Lord knows, Lady Victoria needs some."

It took nearly an hour, but Fiona was finally convinced that Victoria had been sobered up enough to walk back down the stairs and take her leave with her new husband.

"Are you ready, dear?" she asked gently.

Victoria shrugged. "As ready as I'm ever going to be." She glanced down at the blue silk traveling suit she was now wearing. "It seems so silly to change my clothes just to ride over to Wellesley Manor." She hiccoughed loudly, then covered her mouth with her fingers, casting Fiona an embarrassed look. "Sorry."

"Every bride changes out of her wedding gown before she and the groom leave the reception," Fiona murmured, patting Victoria on the shoulder encouragingly.

"Well, it's a stupid waste of effort," Victoria announced. "Especially when that brute is probably going to rip this lovely suit off me as soon as we get to his house."

"Victoria! Why in the world would you call Miles a brute?"

Victoria threw her a pained look. "Because he is," she slurred, hiccoughing again. "All men are."

Fiona turned distraught eyes on the maid, but Rebecca merely shrugged and went back to detaching Victoria's wedding veil from its diamond and flower crown.

"That's not true," Fiona said staunchly. "You and I talked about all of this the other day."

Victoria staggered over to her dressing table and picked up one of the cast-off roses from her veil, sticking it haphazardly into the hair above her ear. "I know what we talked about,

Fiona. I've hardly thought of anything else since. But I also know that all my married friends hate the things their husbands do to them late at night, and I'm going to hate it, too."

Rebecca let out a shocked little gasp at the turn the conversation was taking.

"You may go now, Rebecca," Fiona said sharply. "And please be sure to close the door—and your mouth—when you leave."

Rebecca sighed with disappointment but dutifully made her exit. She only walked about ten feet down the hall, however, before her curiosity got the better of her and she sneaked back, pinning her ear to the bedroom door.

"You're not going to hate it," she heard Fiona saying. "You're going to face it like every other good British bride does. Think of the Queen and how proud she'd be to know that you're doing your part for the future of Britain. Lord knows, she has certainly done hers." Rebecca heard Fiona's soft giggle at her little joke. "Really, Victoria, all you have to do is think of pleasant things and pleasant places and that should sustain you. I'm sure Miles will be considerate of your inexperience and attempt to have the whole thing over with as expediently as possible."

Rebecca heard Victoria mumble something in response to Fiona's bracing speech, but her voice was too thick with drink for her to make out the words through the heavy door.

Fiona's voice rose again. "That's my brave girl. Now come along; your guests are all waiting to throw rice at you and Miles. Let's not delay your departure any longer."

Rebecca scurried away before her mistress found her eavesdropping, but from her vantage point at the end of the hall she saw the door open and Fiona step out, followed by a teetering Victoria.

Rebecca smiled with amusement as she watched Victoria weave her way toward the staircase. Although she'd never been married, she had enjoyed many a roll in the hayloft with various stable boys. One glance at her wobbly mistress and her heart went out to Miles. It didn't look to her as if there would be much loving going on tonight. Tomorrow morning, maybe, but certainly not tonight.

"Ah, the poor man," Rebecca murmured to herself, "and him undoubtedly ready as ready can be." She shook her head in sympathetic commiseration, her fiery curls dancing madly. "Ah, these noble brides. If they'd just quit worrying about the whole thing, they might even enjoy it." Certainly, Rebecca thought, with a man who looked like Miles Wellesley, *she* would!

Miles was, indeed, "ready as ready could be," but one look across the carriage at his semiconscious bride and his hopes of a romantic night were much the same as Rebecca's.

With a disappointed sigh he leaned back against the luxurious seat, crossing his arms over his chest and staring in annoyance at Victoria.

The ride passed in silence as Victoria dozed and Miles brooded. Finally, as they turned up the long drive leading to Wellesley Manor, he reached over and shook her shoulder gently, not wanting Clement to see her in this state and pass unflattering gossip on to every servant in the county.

"Victoria," he whispered. "Victoria!" Groggily, she opened her eyes. "We're home."

"Home?" she murmured in bewilderment, looking out the carriage window. "We're not home. We're at Wellesley Manor."

Miles frowned irritably. "Never mind. I'm going to carry you into the house and straight upstairs."

"You are not!" Victoria protested, sitting up straighter in the seat and glaring at him through glassy eyes. "I'm not drunk and I can walk perfectly well."

"You *are* drunk," Miles insisted, "and even if you weren't, I'd carry you. It's tradition, remember?"

"Oh, yes, so it is," she muttered, grimacing. "Well, all right, but hold me loosely."

"What?"

"You know what I mean. No taking liberties in front of the servants."

"Don't worry about it," he growled.

The carriage door swung open and Clement let down the steps. "Do you need any help, sir?"

"No, I think I can manage just fine." Miles forced a grin and stepped out of the carriage, turning back to lift Victoria off the seat. "Just open the front door for me, will you?"

Clement hurried up the steps, opening the door so quickly that he nearly hit Cedric, who was standing on the other side awaiting his master's approach, in the head with it.

Miles brushed by the two men, saying a quick thank you and rushing up the stairs, his bride in his arms.

Clement and Cedric, who hadn't seen eye to eye on anything in forty years, threw each other knowing looks. "Seems to be in a bit of a hurry, wouldn't you say?" Clement chuckled.

A rare smile curved Cedric's thin lips. "Ah, yes, to be young again."

"Young and randy," Clement added.

For a moment Cedric looked as though he was going to take Clement to task for his disrespect, but, instead, he merely sighed wistfully and nodded. "Yes, indeed, young and randy. I can hardly remember what that was like."

"Neither can I," Clement agreed, shaking his head sadly. The two men cast each other one last sympathetic look, then silently parted, having shared more in the last thirty seconds than they had in the last three decades.

Miles, by this time, had reached the second floor. Hurrying down the hall, he shouldered open the door to the master suite, walking into the flower-filled, candlelit room and setting Victoria carefully on her feet. "We're here," he whispered, breathing deeply of her sweet scent as he reluctantly removed his hands from her waist.

Victoria looked around absently, her eyes settling on the huge bed with its rosebud-strewn silk sheets. Gulping back the sudden surge of nausea that threatened, she croaked, "Are you going to do it now?"

Miles blew out a long, dispirited breath. "No, I'm not going to 'do it now.' What I'm going to do now is leave you so you can get ready for bed."

Victoria, who was beginning to feel truly ill, answered shakily. "It will probably take me a long time."

Miles nodded slowly, fully realizing that her intention was to hold off the inevitable for as long as possible. "I'm a patient man, Victoria. I can wait till you're finished with your toilette. In the meantime, I'll send Hildy in to help you."

"No!"

He looked at her quizzically. "You don't want a maid to help you undress?"

"No. I mean, I . . . I'd rather do it myself. Tonight. You understand."

Miles didn't understand at all, but he was too tired and too depressed to argue, so he merely nodded and left the room, closing the door softly behind him.

He walked down the hall to his own bedroom, slowly removing his clothes and pulling on a dark green silk wrapper. Then he lit a cigar and poured a brandy, pacing the floor while he smoke and drank. When his snifter was empty he refilled it, forcing himself to sit down and relax. It had been a whole hour since he'd left his bride. Surely that was enough time for her to prepare herself.

After making one last check of his appearance in the shaving mirror, he strolled back down the hall. Three paces from the master suite's door, he heard a weak cry, followed by the sound of retching.

Alarmed, he flung open the door, narrowing his eyes as he accustomed them to the dim candlelight. He spotted Victoria, draped over the commode, retching miserably, her face as green as spring grass.

"I'm sick," she announced unnecessarily, turning toward him with a mortified look. "Please, just leave me. I can't do it now."

Miles didn't know whether to laugh or cry. She was so pathetic, so miserably drunk, and *still* her paramount fear was that he was going to leap on her.

"I know you're sick," he soothed, walking toward her. "Here, let me help you."

"No! I don't want you to see me like this. Just go away."

"Nonsense. I'm your husband now." Moving behind her, Miles gathered up her snarled hair, tying it back with a ribbon he grabbed off the dressing table. "Don't you remember this afternoon when we vowed to stand together through better or worse?"

"This is definitely worse!" Victoria groaned, again leaning over the commode.

Miles hurried over to where a pitcher and basin sat atop a small, marble-topped table and poured out some cool water, dipping a clean linen cloth in it and holding it out to her. "I told you that you were drinking too much champagne. Now you're finding out the price you pay for excess."

"I know," she moaned. "I did drink too much. But I just felt I had to."

"Why was that?" he asked solicitously, gently rubbing her back with soothing sweeps of his palms.

If Victoria had been a little less drunk or a little less exhausted, her good judgment might have prevented her from uttering the next devastating words. Unfortunately, good judgment was not a quality in her possession at that moment, and the truth tumbled out before she could stop it. "It was the only thing I could think to do. The thought of being . . . *with* you was just so repugnant that I felt it best to try to numb myself so I could get through it without becoming hysterical. I thought the champagne would help."

Miles took a startled step backward, gaping at his wife in stupefied horror. *Repugnant!* The thought of being in bed with him was repugnant? So repugnant that she preferred a night spent vomiting? Never, at any time in his entire life, had he ever been as insulted as he was at that moment.

His expression hardened until his face was a mask of cold fury. "I'm sorry that the thought of being close to me is so odious to you, Mrs. Wellesley. I won't repulse you with my presence any longer."

Turning on his heel, he stalked out of the room, calling loudly for Hildy. The plump, elderly maid immediately appeared in the doorway of the viscountess's suite, wearing a look of surprised concern. Seeing Miles's black expression, she hurried toward him, trying to imagine what would put such a look on a bride-groom's face on his wedding night. There was only one thing she could think of, and Miles's next words confirmed her suspicions.

"Please go see if you can help my wife. She is ill."

Hildy's eyes filled with sympathy as she watched Miles stalk off down the hall to his bedroom and disappear inside, slamming the door so hard that the frame shook.

Ah, these silly English brides, Hildy thought, shaking her head. Why didn't they just lie back and enjoy it like good German girls did?

With a snort of disgust, Hildy pushed open the door and entered the bridal chamber.

Miles upended the empty bottle of brandy over his equally empty glass. "Gone," he muttered as he tried to shake the last drops of liquid into the snifter. "Now I'm going to have to go all the way down to the cellar to get another one."

Bleary-eyed, he tried to focus on the clock. Was it two o'clock or three? It didn't really matter; it was late. Deep into the wee hours of his wedding night. And instead of being curled up with his bride, basking in the afterglow of love's first sojourn, he was here alone in his room—unwanted, unloved and very much unsatisfied.

He shook his head, trying to clear his vision, but that only served to make him dizzy. "Good God, man," he muttered to himself, "you're as drunk as she is."

Wearily, he threw himself back into a deep cushioned chair,

staring morosely at the rock-ribbed planes of his chest and abdomen.

Why didn't she want him? It wasn't as if he was ugly or fat or old or debauched. God knew, he'd had enough experience with other women to know that most found him attractive. He couldn't even remember how many times, at the most intimate of moments, women had told him how handsome he was, how arousing his hard, muscular body, how satisfying his virile sexual prowess.

But not his wife. Oh, no, not her. His wife found him repugnant. His wife had to drink herself into a stupor to prevent herself from becoming hysterical when he made love to her.

Miles shook his head, wallowing deeper and deeper in an abyss of self-pity. He shouldn't have married her. She had made it clear all along that she hadn't wanted him, and he shouldn't have pressured her.

But he'd wanted her, damn it. Wanted her from the first moment she'd challenged his right to be in her father's stable. She was everything, *everything* he'd ever hoped for in a wife, and the more he'd gotten to know her, the more he'd realized that. And when he had, he'd let himself fall in love with her.

In love. Miles's bleary, liquor-glazed eyes narrowed at the distressing thought. But there was no denying it. He loved Victoria with every fiber of his being.

How had it happened? When?

When had the idea of conquering the reluctant spinster ceased to be an egotistical challenge and become a serious bid for the lady's heart? And what was he going to do about it now that she had irrefutably rejected him, letting him know in the most blatant of terms that she cared nothing for him? That she actually found the thought of making love with him disgusting?

"She'll never know," he vowed angrily. "You may have to be married to her, but you don't have to let her know how much you care—how much it hurts that she doesn't want you. After all, there are plenty of other women out there who can

256 *Jane Kidder*

fill that need." Miles frowned, finding even the thought of another woman's caresses uninviting.

Of course, with the marriage remaining unconsummated, they could just admit their mistake and have it annulled. Victoria would probably be delighted by that suggestion. But, damn it, he didn't want an annulment. An annulment would be tantamount to a public announcement that his wife had rebuffed him. It would be a disgrace—to him, to her, to both their families.

No, an annulment was out. He had married her, and married he'd stay. As Regina always reminded him, he'd made his bed; now he had to lie in it. But, from the way things were going, it seemed inevitable that he was going to be lying in it alone.

Chapter 24

The wedding breakfast was a nightmare.

Victoria, whose head ached so fiercely that she could hardly open her eyes, took one look at the huge platter of lamb kidneys braised with bacon and was afraid she was going to be sick again.

Miles, for his part, tried very hard not to look at anything—especially his bride.

Luckily, the many guests who had reassembled for the breakfast suspected nothing—attributing the bride and groom's hollow-eyed looks to a night spent in romantic bliss.

His bloodshot eyes and the weary droop of his mouth garnered Miles many a congratulatory slap on the back, while Victoria tried desperately to ignore her friends' smiles of commiseration at her exhausted appearance.

Only one member of the party was unconvinced that all was well between the newlyweds. Mary Wellesley, a woman well attuned to the nuances of her children's behavior, looked at her eldest son and frowned. Something was wrong—very wrong. To her astute eye, Miles didn't look tired; he looked miserable.

She guessed rightly that the soft groan she heard when Alexander Shaw clapped him on the back and jokingly asked him how he'd "slept" wasn't caused by sore muscles strained during sensual frolic, but by a head that was pounding from too much alcohol.

Surely, Mary reasoned, a man on his wedding night might share a glass of champagne with his bride, but he didn't get himself soused unless something wasn't going as planned and he was drowning his sorrows.

Mary wished desperately that she dared ask Miles what was troubling him, but now was not the time and she was not the person. Rather, she'd wait until the guests departed, then share her concerns with James, letting him decide whether to invite Miles to confide in him.

Knowing James as she did, she was sure he would speak to his son. That way, at least she'd find out what was wrong. James could never keep anything from her, and Mary knew that even if Miles swore his father to secrecy, there were a multitude of ways in which she could coerce him into talking. She'd have to be patient, but ultimately she would know what was causing Miles to look so dispirited on a morning when he should be radiating an aura of satisfied well-being.

Her gaze swung over to Victoria and she watched with interest as her new daughter-in-law tentatively nibbled a piece of dry toast, then quickly put it down and took a swallow of tea.

Looking back at Miles, Mary noticed that he wasn't eating either, a sure sign that something was wrong. If there was one thing all her sons could do, regardless of what crisis they might be facing in their lives, it was eat.

Even now, little Nathan and Seth were eagerly digging into huge portions of scrambled eggs and bacon, having demanded that Cook fix them some "decent food" after taking one look at the kidneys and loudly proclaiming that they weren't "gonna eat anything that used to hold sheep pee."

Her younger sons' loud protestations of the English delicacy had caused many an aristocratic eyebrow to rise around the room, but Mary had merely smiled benevolently and requested alternate fare. After all, her sons *were* American, and the nearly sacrosanct British tradition of lamb kidneys on toast for breakfast was definitely an acquired taste.

By the time the long ceremonial breakfast finally ended and the last of the guests vacated Wellesley Manor, it was nearly three o'clock. Mary watched as Victoria slowly climbed the stairs and disappeared into the master suite, noting with a pleased expression that Miles followed her almost immediately. Her hopeful smile faded, though, as she saw him pass by his wife's room and go on to his own, closing the door soundly behind him.

"Something's not right between those two," Regina said, walking up behind Mary and shaking her head.

"You noticed that, too?"

Regina shrugged. "How could I not? It's my guess that the silly girl is reluctant to climb into bed with the boy and Miles's very male nose is out of joint."

Mary looked at her mother-in-law and laughed. "I think you're absolutely right. But what are we going to do about it?"

Regina sighed. "There's nothing you and I *can* do. Hopefully James will talk to Miles, and maybe Fiona could be persuaded to speak with Victoria, although now that she has her money from the sale of the estate and she's trying to get those girls of hers ready to leave for America, she's probably too busy."

"Oh, Mother, I think you're being very hard on her. She seems like a lovely, caring woman to me."

"I'm not saying she's not lovely and caring," Regina protested. "I'm saying she's preoccupied. Besides, every available minute she does have is being spent trying to make a match between Georgia and Eric before everyone departs for America. I doubt she'll want to spend any more time counseling Victoria. After all, that's a match that's already made."

"Georgia and Eric!" Mary gasped. "But Eric is just a boy! Whatever would make Fiona think he's ready to marry?"

"She wouldn't if Stuart were here, but he's not, so Eric is the next best thing. She's successfully mated one Wellesley boy to her stepdaughter; why not try for the brass ring and get one of her own daughters married to another?"

"Well, it's absolutely out of the question," Mary huffed. "James and I would not consider letting Eric marry at such a young age, even if he wanted to."

"Then you'd better watch them," Regina advised. "That Georgia Pembroke has a bag of tricks deeper than a court magician's."

Mary clucked her tongue in annoyance. "It's not enough that I have to worry about Miles and Victoria; now I have to deal with Georgia and Eric, too. The next thing you know, she'll be trying to pair Carolina up with Geoffrey!"

"I wouldn't be surprised," Regina chuckled wryly. "After all, Geoffrey may only be fourteen, but he's so big and brawny, he looks five years older. To Carolina Pembroke, that's probably enough."

Mary turned stricken eyes on the older lady, but she relaxed again at Regina's merry laugh. "Thank you for the warning, Mother. I'll speak to James directly."

"Poor James; he's going to be so busy advising his sons on the ways of love that he'll never get in any of that fishing he's so looking forward to."

Mary rolled her eyes heavenward. "Thank the Lord for small favors. Every time that man goes fishing he smells like pond water for a week. Maybe there *is* a positive side to all these little peccadilloes, after all!"

Victoria napped until nearly seven o'clock, but when she finally awoke she felt much better. Pressing a tentative hand to her forehead, she was pleased to find that it no longer throbbed, and her stomach had settled down enough that she felt as if she might actually be able to eat a little something.

Gazing around the sumptuous bedroom, she wondered where Miles was. He'd hardly said a word to her at the breakfast this morning and had disappeared as soon as the last of the guests had departed.

Victoria sighed, realizing how angry he must be. After all, he'd probably had high expectations about what was going to happen between them last night, and she'd done a yeoman's job of foiling them. She grimaced, admitting to herself that Miles did have justification for being put out with her. Somehow, she was going to have to find a way to explain to him that she hadn't meant to get so drunk—that she'd merely been trying to take the edge off a bad case of nerves.

And what are you going to do to take the edge off tonight? a little voice deep inside her asked.

Sitting up, Victoria sighed deeply. Nothing. She wasn't going to do anything more to try to stave Miles off. After all, she was his wife, and as everyone had pointed out to her, it was her duty to accept his attentions. She'd made a fool of herself last night, but she wasn't going to repeat the unpleasant episode. Rather, she was going to "buck up," as Mary Ann repeatedly told her she must and face the inevitable. And she was going to do it tonight.

Getting out of bed, she pulled the cord to summon Hildy.

An hour later, Victoria was dressed in a beautiful amber evening gown, the tight corset Hildy had laced her into nipping her already tiny waist to a minuscule eighteen inches and pushing her generous breasts nearly out of the daringly low-cut bodice.

"I'll never be able to eat," she groaned, struggling to take a deep breath.

"Never mind about eating, my lady." Hildy chuckled. "You look wonderful and that's all that counts. Your husband won't be able to take his eyes off you."

Grateful for the maid's beaming approval, Victoria smiled at her and left the bedroom, slowly walking down the stairs and heading toward the dining room.

Miles, his parents, and his grandmother were seated around the table, their soup bowls sitting empty in front of them.

As Victoria entered the room, James immediately rose and held out a welcoming hand. "Here you are. We were just about to send someone up to see if you were awake."

"I'm sorry if I kept you from your dinner. I'm afraid I slept far longer than I intended."

"You didn't keep us from dinner, dear," Mary assured her. "We all just sat down."

James pulled out the chair next to Miles and Victoria sank gracefully into it, casting her husband a surreptitious glance. He looked wonderful, clad in his favorite buff and brown, with a small ruby stickpin holding his immaculately tied cravat in place. "Good evening," she said softly.

Miles returned her greeting with the briefest of glances. "Good evening, Victoria. Are you feeling better?"

Victoria felt hot color creep up her neck, mortified to think that Miles had probably explained her tardiness by telling his parents of her previous night's excesses. "Yes, thank you."

The stilted conversation came to an abrupt halt and everyone breathed a sigh of relief as a young serving maid pushed through the kitchen door, bearing the soup tureen.

"So, what are you two planning for tomorrow?" James asked, dipping his spoon into his soup. "Getting ready to leave on your wedding trip Wednesday?"

Victoria turned startled eyes on her new father-in-law. "Our wedding trip! Didn't Miles tell you?"

"Tell us what?"

Victoria turned toward Miles, throwing him a perplexed look.

"We decided not to take our wedding trip until you and Mother go back to America," he muttered.

The elder Wellesleys looked at each other, dumbfounded. "Why?"

"Miles felt that he didn't want to be off touring the continent with you here visiting," Victoria explained, "so we agreed to wait until autumn to take our trip."

"But . . ." Mary sputtered, "but it's your honeymoon!"

"It doesn't matter," Miles said dully. "Paris will still be there in October."

Mary turned stricken eyes on James, her heart breaking at the emptiness in Miles's voice. Her mind reeled back nearly twenty-five years to her own honeymoon. She and James had gone to Rome, spending a whole month in that enchanting city. Even now, all these years later, she cherished the memories of that trip—the excitement of being alone with her new husband, the many little personal things they'd learned about each other during leisurely candlelit suppers, the camaraderie that had blossomed between them as they'd explored the ancient city, the intimacies they'd shared nestled together in their bed at the little hotel where they'd stayed . . . Why, Miles had been conceived during that magical month!

And now he and Victoria wanted to postpone their trip. Why would any bride and groom want to put off such a unique and wonderful event? Something was definitely wrong here; even more wrong than she had guessed previously. "I don't think you two should postpone such an important . . ."

"It's all right, Mother," Miles interrupted. "Victoria and I have already discussed it, and we both agree that it's the wisest thing to do."

Wise? Mary thought. They'd been married only a day and they were thinking about what was wise?

"Besides," Victoria added, "I have so many things to do before Fiona and the girls leave—I want to go to Pembroke tomorrow and begin cataloging the wedding presents and writing my thank yous, and Fiona undoubtedly could use my help in packing up the house . . . I think it's a very prudent idea for me to remain here at this time."

Mary shook her head. *Prudent. Wise. What was wrong with these two?* "When did you decide this?" she asked.

"We discussed it this morning," Miles said quickly. "Before the wedding breakfast." He didn't mention that the "discussion" had been in the form of his stopping Victoria at the top of the stairs that morning and telling her that since she obviously found his company so objectionable, he didn't think it was a good idea for them to try to spend a month alone together.

Victoria instantly agreed, causing Miles's male ego to slip yet another notch as he noted the expression of profound relief that crossed her face.

Mary sighed with disappointment. "Well, whatever you two think . . ."

Regina, who had remained silent during this entire conversation, now turned to Victoria. "In my day it was considered perfectly acceptable for a bride to ask her family to help with the organization and cataloging of gifts for thank you notes so that she would be free to go off and enjoy her honeymoon. Of course, the notes would have to be written as soon as she returned home, but gift-givers certainly didn't expect to receive formal thank yous until that time. Have things changed so much in fifty years that people now expect acknowledgment of their gift the same week as the wedding? It seems a bit presumptuous to me."

Victoria set down her spoon and swallowed hard. "I'm sure no one *expects* it, Viscountess, but as long as we're postponing our trip, I feel it's something I should attend to."

"In my estimation there are more important things to attend to the week one is married than writing notes."

Victoria squirmed uncomfortably in her chair, throwing a pleading look at Miles, but instead of leaping into the fray he deftly changed the subject. "How about a game of chess after dinner, Father?"

"Oh, I don't know," James hedged. "I have some reading I'd like to do, and I thought I'd call it an early night. With all the excitement of the last couple of days, I could use a few extra hours of sleep."

Miles tossed James a look that told him very clearly what he thought of his father's lame excuse, but he didn't argue. Instead, he simply nodded and returned his attention to the stuffed capon sitting on his plate.

Mary glanced over at Victoria, wondering how she felt, knowing her new husband preferred to play chess with his father rather than spend the evening with her, but Victoria's head was also bent over her plate as she cut a tiny piece of meat and slowly lifted it to her mouth.

So anxious was everyone to get away from the strained atmosphere around the table that they all declined the offer of dessert.

Victoria rose immediately, causing Miles to look up at her as she leaped to her feet. She saw his eyes hesitate a moment on the creamy swells of her exposed breasts and quickly drew in her breath, smiling at him hopefully.

Miles looked away.

Mortified by his overt rejection, she murmured, "I'm a bit tired myself. If no one minds, I think I'll retire." She paused a moment, casting one last come-hither look at Miles to see if he was going to join her. But he made no move to do so, merely nodding at her disinterestedly and wishing her a pleasant sleep. Picking up her skirts, Victoria fled the room.

After her embarrassed departure, Miles rose also, throwing down his napkin and taking a last swallow of the wine left in his glass. He turned to leave but was brought up short by his father's voice. "I'd like to speak to you a moment before you go."

Miles watched his mother and grandmother hurry out of the room, then sat back down in his chair. "Yes?"

"What on earth is going on between you two?" James asked bluntly.

"Nothing. Why do you ask?"

"Because you've been married twenty-four hours and the two of you won't even look each other in the eye. I think that's a legitimate reason for concern, don't you?"

"Let it be, Father. It's between Victoria and me."

"I understand that," James said patiently, "and I'm not trying to pry. But something is obviously very wrong, and I'd like to help if I can."

Miles pressed his lips into a tight, angry line. "Well, you can't, and although I appreciate your offer, this is a situation that she and I are going to have to work out between ourselves."

James nodded once in silent agreement of his son's demands, but added, "Then work it out, Miles, because the way you two are acting is making everyone uncomfortable."

"I know," Miles admitted. "I'll talk to her."

"You need to do a hell of a lot more than talk to her," James muttered.

"Oh? And what do you suggest?"

James looked at him for a long moment, then said simply, "You should have taken your wedding trip as planned. The two of you need to be alone together."

"No, we don't! In fact, that's the last thing we need. By the way, when are you and Mother planning to return to America?"

His unexpected question took James completely by surprise. "I'm not sure yet. After all, we only just arrived. Why do you ask?"

"Because when you do I'm going with you."

A pleased grin spread across James's face. "Really? I thought you and Victoria were moving over to Pembroke once Fiona and the girls left."

"Well, we're not."

"You mean the two of you have decided to settle in America after all?"

Miles looked at his father for a moment, then again rose from his chair. "The two of us haven't decided anything. I didn't say we were going to accompany you back to America; I said *I* was."

And with that, he walked out of the room, leaving his stunned father to stare after him in speechless disbelief.

Chapter 25

Victoria sank down on the edge of the huge tester bed and buried her face in her hands. She was a fool; a complete and utter fool. Had she really thought that putting on a dress with a daring décolletage and smiling sweetly at her husband over the dinner table would assuage his anger and bring him knocking at her door like a beggar to a banquet? How could she have been so stupid and naive? The only thing her little display tonight had garnered her was her mother-in-law's pity and her husband's disdain.

"I've got to get out of here," she muttered, ripping the pins out of her elegant coiffure and working feverishly at the row of buttons down the back of her beautiful dress. "Leave before things get any worse." How things between herself and her husband could be worse than they were at this moment was almost beyond imagining, but one thing was sure: Miles was too angry to appease and she might as well give up the fight while she was left with some small shred of her dignity. It was obvious after tonight that Miles no longer wanted her, and she couldn't bear to remain with a man who no longer cared.

But where could she go? What could she do?

Shaking her head in abject misery, Victoria ordered herself to think. Think! She breathed deeply a few times, forcing herself to be calm, to consider logically, rationally, what she should do. Suddenly it came to her.

London. She'd go to London and carry out her plan to become a governess—the same plan she'd made when this whole misbegotten marriage had first been discussed. After all, nothing had really changed since that time. Her relationship with Miles was unconsummated, so it wasn't a real marriage. She'd go to the city and find a job; then she'd engage a solicitor and get an annulment. She had read once about a girl whose marriage had been annulled. Of course, that girl had only been sixteen and the groom seventeen, and they'd married at Gretna Green against their parents' will, but still, the fact that an annulment had been granted meant that it was possible under extreme circumstances. And in Victoria's mind her circumstances were every bit as extreme as that luckless couple's had been.

But an annulment was far in the future and she couldn't bear to think about it tonight. Right now she had a far more pressing problem to deal with: money. She'd been unable to sell any of her mother's jewels in the village, but certainly her luck would be better in a city the size of London. She grimaced, realizing that even if she could sell all the jewels her mother had left her, they still amounted to very little. The jeweler to whom she'd offered them had told her that none of the pieces was particularly valuable. Based on his estimate, all of them combined would barely net her enough money for a month's food and lodging in the expensive capital. Still, a month's worth of funds might be enough to see her through. Surely she could find some kind of position in that length of time. But what if she couldn't? What would she do then? Lifting her trembling hands to push back her hair, Victoria's eye caught the flash of fire that shot from her magnificent diamond-and-emerald betrothal ring.

That was it! She'd sell her ring. After all, if there was no marriage, why should she keep the betrothal ring? Slipping it off her finger, she examined it closely. It truly was magnificent. The diamond had to be at least three karats, and the many small emeralds surrounding it would probably be of equal weight when combined. If she could find a reputable jeweler, surely she could get enough for the ring to comfortably support herself until she could find work.

She raced over to the heavy oak armoire, throwing open the doors and peering hopefully inside. Unfortunately, most of her clothes were still at Pembroke, ready to be packed for the ill-fated wedding trip. Thankfully, one traveling suit had been brought over to Wellesley Manor, along with a riding habit and two day dresses. She rummaged around on the floor of the armoire, smiling when she found a pair of sturdy boots. Tossing her meager belongings on the bed, she opened a small valise and stuffed them inside. It wasn't much and they weren't the most appropriate of outfits to wear when searching for a governess's position, but they'd have to do.

Quickly, Victoria slipped out of the amber dress, hanging it in the armoire. She stroked its satin sheen wistfully before closing the doors.

Don't think about it. Don't think about him. Just concentrate on what you have to do.

Catching her trembling lower lip between her teeth, she walked over to the dressing table, picking up a comb and brush, but leaving her perfumes, lotions and powders behind. What did it matter if her skin was soft or carried the scent of an exotic fragrance? No one was going to be close enough to her to notice.

I love the way you smell. Victoria closed her eyes, remembering Miles's whispered compliment the day Harrison Guildford had found them together in the barn. Throwing her head back, she closed her eyes, willing herself not to cry.

Why had she been such a fool last night? Why had she gotten drunk and told Miles that she found his touch repugnant? It was no wonder he hadn't looked at her all day today—no wonder he'd ignored her subtle attempts to apologize tonight.

Even the come-hither look she'd thrown him as she'd left the dining room—a look she'd seen Georgia use on men with astounding success—had been a dismal failure. Miles had merely turned away and asked his father if he wanted to play chess. Chess!

Victoria lowered her head, allowing the tears she'd been fighting to stream down her cheeks. It was obvious that nothing she could do was going to bring him back to her, so it was better that she leave. Better that she end this misery now. If truth be known, Miles would probably be pleased when she advised him that the marriage had been annulled. Once it was, he would be released from all responsibility and would be free to pursue a life without her—to return to America, to find a girl he really cared about and to settle down happily in those mountains he loved so much.

He could even take King's Ransom with him. As long as they were married, the horse was legally his, and if he took him out of the country before the annulment was final, she'd never have the wherewithal to get him back. Miles would finally have all he wanted—all he'd really come to England to get. King's Ransom would be his.

Victoria was surprised to realize that the thought of losing her beloved horse didn't matter much to her. In fact, as she sat down on the edge of the bed to wait for everyone to retire so she could run away, she realized that the horse really didn't matter at all. It was the loss of the man that was shattering her heart.

She closed her eyes, trying to sear Miles's handsome face into her brain so she would remember him during all the lonely days to come. Miles: the tall, handsome, blond, laughing man who had swept into her life, offering her a chance for happiness and love. And she, fool that she was, had turned him away. Had told him his touch was repugnant and made him feel that his company was odious to her.

A great sob of regret tore loose from Victoria's throat. How could she have been such a fool?

How?

Victoria slept for awhile, exhausted by her battle against the twin demons of guilt and remorse. When she opened her eyes the small clock by the bedside proclaimed it to be just after two o'clock.

With a gasp of dismay, she leaped off the bed. She'd meant to be gone by midnight, to be well away by morning just in case Miles felt compelled to follow her. Now she'd already lost two precious hours of travel time.

Grabbing the packed valise, she slipped out of the house and made her way to the stables. Thank God old Samuel was half deaf and snored like a train engine. No matter how much noise she made saddling a horse and riding away, he'd never hear a thing.

Within fifteen minutes, Victoria was on the road, her valise securely attached to the flat saddle she'd chosen. She cantered the little mare she'd taken for a couple of miles, then slowed her to a trot, not wanting to wear out the pretty little horse when they had such a long trip in front of them.

She would ride until daybreak, she decided, then find a rural inn and pass the day there. That way she could get in a few hours of much-needed sleep before resuming her journey tomorrow night.

Even if Miles did come looking for her the following morning, he'd never suspect her to be at an inn. He'd undoubtedly think that she'd be traveling during the day and resting at night, so he'd have no reason to halt his pursuit until evening.

Victoria smiled. It was a good plan and one that was sure to foil any attempts her husband might make to find her. That is, if he even *tried* to find her. He might be so glad to be rid of her that he wouldn't even bother.

Victoria's heart wrenched in her chest. Somehow, the thought that Miles wouldn't care enough to come looking for her made the large knot of misery already weighing her down seem even heavier. She felt the hot sting of tears building behind her eyes and bit her lip hard to stave them off. "You're doing the right thing," she said aloud. "The right thing for everyone."

Now if she could just make herself believe that.

"Have either of you seen Victoria this morning?"

James and Mary looked up from their breakfasts, their surprise at Miles's question obvious.

"Isn't she in your . . . her room?" Mary asked.

Miles shook his head. "No, and Hildy says the bed doesn't look as if it's been slept in."

"What?" James cried, leaping to his feet. "She didn't sleep in her bed?"

"Now, James," Mary said soothingly, rising from her chair and coming around the table to put a hand on her husband's arm. "Don't panic. She must be somewhere nearby. Perhaps she just decided to make her own bed this morning."

Both James and Miles shot her a dubious look.

"Has anyone looked in the gardens?" Regina asked, walking into the room. She'd seen her grandson come thundering down the stairs and, curious to know what was amiss, had followed him into the dining room.

"Hildy and Martha are both looking there now," Miles informed her. "Did Victoria say anything to any of you last night before she retired? Anything about plans she might have for this morning?"

Regina turned a disapproving look on her grandson. "I think it would be far more likely that she'd discuss her day's plans with you than with us. If you were sleeping with your bride as you should be, you'd likely know where she is."

"Mother . . ." James said, his voice heavy with warning. "Now is not the time—"

"Wait a minute," Mary said suddenly, snapping her fingers. "Victoria said last night at dinner that she was going to Pembroke today to begin cataloging the wedding gifts. That's undoubtedly where she is."

"You're right," James concurred. "She did say she was going over there today."

The concern creasing Miles's brow didn't lift despite his parents' obvious relief. "I'm going out to speak with Samuel," he muttered. "If Victoria went to Pembroke this morning, he must have brought the brougham around for her."

Miles no more than turned toward the front door than it burst open, admitting a breathless and red-faced Samuel. He looked around a bit wildly, as if he couldn't quite believe that he'd just entered the main house without knocking.

"Beggin' your pardon for the intrusion, my lady," he panted, his voice hoarse and rasping from the exertion of running across the yard, "but it appears that someone broke into the stable last night and stole one of the horses."

"What?" Regina gasped.

"Which horse is missing?" Miles demanded, stepping toward Samuel so aggressively that the old man danced backward in trepidation.

"Cassandra," Samuel replied promptly. "The pretty little gray mare Miss Victoria has been riding."

"Goddamn it," Miles cursed. "I knew it. She's gone."

"Gone!" Mary cried, her voice suddenly shrill with alarm. "What do you mean, gone?"

"Just what I say," Miles retorted, already heading for the stairs. "She's left me."

"Now, wait a minute, Miles," James called, hurrying to the stairs as Miles bolted up the steps two at a time. "What makes you think Victoria has left you? Maybe she's simply . . ."

Miles threw his father a black look. "She's left me, but if she thinks she's going to end this that easily, she's got another think coming." By this time he had reached the second floor and was already on his way down the hall.

"Are you going after her?" James shouted.

"Yes!"

"Do you want help?"

"No!"

With a nod of understanding, James walked back into the dining room.

"Don't you think you should go with him?" Mary asked. "After all, two people searching is better than one."

James gave his wife a quick kiss on the cheek. "No, I don't. Miles needs to do this himself."

"But, James, what if something has happened to her?"

"I'm sure she's fine. She couldn't have gotten far, and the road is well traveled. He'll find her soon enough."

"James is right." Regina nodded. "Miles needs to handle this on his own. And when he does find Victoria, they need to have a chance to be alone to work things out."

"But," Mary protested, "there are two roads out of the village. What if Miles takes the wrong one?"

"He's not going to take the wrong road, darling," James soothed. "One leads farther into the countryside and the other goes directly to London. That's undoubtedly the one Victoria has taken."

"I suppose you're right," Mary sighed, "but I can't help but worry."

James pulled Mary close and buried his lips in her hair. "I know. Worrying is what you do best."

"Don't fret, Mary." Regina chuckled, seating herself at the table and lifting the cover off a chafing dish. "This may be the best thing that could happen to those two. At least it will force them to face each other and talk over whatever is bothering them. That's certainly an improvement over the icy silence they punished each other with yesterday."

Mary nodded and reluctantly sat back down at the table. "I suppose you're right. I just wish there was something I could do to help."

"If you want to help with something," Regina said, "you can help me."

"Of course. With what?"

"Cedric."

Mary's frown eased and an amused expression softened her face. "What's wrong with the old goat now?"

Regina helped herself to a portion of eggs, then replaced the dish's cover and sat back. "It seems that he's taken to his room and won't come out."

"Oh, no," Mary moaned. "I see a child's hand in this."

Regina nodded. "Exactly. It's Paula this time."

"Paula! What did that little minx do?"

"According to Cook, she threw her entire plate of eggs at Cedric this morning when he insisted she eat them with a fork instead of a spoon."

"Oh, for God's sake," James snapped in annoyance. "Paula's only two years old. I think she's doing damn well to eat with a spoon, much less a fork. Three months ago she was still using her fingers!"

"I agree," Regina nodded, "but Cedric took exception to the child throwing eggs at him, and now I have to try to placate him."

"Placate him, hell," James growled, tearing off a piece of toast and chewing it with a vengeance. "Dismiss the ornery old bugger."

"James!" Mary gasped. "Cedric has been with your family for forty years!"

"I know, and in my estimation that's about thirty-nine years too long."

"I'm not going to dismiss him," Regina stated firmly.

"Of course you aren't," Mary agreed, throwing her husband a shaming look. "Don't listen to James. He always gets this way if someone criticizes his little princess. And don't worry; I'll go eat humble pie with Cedric. I'm sure he'll come around if I'm contrite enough."

"Thank you, my dear," Regina said gratefully. "He may be

an ornery old bugger, but he's the best butler in the shire, and I don't know what I'd do without him."

James sighed in defeat, wondering as he had a thousand times before what special talent God had granted all British servants that allowed them to so easily gain the upper hand over their employers.

Chapter 26

It was late that afternoon when Miles found her.

Correctly guessing that his errant wife would head for London, he took the main road in that direction, stopping along the way at every roadside inn he passed to ask if anyone had seen a woman answering Victoria's description and traveling on horseback.

Finally, shortly before dinnertime, his efforts were rewarded. Walking into a small, cozy inn, Miles sought out the owner, approaching the man and asking the same question he'd already asked eight times that day. This time, however, he got the answer he'd been hoping for.

"Yes, my lord," the innkeeper beamed. "A lady of that description is here now."

"Really?" Miles asked, his heart leaping into his throat.

"Right upstairs in her room, she is."

"And she arrived on horseback?"

"Yes, sir, she did, indeed. A pretty little gray mare. She's back in my stable having a fine dinner. We pride ourselves on tending animals as well as we tend our guests."

"That's very admirable," Miles muttered. "Tell me, what room is the lady in?"

The innkeeper's eyes swept over Miles assessingly, noting the rich cut of his clothing and the expensive leather gloves he carried. "Well, now, I'm not sure I should be giving out that information, sir. The lady, she didn't say anything about expecting a gentleman to be joining her. What if you're here to do her harm? I'd never forgive myself if . . ."

"I'm her husband," Miles announced, interrupting the man's prattle, "and I assure you, I am not intending my wife any harm. I've merely come to collect her and take her home."

By this time the innkeeper's wife had joined her husband behind the counter and was eyeing Miles speculatively. "Collect her? Is she running away from you, then?"

Miles gritted his teeth, incensed that these nosy strangers were demanding explanations about his domestic affairs. With an impatient sigh, he reached into his vest pocket and pulled out a flat wallet. Extracting a large bill, he slapped it on the counter. "I'm going to ask you again. In what room will I find my wife?"

The innkeeper looked down at the bill, then back up at Miles, a wide, nearly toothless grin spreading across his face. "Number six, my lord. Top of the stairs, third door on the right."

With a cursory nod, Miles turned away and took the stairs two at a time, striding down the hall until he reached the correct room.

He lifted his hand to knock, then hesitated a moment. What was he going to say when Victoria opened the door? During this whole mad day of charging about the countryside looking for her, he'd contemplated the tongue lashing he was going to give her when he finally found her. But now, as he stood there facing that moment, he suddenly realized that attacking Victoria with an angry outburst might very well be the death knell of their relationship.

Be calm, he told himself. *Talk to her. Find out why she left.*

Ask her if she really wants to end this thing. Then, whatever she says, abide by her answer.

Even while Miles's brain called for temperance, his heart cried out for him to take a very different tack. *Tell her you want her to come home with you, that you want her to be your wife and that you want to be her husband in every way—body, heart and soul. Tell her you want your marriage to work. Tell her you love her!*

Miles stood in front of the door for a long moment, still unsure how to approach the coming meeting. Finally he shrugged, deciding it was best to simply let the conversation take its natural course. Perhaps when he and Victoria actually started talking, it would become clear to him how to handle the situation. God, but he hoped so!

Lifting his hand again, he softly knocked. He heard a sound from within, confirming that Victoria was, indeed, inside the room, but the door remained closed and he received no answer to his summons. He knocked again, this time louder.

Finally a soft voice queried, "Who's there?"

"Miles."

An interminable silence ensued, lasting so long that Miles thought perhaps Victoria was planning to simply ignore him and leave him standing in the hall. Just as he was about to call to her again, the door opened slowly, revealing his wife standing on the other side.

A great swell of relief rolled over him at the sight of her, making him realize for the first time the abject terror he'd been silently harboring that he might never see her again.

For an endless moment Victoria just stared at him, taking in his muddy boots, his travel-stained cloak and the deep lines of fatigue and worry etched about his beautiful blue eyes.

"How did you find me?"

"I looked."

His simple statement was answered with a slight nod; then she stepped back and gestured for him to enter.

Miles walked inside, scanning the spartan interior of the

small room. There was a bed with a slightly sagging mattress, although the quilt covering it looked clean and the pillows were covered with snowy white cases. A small, marble-topped bureau with a pitcher and a basin sat against one wall, while a rickety table with two mismatched chairs stood under the solitary window.

"Would you like to sit down?" Victoria offered, closing the door and turning to face him.

Miles shook his head. "I want to talk to you."

Victoria clasped her hands tightly in front of her and nodded.

"Why did you leave me?"

His blunt question took Victoria by surprise and she blinked several times before answering. "Because I . . . I didn't see any point in staying."

The obvious honesty of her answer hit Miles like a blow to the chest. "Why not?"

Victoria turned away, no longer able to face his questioning eyes. Walking over to the window, she gazed outside, although her mind absorbed nothing of what her eyes were seeing. "I think we made a mistake."

"You do?"

She turned again, forcing herself to look at him. "Yes. Don't you?"

"I wouldn't have married you if I thought it was a mistake."

"You married me to save my honor."

Miles took a step closer, holding her gaze intently. "I married you because I wanted to."

His quiet, heartfelt words shattered Victoria's closely held control. "But you don't love me!" she cried. "And now, after the things I said to you the other night, it's obvious you don't even want me anymore."

Miles's eyes ran down the length of Victoria's curvy little body, taking in her generous breasts, her tiny waist and her gently flaring hips. "That's not true."

Victoria's breath caught in her throat at his provocative state-ment. She might be innocent in the ways of men, but there was no denying the look he had just given her and the truth in the hoarse comment that had followed. He did still, indeed, want her.

"Why did you ignore me last night at dinner?" she asked plaintively. "I wore that dress because I thought you'd like it, and I made a complete fool of myself in front of your parents by throwing you looks you didn't even notice."

"I noticed," he said softly, moving a step closer.

"But you ignored me!"

"You had hurt me. I wanted to punish you."

Victoria's eyes dropped. "You did an excellent job of it."

When Miles spoke again his voice was soft, contrite. "I'm sorry. It was wrong of me."

Victoria sighed heavily and stared down at her clasped hands. "You were justified in being angry. I said some terrible things to you the other night."

"Yes, you did. Did you mean them?" He was close enough now to reach out and touch her face. Running his knuckles down her cheek, he whispered, "Tory, do you really find my touch repugnant?"

Victoria slowly closed her eyes as she reveled in the heady sensation of his fingers against her skin. "No. I . . . I don't. I never have. I was just scared and . . ."

Suddenly she was in his arms and his lips were on hers, silencing her choked explanation with a kiss so charged with long-denied passion that it made her head swim.

"It doesn't matter anymore," Miles rasped, pressing his soft, warm lips to her ear, her temple, her eyelids. "None of it matters. The only thing that matters is that we're here together now."

"Yes," Victoria breathed. She threw her head back as she felt his mouth move toward her throat. "We're here. Together. Alone."

"I know you're scared about making love, but I'll never hurt you," Miles promised, his voice muffled as he buried his face in her neck.

"I know that," Victoria responded. And in her heart she did.

Reluctantly, Miles lifted his head, forcing himself to halt his caresses. Placing his hands on Victoria's cheeks, he tilted her face up until their eyes met. "Be my wife, Victoria."

Victoria's eyes drooped languidly, and this time it was she who ran her knuckles down his cheek. "Be my husband, Miles."

Slowly, exquisitely, he kissed her, forcing himself to be gentle as he tried to ignore the raging demands his aroused body was suddenly making on him. Swallowing hard, he again lifted his lips from hers. "Do you want some supper?"

With a slight smile, Victoria shook her head. "Not now."

Miles groaned and reached for the top button of her silk blouse. With a flick of his fingers, three buttons were suddenly open, exposing the upper swells of Victoria's breasts to his hungry gaze. He paused, his breath quickening. "I want to make love to you, Victoria, more than I've ever wanted anything in my life, but if you don't want me to, tell me now, because if I unfasten one more button, I don't think I'll be able to stop."

Victoria said nothing. Instead, she slowly lifted her hand and opened the fourth button on her blouse, her eyes never leaving his. "I want to be your wife, Miles."

As her soft admission reverberated through his head, Miles said a quick prayer that he'd be able to find the patience and control to offer this beautiful, trusting woman the initiation into love that she deserved. It had been months since he had indulged in any carnal pleasures and his virile body was already crying out for release, but he closed his eyes tightly for a moment and willed his rampaging lust into submission.

With gentle hands he pulled the bottom of Victoria's blouse out of her long skirt, releasing the remaining buttons and pushing the soft material over her shoulders and down her arms until it fell in a soft heap at their feet. A blush crept up Victoria's alabaster throat, suffusing its swanlike length with the rosy tinge of embarrassment. But, to her credit, she didn't flinch. Rather, she faced Miles proudly, her breasts almost completely exposed beneath the dubious protection of her gauzy chemise.

Miles drew in his breath at the beauty before him and he reached out a shaking hand to lightly trace his finger over the nipple peeping through the sheer cloth. "You're so beautiful," he breathed, lowering his head to kiss her breast.

Victoria remained silent, but a pleased little smile tilted the corners of her mouth. She glanced down at the top of Miles's head as he kissed her breasts, then shyly ran her fingers through his thick, golden hair.

She was hardly aware of when he unfastened her skirt, shimmying it over her hips until it pooled around her ankles. Her petticoat quickly followed, leaving nothing covering her legs but her stockings.

"Come here," he whispered, his voice sounding hoarse and breathless. Taking her by the hand, he led her over to the bed, gently pushing her down to a sitting position, then dropping to his knees between her legs.

Slowly, seductively, he removed her shoes and rolled her stockings down her legs, pulling them slowly off her feet, then bending to kiss her instep and the delicate hollow behind her ankle.

Victoria's heart slammed against her ribs as she felt his hands slide up her bare calves, over her knees, and along her thighs, but she didn't move away. Instead, she closed her eyes and let her mind wander, casting adrift all conscious thought and allowing only the feelings Miles was evoking within her to remain.

"I'm so glad you're not wearing one of those damn corsets." He smiled, running his hands up her narrow ribs until his thumbs met under the swell of her breasts.

"So am I," she murmured.

Burying his hands in her hair, he drew her forward and kissed her again, his tongue running along her lips, seducing her to open to him. Victoria promptly complied, then sighed with the first blush of ecstasy as his tongue tangled with hers and his thumbs brushed provocatively over her now erect nipples.

A streak of pleasure shot downward from her sensitive

breasts, settling deep within her and making her gasp as a hot, liquid coil of desire unfurled. "Oh, Miles," she groaned, unconsciously tightening her legs around his body where he knelt before her. "What are you doing to me?"

"Making love to you," he responded softly.

Tortured by the hampering confines of his clothing, he gave Victoria one last kiss, then got to his feet. Night had fallen since his arrival and the room was now cloaked in darkness. He felt his way over to the small table and lit the stubby candle that sat atop it. Quickly, he shucked his shirt, pants, boots and socks and was just reaching to unfasten his light summer underwear when he heard a shocked gasp coming from the bed.

"What are you doing?"

"Getting undressed," he answered, careful to keep his voice casual. "Making love is most enjoyable if it's done in the nude."

Victoria's eyes rounded to the size of saucers. None of her friends had ever mentioned this! From what they'd said, she had been under the impression that this act was always conducted in the dark, under the covers, and with nightclothes still very much in place.

"That must be an American custom," she said quickly. "I don't think people do it that way in England."

"Yes, they do," Miles assured her, fighting hard to keep his voice calm. "People everywhere do it this way."

"No, they don't," Victoria insisted stubbornly. "Someone surely would have told me if this was expected."

"Nothing is *expected,* Tory," Miles said gently, still standing with his back to her so she wouldn't see his raging erection. "Making love can be done any way a couple wants to . . . any way they feel comfortable."

"Well, I don't feel comfortable with my clothes off," she stated, her voice suddenly taking on a nervous edge.

Miles realized by Victoria's tone that he was in danger of eradicating all the progress they'd made in the last few minutes if he continued to insist they be naked. "All right, then," he said agreeably, "if you prefer, I'll leave my underwear on."

"I do prefer," Victoria nodded emphatically. "I'll leave mine on, too." She hesitated a moment, looking down at her scantily clad figure, then added, "Maybe I should put on my nightgown."

"No," Miles shot back, imagining with horror what kind of high-necked, long-sleeved, voluminous item that would be. "I mean, I like . . . your chemise." His eyes skimmed over her provocatively. "You look gorgeous in it."

Victoria's eyelids fluttered downward at his suggestive compliment. Seizing the moment, Miles turned and sauntered back to the bed. He had just about reached it when he heard her whisper, "You forgot to put out the candle."

Damn it! he thought, feeling his erection start to flag. What more could she say to break the mood? Maybe it was a good thing after all that he hadn't been with a woman in so long. If he was any less horny, his desire would never last through this nitpicking session.

"Sweetheart," he said patiently, placing one knee on the bed and pulling Victoria into his arms, "making love by candlelight is very romantic."

"But Mary Ann said that it's always done in the dark!"

Miles felt his jaw start to clench, but he tamped down hard on his growing irritation. "Let's compromise. I'll keep my underwear on because you want me to, and you agree to keep the candle lit because I want to. How's that?"

"Well, all right," Victoria acquiesced, her strict code of do's and don't's quickly starting to unravel as Miles began kissing her again.

Gathering her closer, Miles lay back on the bed, pulling her down on top of him and deepening his caresses. He ran his hands slowly down her back, sliding them along her hips, then dragging them upward again, bringing the short chemise with him until he'd successfully uncovered her bottom.

Turning her in his arms, he moved her over onto her back, pleased to see that the chemise had twisted itself around her middle, effectively baring her from the waist down. Bracing his arms alongside her, he leaned forward, blazing a hot, sensual trail with his tongue along the sensitive cords of her neck and down to her breasts. He paused a moment when he heard her sharp intake of breath, then continued on, running his lips erotically across the soft, round globes until his mouth settled over a nipple.

Victoria let out a little cry of pleasure as he gently sucked and teased the sensitive bud, her hands clutching at his shoulders as if she couldn't decide whether to push him away or draw him closer.

"Do you like this?" Miles asked softly, lifting his head.

"Oh, yes." She sighed. "It feels so . . ."

"Good?"

"Yes. Better than good. Wonderful."

Miles, whose lusty desire had returned with a vengeance the moment he'd begun kissing her again, realized that now was the moment. He had to get the damn chemise off of her, or he was going to go crazy. Drawing in a shaky breath, he whispered, "You know what feels even better?"

"Nothing could," Victoria moaned as he continued to toy with her breast.

Again he ran his tongue across her nipple, causing another little shriek of pleasure to escape her. "Oh, but there is something."

"Then do it!" Victoria cried, tossing her head back and forth on the pillow.

Miles's eyes widened at his wife's unexpectedly wanton comment. "We have to take our clothes off," he murmured.

Victoria's eyes snapped open. "We do?"

Lowering his head, Miles gently nipped at her exposed stomach. "Yes. It feels so much better. Trust me, sweetheart. Skin touching skin is wonderful."

Victoria hesitated for a moment, as if debating whether she could actually throw away a lifetime of teaching on the basis of this man's promises. Then, with a tremulous little sigh, she sat up and pulled her chemise over her head.

Miles's breath caught in his throat as he witnessed Victoria's beautiful body fully exposed to him for the first time. The candlelight threw its mellow glow across the perfect slope of her shoulders and cast dusky shadows across the ivory hills of her breasts. Her nipples were small, perfect and rose-colored, the skin taut and excited beneath his hungry gaze. Her hair fell over her shoulders like a dark cloud, shadowing her cheeks and making her smoky eyes appear large and luminous.

"You are the most beautiful creature I've ever seen," he breathed, his mouth dry and his pulse pounding. He continued to look at her, his eyes drinking in every curve and hollow of her body as his erection grew and strengthened with primal male appreciation.

Victoria's lowered eyes raised, skimming over her husband's massive chest and wide, muscular shoulders with equally rapt feminine curiosity. "All right, Mr. Wellesley," she whispered, reaching out and running a tapered nail shyly down his chest, "I'm naked, just as you wanted to see me."

"Everything about you is just as I wanted. Now the question is, do you want to see me?"

Victoria licked her lips unconsciously, her curiosity warring with her fears. "I . . . I don't . . . Yes."

Miles closed his eyes, thanking whatever god had just seen fit to smile down upon him. Slowly he stood up, pulling off his underwear, and then turned to face his bride in all his magnificent, golden splendor. "Just as God made me," he murmured.

Victoria's gaze slowly dropped from his face to his chest to the ribbed muscles of his abdomen and then . . . lower. Her eyes settled on his pulsing arousal, staring at the hard, velvety shaft so long that Miles actually felt a twinge of embarrassment.

"You look like King's Ransom," she said softly.

It was the last thing in the world that Miles expected to hear from his prudish little bride and, despite the intensity of the moment, a rumble of laughter rose in his chest. "Thank you very much."

Victoria looked at him in bewilderment. "Was that funny? I didn't mean it as a joke."

Miles saw the confusion in her eyes and his laughter faded. "I've just never been compared to a stallion before."

Victoria blushed crimson. "I shouldn't have said anything."

"No, no," he said, chuckling again. Leaning forward, he drew her into his arms. "I'm flattered, believe me." His voice and his laughter trailed off as Victoria's bare breasts rubbed sensuously against his chest.

Again he lowered her into the softness of the mattress, his caresses growing ever bolder as his hot kisses blazed a sensuous trail down the length of her body. He moved slowly over her stomach and abdomen, pausing finally with his mouth just inches away from the core of her womanhood. Blowing gently on the soft triangle of dark hair at the juncture of her thighs, he allowed her time to accustom herself to this newfound intimacy. Then, raising up on one elbow, he kissed her there, his lips soft and warm as they pressed against her sensitive skin.

Victoria moaned, causing him to glance up at her. He smiled when he saw the expression of sublime ecstasy on her face and redoubled his efforts, running his tongue erotically along the crease where her leg met her body.

She shifted restlessly beneath him, unconsciously changing her position so that her womanhood was again beneath his lips. Her unknowingly provocative movement brought Miles close to the brink of his control, and again he moved upward, his arms shaking as he positioned himself above her.

Running his tongue along her parted lips, he whispered, "Victoria?"

"Yes?" she mumbled, not bothering to open her eyes.

"Sweetheart, look at me."

Her eyes, glassy with passion, slowly opened. "Are we going to do it now?"

Miles nodded slowly. "Yes, and this first time it's going to hurt you a bit."

Victoria's eyes widened and, to Miles's consternation, filled with fear. "This is the bad part, isn't it?"

"There is no bad part, darling," he assured her. "But this first time it is going to hurt, and there's nothing I can do to stop that."

"I know. Everyone has told me how awful it is."

Miles closed his eyes, cursing the women who had felt it their duty to instill these ridiculous fears in her.

"It only hurts this once, Tory. I promise you, just this once." Slowly, with infinite gentleness, he lowered himself between her thighs and entered her. Their long, slow foreplay had made her wet and ready for him, but still, as he slipped inside her tight sheath, he could feel her wince and begin to draw away. Knowing that the best way to get past the pain was simply to do it, he shifted his hips, thrusting forward and breaking through her maiden's barrier, then covering her mouth with a passionate kiss as she cried out at the painful invasion.

"I'm sorry," he murmured, his lips against hers. "It's over now."

Victoria closed her eyes, trying hard to hold back the tears she felt building, but before they reached her eyes, the pain began to recede, to be replaced by another, far more pleasant sensation. She felt Miles begin to gently rock above her, and with each long, delicious stroke, a tingle of pleasure shot through her entire body.

She gasped as his rhythm increased, then began moving her hips in cadence with his. The exquisite pressure building inside her made her feel as if she was reaching for something— something nebulous and undefined but which promised an incredible reward if she could just seize it. She rose higher, higher, trying to grasp the elusive prize before her, then suddenly let loose with an ecstatic scream as she reached her goal and the spasms of fulfillment began to shake her.

She heard Miles's shout of masculine triumph, then felt a

sublime warmth filling her, suffusing her entire body with a sensation of completion and well-being that she'd never even dreamed existed.

Gradually their rhythm slowed, and Victoria wrapped her arms around her husband, easing him down on top of her, their bodies still intimately joined.

They lay there together for a long moment; then Miles slowly raised his head, smiling down at her lovingly. "Are you all right?"

Victoria was so overwhelmed by the experience they'd just shared that she couldn't answer. Instead, she merely nodded and urged his head back down again.

Much later, when their hearts had slowed and their bodies had cooled, Miles rolled away, pulling Victoria up against his side and rubbing her back with long, languid strokes.

Victoria smiled dreamily at his loving caress, then whispered, "You were right, Miles. There is no bad part."

"It only gets better," he promised. "Next time there won't be any pain. Just pleasure."

She sighed, stretching luxuriously. "I don't know why my friends don't like this. They must do it differently than we did."

Miles grinned with pleased satisfaction, his eyes closed, his body sated. "Yes, they must."

"There is one thing I'm disappointed about, though."

Opening his eyes, he looked over at her anxiously. "Disappointed? About what?"

"That we can only do it once a week."

"Once a week! Who told you that?"

"Mary Ann. She said that she and Tom do it once a week on Saturday nights. That's the only time."

"Oh, God," Miles groaned. "Poor Tom."

"What?"

"Never mind." He watched as Victoria's eyes drifted closed. "Tory?"

"Hmm?"

"Listen to me for a minute. Open your eyes."

With an effort, Victoria forced her eyes open. "Yes?"

"There aren't any rules about lovemaking, sweetheart. No schedules. We can do this as often as we want. Not just on Saturdays or Tuesdays or any other specific day. We can do it every night if we want to. Twice a night, for that matter."

"Twice a night?" Victoria gasped, her eyes snapping open. "You mean we could do it again right now?"

"Well, not *right* now," Miles chuckled, "but in a little while."

"How soon?"

He started to laugh and leaned over to kiss her. "My God, I've unleashed a monster! I'll tell you what: How about if we sleep for a couple of hours; then, if you want to, we'll do it again."

Victoria nodded happily and snuggled closer to him. "I will want to, but sleeping for awhile does sound good."

Miles gazed down at the beautiful woman lying next to him, his heart overflowing with tenderness. Sighing, he nestled her head deeper into the hollow of his shoulder. "You know, I think I would have lost my mind if I couldn't have found you."

Victoria smiled sleepily. "Do you really mean that?"

"Absolutely. Promise me that you'll never leave me again."

"I promise," she sighed, running a limp hand across his chest. "Now will you promise me something?"

"Anything."

"Promise me that you'll go to sleep now so that we can wake up and make love again."

Miles smiled with utter contentment. Who would have ever thought that this terrible day would end so wonderfully?

He closed his eyes.

Chapter 27

Victoria's eyelids fluttered open, then immediately closed again as a bright shaft of sunlight streaming through the window rudely stabbed her.

Reluctantly, she forced her eyes open again, looking around groggily as she tried to place where she was. A slight stirring next to her suddenly brought her to full awareness. She was in bed with Miles.

A flush of embarrassment washed over her as memories of the previous night flooded her mind. Raising the quilt a few inches, she glanced down at herself. Her blush deepened. She was completely naked.

Slowly turning her head, Victoria glanced over at the equally nude man lying next to her. Miles was still asleep, lying on his back with one arm over his head and the other thrown across her bare abdomen.

Victoria hastily reminded herself that this golden Adonis lying so intimately near her was, after all, her husband. Still, she suspected that there wasn't another married woman in her acquaintance who was waking up this morning to find herself naked in her husband's embrace. It simply wasn't proper—married or not.

Their lovemaking the night before had been scandalous enough, but at least it had been dark in the room, and even the candle that Miles had insisted upon had cast only a slight luminance over their naked forms. Now, however, the room was awash with sunlight. In fact, it was downright *bright* and their provocative state of undress, coupled with Miles's hand resting so possessively against her abdomen was shockingly risqué.

Moving as carefully as she could so as not to disturb her sleeping husband, Victoria attempted to slip out of bed. She simply had to cover herself before he woke up.

Unfortunately for her, her attempts to slide out from under Miles's hand only served to make matters worse. Her movements caused him to shift restlessly, running his hand up the length of her body until it settled over one of her bare breasts, then kicking the hot blanket off so his entire body was exposed to her wide-eyed gaze.

Victoria squeezed her eyes shut, telling herself that it was totally inappropriate for her to be gaping at her husband in his present naked state, but, almost against her will, her eyes popped open again.

Glancing up at Miles's face, she was vastly relieved to see that he was still asleep, his lips slightly parted and his breathing deep and even.

Slowly, despite her silent admonishments, Victoria looked down. Although she had seen Miles's manhood last night when he'd turned toward her in the candlelight, this morning it looked entirely different. Lying soft and flaccid, it now appeared more gentle and less intimidating than it had the previous evening. Victoria smiled, touched by how sweetly it nestled in its warm, golden nest, but her tender smile soon turned to a little moue of surprise as the object of her musings suddenly surged upward, stiffening and beginning to lengthen right before her astonished eyes.

She forced her gaze away, mentally chastising herself for watching this shocking phenomenon. Nervously, she looked again at Miles's face. His eyes were still peacefully closed. Was it possible that a man could accomplish this astonishing feat when he wasn't even conscious? It was absolutely incredible!

Despite her mind screaming at her to turn away, Victoria found herself powerless not to take one more peek. Bracing herself on one elbow to get a better view, she watched in rapt fascination as Miles's erection continued to grow. It was now jutting out from his body, no longer looking pale and tame. Rather, it was stiff and red, pulsing with lusty male vigor.

To Victoria's amazement, looking at Miles's thick, hard shaft seemed to create strange little spasms deep within her own body. She gasped aloud as she felt that same warm, liquidy rush that she had experienced last night. Squirming uncomfortably, she straightened her legs, trying to calm the sudden cravings she was feeling at the center of her being. It didn't help.

Rather, her breathing continued to quicken and her heart began to pound so hard that she was afraid it was going to jump out of her chest.

Stop this! she commanded herself. *What kind of woman are you? Ladies don't look at men this way. Close your eyes!*

But she didn't. Instead, she sat up, staring hungrily at the throbbing erection standing so proudly just inches away from her hand. She clenched her fingers into a tight fist and pulled her hand back against her chest, scandalized by the nearly overwhelming urge she had to reach out and stroke it.

So mesmerized was she by the erotic display in front of her that she nearly jumped out of her skin when a husky voice behind her murmured, "Go ahead, sweetheart. Touch it."

Jerking her head around, she stared in abject horror at Miles's smiling countenance. "Touch me, Victoria. I want you to."

"No!" she cried, wishing she could pull the quilt over her head and disappear. "I can't . . . I mean, I shouldn't . . . it's not proper."

"It's perfectly proper," Miles said softly. Covering her hand with his own, he slowly, inexorably moved it down and placed it against his arousal.

As if of its own volition, Victoria's hand unclenched. Gently, almost reverently, she curled her fingers around him, shivering in sensuous delight at the hot, velvety sensation of holding him within her hand.

Miles groaned throatily, his excitement heightened by the look of sublime pleasure that came over Victoria's face as she fondled him.

His eyes glazing with passion, he watched his wife stroke his turgid length, nearly coming off the bed when she reached lower to cup the soft, round globes beneath. "Come here," he growled suddenly, pulling her down on top of him so that the entire length of their bodies touched.

"I didn't do anything wrong, did I?" Victoria asked, puzzled as to why he'd interrupted her fascinating exploration.

"No," Miles rasped, rubbing his erection seductively against her. "In fact, you're doing everything just a little too right."

"Too right? What does that mean?"

"It means that if we don't slow down a little bit, things are going to be over way too fast."

Victoria had absolutely no idea what Miles was talking about, but she was so aroused by the feeling of his erection rubbing against her that she couldn't seem to form a coherent enough thought to ask any more questions.

"Is it all right to do this in the morning?" she asked, her voice tremulous.

"Like I told you last night, sweetheart, there aren't any rules. We can do it anytime we want to."

"But this seems so wicked. After all, it's broad daylight."

"Yes." Miles chuckled, turning her over and teasing a swollen breast with his tongue. "Great, isn't it?"

Victoria gasped as streaks of molten desire shot through her. "I feel like a wanton."

"And I feel like all my dreams have come true." Sliding downward, Miles kissed the soft skin on her stomach, then dipped his tongue into her navel, causing gooseflesh to appear all over her body.

Slowly rising, he knelt next to her, his eyes raking boldly over her body. "Do you know how beautiful you are? Every time I look at you, I feel like my blood's going to boil."

Victoria knew she should be embarrassed by Miles's intimate perusal, but instead she felt liberated by his sensuous compliment. Reaching up, she lightly drew her nails down his chest. "You're beautiful yourself."

Miles drew in a deep, shuddering breath as her hand continued its downward journey, then released a groan of ecstasy as she again began to stroke him.

"I like to touch you here," Victoria confessed, her voice barely audible.

"And I like to have you touch me there," he answered hoarsely. Reaching out, he ran his fingers over her abdomen, slowly trailing them lower and lower until they reached the juncture of her thighs. "I want to touch you there, too."

Victoria closed her eyes and held her breath, releasing it in a long, trembling sigh as she felt his fingers slide seductively over her slick, moist flesh and then disappear deep inside. Miles's intimate caresses started the delicious pressure building again, and she tossed her head back and forth, clutching the edges of the pillow and biting down hard on her lip. "Oh, Miles. Oh, God, Miles! Please . . ."

Miles smiled, knowing that with her limited experience, Victoria was hardly aware of what she was pleading for. But he knew exactly what she wanted and was more than happy to grant her surcease. Moving between her thighs, he lowered his head, kissing her and stroking her intimately with his tongue.

Victoria felt his mouth against her sensitive flesh and reflexively bucked her hips, a little scream of delight tearing from her throat.

Her lusty call was nearly Miles's undoing. Catching one of her flailing hands, he pressed it against his pulsating erection, then lowered himself over her.

Despite her modest upbringing, Victoria was a highly sexual woman. With sure instinct she guided him to her, lifting her hips to ease his entry, then hooking her heels behind his thighs and pressing downward. She gasped as she felt Miles's hard, thick length fill her, the sensation of him sheathed deep inside, coupled with the sheer eroticism his tongue had wrought, causing the climactic spasms to start even before he began love's ancient dance.

Miles felt Victoria begin to climax and let himself go, releasing his hot, potent seed after only a few thrusts. Their cries of completion mingled in the quiet morning air, filling the tiny room with the sounds of their shared pleasure. Finally they quieted, their groans of ecstasy fading to sighs of replete satisfaction.

Miles lifted his head from the hollow of Victoria's shoulder and shot her a teasing smile. "You know, for a proper young British matron, you sure do like your loving hard and fast."

Victoria squeezed her eyes shut, embarrassed to the core by his frank observation. "Is that bad? Is there something wrong with me that I like this so much?"

"God, no, there's nothing wrong with you!" he retorted, giving her a searing kiss. "In fact, everything is completely right with you, and that rightness has made me a very happy man."

Victoria's eyes widened with pleased surprise. "Really? Do I really make you happy, Miles?"

"If you make me much happier, I'll never be able to muster the energy to go home today."

Victoria grinned, vastly pleased with herself, her husband and the world in general. Turning toward him, she began drawing slow, lazy circles on his chest. "Miles?"

"Yes?"

"Do we have to go back today?"

Arching an inquisitive brow, Miles gazed at her in surprise. "Don't you want to go home, Tory?"

"Not today," she murmured, lightly grazing his pebbly little nipple with her fingernail. "Couldn't we just stay here for a few days?"

"Stop that!" he commanded, pointedly lifting her hand from his chest and placing it on the bed between them. "You're making me crazy. I can't talk if you do that."

Victoria smiled smugly, reveling in her newly discovered sexual powers.

Miles glanced around the shabby little room. "Do you really want to stay here? This room is hardly what I had in mind for our honeymoon suite."

"I love it." She sighed. "This bed is so comfortable."

"This bed is so *small.*"

"Cozy," Victoria corrected, snuggling closer, "not small. Cozy."

"I don't want to go home yet, either," Miles confessed, "but we could probably find more luxurious accommodations somewhere if you want to spend a few days alone."

"I definitely think a few days alone is a good idea," Victoria agreed languidly. "And if you really don't like it here, I suppose we could move. There's a village down the road a ways. Do you suppose they'd have a better inn?"

"That would be Wigginton," Miles mused. "I've been there a couple of times and I don't remember seeing anything much different than this. We'd probably have to ride to Newmarket to find something significantly better."

"That's half a day's ride." Victoria groaned tiredly. "I don't think I'm up to that right now."

Miles smiled in understanding, realizing that his innocent little wife probably was a bit tender after their passionate night and morning. Turning to face her, he pulled her into his embrace. "Let's just stay here, then."

Victoria yawned, the relaxing effects of their lovemaking getting the better of her. "Yes, let's," she mumbled. "I really do like this inn better than anywhere I've ever stayed." Her voice trailed off, replaced almost immediately by the sound of deep, even breathing.

Miles gazed down at her sleeping form and smiled tenderly. What a surprise the last twenty-four hours had been. He sighed, knowing that he'd never felt happier or more content in his life. Brushing a tousled lock of Victoria's hair back from her face, he gently kissed her forehead, realizing that if she'd told him she wanted to camp under a tree for the next few days, he would have agreed.

Shifting uncomfortably on the saggy old mattress, he muttered, "Cozy, Wellesley. Not small, cozy."

And closing his eyes, he sought his own rest.

Chapter 28

The next few days were halcyon. After sending his family a message, explaining that he had found Victoria and that they were going to spend a few days alone, Miles settled down to get to know his wife.

They spent their days taking long walks, snooping about the quaint little shops in the nearby village of Wigginton, sharing picnics and dreams in the verdant meadow behind the inn, making love in their cozy little bed.

Once the innkeeper and his wife found out that Victoria and the angry man who'd come to "collect" her were, in reality, a honeymooning couple who'd simply had a minor disagreement, they went out of their way to make their stay as pleasant as possible. Special meals were prepared, vintage wines in dusty bottles found their way up from the cellar and onto their dinner table, and small vases of fresh flowers magically appeared on the small bureau each morning after their room was cleaned.

One week stretched into two and then to three, causing the ecstatic innkeeper to begin joking with his friends that the free-spending nabob and his beautiful bride were never going to leave.

Finally, however, toward the end of the third week of their impromptu wedding trip, Miles told Victoria he thought it was time to go home. "Fiona and your sisters are going to be leaving next week," he reminded her, "and you and I need to sit down and figure out next year's breeding schedule for King's Ransom. It's time we got back."

Victoria looked up from the plate of roasted lamb she was eating and stared at her husband in astonishment. "You want to go over Ransom's breeding commitments with me?"

"Of course. He's your horse. Why wouldn't I?"

Victoria grinned, barely able to contain her delight. "I just thought that once we were married and my horses legally became your property, you probably wouldn't . . ."

". . . care what you thought?" Miles finished for her. "I can't believe you'd think that of me."

Victoria looked down at her food, her pleased grin fading to a shy smile. "You're surprising me in a lot of ways, Miles."

Miles reached across the table, picking up Victoria's hand and placing a gentle kiss in her palm. "Is that good or bad, my lady?"

"Good," she whispered, "all good."

Their eyes met, exchanging a heated message. Suddenly, the dinner laid before them no longer held any appeal. Simultaneously, they rose from the table. Miles grabbed the wine bottle and their yet unfilled glasses, and together they headed for the staircase leading to their room.

The innkeeper's wife, who was hovering near the door of the dining room, looked over at her husband in distress. "I'm afraid those two are going to lose five stone apiece before they leave here. They never seem to finish a meal."

The innkeeper chuckled and winked broadly at her. "Ah, Clairie, they've no need for food right now. They're living on love. Don't you remember those days, girl?"

Fifty-four-year-old Clairie Winestock looked over at her fifty-seven-year-old husband and nodded in fond remembrance.

"Of course I do, Will," she said. "Even though it's been thirty-five years, no woman ever forgets those days."

Will put his arm around his corpulent wife's waist and drew her close. "You were a pretty maid at sixteen, you were. Hard for a man to resist."

Clairie blushed and gave her short, bald husband an affectionate little shove. "Get back to your tap, Will Winestock, before you get me to thinking about such things as will prevent me from getting my work done."

Will nodded, but before he returned to the bar he laid a smacking kiss on his wife's plump cheek, thinking that if the couple upstairs found as much happiness as he and Clairie had, they'd be lucky indeed.

Victoria and Miles's return home was joyful. They had barely reached the top of the drive to Wellesley Manor before Seth and Nathan excitedly burst out of the house and onto the steps, shouting exuberantly, "Ma, Pa, come quick! Miles and that lady he married are back!"

James and Mary hurried outside to greet their son and his bride, welcoming them with heartfelt hugs. Mary looked closely at Victoria as she climbed off her horse, then broke into a relieved smile. It was obvious from her daughter-in-law's contented smile and relaxed demeanor that all was well between them.

"So, where have you two been?" James asked as they trooped into the house.

"We stayed at a little inn outside the village of Wigginton."

James nodded. "You mentioned that in your message. Where else did you go?"

"Nowhere. We just stayed there. It was . . . a very pleasant place."

"Obviously." Looking over at his wife, James threw her a wink and was rewarded by an answering smile.

"I'm so glad you got home in time for dinner," Mary told Victoria. "James and I can't wait to hear about your trip."

Victoria forced a smile, then tossed a pleading look at Miles. He responded with a good-natured shrug, knowing that she was worried about how they would explain to his parents that in three weeks away they'd barely left the inn.

"I think we'll go freshen up a bit before we eat," he said, catching Victoria by the elbow and propelling her toward the stairs. "Can dinner wait fifteen minutes or so?"

"Certainly." James nodded. "It can even wait a half hour if you like, so don't feel rushed. You've plenty of time to get whatever it is you need to get done."

Miles nodded and headed up the stairs while Mary gave her husband a playful poke in the ribs. "Shame on you!" she whispered, trying hard to conceal her laughter.

"What do you mean?" James protested innocently. "It sounds as if they stayed in the same little inn for three weeks without ever venturing outside. After keeping that kind of romantic schedule I'm sure they're half starved for each other after being forced to ride on separate horses all day."

Mary laughed aloud at her husband's bawdy assumptions, never seriously considering how right he was.

Miles barely had the master suite's door closed behind him before he grabbed Victoria and pulled her into his arms for a lusty kiss.

"Miles! I haven't even taken off my hat yet!"

"Your hat isn't what needs to come off," he answered huskily, cupping her bottom and pressing her hips against his. "Just feel what you've done to me."

Victoria responded by giving her suddenly ardent husband a scathing look. "Miles Wellesley, you stop that now! We only have fifteen minutes till dinner, and I have to change into something suitable."

"I know," he rasped, his fingers flying down the front of her bodice, "and I'm going to help you."

Victoria's next words were muffled as Miles again covered

her mouth with his own, thrusting his tongue seductively into the warm, dark cavern. Whatever argument she had been planning to voice died on her lips as his erotic play replaced her words with a throaty moan.

Miles peeled off the jacket of her traveling suit, throwing it haphazardly across the room as his mouth feasted on her partially exposed breasts.

"We don't have time," Victoria groaned, even as her hands fumbled with the front of his trousers.

"Yes, we do." Stepping away for a brief moment, Miles tore off his boots and socks, then peeled down his trousers and underwear, stepping out of them and turning toward her again.

Victoria watched breathlessly as his impassioned manhood sprang free from the confines of his clothing, then redoubled her efforts to hasten the removal of her skirt, petticoat and drawers, leaving her clad only in her gaping camisole.

"The bed!" she whispered. "If we muss the bed, the maids are sure to guess what we've been doing when they come to turn it down, and by morning the entire household will be snickering."

"Don't worry about it. We don't need the bed." At Victoria's befuddled look, Miles closed the space between them and backed her up to the wall.

"What are you doing?"

"Something new," he answered with a grin. Cupping his hands around her slender thighs, he lifted her. "Wrap your legs around my waist."

His provocative suggestion caused a jolt of excitement to run down Victoria's spine, and without hesitation she did as he bade. He, in turn, braced her against the heavy velvet drapes to cushion her back, then thrust eagerly into her welcoming warmth.

Placing his hand on the back of Victoria's head, he buried her face against his shoulder to muffle the shrieks of surprised delight he could hear building.

Seconds later, they climaxed together. As their shuddering

release faded, Miles slowly lowered Victoria back to the floor, then held her limp body close, stroking her mussed hair and whispering unintelligible words of love.

A full minute passed before Victoria felt that her legs would hold her. Clapping a hand over her mouth to hide her giggles, she turned shining eyes on her husband. "I can't believe we just did that! Look, we've crushed your grandmother's draperies."

"They'll hang out." Miles shrugged. Pulling his watch out of the pocket of the vest he still wore, he glanced down at it. "My, my, Mrs. Wellesley," he teased. "You are getting adept at this."

Victoria walked over to the commode, dipping a piece of linen into the basin and pressing it against her flaming face. "What do you mean?"

Miles swaggered over and dangled the watch in front of her. "All that, and we've still eight minutes to spare before dinner!"

Dinner was a riotous affair. All six of the younger Wellesley children were allowed to eat with the adults in honor of Miles and Victoria's return, creating an atmosphere around the huge table that could only be described as controlled chaos.

Finally, when the younger members of the family had finished their desserts and departed for their respective after-dinner entertainments, the adults sat back to enjoy their brandies and catch up.

James held up a cigar and raised his eyebrows questioningly, silently asking the ladies' permission to light it. When both of them nodded he puffed it to life, then blew out a long stream of smoke. "By the way, Miles, your mother and I have booked passage for America on October second. What have you and Victoria decided about going back with us?"

Victoria's eyes widened in stunned amazement. Jerking her head around in her husband's direction, she stared at him in disbelief. "America? What's this about us going to America?"

Miles frowned and threw his father an annoyed look. "Actually, Father, Victoria and I haven't discussed it yet."

James winced, mortified by his faux pas. "I'm sorry. I thought by now that you would have . . ."

"We haven't."

"Well, no matter," Mary interjected brightly. "There's plenty of time yet."

Miles could feel Victoria's eyes boring into him, but he remained staring stubbornly forward, refusing to meet her eyes. "So, Grandmother, how are things with the horses?"

Regina's gaze flicked between her grandson and his wife, wondering what she could possibly say to fill the angry chasm that had suddenly yawned between them. "The horses are all fine, dear. You missed the races at Ascot while you were gone, but we did very well. In fact, we were in the money in all but two that we entered."

Miles's gloomy expression lightened at this news. "Really? Any wins?"

Regina shook her head. "No, but we placed in two and showed in three more. Considering how young and inexperienced our stock is, I'm very hopeful for next year."

Miles nodded, agreeing that the following year could be a very big one for the Wellesley racing string.

"Oh, Victoria," Mary piped up, "you might be interested to hear this: I was over at Pembroke visiting with Lady Fiona last week and your stableman . . . what is his name?"

"George," Victoria supplied, her voice dull and lifeless.

"Yes, that's right, George. Anyway, while your stepmother and I were having tea, he came in to report that a mare named Spring Daffodil is in foal to King's Ransom. Lady Fiona seemed to think that you'd be pleased to hear that."

"I am," Victoria said quietly.

"You bred Spring Daffodil to Ransom?" Miles asked, his face betraying his pleasure at this news.

Victoria's voice was stony. "Yes."

"That's great. I was hoping you'd take my advice on that."

"Your advice had nothing to do with it," Victoria lied, still not looking at him. "George and I felt it would be a good match."

Miles's pleased grin disappeared. "I see. Well, at least we're all in accord as to what good potential that mating has."

Victoria shot him a cold look, then threw her napkin down and rose. "If you'll excuse me, I'm going to retire. It was a long ride today and I'm very tired."

"Certainly, dear," Mary murmured. "Sleep well."

With a parting nod, Victoria turned on her heel and stalked out of the room.

"Miles, I'm sorry," James blurted as soon as Victoria was out of earshot. "I had no idea that you hadn't discussed the idea of going to America with her."

"I should have," Miles admitted. "I just never seemed to find the right time to bring it up."

"There's no reason in the world why you should," Regina snorted. "You and Victoria have Pembroke to run, not to mention the fact that I was hoping you'd help me take over the management of Wellesley. Why in the world are you contemplating going to America when you have so many responsibilities here?"

"Because it's my home!" Miles barked, his voice much sharper than he'd intended. Seeing how shocked his grandmother was by his rudeness, he quickly added, "I've been hoping that Victoria and I could agree to live six months here and six months there."

"That seems like a somewhat rootless existence," Regina muttered. "After all, you're not vagabonds."

"Mother," James said quietly, "Miles and Victoria are adults. It's their decision, not ours. I'm sure they'll come to some agreement that will be acceptable to all parties involved."

"Right you are, my dear," Regina acquiesced, "but based on Victoria's reaction this evening, I'm afraid that agreement may be a bit difficult to achieve."

Miles sighed heavily. The last thing he'd wanted to do tonight was become embroiled in a heated discussion with his bride, but it looked as if there was no avoiding it. "I think I'd better go upstairs and talk to my wife," he said, getting to his feet and tossing back the remainder of his brandy. "I'll see you all in the morning."

Miles wasn't even through the bedroom door before Victoria lashed out at him. "How could you? How *could* you make plans to go to America without consulting me? Or was it that you weren't going to ask me to go with you? Perhaps you were planning to return home with your parents and leave your unwanted wife behind!"

"Actually, you're right," Miles snapped, his anger far out-stripping his judgment. "I *did* tell my father that I was going back to America with them and leaving you behind, but that was the night after we were married. Before the inn."

Victoria stared at him in horrified disbelief, her expression now more hurt than angry. "I see. You mean before I came to heel and crawled into your bed. And now that you've discovered what round heels I have when it comes to your legendary masculine charms, you've decided to keep me around?"

Miles's eyes darkened to a stormy gray. "I refuse to even dignify that comment with a response, madam." Whipping off his frock coat, he tossed it over a chair, then angrily began stripping off his trousers.

"What are you doing?" Victoria gasped.

"What does it look like? I'm getting ready for bed."

"Bed!"

"Yes, bed!" Gripping the back of the chair in frustration, Miles blew out a long, calming breath. "Look, Tory, we're both tired and neither of us is in the right frame of mind to discuss this, so let's just agree to leave it till morning. I think the thing to do now is go to bed."

"I think not!" Victoria countered. "After all this, do you

seriously expect to climb into bed with me? Because if you do, you're badly mistaken. You can take your rest elsewhere."

"You're damn right I expect to climb into bed with you!" Miles thundered. "And that's something else that we need to get straight. If you think that every time you get angry with me you're going to ban me from our bed, then *you're* badly mistaken. I refuse to be sent off to another room to sleep just because you're suffering a fit of pique. This is our bedroom, this is our bed and this is where I intend to sleep. Period."

"Well, fine!" Victoria huffed. "You just do that. *I* will sleep somewhere else."

"Suit yourself."

Turning away, Miles yanked at his tie, nearly choking himself as the recalcitrant material knotted around his throat. "God*damn* it!" he cursed, ripping the stubborn bit of silk in two and flinging the pieces at the wall.

In the midst of his rage, he heard the bedroom door close and whirled around to find himself alone. "Goddamn *her!*"

With a vicious kick, he sent a small, tapestried ottoman flying across the room. "And goddamn me for being such a fool as to think that anything had changed!"

Chapter 29

Miles turned over in the huge bed and irritably punched his pillow. Squinting, he glanced over at the clock on the mantel. Four o'clock and still he hadn't slept.

For three weeks he had squeezed into that tiny, lumpy bed at the inn and had slept like a baby every night. Now, here he was, lying on a feather mattress with down pillows beneath his head and covered by a satin comforter—and he couldn't sleep a wink. Of course, there had been one major difference between then and now: Victoria had been snuggled up with him at the inn. Now he was alone.

He kicked off the luxurious quilt and sat up. Why had he let the situation tonight get so out of hand? And why did Victoria seem to think that the solution to every domestic problem was to sleep in another room? Miles glared angrily at the door, wondering if she was having as much trouble embracing Morpheus as he was.

"Probably not," he snorted. "She's probably sleeping like a baby."

And why shouldn't she? his conscience asked. *After all, this was your fault, not hers. She was perfectly justified in being angry and hurt.*

Miles shook his head, trying to dispel the annoying little internal voice, but the niggling guilt wouldn't go away. The problem they'd had tonight *had* been his fault. He should have talked to Victoria, should have broached the subject of returning to America with his parents. There had been plenty of opportunities during their stay in Wigginton to bring it up. So why hadn't he?

"Because you knew she was going to object," he said aloud, "and you didn't want to upset things when they were going so well."

Still, it had been wrong of him not to tell Victoria of his desire to live in America part of the year. After all, she was his wife now, and she deserved to know his thoughts on such matters. That annoying little voice was right. He had no one to blame for their argument tonight except himself.

Go tell her you're sorry, his conscience prodded. *Go now!*

Miles stood up, pulling on his green silk wrapper and walking purposefully out of the master suite and down the hall to his old room. He didn't knock, but cracked the door and peeked in, not certain that this was even where Victoria had decided to sleep.

The only light in the room was afforded by a small candle burning on a stand near the bed. Despite the dimness, Miles could see that she was there. As he crept closer, he noticed that her eyes were open and she was watching him.

"Tory?" he whispered.

"Oh, Miles," she breathed, sitting up and holding out her arms to him. "I'm so sorry . . ."

"No," he responded, pulling her into his embrace and burying his head in her neck. "Don't apologize. I'm the one who's sorry. I should have talked to you weeks ago about the fact that I'd like for us to live at least part of the time in America."

"It's all right," Victoria cried, tears of relief streaming down her cheeks. "I don't care where we live, as long as we're together. If you really want to live in a primitive cabin in the wilderness, then we will."

Despite the poignancy of her words, Miles couldn't help but smile. Raising his head, he looked down at her, brushing her tears away with his thumbs. "Victoria, my parents' home in Colorado is hardly a 'primitive cabin.' It's two stories with eight bedrooms, four bathing chambers, servant's quarters for six, and a front room big enough to host a party for two hundred."

"But that's your parents' home," Victoria murmured. "I don't think I'd be comfortable living with them all the time. Couldn't we have a house of our own?"

"Of course we can. I'll build you any house you want. A mansion to rival Pembroke, if that's what you desire."

"Oh, I don't need anything that grand." She giggled.

"Then how about something in between a sod hut and a palace? How would that suit you?"

"Perfectly," Victoria murmured, throwing her head back as he began kissing her neck. "But Miles?"

"Yes?" His voice had become thick and muffled as he began to lose interest in the conversation and concentrated instead on kissing the ripe curves of her breasts.

"Do we have to go back with your family in October?"

Slowly, he lifted his head, the expression on his face perplexed. "You don't want to?"

Victoria smiled shyly. "I'm not sure it would be a good idea."

"Why not?"

Victoria looked away, and despite the deep shadows, Miles could see a blush color her cheeks. "Because I think you're going to be a father in the spring, and I'd really like our first child to be born here in England."

Miles's mouth dropped open in astonishment. "You're going to have a baby? Already? My God, Tory, we've only been married a month. How could you even know yet?"

Victoria raised shining eyes to his. "I'm not absolutely sure yet, but I'm ... well, I'm ..."

"Late?" He smiled.

If possible, the embarrassed hue in her cheeks turned an even deeper shade of rose. "Yes."

Miles sat for so long without moving that Victoria began to worry that he was not pleased to hear her news. Then, suddenly, he reached for her, gathering her close. "Oh, sweetheart," he sighed, kissing her tenderly, "you've just made me the happiest man on earth."

Victoria smiled tremulously and, again, her eyes filled with tears. "I'm so glad you're not upset," she confided. "I was afraid that . . ."

"Upset!" Miles blurted. "Why would I be upset?"

"Well, because it happened so fast. I thought maybe you'd rather we didn't have any children for awhile."

"Nonsense! I want a big family, and the sooner the better. In fact, I hope we have as many children as my parents did."

Victoria smiled with pleasure at his exuberance, although the thought of raising a tribe of children the size of Miles's family was still a bit daunting. "I think you're getting a bit ahead of yourself, Mr. Wellesley. One is plenty for now."

"Well, yes, for now."

"And remember, I'm not really sure yet. It could be a false alarm."

Miles shook his head. "*I'm* sure. It's not a false alarm."

Victoria giggled and lay back against the plush pillows. "Oh? And how can you be so sure?"

"A father knows these things." Miles grinned. Pulling back the blanket, he crawled into bed beside her, pulling her into his arms. "I love you, Tory."

Victoria's breath caught in her throat. Never, during all the time they'd known each other, and even during their three glorious weeks in Wigginton, had Miles ever said those words to her. She turned toward him, her eyes soft. "I never thought you were going to say that to me."

Miles's brow furrowed. "What do you mean? I've said it before."

Victoria shook her head. "No, you haven't, and I've been waiting and waiting."

"I'm sure I've said it before," Miles argued, frowning in consternation. "You probably just haven't heard me."

"Believe me, if you had said it, I would have heard you."

"Well, maybe I just *thought* it, then."

"Maybe . . ."

"Regardless," he whispered, running a finger gently down her cheek, "whether I've thought to say it out loud or not, it's true, and has been for a very long time now."

Victoria was so touched by Miles's quiet declaration that for a moment she thought she was going to cry again. Instead, she looked at him, her eyes overflowing with love, and said, "It's true for me too."

"Really, Tory? Do you really mean that?"

"Yes," she whispered. Raising herself on one elbow, she kissed him with all the love she'd felt for so long. "I love you with all my heart, my beautiful husband."

Miles sighed and closed his eyes, sure that if he lived to be a hundred, he would never be happier than he was at this moment.

Rebecca walked into the library where Victoria and Fiona were sorting through some of Sir John's belongings and cleared her throat nervously. "Lady Victoria?"

Victoria looked up from the stack of papers she was reading. "Yes?"

"You have a . . . message."

Victoria's hands tightened around the documents she held. Swallowing hard, she forced a calmness into her voice she was far from feeling. "A message from whom, Rebecca?"

"Lord Guildford," Rebecca mumbled. Stepping forward, she thrust the sealed envelope into Victoria's hand. "This is the third one this week, my lady."

"I know," Victoria acknowledged. "Is the messenger waiting for a response?"

"Yes, my lady."

"Well, please tell him there will be none and send him on his way."

Rebecca curtsied and hurried out of the library. As soon as the double doors were securely closed behind her, Fiona whirled around, eyeing Victoria accusingly. "Have you told Miles about the notes Harrison keeps sending?"

Victoria threw the envelope down on the desk and returned to shuffling papers, stubbornly remaining silent.

"Victoria Ann, did you hear me?"

Victoria sighed, wondering why it was that whenever an elder called you by both your given and your middle name, it immediately made you feel as if you were eight years old and in big trouble. "Yes, I heard you, Fiona."

"Then please show me the courtesy of answering my question. Have you told Miles about these notes?"

Impatiently, Victoria threw the papers down. "No, I haven't told him. Now that I've answered your question, could we please get back to work? We have a lot of documents still to go through and not a lot of time."

"We're not going to do anything until you open that message and tell me what it says."

With a mutinous glare, Victoria grabbed the envelope from the desk and ripped it open, quickly scanning the brief message and then handing the single sheet to Fiona.

Fiona looked down at the hastily scrawled words, her hand circling her neck in distress as she read.

Victoria,

I *must* talk to you as soon as possible. Why have you ignored my previous messages?

It is imperative that we decide what we're going to do to get you out of this unfortunate situation you're mired in.

Meet me at the Pembroke stables at eight o'clock tomorrow night or I will be forced to tell Wellesley all about us.

Yours,
Harrison

"Good God in heaven!" Fiona cried. "What is going on between you and this man? Have you actually told him that you want him to help you extricate yourself from your marriage to Miles?"

"Of course not!" Victoria retorted. "And there's nothing going on between Harrison and myself, I swear it! I don't know what has gotten into him, Fiona. You know very well that we were never more than friends, and yet, ever since Miles started courting me, Harrison has acted like a jilted suitor."

Fiona shot Victoria a quelling look. "You *must* tell Miles about this, Victoria. Obviously, Harrison believes that there was more between the two of you than simple friendship, and these notes are beginning to sound almost threatening. You must let Miles handle this situation."

Victoria sighed tiredly. "I don't want to upset Miles with this. He's never liked Harrison and I'm afraid if I tell him, there will be real trouble between them."

"There may well be," Fiona acknowledged, "but the fact still remains, someone must make it clear to Harrison that these notes will not be tolerated. As your husband, it is Miles's duty to do so."

"I just keep thinking that if I ignore the messages, Harrison will give up and stop sending them."

"I don't think that's going to happen," Fiona stated flatly. "How many have you received now?"

"Five."

"And every one you've shown me becomes more demanding. I don't believe Harrison has any intention of giving up. Now promise me that you will show this to Miles and let him handle Harrison as he sees fit."

Victoria stared down at her clenched hands, refusing to make that promise.

"Victoria?"

"All right," she snapped. "I'll speak to Miles."

"Tonight?"

Victoria looked at her stepmother with anguished eyes. "I can't tonight, Fiona. Tonight is the viscountess's ball, and if I tell Miles about this, it will ruin the evening for both of us."

Fiona nodded reluctantly. "All right, then; first thing tomorrow. Promise?"

Victoria sighed heavily. "All right. I promise."

"If you'll all gather around for a moment, Victoria and I have something we'd like to say."

Three hundred faces lifted toward Miles where he stood atop a small dais at the end of his grandmother's ballroom. Regina had insisted on giving a party before Fiona and the twins left for America and, despite the short notice, nearly everyone on her extensive list had accepted.

Miles drew Victoria up beside him and, at her inquisitive expression, gave her a quick, reassuring smile. Turning back to the waiting crowd, he said, "First of all, we'd like to thank you for coming tonight. Although it is a sad occasion for all of us to see Lady Fiona and Ladies Georgia and Carolina leave us, we are happy we could get all of you together tonight to wish them Godspeed."

Turning to look at the misty-eyed Fiona, he bowed slightly. "I would like to personally thank you, Lady Fiona, for all you have done for my wife. So often we hear stories of wicked stepmothers and sorely neglected stepchildren. You, however, are an ideal example that this relationship can be as warm and loving as that between a mother and her natural daughter. I know how much you mean to Victoria and I want to assure you that even though we are going to be living on different sides of the Atlantic . . ." He paused a moment to whisper to

Victoria. "Most of the time anyway . . . you will always be with us in our hearts. And we want you and Georgia and Carolina to know that we look forward to your visiting us here very soon and to our visiting you in Virginia." Lifting the champagne glass he was holding, he added, "To the ladies Pembroke! May your journey be safe and your new life everything you dreamed of."

The crowd chorused his toast with "To the ladies Pembroke!" as the air rang with the tinkle of three hundred glasses clinking together. Once everyone had sipped their wine, they again turned toward Miles.

"Oh," he chuckled, "so you guessed I hadn't quite finished, had you?"

The crowd laughed heartily.

Putting an affectionate arm around Victoria's waist, he added, "Well, you were right. I know that my wife may be a little put out with me for making this announcement, but I am so elated with this news that I want to share it with everyone—and especially with Lady Fiona before she departs tomorrow morning."

He heard Victoria's sharply indrawn breath and threw her a sheepish look. "Don't be angry," he whispered.

Turning back to the crowd, he said, "I am happy and proud to announce that in May of next year, Victoria and I will be welcoming our first child."

A ripple of surprise and excitement ran through the crowd, followed by a spontaneous round of applause. Mary Wellesley clapped her hands to her cheeks and turned delighted eyes on Regina, who was smiling equally broadly.

Fiona let out a little shriek of glee and raced up onto the dais to hug Miles and Victoria exuberantly. Georgia and Carolina were awash with happy tears and James just grinned, throwing his eldest son a triumphant look.

Victoria didn't know how to react to Miles's unexpected announcement. Although she now knew beyond a doubt that she was, indeed, pregnant, she hadn't planned to tell anyone outside the family about her condition for at least another month. Miles had certainly put a crimp in those plans, so she decided she might as well just smile and accept the multitude of congratulations that were being shouted at her from every direction.

Her eyes scanned the enthusiastic crowd, settling on the one person who was not smiling. Harrison Guildford met her gaze with an icy look of contempt, his expression a mask of rage and his frown so deep that his mouth appeared to be nothing more than a cruel slash across his face.

Victoria drew in her breath in surprise, stunned by his sinister look. Quickly turning back to Miles, she smiled wanly. "Can we dance now?"

Miles looked at her in bewilderment. "What's wrong, Tory? You're not really upset that I told everyone, are you?"

"No," she said, glancing over her shoulder to find Harrison still staring at her. "I'd simply like to dance."

Miles studied her for a moment, perplexed and concerned by the apprehensive expression in her eyes. "Are you sure you're all right? You look a little strange. You feel all right, don't you?"

"I'm fine," Victoria gritted through clenched teeth. "I just want to dance!"

Miles shook his head, convinced that something was very wrong but not knowing what more to ask without further angering his wife. At last he decided to accede to her wishes. Holding out his arm, he said cordially, "May I have the pleasure of this dance?"

Victoria threw him a relieved smile, and together they stepped down from the dais, mingling with the congratulatory crowd as the orchestra struck up a waltz.

They had barely made it once around the dance floor before Miles felt a hard jab to his shoulder. Remembering when he'd last felt that same rude gesture, he wasn't surprised when he turned and found Harrison Guildford at his elbow.

Their eyes met, and immediately Miles knew he had an enemy. "What do you want, Guildford?" he asked coldly.

"I want to dance with Victoria," Harrison announced bluntly. "Since I wasn't offered the courtesy of an invitation to your wedding, I've not yet had a chance to congratulate her on your nuptials. Now I see that you two have moved way past that point and on to the next step. Or perhaps I have that backwards. Which did come first, Wellesley? The nuptials or impending parenthood?"

Miles's eyes turned stormy and Victoria saw his fists ball at his side. "I'm afraid I'm going to have to refuse your most graciously articulated request, Guildford. Since Mrs. Wellesley is in a delicate condition she has to limit her dance card from now on. Of course, I have claimed this first waltz and then we're going to sit down and rest for the remainder of the evening. I'm sure, however, you'll understand, especially considering your eloquence tonight in expressing your happiness for us."

The hatred in Harrison's eyes as he glared at Miles was terrifying, and suddenly Victoria was glad that Miles wasn't going to permit him to dance with her. She breathed an audible sigh of relief when Miles turned his back on the seething man and danced her away.

"Thank you," she whispered, leaning her forehead against his shoulder. "I really didn't want to dance with him. I don't know what's come over him lately. He used to be such a nice man. My heavens, we were friends for years. Now, he always seems to be angry."

"He *is* angry," Miles growled. "I married the woman he wanted and he's not taking his defeat graciously."

"Oh, Miles, Harrison and I never had that kind of relationship!"

"Perhaps in your mind," Miles muttered. "At any rate, I don't like him and I don't trust him. Unless you have an objection, I don't want him anywhere near you."

"I think you're overreacting a bit," Victoria chided gently, "but the man means nothing to me and I have no objection to not seeing him anymore. I don't even know who invited him here tonight."

"I think he was on Fiona's list."

"Probably. Harrison was a great favorite of my father's, and despite how strangely he's been acting toward me since our marriage, I suppose Fiona really didn't feel that she could exclude him."

Miles looked at Victoria, his expression startled. "What do you mean, 'since our marriage'? When have you seen Guildford since we married?"

"I haven't, but he . . . well, he's sent me a couple of rather strange notes."

Miles stopped dancing. "What are you talking about?" he demanded. "What kind of notes?"

Victoria looked around apprehensively, noticing how many people were suddenly staring at them. "Lower your voice," she pleaded. "I don't want to discuss this now. I'll tell you about it later."

"No. You'll tell me about it now." Taking her hand, Miles led her off the dance floor and out into the foyer. Glancing around hastily to make sure they were out of earshot of the many milling guests, he said, "Now, what is this all about?"

"Oh, God," Victoria groaned. "I wish I hadn't said anything."

Miles remained silent, but his eyes bored into hers, demanding an answer to his question and brooking no argument.

Victoria drew a deep breath. "I have received several notes from Harrison since we returned from our trip."

"What kind of notes?"

"Strange little messages, asking that I meet him. In each one, he's written that it's imperative he talk to me alone."

A dark cloud of anger built in Miles's blue eyes. "And what have you answered?"

"I haven't."

"You've just ignored him?"

"Yes."

Miles nodded approvingly. "You did the right thing, although I wish you'd told me about this sooner."

"I didn't want to upset you."

"Tory, what upsets me is you keeping secrets from me."

Victoria smiled, loving the care and concern in his voice. "All right, Miles. If I get another note from him, I'll show it to you."

"You won't get another note," Miles growled. "I'll see to that." Holding out his hand, he forced a thin smile. "Come on, we'd better go back inside."

Arm in arm, they strolled back into the ballroom. Miles directed Victoria to sit beside Fiona, then strode aggressively across the dance floor to where Harrison stood talking to another man.

"I need to speak with you," he demanded, interrupting Harrison in midsentence. "Now."

Harrison raised his eyebrows haughtily. "I'm in the middle of a conversation, Wellesley. You'll have to wait."

"Either we talk privately," Miles gritted, "or we talk here in front of Mr. Fitzpatrick. The choice is yours."

Harrison's mouth thinned, but he excused himself from his friend's company and followed Miles out onto the balcony.

They were barely outside when Miles turned on him, stepping so close that their noses almost touched. "Stay away from my wife, Guildford, or by God, you'll be sorry. Do you understand me?"

Harrison was taken aback by the threat in Miles's words, but he covered his trepidation with a smug smile. "There are a lot of things between Victoria and myself that you have no knowledge of, Wellesley, and if you think that coercing her into a marriage she didn't want is going to wipe out all that we've shared—and will continue to share—I'm afraid you've greatly underestimated us."

Miles grabbed the front of Guildford's starched shirt and slammed him up against the ballroom wall. "You listen to me, you bastard. You send another note to my wife and you'll find it's me who answers your summons."

"Take your hands off me!"

"Certainly," Miles replied, releasing the man, then looking at his hands as if they were dirty. "Just remember what I said. Stay away from Victoria or you'll answer to me."

"Do you seriously think you can scare me with physical threats, Wellesley? How pathetic it is that at the first sign of a challenge, you have no more intelligent response than to resort to your crude American ways."

Miles smiled coldly. "You're right, Guildford. I *am* an American, and just as you say, we're a crude—and violent—lot. We have dozens of primitive traditions in my country, and one of them is the method we use to handle men who are foolish enough to try to move in on our wives. We don't settle matters as you gentlemanly Brits do with orchestrated duels or refereed boxing matches. We just get down on the ground and brawl." Miles paused, shrugging elaborately. "Unfortunately, it isn't uncommon for somebody to end up dead—usually the person who is the least accomplished at brawling. And since I've been using this method to settle differences since I was a boy and I very much doubt that a gentleman of your esteemed stature has, you'd probably be well advised to heed my words. Simply put, Guildford, if you continue to bother my wife, I'll kill you."

Miles ended his speech by raking his eyes over Harrison as if he were of no more consequence than an annoying insect. Then, with a last sneer of disgust, he turned and sauntered back into the ballroom.

Chapter 30

Harrison Guildford reclined in his plush bed, a glass half filled with gin dangling from his fingers and a drunken sneer contorting his handsome face.

So the prissy bitch was pregnant, was she? Well, maybe Wellesley was a better man than he'd given him credit for. Either that, or the most potent one he'd ever met. Harrison closed glassy eyes, trying to imagine tight-lipped, starchy Lady Victoria Pembroke writhing in the throes of passion, but the vision just wouldn't come. Knowing Victoria as he did, it was more likely that while Wellesley thrashed around atop her, she was probably concentrating on doing her duty to God and Queen.

Still, Harrison had to hand it to Miles. The American had got the little prig with child far more quickly than he would have ever guessed possible.

Unfortunately, the fact that Victoria was now in the family way tied her to Wellesley so firmly that for the first time Harrison had to seriously face the possibility that he might not be able to drive a wedge between them.

He shook his head angrily. Things had appeared to be going

so well. Everyone had said that the marriage between Miles and Victoria had been one of opportunity on her side and convenience on his. And Harrison knew for a fact that Victoria had fled her bridegroom the night after their wedding; the man he'd hired to spy on them had been hiding in the bushes at the edge of the Wellesley estate and had seen her take flight.

Somehow, though, between that night and the day three weeks later when his agent reported that Mr. and Mrs. Wellesley had returned from wherever it was that Miles had finally run Victoria to ground, the couple had managed to put their relationship to rights—at least right enough to have conceived a child together.

Harrison chuckled as he remembered the stunned look on Victoria's face when, at the party that night, he'd alluded to the fact that it was possible the pregnancy had come before the wedding. Was she really so naive that she didn't know that people all over the shire were bound to jump to that conclusion?

"Well, what the hell," he slurred, upending his glass and draining it. "She wasn't much, anyway." He stared morosely at the wall, knowing that even as he tried to convince himself he didn't care, he actually cared very much. All the plans he'd made, all the dreams he'd had of owning the vast Pembroke estate and the superlative herd of horses that went with it were now shattered.

It was a terrible blow to his ego to admit that he'd failed to win Victoria. For years he'd set his sights on the beauteous Georgia, but she had never so much as given him a look. Finally he'd decided he had better concentrate his efforts on Victoria, even though she was not the kind of voluptuous, eye-catching woman he favored. Surprisingly, as they'd gotten to know each other better, he'd found that he actually enjoyed her company, despite the fact that she didn't set his loins on fire the way her younger sister did.

How could he have failed? He'd done everything exactly right: taking his time with the standoffish spinster, never press-

ing her physically, never demanding more from her than she
was willing to give—and that had been precious little, indeed.

He could see now that doing a slow dance with Victoria's
affections had been a mistake. But who would have ever
guessed that someone as unpolished and earthy as Miles Wellesley would move in on her? Harrison shook his head, still hardly
able to believe that Victoria had actually fallen for the crass
American, married him and conceived a child all within a few
months' time.

With a grunt of disgust, he reached for the decanter next to
his bed and splashed another liberal portion of gin into his
empty glass.

"Goddamn it, it's not fair," he cursed, sinking lower and
lower into an abyss of self-pity. "A whole year wasted on her.
The least I deserve is some recompense for my time."

He closed his eyes, picturing King's Ransom. There was the
real loss. What couldn't he have done with that horse! Run
him, bred him, sold him. The stallion was a veritable money
pot just waiting to be dipped into, but Harrison seemed to be
the only one who realized it. Despite all his subtle suggestions
to John Pembroke to expand the stallion's breeding book, the
old fool had clung stubbornly to the idea that limiting the
horse's output would drive up the price of his foals.

"Utter nonsense," Harrison snorted, taking another long swallow. Breed the hell out of the horse, and even if the price of
his offspring did drop, the loss would be more than compensated
for by doubling the number of available foals for sale each
year.

"I could have made a fortune," Harrison groused. "*Should*
have made a fortune. The damn horse should have been mine."

Suddenly he straightened, pushing himself up against the
mountain of pillows at his back as an idea dawned.

He could still salvage his dream. Nobody guarded the Pembroke stables at night. He could simply take the horse, hide
him somewhere until the inevitable fury died down, and then
sell him. Surely there were breeders in France or Italy who

would pay a pretty price for a Thoroughbred of King's Ransom's quality. It might not net him the long-term money he could have made through ten years of heavy breeding, but the cash the stud would command would set him up for a good long time. And cash was something he desperately needed. Something his philandering, gambling father had left him with very little of.

"I deserve it," he intoned righteously. "If I can't have the girl, then the least I deserve is the money that horse will bring and, by God, I'm going to have it."

His plans made, Harrison sank back into the pillows, closing his eyes as he fell into an inebriated stupor. The glass of gin slid out of his limp fingers and hit the floor with a muffled thump.

"Victoria, what a wonderful surprise! Come in, my dear, and let's have a cup of tea."

Victoria smiled warmly at Mary Ann Parks and stepped into the foyer of her lavish home. "I know it's horribly rude of me to just drop by, but I was out riding and . . ."

"Nonsense!" Mary Ann interrupted. "I'm delighted to see you. I've been meaning to send you an invitation for tea, but I've been so busy directing the servants in finishing the summer housecleaning that I haven't had a single minute to myself."

Victoria looked around the immaculate house, smiling with secret amusement. Like many other young wives, Mary Ann subscribed to the theory that her house was never quite as clean as it could be and nearly drove her servants to distraction in her endless quest to unearth and destroy a forgotten bit of dust.

Mary Ann led Victoria down the hall and into the parlor, gesturing toward the same chair she'd sat in the last time she'd been there. They seated themselves and, after ringing for tea, Mary Ann turned to her guest. "The viscountess certainly gave a wonderful party last week. Tom and I had such a good time."

"Yes, it was lovely, wasn't it?" Victoria agreed. "I just wish the occasion hadn't been a farewell party for Fiona and the twins."

Mary Ann looked at her sympathetically. "Did they get off all right?"

"Yes," Victoria answered sadly, "and I miss them already."

"I'm sure you do. I know how close you all are."

A silence fell between the two friends; then Mary Ann said brightly, "But your wonderful news! That certainly must be perking up your spirits. You're so lucky, Victoria, to already be with child. Here I have been trying for nearly five months with no success, and you ... why you've barely been married a month!"

Victoria nodded happily. "Those were Miles's words exactly."

Mary Ann sighed and shook her head wistfully. "And besides having a baby to look forward to, now you don't have to ... well, you know. What we talked about before. Just think, since you're already in the family way, you don't have to even consider that responsibility until next summer. I envy you so."

Victoria cocked her head, gazing at her friend speculatively. "That 'responsibility' is one of the things I wanted to talk to you about, Mary Ann."

At Mary Ann's perplexed look, Victoria continued. "Do you know if it's all right to keep on doing ... well, you know, what we talked about before, even if you're already with child?"

Mary Ann's eyes widened with astonishment. "Actually, I've never heard that it's *not* all right, but then, I've never talked to anyone who wanted to." She paused a moment; then her eyes widened even further. "Victoria, are you saying that you actually *enjoy* Miles's attentions?"

Victoria blushed a deep crimson. "I suppose it's scandalous to admit it but, yes, I do enjoy Miles's attentions."

Mary Ann was clearly flabbergasted. "You enjoy it ..." she mused, staring off into space and shaking her head. Returning her gaze to Victoria, she wrinkled her nose with obvious distaste. "Don't you find it ... messy?"

"Messy?" Victoria giggled. "No."

"Or boring?"

Now it was Victoria's turn to look flabbergasted. "Boring? Never!"

Mary Ann tried again. "But don't you think the whole thing is sort of, well, primitive and . . . uncouth?"

Victoria thought for a moment, then shrugged. "I guess in a way it is, but, oh, Mary Ann, the way Miles makes me feel!"

"Feel? You mean, uncomfortable?"

"No! When Miles kisses me and . . . all those other things people do in the marriage bed, I feel . . . transported."

"Transported," Mary Ann repeated, sounding as if she'd never heard the word before. "Transported where?"

Victoria smiled shyly. "To heaven."

Mary Ann's mouth dropped open. "You're joking, aren't you?"

Victoria's dreamy expression answered that question before she ever opened her mouth. "Not at all. I love being in Miles's arms, having him kiss me and whisper little things to me. I know it's probably terribly improper, but I just love it."

"He whispers to you?"

"Oh, yes, and that's one of the best parts. Doesn't Tom ever whisper sweet words to you?"

Mary Ann leaned back in her chair, casting Victoria a dubious look. "No, Tom doesn't whisper to me, Victoria, and neither do any of our other friends's husbands that I know of."

"Well, what *do* you two do?" Victoria blurted.

Mary Ann thought a minute, then said, "We don't do much, actually. Tom and I have reached a sort of understanding about this. We both know that we're going to do it on Saturday nights from eleven till eleven twenty. But, believe me, we don't discuss it."

"Well, maybe you should," Victoria suggested. "And maybe you should try being more adventurous."

"Adventurous?" Mary Ann straightened in her chair, her curiosity piqued. "How?"

"Well, for instance, try it on a Tuesday morning. It's a completely different experience in the daylight."

"Tuesday morning!" Mary Ann gasped. "Now I know you're teasing."

Victoria shook her head and raised her eyebrows meaningfully.

"You're not teasing?" Mary Ann squealed. "You and Miles . . . on Tuesday *mornings?*"

"And Wednesday mornings and Monday afternoons and . . .'

Mary Ann clapped a hand over her mouth and gaped a Victoria incredulously. "I think I'm beginning to understand why you're already with child. How could you not be?"

Victoria had the good grace to blush, but her self-satisfied little grin belied any real embarrassment.

"And you say you enjoy it," Mary Ann repeated, as if she still couldn't quite believe that was possible. "Every time?"

"Every time."

"And you never get . . . tired of it?"

"Never."

Mary Ann exhaled a wistful breath and shook her head. " wish I knew your secret—and don't tell me it's doing it in the morning, because Tom finally caught me one Sunday and know it's not just that—unless, of course, Tuesdays are a lo different than Sundays."

"Tuesdays are no different than Sundays." Victoria laughed "And you're right. It is a lot more than just the time of day But there is no particular secret, Mary Ann, that I know of anyway—except that maybe practice makes perfect."

"Practice makes perfect? Do you really believe that?"

"Absolutely. The more you do it, the more fun it is."

Mary Ann looked at Victoria, her eyes dancing with mischie "Do you think I should try that?"

Victoria nodded encouragingly. "It certainly couldn't hur And you might be surprised just how un-boring things could b if you offered Tom a little romantic diversion some afternoon.

Mary Ann's animated expression seesawed back and fort

between scandalized and intrigued. "What day is today?" she asked suddenly.

"Friday."

"Tom always comes home early on Friday afternoons."

Victoria broke out in a melodic little laugh. "Well, then. There's your opportunity."

"You're right." Mary Ann giggled. "There's my opportunity. And if there's one thing my mother always stressed to me, it was never to pass up an opportunity!"

After sharing a light lunch together Victoria left Mary Ann's house and headed back to Wellesley Manor. Knowing that her little mare knew the way to her barn, she jogged along the path with a loose rein, gazing at the verdant midsummer wildflowers that bloomed along the side of the road.

Her contented reverie came to a startled end, however, when a big roan gelding suddenly lunged out of the woods and leaped up on to the road in front of her.

Cassandra let out a frightened little snort and reared so abruptly that only Victoria's superlative riding skills allowed her to remain in the saddle. Finally bringing the mare under control, she glared furiously at the other rider.

"Just what do you . . . Harrison!" Victoria's angry cry died in her throat as she identified the rider positioned crosswise in the road ahead of her.

"Good afternoon, Mrs. Wellesley," he said silkily.

Victoria's expression became wary at his odd tone. "Good afternoon. You gave me a fright. I was afraid you might be a highwayman."

"Hardly. They usually confine their activities to the nighttime, I believe."

Victoria reined her mare around and nudged her back into a walk. "What brings you out this way?"

Careful to keep his voice casual, Harrison replied, "Oh, nothing in particular. I was just out for a ride."

Victoria looked at him askance. "You were riding in the woods?"

Harrison ignored that question. "Where are you headed?" he asked, reining his horse into position beside hers.

"I've been visiting Mary Ann Parks and I'm on my way home."

"You're going to Pembroke?"

Victoria shook her head and looked at him again, unable to quell the feeling of unease that niggled at her. "No, I'm going to Wellesley Manor."

It was all Harrison could do to control the anger that surged within him. "You consider Wellesley Manor *home* now?"

Victoria shot him a haughty look. "Home is wherever my husband is residing. Right now, that's Wellesley Manor."

"Ah, yes," Harrison growled, "your husband. How is the American?"

Victoria's sense of unease was growing with every passing second and she subtly urged Cassandra into a faster gait. "Miles is fine, thank you. I'll tell him that you asked after him."

"Don't bother."

Victoria licked her lips nervously and gave the horse another little nudge with her foot. "Harrison, it has been lovely to see you, but I really do have to get home."

Kicking his horse to catch up with Victoria's suddenly accelerated pace, Harrison reached out and grabbed her reins, pulling the mare to an abrupt stop. "Come away with me, Victoria," he blurted, his voice hoarse and urgent. "I know you don't love Wellesley, that you only married him for his money. We'll take King's Ransom and go to France—or Italy, if you prefer. We can sell the horse on the continent for an excellent price, and the proceeds will set us up very nicely for a long time."

Victoria stared at him aghast. "Good Lord, Harrison, have you completely taken leave of your senses? I'm a married woman now, and Miles and I are expecting a child in the spring. Whatever makes you think that I would consider running away with you?" Wrenching her reins out of Guildford's hands, she spurred Cassandra into a canter.

"Because we were meant to be together!" Harrison yelled,

charging after her. His big gelding had little trouble catching the delicate mare, and Victoria sent an apprehensive glance over her shoulder as she heard him come storming up behind her.

"Victoria, stop!" he shouted. "I need to talk to you. Stop, I say!"

Seeing the gate to Wellesley Manor looming up in front of her, Victoria decided that it was more prudent to slow down and finish this discussion away from the gardeners' ears than to gallop up the drive with Harrison in hot pursuit yelling after her. Again, she reined in her mare, pausing just outside the gate.

"Admit it, Victoria," Harrison panted, pulling up beside her, "marrying that American clod was a mistake—a terrible error in judgment on your part. But at least it's easily rectified. We can just disappear someplace where Wellesley will never find us."

Victoria's lips thinned with outrage. "This is insanity, Harrison, and I refuse to listen to another word. Miles is my husband and the father of my child. I have no intention of leaving him for you or anyone else."

Looking around a little desperately, she suddenly spotted Samuel, the stablemaster, who was checking a pasture fence not fifty feet from where they stood. She watched as the old man cupped a hand over his eyes to shade them from the midafternoon sun while he identified the unexpected visitors. Seeing Victoria, he waved and went back to his work.

"There's Samuel," Victoria said quickly, relief evident in her voice. "I need to talk to him, so I'll be saying good-bye now."

Harrison shot her a killing look. "What possible business could you have with the viscountess's stableman?"

Victoria cast about in her mind for a suitable response, but none came. Finally she sighed and said simply, "Harrison, I have to go. Good-bye."

Harrison's eyes narrowed menacingly. "You're making that *goodbye* sound very final, Victoria."

Victoria looked at him steadily. "It is, Harrison. *Very* final."

"Maybe not quite as final as you think," he snarled. Wheeling his horse around, he galloped off down the lane.

Harrison stood in the darkened parlor of his house, swilling gin and staring moodily out the window into the black night.

He'd tried, he really had. He'd given Victoria one last chance to right the wrong she'd done him, but the foolish woman had rejected him yet again.

Well, it was her loss. Now he would be forced to put his original plan into action, and if somebody—like Wellesley— got hurt because of it, Victoria would have only herself to blame.

Harrison sneered with contempt as he took another long swallow of his drink. It was disappointing, really. He'd never thought of Victoria as a stupid woman. But she was. And now she'd have to pay for that stupidity.

Chapter 31

Miles was standing in the foyer waiting for Victoria when she came through the door.

"Where have you been, pretty lady?" he asked, hooking an arm around her neck and kissing her soundly.

"Visiting Mary Ann Parks," Victoria answered. She forced a smile and ducked away from Miles's playful embrace, hoping she didn't sound as flustered as she felt. Her unexpected encounter with Harrison had upset her a great deal, but the last person she wished to know about it was her volatile husband.

Miles's brow furrowed as Victoria danced away from him, but he didn't try to stop her. Following her up the stairs, he asked, "And how is everything with the Parkses?"

"Fine," Victoria answered. "Mary Ann and I had a nice visit."

"Good. What did you talk about?"

Victoria could feel the color creeping up her neck as she thought back on her conversation with Mary Ann. She could only imagine what Miles would think of her if she admitted that she'd spent the afternoon bragging about his sexual prowess to her friend. Suddenly she was very grateful that he was a pace behind her and couldn't see her flaming face. "We didn't talk about anything in particular," she said, hoping she sounded nonchalant.

Again Miles's forehead wrinkled. Rarely was Victoria so noncommittal when he chatted with her. It was almost as if something had happened during her time away from the house that she didn't want him to know about. He followed her into the bedroom, gazing at her reflection in the pier glass as she removed her hat. "Is something wrong, sweetheart?"

Victoria made a great pretense of carefully straightening the small veil on her riding hat; then she turned toward him and smiled brightly. "Of course not. What could be wrong?"

Miles shrugged. "I don't know. You're just acting a little strange."

"Strange?"

"Yes, as if you're nervous or upset or something."

Victoria hurried over to the armoire, taking advantage of the brief moment during which her back was turned to draw in several calming breaths. "I can't imagine why I'd be giving you that impression, Miles. Everything is perfectly fine. It's probably just that I cantered most of the way home so I'd be here in time to help with afternoon tea."

Miles came to loop his arms around her waist, turning her so that she faced him. "Don't overdo, Tory. You're in a delicate condition now and I would be very upset if anything happened to you because you were hurrying home to fix tea. We have plenty of servants who are paid handsomely to perform those tasks, so you just take it easy. Promise?"

Victoria lowered her head and nodded contritely, hating herself for lying. "All right, Miles, I promise."

His good humor restored, Miles tipped up her chin and placed a soft kiss on her lips.

Victoria eagerly responded to his gentle caress, realizing that his touch was exactly what she needed to put her world back to rights after her disturbing meeting with Harrison.

"Mmm," Miles groaned as Victoria's mouth parted beneath his and she wrapped her arms around his neck. "Maybe you should go away more often if this is the reception I get when you come back home."

"I missed you," Victoria whispered, threading her fingers through his soft, thick hair.

Miles chuckled with delight. "You were only gone a couple of hours."

Victoria's lips brushed his provocatively. "I know, but I missed you anyway. Mary Ann and I were talking about you, and it made me long to be with you."

Miles ran his tongue along the seam of her lips, causing a delicate little shudder to ripple through her. "Talking about me? What were you saying?"

"I was telling her what a wonderful lover you are," Victoria responded, deciding to tell him the truth.

Miles laughed, not believing her for a second. "Sure you were."

"I was!"

"Well, whether you were or not, I'm very glad that you appreciate my finer qualities." He threw her a look that could only be described as a leer and quickly unbuttoned the front of her riding habit.

Peeling back the jacket, Miles bent to kiss her breasts but paused as he felt the stiff bones of her corset beneath his fingers. He lifted his head, the flaring passion Victoria had just seen in his eyes quickly fading. "Why the hell are you wearing a corset?"

Victoria looked at him in complete surprise. "I have to, or I wouldn't be able to get my jacket buttoned."

Miles's frown clearly told her that he didn't consider that an adequate answer. "I told you before, Tory, that I don't want you wearing these damn things anymore. It can't be good for the baby to have you squeeze yourself in like this. Why, this thing is so tight, you can hardly take a deep breath."

"But Miles, none of my clothes will fit without a corset."

"Have new ones made," he barked. "You're going to need

a new wardrobe soon anyway. You might as well get started now."

"Oh, that's ridiculous," Victoria protested. "I've only been with child for a few weeks. I certainly don't need new clothes yet. I'll bet I haven't gained an ounce."

Miles rammed his fingers through his hair, completely frustrated by Victoria's continued obstinacy. "I'm not saying that you need to dress for confinement, damn it! I'm just saying that I want you to get some more comfortable clothing that don't require a corset."

"All right," Victoria acquiesced, secretly pleased by his concern. "I'll call Mrs. Livick tomorrow."

Miles nodded approvingly. "Good. In the meantime, let's get this thing off you." With nimble fingers, he began to unlace the corset strings.

Victoria looked at him wryly. "You know, I don't think you're concerned in the least about my comfort. I think you're just looking for an excuse to undress me."

Lowering his head, Miles placed a series of nibbling kisses on the sensitive skin beneath her ear. "That's not true," he whispered huskily, "I'm very concerned about your comfort. The fact that the best way to make you comfortable is to undress you is just a lucky coincidence for me."

Victoria exhaled a long, languorous sigh as the confining corset fell away and Miles gathered her full breasts in his hands. "You're so beautiful," he breathed, burying his face in the soft fullness of her bare bosom. "The most beautiful woman I've ever known."

Victoria insinuated her hand between their bodies, lightly stroking his rapidly swelling erection through his trousers. "You're beautiful, too."

Miles's eyes lit with desire at her seductive touch. Placing his hands on either side of her face, he gave her a scorching kiss, his tongue tangling provocatively with hers. "Do you realize that we haven't made love in three days?"

"I know," Victoria answered throatily, releasing his hot, aroused manhood from his clothing and stroking it.

Miles groaned in primal appreciation of her sensual touch, and when he spoke again his voice was so ragged that Victoria could hardly understand him. "Why do you suppose that is?"

"I don't know," she murmured, slowly sinking to her knees and shinnying his trousers down over his lean hips, "but let's not wait any longer."

Miles smiled down at the sight of his wife pressed so intimately against his abdomen; then all rational thought fled as he felt the warm silkiness of her tongue glide across his hot, wet tip. "Oh my God," he moaned, throwing his head back and closing his eyes. "Who taught you how to cast this spell?"

"A very accomplished sorcerer," Victoria whispered. "He showed me how good it felt when he did this to me, so I thought I'd see if the pleasure works both ways."

"I assure you it does," Miles rasped, burying his hands in her hair and locking his knees to keep them from buckling.

"Good," Victoria murmured. "And how about this?" Leaning forward, she drew him into her mouth, her tongue swirling round and round his thick, hard length.

Miles let out a long moan of ecstasy, then suddenly pulled away, grabbing Victoria under her arms and lifting her to her feet. "Come here, my little temptress."

Tossing her playfully onto the bed, Miles straddled her, his grin devilish. "You're a fraud, Victoria Wellesley," he accused, pushing her long, full skirt up around her hips.

"A fraud?" Victoria gasped. "What do you . . ." Her words were cut off by a delighted little cry as Miles entered her in one smooth lunge. ". . . mean?"

Miles sat back on his haunches, teasing her unmercifully by giving her his full length and then slowly pulling back until he nearly withdrew. "You make everyone think you're a prim and proper young matron until you get into the bedroom. Then you magically turn into such a wild little seductress that no one would ever believe it—not even me if I wasn't here witnessing it firsthand."

"Magically, eh?" Victoria giggled, her expression turning from amusement to bliss as Miles again thrust into her. "Do you really think I'm magic?"

"Oh, you're magic, all right," he groaned, increasing his rhythm.

"As are you, Mr. Wellesley," she returned, her voice as breathless as his. "And I'd be most appreciative if you'd perform a little of your special magic on me."

"With pleasure, Mrs. Wellesley."

And, for the next few minutes, Mr. and Mrs. Wellesley performed love's magic on each other in a most delightful—and satisfying—way.

"Mrs. Wellesley, a man named George who says he's from Pembroke is here to see you."

Victoria looked up from the shirt she was darning for Miles, a perplexed expression on her face. "George? The stablemaster?"

Cedric shrugged elaborately, his frown of disapproval telling her quite eloquently that he felt her visitor to be far beneath his notice. "All he said was that his name was George, my lady."

"It must be our stablemaster. I certainly hope nothing is wrong at Pembroke."

Laying aside her sewing, Victoria hurried into the foyer, holding her hands out in a gesture of welcome as she spotted the old man standing uncertainly near the front door. "George," she said warmly, "what brings you to Wellesley Manor?"

"A private matter, my lady," he muttered, looking askance at the hovering Cedric.

Victoria read his cue and turned to Cedric, smiling sweetly. "That will be all, Cedric, thank you."

Cedric's mouth pursed with offense at her abrupt dismissal, but he obediently turned and stalked off into the dining room.

Victoria turned back to the stablemaster. "Tell me what brings you here, George. Is something wrong at home?"

The old man wrung his beat-up old hat between his gnarled hands and nodded miserably. "Indeed it is, Lady Victoria. It appears that someone broke into the barn during the night and stole King's Ransom."

Victoria blanched and raised a shaking hand to clutch at her throat. "You're sure? King's Ransom is gone?"

The old man's face crumpled, and for a moment Victoria thought he was going to weep. "Yes, my lady. He's gone, and without a trace."

Victoria's initial look of shock gradually gave way to frowning suspicion. "Are any of the other horses missing?"

George shook his head. "No, just Ransom. Nothing was disturbed in the barn either. It's almost as if whoever took him knew who he was after and didn't waste his time with anything else."

Victoria nodded slowly, her suspicions more firmly planted with every passing moment. "I assume you have a search party out looking for him."

"Yes, every available man on the place. We saw his hoof prints and a man's boot tracks leading out of the barn, but once they hit the bricks outside, there wasn't a trace. Whoever stole him must have ridden him across the near pasture. I was going to notify the authorities, but I figured I'd better come tell you first."

"You did the right thing." Victoria nodded, patting George absently on the shoulder. "There's no reason to bring the authorities into this unless we have to."

George's old eyes became bleary with tears and he lowered his head. "I feel terrible about this, my lady. The stables is my responsibility, and if I weren't such a sound sleeper . . ."

"Don't be silly," Victoria soothed. "This is not your fault. What would you be doing in the middle of the night except sleeping?"

"What're you going to do my lady? Call the authorities or let Mr. Wellesley handle it?"

"Neither," Victoria answered quietly. "This is Pembroke business and I will handle it myself."

George kneaded his hat relentlessly, carefully phrasing his next words. "Beggin' your pardon, Lady Victoria, but we're talking about a horse thief here. I don't think this is something you should be getting yourself involved in. It could be dangerous."

"Nonsense," Victoria protested, waving her hand in dismissal of George's concerns. "I'm quite sure that I know who took Ransom, and I'll be in no danger getting him back."

George's eyes widened incredulously. "You know who took him? You mean you think it's someone we know?"

Victoria sighed heavily. "I'm afraid so, but I think that if I just reason with the man, I'll have the horse back in his stall before noon. So, you see, there's no reason to upset Mr. Wellesley with this, or to call in the authorities."

George cast her another doubtful look, but having experienced Victoria's stubborn streak for many years, he knew it would do no good to argue with her. "Very well, my lady, whatever you think is best. Is there anything I can do?"

Victoria thought for a moment. She was convinced it was Harrison who was behind the disappearance of King's Ransom, and it would be helpful to have George with her when she confronted him. That way, when Harrison realized how senseless his actions were and agreed to return the horse to her, as she was convinced he would, George would be there to take the horse home. But, on the other hand, letting George accompany her would also mean that he would know the identity of the perpetrator of this foolish crime and might possibly tell Miles. The last thing Victoria wanted was for Miles to find out about Harrison's latest escapade. With his intense dislike of her former suitor, coupled with his famous Wellesley temper, there was no telling what he might do in retaliation.

"No, George," she said slowly, making up her mind to confront Harrison alone, "I will handle this myself. You just go back to Pembroke and say nothing to anyone until I have a chance to set this to rights."

The expression on George's wizened old face stated very clearly that he wasn't pleased with her decision, but he dared not say more. After all, since her father's death and her stepmother's departure for America, she was his employer, and he really had no choice but to obey her order. "All right, my lady," he said, nodding, "if you're absolutely sure."

"I'm sure." Victoria smiled, touched by the old man's obvious concern for her welfare. "And I'm also sure that by this afternoon the whole unfortunate affair will be behind us."

George nodded again, but his expression was still dubious as he turned and mounted his old gelding. With a gentle nudge to the horse's ribs, he shambled off down the drive.

Victoria watched him go, a fond smile curving her lips. As he disappeared around the bend, though, her smile faded, replaced by an angry, set expression. With a purposeful stride, she set off for the barns, determined to ride over to Harrison's estate and have it out with him once and for all.

The man had really crossed the line this time, and she was going to let him know in no uncertain terms that she would tolerate no more of his outrageous behavior.

This nonsense was going to stop now.

Chapter 32

"Mother, have you seen Victoria?"

Mary Wellesley looked up from her embroidery and shook her head. "No, dear, I haven't. She and I had planned to do some sewing together this morning, but I've been in here for almost an hour and I haven't seen her yet." Mary gestured to a heap of white linen material thrown on a table near the door. "I think she must have been here earlier, though, because that looks like the shirt she was working on."

Miles frowned. "This is very strange. Father hasn't seen her since breakfast, and you haven't seen her at all. I can't imagine where she is."

"Maybe she was called away on an unexpected errand of some kind," Mary suggested. "Since she left her sewing sitting there, I'm sure she'll be back in a few minutes."

Miles stared at the half-made shirt for a moment, then turned and walked back into the foyer. Spying Cedric, he quickened his pace. "Cedric, have you seen my wife?"

"Not since she left with that unkempt man, sir."

Miles's eyebrows shot up with alarm. "What unkempt man?"

"A man came to the door this morning, looking for Lady

Victoria. He said he was from Pembroke, although in my estimation, he looked more like a vagabond. I can't remember when I've seen a shabbier hat than the one he was wearing."

Miles frowned, annoyed that Cedric was wasting time elaborating about the unknown man's clothing. "I don't care what his hat looked like, Cedric. Did he give you his name?"

"Yes, sir. He said his name was George. I nearly didn't announce him, considering his appearance, but he was most adamant about speaking with your wife."

"George," Miles muttered. "Must be Pembroke's old stablemaster. Did Mrs. Wellesley seem to know him?"

"Oh, yes, sir. In fact, she greeted him most warmly. Then, for no reason whatsoever, she banished me from the room. Obviously they wanted to talk privately about something."

Miles's frown darkened. "Privately?" What in the world could Victoria have to discuss with George that would necessitate privacy?

"What happened then, Cedric?"

Cedric drew himself up to his full, spidery height and looked haughtily down his nose. "I'm sure I don't know, sir. As I said, I was dismissed and . . ."

"Yes, yes," Miles interrupted impatiently, "and you went around the corner into the dining room and eavesdropped on everything they said. Now tell me, what happened?"

Cedric pursed his mouth so tightly that it nearly disappeared. "Master Miles, really . . ."

"Oh, come now, Cedric! I don't give a damn that you were eavesdropping. Everyone knows that you do it all the time and have for the past forty years. I just want to know what George said to Victoria."

Cedric cast Miles an offended glare but said, "I didn't hear much, but the man was talking rather loudly and I was right in the next room . . ."

"Yes, yes; go on."

"Well, I did hear him mention something about someone stealing King's Ransom."

"What?"

"That's what he said, sir. That someone had stolen King's Ransom."

Miles's face went white as a sheet. "You're absolutely sure that's what he said?"

Cedric nodded. "Absolutely. But Mrs. Wellesley didn't seem to be overly concerned. She told the man that she thought she knew who had taken the horse and that she would see to having him returned."

Miles eyes darkened with anger. "And you never thought to tell me about this?"

Cedric had the good grace to look chagrined. "Really, sir, it all happened very quickly, and then the two of them went outside and . . ."

"Never mind. How long ago did this occur?"

"Perhaps an hour, no longer."

Miles nodded grimly. "All right. Run out and tell Samuel to saddle Summer Storm for me."

"Run, sir?" Cedric gasped. "You want me to *run?*"

"Yes, goddamn it! Now go!"

Cedric's brows rose so high that if he had had a hairline, they would have surely disappeared into it, but seeing Miles's enraged expression, he sprinted out the front door and galloped across the lawn faster than anyone had seen him move in twenty years.

Miles tore into the library, searching frantically for his father. Spotting him buried behind a copy of the London *Times,* he cried, "Quick, Father; I need your help!"

James looked up from his paper, his heart leaping into his throat when he saw the expression on Miles's face.

"What's wrong?"

Miles swallowed hard, clamping down on his fear and anger so that he could give his father a rational accounting of what he'd just learned. "It appears that Harrison Guildford has stolen King's Ransom, and Victoria has gone over to his home alone to try to talk him into returning him."

James jumped out of his chair, his newspaper forgotten. "You must be joking!"

"Do I look like I'm joking?"

"No, of course not," James muttered. "I'm sorry. Are you going over to Guildford's?"

"Yes. Cedric is seeing about having my horse saddled right now. I just hope Victoria is all right. She had no business . . ."

"Now calm down," James ordered. "What do you want me to do? Call the authorities?"

"Yes. Tell them to meet me there as quickly as they possibly can."

"I'm on my way," James said, rushing past Miles as he headed for the front door. Miles was only a step behind him, however, and as the two men raced down the front steps, James turned toward his son and clapped a restraining hand on his forearm. "Don't do anything foolish, Miles. Just get Victoria out of there, if indeed she's actually at Guildford's, and let the authorities handle the rest."

"Oh, she's there, all right," Miles raged. "It's just like her to decide to try to handle something like this by herself. But I'll tell you one thing, Father: If that son of a bitch has done anything—*anything*—to my wife, by God, I'll kill him with my bare hands, and to hell with the authorities."

"Miles!" James thundered, tightening his hold as Miles tried to break away from him. "You're talking like a fool. Harrison Guildford isn't going to harm Victoria, and nobody is going to kill anyone. Do you understand? Now, please, do as I say. Assess the situation, make sure your wife is in no jeopardy, then wait until I get there with the authorities."

"All right." Miles nodded reluctantly. "Now let go of me. I have to get over there."

James released Miles's arm and watched fearfully as his son ran across the lawn. "Use your head, boy," he muttered, "please use your head."

At least there was one thing to be thankful for in all this, James thought as he hurried toward the barn; Miles was probably the most levelheaded of all his sons. If something like this had happened to Geoffrey, with his flash-fire temper and big, burly body, he probably *would* kill the man first and ask questions later. James could only pray that Miles would be more prudent.

Miles galloped down the lane toward Harrison Guildford's estate as if all the demons in hell were after him. His thoughts careened back and forth between worrying about Victoria's welfare and cursing her for putting herself into such a precarious situation. "Damn her, anyway," he cursed as he flew down the road. "Once I get her back home, I swear I'm going to chain her to the bedpost!"

Pembroke House loomed up on his left and, without warning, he reined in his horse and thundered up the drive. Leaping off the winded gelding's back, he burst into the old stone barn. "George! George, are you in here?"

The old man appeared at once, a look of profound relief on his face when he spotted Miles. "Oh, thank God, sir, that you're here."

"Where is my wife?" Miles asked without preamble.

"I'm not sure."

"What do you mean, you're not sure? You're the one who summoned her this morning, aren't you?"

"Yes, sir, I am. I came to Wellesley Manor to tell her that King's Ransom was stolen during the night."

"And . . ."

"And she told me that she thought she knew who had taken him and that she would put the situation to rights personally. Then she went to the barn and ordered that her horse be saddled. I offered to accompany her to wherever it was she was going, but she refused me. I also suggested that I notify you and the authorities," he added hastily, "but she was very firm about wanting to handle this on her own. She told me to say nothing to anyone and sent me home to wait for further word from her. I hope I did the right thing."

Miles pinned the flustered old man with a killing look, making it abundantly clear that, in his opinion, he had definitely *not* done the right thing. "Do you think Harrison Guildford might have taken the horse?"

George's expression changed from chagrined to incredulous. "Harrison Guildford? Why would he steal King's Ransom?"

"I have no idea, but there's a distinct possibility that he's at the bottom of this."

"Oh, I don't think Lord Guildford would do anything like that," George protested. "After all, he and Lady Victoria are friends—have been for years. In fact, your man, Samuel, told me that he'd seen them out riding together just yesterday."

It was Miles's turn to appear incredulous. "Samuel saw Guildford and Victoria together yesterday? Are you sure?"

"That's what he told me, sir." George nodded. "He and I were down at the pub last evening hoisting a few, and he said he was mending the front pasture fence yesterday afternoon when the two of them came riding up together. Samuel said Lord Guildford left Lady Victoria at the front gate of Wellesley Manor."

Miles's mind flew back to Victoria's arrival home yesterday. She had said that she'd spent the afternoon with Mary Ann Parks, but Miles recalled that she'd been flushed and breathless when she'd entered the house. And when he'd asked her if anything was wrong, she'd avoided his question.

A myriad of conclusions—all of them painful—hit Miles like a blow to the chest. Was it possible that his wife was cuckolding him? Immediately, he dismissed that idea. She hadn't been in the house ten minutes yesterday before they'd been all over each other—and their lovemaking had been some of the most intimate they'd ever shared. Never had Miles known Victoria to be so uninhibited, so abandoned, so boldly sensual. He squeezed his eyes shut, refusing to believe that Victoria's overt seduction of him had been prompted by guilt. But why had she been out riding with Guildford? And why hadn't she told him?

Why?

Without so much as a word of farewell to George, Miles rushed out of the Pembroke stables. There was only one way to find out what the hell was going on between Victoria and Harrison and, by God, he intended to know the truth before the afternoon was over.

Harrison Guildford opened the front door of his ancestral home, a satisfied smile playing about his handsome mouth. "Ah, Victoria," he greeted, "how nice of you to visit. Won't you come in?"

"I'm not here on a social call and you well know it," Victoria spat, stepping into the house and yanking off her gloves. Whirling around, she glared at the still smiling man. "Why did you steal King's Ransom, Harrison?"

Harrison's smile faded. "You're a very astute woman, Victoria, to have figured it out so quickly. But then, I always was impressed by your intelligence."

"You can skip the flattery, Harrison. Just tell me why you took my horse."

Harrison smiled again, a self-satisfied smirk that made a little prickle of apprehension skitter up Victoria's spine. "Let's put it this way, my dear. I decided that I deserved some recompense for all the time I wasted courting you."

"Courting me! You never courted me, Harrison. We were friends, that's all."

Harrison clapped a hand dramatically over his heart. "You wound me, Victoria. Have you forgotten that I asked you to be my wife?"

"No, I haven't forgotten," Victoria stated flatly, "and I also haven't forgotten that I didn't accept you."

Harrison's smile disappeared, replaced by an ugly sneer. "You accepted Wellesley fast enough, though, didn't you? It

makes my head spin to think how fast you leaped into his bed."
He paused, lowering his eyes insultingly to her abdomen. "And
how fast you let him get you with child."

Victoria shot him an outraged look. "I refuse to stand here
and listen to your insults. What's between my husband and
myself is none of your business. Now, please, just give me
your word that you'll return my horse and I'll try to forget this
ugly incident ever occurred."

Harrison suddenly moved forward, pinning Victoria against
the wall and rubbing his body insolently against hers. "So you
don't want to talk about your relationship with the American,
eh? Why is that, Victoria? Are you embarrassed by what he
does to you? Do you close your eyes and try to pretend you're
somewhere else while he's making love to you?"

Victoria gasped in stunned disbelief at Harrison's words.
Ducking under his arm, she bolted for the front door. Her abrupt
movement threw Harrison off balance for a moment, but he
quickly righted himself and lunged after her, catching her by
the arm and slamming her against the door.

"Stop this!" Victoria shrieked, pushing at his chest with all
her strength. "What is the matter with you? Have you gone
completely insane?"

Her anguished demand seemed to somehow penetrate the
red haze of anger enshrouding Harrison and he stepped back.

She reached up and dashed away the terrified tears that
streamed down her face. "Please, Harrison, don't do this crazy
thing. Tonight, after everyone is asleep, put King's Ransom
back in his stall, and no one will ever be the wiser."

Again, Harrison's lips spread with a self-satisfied smile. "I'm
afraid I can't do that, my lady. You see, I've sold him."

"Sold him? You're lying! You couldn't have possibly sold
him so quickly, especially when you don't have any ownership
papers on him."

"Ownership papers are easily forged," Harrison smirked,
"and foreign buyers aren't nearly as careful about checking
signatures and seals as we British are. So, you see, Victoria,

King's Ransom is gone. Sold, shipped and out of your reach forever."

"You won't get away with this," Victoria warned brazenly. "Miles will have you brought up before the magistrate. You'll go to prison, or worse. Surely you know that the theft of a horse as valuable as Ransom is a hanging offense."

Harrison shook his head, his smile never slipping. "They can't touch me, Victoria. It'll be your word against mine, and you have no evidence. If you tell anyone about this conversation, I'll simply deny it ever took place. Who do you think the authorities will believe? An overwrought, hysterical woman, or a peer of the realm with impeccable credentials?"

"King's Ransom is gone!" Victoria cried. "That's evidence enough."

"Evidence that he was stolen, perhaps," Harrison sneered, "but not that I had anything to do with it. Besides, I have an unshakable alibi for last night. I was with a friend ... a lady friend who will be more than happy to testify that I was with her all evening."

Victoria stared at her childhood friend, a sad, beseeching look on her face. "Why are you doing this, Harrison? Why would you want to hurt me? You know that King's Ransom was my most prized possession. Why would you want to take him away from me?"

"I didn't take him away from you, Victoria. Once you married Wellesley, Ransom became his possession, not yours. I took the horse away from him, just as he took you away from me."

Victoria closed her eyes, trying to make some sense of Harrison's twisted logic. "You won't get away with it," she vowed. "Somehow, some way, I'll prove what you've done."

"As I said, my dear, it will be merely your word against mine."

"Not merely, Guildford," came a deep voice from down the hall.

"Miles!" Victoria cried, wrenching out of Harrison's grasp

and racing over to where her husband stood in the doorway leading to the kitchen. "Oh, God, I'm so glad you're here!"

At the sight of Miles standing so calmly in his hallway, a black rage engulfed Harrison. With a sharp, guttural cry, he grabbed a heavy vase sitting on a stand by the front door and lunged toward his nemesis.

Miles pushed Victoria out of the way, his feet tangling in her full skirt as he tried to free himself from her clutching hands. Harrison launched himself at Miles and the two men crashed to the floor. For several agonizing moments they rolled over and over, each of them pounding mercilessly at the other. Finally Miles gained the upper hand and delivered a brutal undercut to Harrison's jaw. Harrison's head snapped back and hit the floor with a sickening thud, but as Miles rose to his knees, Harrison raised the vase over his head and brought it smashing down on Miles's skull.

Victoria screamed as she saw Miles crumple and fall to the floor. Realizing that she was now at Harrison's mercy, she glanced around wildly, spying a pair of ancient crossed sabers hanging on the wall. Pulling one down, she turned on Harrison, waving the sword in a wicked, swinging arc as she came toward him.

"Put the saber down, Victoria," Harrison ordered. "You know you're not going to cut me, so put it down before you hurt yourself."

"Oh, yes, I am going to cut you," Victoria hissed. "In fact, I'm going to kill you."

Harrison laughed, but still, he backed up a step. "You, Victoria? You're going to kill me? Oh, come now, my lady. Do you really expect me to believe that?"

"Don't taunt me, Harrison," Victoria warned, thrusting the swordpoint menacingly toward him. "You might be very surprised at what we *ladies* are capable of when someone we love is in jeopardy."

As she moved forward another step, the vengeful gleam in her eyes gave Harrison his first moment of real fear. "Victoria,

listen . . ." He made the mistake of backing up another step as
he uttered her name, and the next thing Victoria knew, he was
lying on his back where Miles had grabbed his legs and pulled
them out from under him.

Victoria watched in astonishment as her husband, whom
she'd been so bravely defending, suddenly lunged to his knees
and began pummeling Harrison's handsome face. Guildford
put up a token resistance, but the back of his head had hit the
floor hard when Miles had tripped him and that, coupled with
the punishment Miles was now inflicting, caused him to be
quickly subdued.

"Miles, stop!" Victoria cried as he continued to brutalize his
foe, even after it was evident that Harrison was beaten. "Stop!
You're going to kill him!"

She rushed forward, pulling ineffectually at Miles in an effort
to stop his killing rage, but again she found herself being pulled
out of the way as James Wellesley burst through the front door.

"Miles, that's enough!" James bellowed, jerking his son off
Guildford's prostrate body. Hauling him to his feet, James held
Miles's shoulders in an unrelenting grip until he saw the blood
lust fade from his eyes. "That's enough," he said again.

Miles nodded, then turned to Victoria, hauling her into his
arms and burying his bruised and bleeding face in her hair.

Suddenly the room was filled with men as the village sheriff
and several of his deputies poured in through the front door.
The sheriff took one look at the battered Miles and the prostrate
Harrison and shrugged. "Looks like there's not much here for
me to do."

"Lord Guildford stole our prize stallion," Victoria cried,
pointing an accusing finger as the deputies helped Harrison to
his feet. "He confessed to me that he took the horse and sold
him to a foreign buyer."

"Is what she says true, Guildford?" the sheriff demanded.

"Of course not," Harrison scoffed. "The woman is mad. She
probably sold the stud herself and is trying to pin the loss on
me so her husband won't find out."

"That's a lie!" Victoria cried. Turning again to the sheriff, she added, "He told me that you'd never be able to prove anything against him. He even said that he'd arranged an alibi with some woman so that it would only be my word against his."

The sheriff looked around uncomfortably, not quite sure how to handle the accusations.

"My wife is telling the truth," Miles said, stepping forward and looking the sheriff directly in the eye. "I heard the entire conversation from the kitchen."

"Are you going to believe him?" Harrison cried. "Of course he's going to back up this ridiculous story. Any husband would feel bound to protect his wife by lying for her."

"Mr. and Mrs. Wellesley are not lying," came a soft, shaky voice from behind them. "I heard the conversation, too."

Everyone turned to stare at an elderly maid who stood hovering in the kitchen doorway.

"Exactly what did you hear, ma'am?" the sheriff asked.

The maid cast an uneasy glance in Harrison's direction, but then squared her shoulders and said, "Well, sir, the lady, she accused my lord of stealing her horse and he admitted to her that he had, but then he said that she'd never be able to prove it. He told her that he'd already sold the animal, and that she'd never find it. Everything the lady told you is true."

"She's mad!" Harrison shouted, trying desperately to break out of the deputies' hold and lunge toward the old woman. "She's a scullery maid. You can't believe anything she'd say."

"Oh, but I do," the sheriff answered blandly. Straightening, he faced Harrison squarely. "Lord Harrison Guildford, in the name of the queen, I arrest you for the crime of horse theft. Take him in, men."

As the deputies dragged the cursing, resisting Harrison out the front door, Victoria turned back to Miles, raising her hand to his battered cheek and stroking it gently. "Are you all right?"

Miles attempted a smile, but ended up grimacing in pain. "Actually, I hurt like hell, but I'll be all right."

James stepped up and put an arm around his son's shoulder. "Sorry I was so rough with you, Miles, but I really was afraid you were going to kill Guildford."

"It's all right, Father. If you hadn't come along when you had, I very well might have. I didn't realize I could become so angry."

James gave Miles's shoulder a paternal squeeze. "Don't worry about it, son. Any man can be driven to violence if he's severely enough provoked. Now, let's go home. Miles needs patching up, Victoria needs a nap and I think all three of us need a drink!"

Chapter 33

Victoria sat down on the edge of the huge tester bed and
gently pressed a cold cloth to Miles's bruised cheek. "Are you
in a great deal of pain?" she asked quietly.

Miles squinted at her from his rapidly swelling black eye
and tried valiantly to smile. "I've got a hell of a headache."

"That was a hell of a vase," Victoria returned sympathetically.

Miles's jaw dropped at Victoria's unprecedented use of pro-
fanity. "I'm afraid I'm a bad influence on you." He chuckled.

"Oh, I know you are, and in more ways than one." Smiling
at him, she placed the damp cloth on his forehead.

"That feels good." He sighed. "My head feels like it's on
fire."

"I'm not surprised. You look like you were in a barroom
brawl."

"I *was* in a brawl, just minus the barroom."

Victoria clasped her hands in her lap, staring at them dismally.
"Miles, I'm so sorry about everything. If I hadn't been so
foolish as to think that I could handle Harrison, none of this
would have happened."

Miles ran his hand caressingly down Victoria's cheek. "It's behind us now, sweetheart. Don't think about it anymore."

"How can I help but think about it? You've been beaten to a pulp . . ."

"Hey, hey," Miles interjected. "Give me a little credit here. After all, it's Guildford who had to be carried out."

"I know," Victoria mumbled, "but, still, you were hurt, King's Ransom is gone and it's all my fault."

"It isn't your fault, Tory, except that perhaps you led Harrison on a bit."

In a split second Victoria's chagrined expression turned defensive. "What do you mean, led him on? I never led Harrison on. Not for a single moment!"

Miles sighed, cursing himself for letting that one slip. True, he did want some answers from Victoria as to why she'd told him she was visiting Mary Ann when, in actuality, she was out riding with Guildford, but now was definitely not the time he'd planned to have that discussion. "Never mind," he muttered. "I shouldn't have said that."

Victoria stood up, pacing to the window and then whirling around and facing him again. "I know you don't feel well, Miles, and the last thing I intended when I came in here was to have an argument with you, but I really want to know what you meant by that comment. Do you seriously believe there's something going on between Harrison and me?"

Miles closed his eyes, steeling himself for the inevitability of the confrontation. "No, I don't believe that," he said truthfully, "but I *am* upset that you've lied to me about your whereabouts recently."

"Lied to you? I've never lied to you! What are you talking about?"

"You told me yesterday that you spent the afternoon visiting Mary Ann Parks."

Victoria looked at him in bewilderment. "I did. Why would you think that was a lie?"

Miles turned his face away, not wanting her to see how disappointed he was that she was continuing to deceive him.

"Miles, I asked you a question. Why do you think I was lying when I said I was visiting Mary Ann?"

Whipping back his head to face her, he barked, "Because Samuel was mending fences yesterday afternoon and saw you out riding with Guildford!"

Victoria's jaw dropped. "And you think . . . Are you saying that you think I made up a story about going to visit Mary Ann to cover the fact that I was out having some sort of romantic tryst with Harrison? And that then I came home from this supposed assignation and made love with you? My God, Miles, how *could* you think that?"

His aching head forgotten, Miles pushed himself up in bed. "I just told you: Samuel saw the two of you together. He said that Guildford escorted you right up to the gate, and that you seemed to be having a very pleasant conversation."

Victoria's hands clenched at her sides and it was all she could do to keep herself from punching her husband in his other eye. "I don't believe this," she cried angrily. Walking back to the bed, she stared at Miles unflinchingly. "You want the truth? All right, I'll give it to you. Samuel did see me with Harrison yesterday. I was on my way home from Mary Ann's and I met him on the road. He . . ." Her voice trailed off.

"He what?"

"He and I had words and I rode away from him, but he followed me."

"If you two had words, why did Samuel see you chatting amicably at the gate?"

"We weren't chatting amicably! Harrison was pressing me to go away with him and I told him that he was being ridiculous and that I was going into the house."

"He wanted you to go away with him?" Miles gasped.

"Yes. That's how I knew who took King's Ransom. Harrison told me he had a plan all worked out. We'd run away together and take Ransom with us. Then we could sell the horse on the

Continent and use the proceeds to set ourselves up financially. I told him he was crazy and that I wanted no part of his scheme, but when Ransom disappeared that same night, I knew he was behind it."

"That son of a bitch . . ." Miles snarled. "If I'd known any of this, he'd be a dead man right now." Glaring at Victoria, he demanded, "Why didn't you tell me about this?"

"Because I knew you'd react exactly as you are right now!"

"So, instead of being truthful you decided to distract me by telling me that ridiculous story of how you spent the afternoon extolling the wonders of my sexual prowess to Mary Ann Parks."

"That wasn't a lie either," Victoria blazed. "Mary Ann and I did have a long talk about . . . personal things. Women do that, you know."

Miles could see by Victoria's furious glare and crimson cheeks that she was telling him the truth. Embarrassed by his outburst, he tried a conciliatory smile. "I'm sorry. I didn't know ladies talked about such things."

"Well, we do."

"I appreciate your enlightening me," he said softly. "I thought that ladies only discussed subjects like servant problems and the rising cost of tea and . . ."

"We discuss those things, too," Victoria interrupted, "but we also talk about our husbands and our marriages and . . ."

". . . lovemaking?"

Victoria's indignant expression softened. "Occasionally." Sitting back down on the bed, she pushed an errant lock of blond hair off Miles's forehead. "Remember when I told you that Mary Ann said she and Tom confine their . . . lovemaking to Saturday nights?"

Miles chuckled. "Yes, and I also remember feeling very sorry for Tom."

"Well, I felt sorry for Mary Ann, too, so I decided to tell her that, perhaps, with a little imagination, things between them could be more exciting."

"Spoken like a woman of vast experience," Miles commented wryly.

"No, Miles," Victoria responded softly, "spoken like a woman who has found true love."

All traces of amusement fled Miles's eyes, and he pulled Victoria down next to him. "I love you, Tory," he whispered. "I'm sorry I ever doubted you."

Looking into his beloved face, Victoria smiled. "I love you, too, Miles, and I want you to believe me when I tell you that there's never been anyone but you. Never."

Miles gathered her close, wincing slightly as he pulled her against his bruised ribs. "I know that now, sweetheart. I've just been so damn scared that I would lose you to Harrison that I've acted like a jackass."

Victoria shook her head in disbelief. "Oh, Miles, that's so silly. Harrison has never meant anything to me. Until you came along, I'd never met any man who interested me. Remember, all the bachelors in the shire think I'm the cold, unemotional Pembroke sister, and they had good reason to think that."

Miles braced himself up on one elbow, gazing down at his wife with a smug smile. "That's only because none of the titled, noble bachelors in this shire were smart enough to find the hot little temptress who hides behind that cool, untouchable demeanor of yours."

Victoria giggled delightedly at his provocative compliment. "I guess it took a big, arrogant American to discover that. Even I didn't know it."

Untying the sash of Miles's bathrobe, she ran a tapered nail lightly across his chest. "In fact, you've taught me a whole lot of things I didn't know before I met you."

"Sometimes I think you know too much," Miles groaned, pushing her hand away.

"Am I hurting you?"

"No, but you're starting something that I'm probably too beat up to finish."

Victoria turned over onto her stomach, gazing at Miles seductively. "What if I start it and finish it, too?"

A spark of pleased surprise lit Miles's eyes. "What do you have in mind?"

Victoria flipped his robe open, exposing his already swelling manhood to her hungry gaze. Closing her hand around him, she fondled him sensuously. "Just something I read once in a scandalous French novel."

"A scandalous French novel," Miles moaned, his hips already moving beneath her stroking fingers. "When did you start reading those?"

"In boarding school," Victoria confided, getting to her knees and beginning to kiss him. "All of us girls read them, but I never thought I'd have a chance to put any of their lessons to use."

"Dare I hope that you're going to now?"

Victoria's tongue swirled around the tip of his erection, causing him to nearly come off the bed. "Do you want me to?" she purred.

"Let me put it this way," Miles rasped. "I'm completely, and I mean *completely,* at your mercy."

As Victoria felt her husband grow hard and hot in her mouth, her own body began to pulse with excitement. Still, she ignored its heated demands and continued her lovemaking until they were both frenzied with desire. Only when Miles cried out her name and begged her to put an end to the delicious torture she was inflicting upon him did she finally lift her head. Pulling her robe up around her waist, she straddled his hips, holding herself just inches above his throbbing shaft. "Are you sure you're up to this?" she murmured coyly.

His strangled, "God, yes!" was all the answer she needed. With a smile full of erotic promise, she slowly lowered herself onto him.

Miles slid within Victoria's warm, moist depths, his cry of carnal pleasure reverberating loudly off the high ceilings of the massive chamber. Responding to his passion, Victoria moved her hips in rhythmic circles, finding the sensation of being filled so completely more exciting than anything she'd ever experienced.

Reaching up, Miles placed his hands on either side of her hips, moving her up and down with increasing rapidity. "You're making me crazy!" he panted, rubbing his lips against her full breasts as she bent over him.

Straightening, Victoria threw her head back, her long, dark hair brushing tantalizingly against his hips. "Then do it," she cried. "Please, Miles! Do it now!"

Her plea was like a siren's call, and with a hoarse shout, Miles surged within her, filling her with his essence as, together, they hurtled over love's great pinnacle and descended into the sweet abyss of completion.

Victoria collapsed on Miles's chest, listening to the thundering of his heart. "That was wonderful," she breathed, tightening her internal muscles around him playfully.

"Don't you start up again," he groaned, slipping out of her and pulling her down next to him. "Try to remember, lady, that I'm injured."

"You didn't act injured a few minutes ago," she teased.

"I know," he returned, "but what Harrison Guildford started, you just finished. I'm completely done in, girl."

Victoria looked up at him in alarm. "You're not serious, are you, Miles? I didn't really hurt you, did I?"

Miles moaned dramatically. "As I said, I'm completely done in . . . for at least an hour."

"Oh, you!" Victoria admonished. Then, sighing happily, she cuddled up next to her husband. A moment later they were both fast asleep.

"Seth, wait till you see the terrific outlaw fort I found!"

Nine-year-old Seth looked up at ten-year-old Nathan and wiped a thick layer of cake crumbs off his mouth. "Go on, Nate! Where would you find a fort in the middle of England?

They don't even have outlaws here; leastwise not real ones, like we've got at home."

"I'm tellin' you, I found a fort," Nathan insisted. "I was out scoutin' around down by the creek and I found this empty building. It's kind of a mess, and most of the roof is gone, but it's still a perfect place for you to hide out when we're playin' sheriff and outlaw."

Seth eagerly jumped down from his chair and grabbed his brother's arm. "Well, come on, then; show it to me!"

The two boys sped out the front door of Wellesley Manor and headed off for the woods. They'd only walked for about ten minutes, though, when Seth turned to Nathan and demanded, "Just how far is this place, anyway?"

"It's not much farther," Nathan assured him. "What's the matter? Are you tired already, you big sissy?"

" 'Course I'm not tired," Seth retorted hotly. "I just think you're lost, or else there isn't any fort at all and you're just makin' all this up."

"I'm not makin' it up and I'm not lost. I did find a fort. It's right up yonder through those trees." Nathan pointed to a dense stand of oaks directly ahead of them.

"Well, okay, but you'd better be right, or else I'm goin' back to Grandma's."

"I *am* right. Quit bein' such a baby!"

The two boys trudged on, entering the heavy copse of trees and exiting the other side a few minutes later. "See?" Nathan cried. "There it is! Just like I said."

Seth's blue eyes widened with glee. Grabbing Nathan's arm, he began running toward the partially demolished crofter's cottage. "You were right, Nate. It *is* perfect, and I'll bet it really was some outlaw's hideout. I wonder what happened to it, though. Practically the whole roof's gone."

"It probably got burned off when the police came lookin' for the outlaw," Nathan speculated. "I bet he was holed up inside with millions of guns and wouldn't come out, so the lawmen had to burn the roof off to get to him."

Seth nodded excitedly, squinting up at the remnants of the thatched roof. "I bet you're right."

By this time they had reached what was left of a flagstone walkway leading up to the house. "Want to go in and explore?" Nate asked.

Seth's enthusiasm faded a bit as he peered through a gap in the wall that had once been a front door. Despite the fact that the roof was rotted away, it was a dreary day and the interior of the abandoned building was dark and shadowy.

"Well, do you want to go in or not?" Nathan demanded.

"I guess so," Seth muttered. "You don't think there's any snakes or wild animals in there, do you?"

Nathan looked warily at his younger brother, trying hard to hide the prickle of apprehension his suggestion had wrought. "Naw," he said, forcing himself to swagger up the path toward the yawning doorway. "And even if there are, I'll beat 'em off with my club." Holding up a stout stick he'd picked up along the way, Nathan waved it around menacingly. "Come on, Seth, quit actin' like such a baby. I'll protect you."

"You don't need to protect me," Seth announced, trying desperately to match his older brother's bravado. "I can take care of myself."

"All right, then, come on!"

Together, the two boys approached the front door, their steps slowing as the dim opening drew even closer. Suddenly Seth heard a rustling sound from within, as if someone was scuffing through a pile of straw. Stopping dead in his tracks, he grabbed his brother's arm. "Did you hear that?" he whispered, his eyes bulging with fear.

"Hear what?"

"Shh! There's somebody in there."

"Aw, you're crazier than a coot. Nobody's in there."

"Yes, there is. I heard somethin'."

"Well, what was it?"

"I don't know. It was a sound, like somebody walkin' around."

Nathan turned on Seth impatiently. "Just who do you think would be in there walkin' around? I swear, if you're gonna be this much of a scaredy pants, then you might as well go back to Grandma's and I'll scout the place alone."

Seth drew himself up to his full four feet, six inches and glared belligerently at his older brother. "I am not a scaredy pants! You take that back, Nate, or I'll sock you a good one."

"I'm not takin' it back," Nathan returned hotly. "You're a scaredy pants and a fraidy cat, too. Why, little Paula's braver than you are. Maybe next time I go scoutin' I'll take her with me 'stead of you."

True to his word, Seth drew back his arm and punched Nathan in the stomach.

Nathan bent double for a moment, then straightened up, glaring angrily at his brother. "Cut it out, Seth! We ain't here to fight; we're here to explore. Now, are you comin' or not?"

Seth shot Nathan a superior smile, well pleased with the blow he'd landed. "Ma says you're not s'posed to say 'ain't,' Nathan."

Nathan threw him an arrogant look. "Well, Ma's not here, so I guess I can say whatever I want to. Now, are you comin', 'cause I'm goin' in."

Bolstered by the fact that he'd just bested his older brother, Seth hitched up his pants and spit on the flagstones. "Damn right, I'm comin'."

"Seth! If Pa heard you cussin' like that, he'd skin you alive for sure."

"Well, Pa's not here either," Seth smirked, "so I guess I can say what I want to, too."

Turning back to the business at hand, the boys again proceeded up the walk, stepping carefully onto the rotting porch boards and peeking in through the front door.

Suddenly a loud movement from the back of the dwelling sent them both screaming back down the walkway, clutching at each other in full-blown panic.

"There *is* somebody in there!" Nathan yelped.

"I told ya there was! Come on; let's get out of here and go home."

They raced past the crumbling stone wall surrounding the property and started back down the path toward the woods, but they'd only gotten about fifty feet when Nathan suddenly stopped, pulling back on Seth's arm to halt him, too. "I've changed my mind, Seth. I'm not goin' home yet. I've just gotta know what's in that old place."

"Are you crazy?" Seth yelled. "It's probably some wild animal. You go in there and provoke it and it'll probably eat you!"

"I don't care," Nathan said staunchly. "I've gotta know what it is. This is an adventure, and Geoff always says that a real man never passes up a chance for adventure."

"Yeah," Seth nodded, "but Eric always says that only a fool puts himself in danger for no reason."

"Oh, who listens to Eric, anyway?" Nathan scoffed. "The most dangerous thing he does is climb up on the ridge behind the house and paint the mountains."

Seth pondered Nathan's reasoning for a moment, then said, "Are you really goin' back?"

"Yup, and I'm goin' inside, too. I've got my stick if I need it, and I'm not afraid of any old critter that might be livin' in there."

Seth's curiosity finally won out over his fear. "All right. If you're goin' back, then I am, too."

With identical nods, the two boys turned around and headed back for the abandoned cottage. Strutting up the walk with a confidence neither of them was truly feeling, they peeked in the door again, peering through the dimness toward the corner from which the rustling sound had come.

"There *is* something back there," Seth whispered. "I can see it."

Nathan nodded. "I can, too. And whatever it is, it's a monster!"

At that moment the "monster" took a step forward and nickered a greeting.

"It's a horse!" Seth shouted, gaping at his brother in astonishment. "What do you s'pose a horse is doin' way out here?"

"It's probably a wild horse," Nathan conjectured. "You know, like a mustang."

"A mustang! There ain't any mustangs in England."

"I didn't say it *was* a mustang," Nathan announced, fumbling for a length of rope tied around his waist. "I said it was *like* a mustang." Finally succeeding in untying the rope from his belt, he moved slowly forward.

"What in tarnation are you doin'?" Seth gasped.

"What does it look like I'm doin'? I'm gonna catch him and take him back to Grandma's with us."

Seth looked at his brother incredulously. "What for? The last thing Grandma needs is more horses."

"This won't be Grandma's horse," Nathan explained as he moved stealthily toward the stallion. "I'm gonna take him back to Wellesley Manor and break him. Then he'll be *my* horse."

"Yours! What about me? I'm the one who saw him first."

Nathan shrugged. "But I'm the one who has the rope, so I guess that makes him mine."

Seth frowned angrily but could think of no argument that would defeat Nathan's logic. "You'd better be careful," he warned, "he might try to kick or bite."

"No, he won't. Horses always like me." By now Nathan had reached the stallion, who was dancing nervously at the sight of the swinging rope but showed no signs of hostility.

Nathan looped the rope around the horse's neck, then clucked to him softly, leading him toward the door. The horse followed along amiably and as they stepped outside, both boys turned to look at him.

"Whoa. He's a beauty, Nate!" Seth enthused, stepping forward to gently pet the stallion's neck.

Nathan grinned. "Yup, he sure is. And he's all mine."

Seth nodded wistfully. "I guess you're right. You did think to bring the rope."

"I *always* carry a rope," Nathan boasted. "You never know

when you're gonna need one. Let that be a lesson to you, little brother."

Seeing Seth's downcast expression, he quickly added, "Tell you what. Since you came with me today, once I get him broke, I'll let you ride him sometimes."

Seth immediately perked up. "You will? Really?"

"Yes. Now, come on; let's get him back to the house so I can show him off to everybody. I can't wait for Geoff to see him. He always actin' so stuck up, braggin' about his adventures in the woods. Just wait till he hears about this!"

Chapter 34

Samuel thundered up the steps of Wellesley Manor and doubling his fist, beat frantically on the front door. "Master James! Master James, come quick!"

Hearing the unprecedented commotion coming from the porch, Cedric hurried to the door and flung it open. "Samuel! Have you taken leave of your senses? Stop this shouting at once!"

"Where's Master James?" Samuel demanded, ignoring Cedric's haughty order and pushing past him into the foyer. "Master James!" he yelled.

James came rushing to the library door, a sheaf of documents clutched in one hand. "What is it, Samuel? Is something wrong?"

"No, sir," Samuel answered, pulling off his cap and acknowledging his employer's presence with a quick bob of his head. "But you need to come outside right now. You won't believe who's coming up the drive!"

Cedric drew in an outraged breath and glared at Samuel furiously. "Do you mean that this unforgivable outburst of yours is over a visitor? My God, man, what is wrong with you?"

Samuel threw an impatient look at the enraged butler, then turned his attention back to James. "Please, sir, come quickly."

James pulled off his spectacles and laid them and the papers he was holding on a table. "All right, Sam, I'm coming."

"Cedric," Samuel ordered, "go find Master Miles and Lady Victoria. Tell them to come outside, too."

"I beg your pardon?" Cedric gasped. "Are you giving *me* orders?"

"Just do it!" the stablemaster barked. Catching James by the arm, he unceremoniously pushed him out the door. "Over there," he pointed. "Look who Master Nathan and Master Seth are leading up the drive."

James gazed off in the direction in which Samuel pointed, then drew in a startled breath. "My God, where did they find him?"

Leaping down the front steps, James sprinted across the yard toward his sons. "Boys! Where did you get that horse?"

Nathan and Seth exchanged proud looks, then turned back to their father. "Isn't he great, Pa?" Nathan enthused. "We found him out in the woods . . ."

"In an abandoned building we're going to use as a fort," Seth finished.

Nathan threw his younger brother a quelling look, furious that Seth was obviously trying to steal his thunder. "His name is Outlaw and I'm gonna break him to ride, then take him home with me when we go. Just look at him, Pa. Ain't he a fine horse?"

"*Isn't* he," James corrected automatically. "And, yes, Nathan, he's a very fine horse, but his name isn't Outlaw."

Nathan looked at his father blankly. "What do you mean?"

James gazed at his son sympathetically, regretting that he was going to have to dash the boy's excitement. "That horse is King's Ransom, Nate."

Nathan continued to stare at his father uncomprehendingly. "Who's King's Ransom?"

James put his arm around his son's shoulder and gave him

an affectionate squeeze. "King's Ransom is the stallion that Harrison Guildford stole from Pembroke stables last week."

"You mean the one that Victoria has been so upset about? The one that Miles got into that big fight over?"

James nodded. "That's the one."

"But it can't be the same horse, Pa. Me and Seth found this one way out in the middle of the woods. We figure he's a wild horse; you know, like the mustangs at home. He probably just looks like the horse that was stolen."

James shook his head a bit sadly. "No, Nathan, he doesn't just look like King's Ransom. He *is* King's Ransom."

Nathan's expression became mutinous. "But Pa, if somebody stole a horse, why would they leave him in the woods by himself?"

"I'm not sure why," James admitted. "Lord Guildford confessed that he had stolen the horse to sell him to a foreign buyer. Maybe he was hiding him in the woods until he could arrange passage to ship him to the continent. When the authorities caught Lord Guildford he must have decided that he'd rather have the horse die in the forest than return him to his rightful owner, so he just left Ransom to forage for himself."

"That was a terrible thing to do!" Seth proclaimed angrily.

"Yes, it was," James agreed. "Lord Guildford is a very troubled man. Unfortunately, there are a lot of people in this world who aren't as nice as we'd like them to be."

Nathan looked at the stallion longingly, trying hard to fight back the tears that threatened. "I guess this means I can't have him, huh?"

"I'm afraid so, son," James said quietly, "but think about what a fine thing you've done by bringing him back. Lady Victoria will be very happy, and it's all because of you."

"I helped, too, you know," Seth piped up. "In fact, I'm the one who found him in the first place. Nathan just said the horse was his because he had a rope to catch him with and I didn't."

James smiled at his younger son lovingly. "Then you're a hero, too, Seth. Both of you boys are. You've rescued a very valuable animal from what could have been a terrible fate. King's Ransom isn't used to being out in the woods alone, and there's no telling what might have happened to him if you two hadn't found him."

Just then the front door opened, and Victoria and Miles stepped out on to the porch, both of them wearing quizzical expressions. Catching sight of King's Ransom standing in the drive, Victoria let out a little shriek of delight and flew off the steps, racing over to the horse and throwing her arms around his neck. Miles was just a few steps behind her, and when he reached the little gathering he looked back and forth between his two brothers in astonishment. "What in the world is going on here?"

"We found Victoria's horse," Nathan said dully, handing the rope to Miles.

Miles looked at his father, bewildered by Nathan's downcast tone.

"The boys found Ransom in an abandoned building out in the woods," James explained. "Nathan thought he was a wild horse and decided he'd keep him for his own."

Miles nodded with dawning understanding, then clapped a hand on Nathan's shoulder. "You know, Nate, there's a big reward posted for the return of this horse. I guess all that money is rightfully yours now."

Nathan shrugged disinterestedly.

Victoria, who was running her hands over Ransom's flanks to check that he wasn't injured, turned to smile at her young brother-in-law. "And do you know what else, Nathan? If for some reason the person who found the horse doesn't want the money, Pembroke stables is offering a champion colt instead."

Nathan's eyes widened. "You mean, I could get another horse as a reward for bringing this one back?"

"You certainly can," Victoria grinned, "and there are several you can choose from, too."

"Any white ones?" Nathan asked hopefully.

"I'm not sure about that," Victoria hedged, sending Miles a worried look.

Correctly interpreting her plea, Miles jumped back into the conversation. "I don't know about white, Nate, but I have seen a very handsome gray colt out in the pasture who I think you'd really like."

Nathan grinned with renewed excitement. "Gray, huh? Well, gray's a good color, especially for a sheriff. Helps him blend into the rocks when he's trackin' outlaws, you know. Okay, when can I see him?"

"Today," Miles promised. "We'll go over to Pembroke after lunch and you can take a look at all the colts and then make your choice."

"That's great!" Nathan shouted. "Isn't that great, Seth?"

Seth, who had been standing with his head down, scuffed the toe of his boot in the dirt. "Yeah, great."

James and Miles's eyes met and James said, "You know, Victoria, Seth helped Nathan rescue King's Ransom. In fact, it was Seth who actually first found him."

Victoria had caught the look that had passed between her husband and his father. Immediately understanding the problem, she walked over to the disconsolate child and squatted down in front of him. "You know what, Seth? If Nathan is going to be a sheriff, then I think he needs an outlaw to chase, don't you?"

"I s'pose so," Seth muttered.

"And outlaws need horses, too," Victoria continued. "I've heard black ones are very popular with outlaws in the American west. Is that true?"

Seth nodded, looking up at her for the first time.

"Well, then, I think it's only proper for you to have a horse, too." Turning to Miles, she said casually, "Do you know if there are any black colts in the Pembroke pastures?"

"Oh, I think there may be one or two," Miles answered, smiling at his wife gratefully.

Victoria turned her attention back to the now smiling Seth.

"Would you like a black colt to take back to America with you?"

Seth's blue eyes widened with excitement. "Would I!" Turning to Nathan, he shouted, "Did you hear that, Nate? We're both gonna have new horses! And we'll train 'em to run so fast that no one will ever be able to catch us."

"You bet we will!" Nathan enthused. "Come on; let's go tell Eric and Geoff! Boy, are they gonna be jealous!" Together, the two boys raced off toward the house.

Mary Wellesley, who had quietly joined the group in the midst of all the excitement, now turned to her daughter-in-law and kissed her on the cheek. "That was very, very kind of you, Victoria." Reaching out, she gently patted Victoria's stomach. "You're going to make some lucky child a wonderful mother."

"Not to mention that she's already made some lucky parents a wonderful daughter-in-law," James added.

"And this lucky man a wonderful wife." Miles grinned. Reaching out, he pulled Victoria into his arms and, despite the fact that his parents and half the stable help at Wellesley Manor were gathered round, kissed her soundly.

Everyone laughed as Miles bussed his wife; then the happy group returned to the house to regale Regina with the story of her grandsons' heroic rescue of the stolen horse.

Late that night Victoria was seated at her dressing table brushing her hair when Miles walked into the bedroom, a rolled up piece of paper in his hand.

"I have something for you," he whispered, leaning down and kissing her neck as he dropped the document in her lap.

Victoria set down her brush and looked at the paper quizzically. "What is it?"

"Unroll it and see," Miles suggested. He walked over to his wardrobe, shedding his clothes and pulling on a silk wrapper as Victoria untied the ribbon circling the document and carefully unrolled it.

Holding it close to a lamp, she quickly scanned it, then looked up at Miles, her eyes shining. "It's Ransom's ownership certificate, and it's in my name."

"I know. It arrived from the registry about a week ago, but I didn't think it was appropriate to give it to you then."

Victoria shook her head in bewilderment, perusing the document again. "I don't understand, Miles. I thought Fiona signed King's Ransom over to you when we married. Wasn't that part of the deal?"

Miles pulled Victoria up off her stool and wrapped her in his muscular arms. "Who told you there was a deal, sweetheart?"

"Well, no one, really; I just assumed there was. I knew when you married me that what you were really after was Ransom, and I just figured that when the financial agreements were signed between Fiona and you, Ransom's ownership was part of them."

"Tory," Miles whispered, placing feathery little kisses against her temple, "there were never formal agreements signed, except for a bill of sale on the estate, and there was never any 'deal.' I married you because I wanted you, not because of your horse, not because of your title, not because of your estate. I wanted *you*, and I wouldn't have cared if you hadn't a shilling to your name."

Victoria looked up into Miles's beautiful blue eyes, her expression so full of love that it made him catch his breath. "You really wanted me?" she breathed. "But why? You could have had any girl in England. Why me?"

Miles chuckled and shook his head. "Because you're the most beautiful, intelligent, spirited woman I've ever known, and I think I fell in love with you that first day when you threw me out of your barn. I've told you this before, sweetheart. How many times do I have to say it before you believe me?"

"I do believe you, my darling," Victoria smiled, snuggling up against his solid chest, "but I still love to hear you say it."

"Oh, I see." Miles laughed. "Fishing for compliments, are you?"

Victoria blushed. "You've found me out."

"Yes, I have, but I'm more than happy to comply. Now, just how often would you like me to tell you that I think you're the most fabulous woman in the world?"

"I don't know," Victoria teased. "Once or twice a day for the rest of our lives should do it."

Miles tilted Victoria's head back and kissed her softly, his eyes promising a lifetime of tender moments and a love everlasting. "Agreed, my lady. *Now* we have a deal."

Epilogue

Miles sat down on the side of the bed and watched lovingly as his wife nursed their newborn son.

Victoria gazed up at him, her face betraying the exhaustion of her long labor, but her eyes shining with happiness. "If it's all right with you, I'd like to name him John after my father," she whispered.

Miles smiled and nodded. "That was going to be my suggestion, too. John Pembroke Wellesley. It has a nice solid sound to it."

"Oh, Miles," Victoria sighed, leaning her head against his chest. "I never knew it was possible to be so happy."

"Nor did I," Miles confessed. "You have truly given me everything I ever wanted in life, Tory, and I love you more than words can express."

Victoria gazed serenely at the blond, blue-eyed baby who showed every sign of growing up to look just like his handsome father. "He's beautiful, isn't he?"

Miles grimaced. "Actually, I think he looks kind of like a troll."

"Oh!" Victoria gasped, swatting her husband on the arm.

"What a terrible thing to say! He doesn't look like a troll. He looks just like you."

Miles laughed heartily at her comment. "Thanks a lot, lady. Now I know what you really think of my looks."

"Oh, stop," Victoria admonished good-naturedly. "You know I think you're the most handsome man in the world, and John is going to be just as handsome."

Miles grinned, greatly pleased by her compliment. "Actually, I know of a lady who also gave birth to a son today, and he's far more handsome than our son is."

Victoria looked up at him in genuinely outraged maternal offense. "Who? Someone I know?"

"I think so. Her name is Spring Daffodil, and she had a son today, too, who is, without a doubt, the most handsome young man I've ever seen."

Victoria smiled with delight. "Really, Miles? Daffodil foaled today? Is she all right?"

"She's just fine, but I'm telling you, Victoria, her son is far more advanced than ours. He's already standing up and walking, and he's not all red and wrinkled like John is. But, best of all," he added, his voice becoming serious, "he's not cowhocked."

"Are you saying you think our baby is going to be cowhocked?" Victoria giggled.

"Hardly." Miles chuckled. "But I'm so pleased with the way Daffodil's foal turned out that I think we should breed her back to Ransom again this year. Hopefully, we'll get another baby just like this one."

Leaning over, Miles touched a gentle finger to his son's soft cheek. "And even though he looks like a troll, I'm also very pleased with the way this little boy turned out. In fact, I think we should start thinking about trying for another one just like him, too."

Victoria threw Miles a withering look. "You're incorrigible, do you know that? Your son is only three hours old and already you're thinking about another one."

"I know." Miles laughed, wiggling his eyebrows and shamelessly leering at his wife. "I told you I like children." Leaning down, he placed a soft kiss on Victoria's lips. "I like his mama a lot, too."

Victoria threw him a saucy grin. "Well, since you put it that way, I'll think about it. Maybe we can try for another one some Saturday night between eleven and eleven twenty."

"What?"

Victoria yawned expansively. "You know, like Tom and Mary Ann. Remember?"

Handing him the sleeping baby, Victoria slid down in the big bed and closed her eyes. The last thing Miles heard her say before she drifted off to sleep was, "But then again, if you're really good, I might also consider trying on Tuesday mornings and Monday afternoons and Friday at lunch time and . . ." Her voice trailed off with a contented sigh.

Quietly, Miles placed the baby next to Victoria and put out the lamp. "Anytime, my precious wife," he whispered. "Anytime at all." Straightening, he chuckled softly. "And that includes every Saturday night from eleven to eleven twenty."

WATCH FOR THESE HOT ROMANCES
NEXT MONTH

PROMISE ME   (0-8217-5336-3, $4.99)
by Elaine Kane
Deidre Ramsey, new Countess of Ramshead, is the lonely mistress of
a barren ancestral estate. The tender promises of seductive Jared
Montgomery, Marquess of Jersey and society's most eligible bachelor,
are most tempting. But then Deidre learns the truth—Jared has secretly
wanted Ramshead all along. Dare she trust he covets her as well?

GENTLE HEARTS   (0-8217-5337-1, $4.99)
by Clara Wimberly
As the Civil War raged, Lida Rinehart was content in her simple Amish
world. But when her brother dies helping a slave escape to freedom,
she struggles to carry on his mission with the help of John Sexton. An
outsider to her people's ways and a threat to all she believes, John awak-
ens Lida's desire and demands what she is forbidden to give: her love.

NO PLACE FOR A LADY   (0-8217-5334-7, $4.99)
by Vivian Vaughan
Spoiling for reform, suffragette Maddie Sinclair hasn't counted on the
complication of sinfully handsome Tyler Grant having a mission of his
own. The six-foot-tall hunk has secretly sworn revenge against Maddie's
brother, and she fits perfectly into his scheme. Falling in love could
prove disastrous, as warring passions heat up for a showdown that could
set one incendiary town and two blazing hearts—on fire.

HEARTS VICTORIOUS   (0-8217-5335-5, $4.99)
by Marian Edwards
Bethany of North Umberland is the beloved mistress of Renwyg castle
until she is suddenly stripped of power and imprisoned, slave to Norman
conqueror Royce de Bellemare. Determined to outwit her captor, she
soon finds that when it comes to her seductive enemy, passion has no
allegiance.

*Available wherever paperbacks are sold, or order direct from the
Publisher. Send cover price plus 50¢ per copy for mailing and handling to Penguin USA, P.O. Box 999, c/o Dept. 17109, Bergenfield, NJ 07621. Residents of New York and Tennessee must
include sales tax. DO NOT SEND CASH.*

DON'T MISS THESE OTHER THRILLING ROMANCES BY BEST-SELLING AUTHOR COLLEEN FAULKNER!

O'BRIAN'S BRIDE   (0-8217-4895-5, $4.99)

Elizabeth Lawrence left her pampered English childhood behind to journey to the far-off Colonies . . . and marry a man she'd never met. But her dreams turned to dust when an explosion killed her new husband at his powder mill, leaving her alone to run his business . . . and face a perilous life on the untamed frontier. After a desperate engagement to her husband's brother, yet another man, strong, sensual and secretive Michael Patrick O'Brian, enters her life and it will never be the same.

CAPTIVE   (0-8217-4683-1, $4.99)

Tess Morgan had journeyed across the sea to Maryland colony in search of a better life. Instead, the brave British innocent finds a battle-torn land . . . and passion in the arms of Raven, the gentle Lenape warrior who saves her from a savage fate. But Tess is bound by another. And Raven dares not trust this woman whose touch has enslaved him, yet whose blood vow to his people has set him on a path of rage and vengeance. Now, as cruel destiny forces her to become Raven's prisoner, Tess must make a choice: to fight for her freedom . . . or for the tender captor she has come to cherish with a love that will hold her forever.

Available wherever paperbacks are sold, or order direct from the Publisher. Send cover price plus 50¢ per copy for mailing and handling to Penguin USA, P.O. Box 999, c/o Dept. 17109, Bergenfield, NJ 07621. Residents of New York and Tennessee must include sales tax. DO NOT SEND CASH.

DON'T MISS THESE ROMANCES FROM BEST-SELLING AUTHOR KATHERINE DEAUXVILLE!

THE CRYSTAL HEART   (0-8217-4928-5, $5.99)

Emmeline gave herself to a sensual stranger in a night aglow with candlelight and mystery. Then she sent him away. Wed by arrangement, Emmeline desperately needed to provide her aged husband with an heir. But her lover awakened a passion she kept secret in her heart . . . until he returned and rocked her world with his demands and his desire.

THE AMETHYST CROWN   (0-8217-4555-7, $5.99)

She is Constance, England's richest heiress. A radiant, silver-eyed beauty, she is a player in the ruthless power games of King Henry I. Now, a desperate gambit takes her back to Wales where she falls prey to a ragged prisoner who escapes his chains, enters her bedchamber . . . and enslaves her with his touch. He is a bronzed, blond Adonis whose dangerous past has forced him to wander Britain in disguise. He will escape an enemy's shackles—only to discover a woman whose kisses fire his tormented soul. His birthright is a secret, but his wild, burning love is his destiny . . .

Available wherever paperbacks are sold, or order direct from the Publisher. Send cover price plus 50¢ per copy for mailing and handling to Penguin USA, P.O. Box 999, c/o Dept. 17109, Bergenfield, NJ 07621. Residents of New York and Tennessee must include sales tax. DO NOT SEND CASH.